PRAISE FOR PETER STENSON

"Shockingly personal....*Shaun of the Dead* meets *Trainspotting.*"

—MTV.com on *Fiend*

"This novel is a provocative, thoroughly gripping ride."

—*Publishers Weekly* on *Thirty-Seven*

"A book that manages to break your heart, make you dizzy, and punch you in the gut all at once. You will be hard-pressed to find a novel as dark or intense in any bookstore."

—*Kirkus Reviews* *Starred* review on *Thirty-Seven*

WE, ADULTS

Peter Stenson

Regal House Publishing

Published by
Regal House Publishing, LLC
Raleigh, NC 27605
All rights reserved

ISBN -13 (paperback): 9781646034277
ISBN -13 (epub): 9781646034284
Library of Congress Control Number: 2023934866

All efforts were made to determine the copyright holders and obtain their permissions in any circumstance where copyrighted material was used. The publisher apologizes if any errors were made during this process, or if any omissions occurred. If noted, please contact the publisher and all efforts will be made to incorporate permissions in future editions.

Cover images and design by © C. B. Royal

Regal House Publishing, LLC
https://regalhousepublishing.com

The following is a work of fiction created by the author. All names, individuals, characters, places, items, brands, events, etc. were either the product of the author or were used fictitiously. Any name, place, event, person, brand, or item, current or past, is entirely coincidental.

Printed in the United States of America

For Lindsay, my partner and best friend

LEAKY VESSELS

I

Hanger Integrity—Elliot Meets Boy—Skunk—A Bitch is a Bitch is a Bitch

It was all a matter of *Hanger Integrity*—a four-point system of checks, each descending in obviousness, but as was so often clarified, not *importance*—that served as a mantra to be spewed around the waxed floors and white built-in shelves of the thirty-seventh highest grossing Talbots in America (second in the state, but what store could compete with the foot traffic of The Mall of America?) right there in Roseville, Minnesota. It was delivered with varying inflections, each denoting an unsaid sentiment: H.I. ladies! (I-can-poke-fun-at-myself-but-pick-it-up); how's your integrity on those cashmere cowls? (motherly-raising-of-voice-about-to-quit-with-the-smile); those triple-pleat cuffed slacks are lacking in both style *and* integrity (you're-pretty-much-worthless-and-trust-me-you're-not-fooling-anyone-with-the-belt-cinched-around-your-bottom-two-ribs-about-the-fact-you've-birthed-your-hips-into-a-size   twelve). These bits of biting encouragement were given from one of the six Floor Leads, the Assistant Manager, the Manager, or during peak times, as Thanksgiving was, the Regional Director of Marketing.

But perhaps mostly, Hanger Integrity was championed by Carolyn Sheppard, the closest woman in age and body weight to Elliot Svendson, which is to say Carolyn wasn't sweating with the lack of estrogen or just plain fat, but definitely chubby, or at least rounded, her thirty-three years softening her features to the point of puffy, her power animal more than likely a blow fish. Carolyn wasn't a Manager. Not an Assistant. Not even a Floor Lead with their extra fifty cents an hour. She was Part-Time (non-benefited), and since Elliot was Seasonal, and younger, and better looking, and not trying to move up the goddamn retail chain of the thirty-seventh highest grossing Talbots in a shitty suburb of St. Paul, this somehow gave Carolyn the right to be a bitch.

For the hundredth time, Carolyn was using her communicating-with-an-imbecile voice to explain the four tenants of Hanger Integrity. They stood next to the merino sweater coats, front left of the store

(73 percent of the time, the first direction a customer will turn upon entering, therefore the most important and most heavily abused). It was Elliot's section to fluff, a term she seemed to be the only one who understood an alternate meaning for. Carolyn had her cornered. She'd already started in on the most obvious check, that each hanger be slung around the metal poles front to back. Next was the equally obvious fact that the Talbots logo etched into the aspen wood be facing the same direction.

"And here is where you seem to…where you could *improve*," Carolyn was saying, spreading her fingers through the hung sweaters. "Spacing. Equal spacing. You see how I'm doing this? Each hanger should be an *equal* distance from the one in front and behind it."

Elliot looked at Carolyn's hands. They weren't attractive hands, not ones she could imagine any man liking to touch his face, not even his body, too Scandinavian, blotchy even with over-lubrication. Elliot looked at the princess-cut diamond strangling Carolyn's ring finger, feeling sorry for a man stupid/desperate enough to view Carolyn as any sort of take-home prize.

"Oh, and it goes without saying, everything needs to be size-run."

Elliot nodded. Carolyn kept staring. Maybe she'd looked good in high school. Elliot could see Carolyn being attractive simply because she was blond and had breasts and the ruthless bitchiness of those striving to keep others subjugated, and her husband was probably varsity something, tight end maybe, and it'd been juvenile love or convenience and an early marriage, and well, fifteen years later, they were living out their continuation of a dream that sounded better during prom. Carolyn glanced down at the rack of merino sweaters. Oh, Elliot was supposed to be doing something. She noticed an 8 was in front of a 6. She rolled her eyes and switched the hangers and Carolyn kept staring and Elliot slid her fingers between the hangers to ensure equal spacing.

"Good," Carolyn said. She gave the smile of the victorious. Her gentle tap on Elliot's arm felt aggressive. She walked back toward the cashiers.

And there Elliot stood.

She stared out at people walking by, people looking at the red font of Talbots, before turning back to their phones or conversations or leering at teenage girls. Nobody wanted to be in Talbots, certainly not Elliot, who at twenty-nine years old wondered how in the fuck she'd come to be staring through the wrong side of the glass. Talbots seemed like an admission of age, of failure, of hips that never bounced back, were never there in the first place, of an interest in the softness of fabrics, a preference for those that draped away from the body, that showed less of your muffin top. But this was not Elliot Svendson. She hadn't yet hit thirty. Her body was still tight-ish. Her brownish-blond hair wasn't extravagant, but it wasn't the boy-short wispy uniform of most Talbots patrons, and yeah, there were a few split ends, but it wasn't like any man was getting close enough to notice. She was an attractive woman who feared her face to be too wide, not heart-shaped, but more like a genetically modified strawberry, all top and no chin. These were unfounded fears. In certain circles, say a plastic surgeon's office in West Hollywood, a case could be made for a weak chin, a lack of definition, which, if not careful, could lead to a gentle slopping from jaw to base of neck, but that wasn't the circle Elliot lived in, not before, not now. And by Roseville, Minnesota, standards, Elliot was most definitely attractive, even *hot*, a hundred and nineteen pounds, breasts that gave no hint of sagging while in a bra, a butt on the sexy side of full, and when taken with the knowledge of her three-year-old son, people would stamp her with the demeaning-yet-sought-after title of *MILF*.

Elliot thought Hanger Integrity was fucking stupid.

And Carolyn.

And Talbots.

And the Rosedale Mall.

And the fact she was so close to thirty, past the point of teetering, past the flirty arm touch of late twenties, her birthday less than three weeks away, a day she knew would come with the fanfare of being woken up in her childhood room by her mother and father armed with a *we're-so-funny* Disney Little Mermaid birthday card, a pen-drawn zero added after the printed three. People said thirties were the new twenties, but it was thirty-year-olds saying these things, people who had no dog in the fight for their drunken/whorish previous decade. Sure, maybe she'd be more secure. Less likely to do stupid things for the sake of being accepted. People were always talking about a self-confidence that magically appeared in their thirties, but really? She'd already married, already birthed a little boy. She'd owned a home and paid off student loans. She'd hosted dinner parties with three forks and flip-flopped on cloth diapers before deciding one extra boy's Pampers wouldn't ruin the ozone. She'd experienced the supposed grounding joys of the previous generation's thirties. And she thought they were fucking stupid. They'd teleported her back twelve years, back to the same childhood room with a window looking into the neighbor's second-story bathroom (Mr. Henderson was not a pretty sight to see in the nude), the same walls painted red in an act of sixteen-year-old rebellion, a vanity she'd sat at every night trying to excavate blackheads from the corners of her nostrils, and now, three weeks away from thirty, the only difference between her now and then was her son, Jacob.

Elliot helped a woman who could easily be her mother. She was looking for something to wear to Thanksgiving dinner. She informed Elliot of a style she'd seen on TV, a blouse over a different colored long-sleeve shirt, a style she'd seen on that show about the polygamists who lived in Las Vegas.

Elliot knew the show. She knew the look. It was a pathetic attempt at wearing cute empire-cut blouses while hiding the fact your armpit was a coalmine, your triceps pterodactyl wings. Elliot brought her to Carolyn's section. Carolyn pretended to be working on the equal distance tenant of H.I. while eavesdropping, waiting for Elliot to mess up and blow the sale, in which case Carolyn would swoop in with her *Finding Nemo* face, full of bullshit tidbits about that show being *so good, so interesting, can you imagine having to care for all those children?*

But not today.

Not with Christmas coming, and she needed it to be good for Jacob, him three, him suddenly being able to connect the ads he saw on TV with toys that should be his, him drawing stick figures of their family, Devon off to one side, Jacob in the middle, Elliot the Godzilla-sized figure looming over his entire worldview. She needed commission. She needed to flood Jacob's life with plastic toys. To buy his forgiveness. His love. For him to realize she did what needed to be done, because whatever that stupid reality show about polygamists in Vegas championed, nobody wanted to be stuck at home with a colicky baby while her husband ate the pussy of one of his undergrad students.

Elliot spoke the language of retail:

These two would go so well with one another.

No, no, that's part of the look, the almost-clashing. It's really hot right now. Bold. Youthful. Fun.

A 12? You're crazy, I would've put you in an 8!

Would you like to save ten percent on your purchases today by opening an exclusive Talbots Visa?

And this was Elliot's life—the doling out of flattery to dumpy women, the verbiage of Hanger Integrity, a misplaced competitive streak on Carolyn's behalf (maybe a little on Elliot's behalf too), and fluffing, folding, touching fabrics in order to affect busyness, all of it for $9.75 an hour, in heels, mind you, her right foot growing a goddamn bunion in two weeks to the day, a bunion or maybe a corn before she was thirty, not to mention a divorce before she was thirty, and a retreat from Denver, Colorado, to Roseville, Minnesota, from a cute bungalow in a hip-yet-gentrifying section of The Mile High City to her parents' home with faux wood paneling, the wall decoration of choice.

"Oh, and one other thing," Carolyn said. She'd snuck up to Elliot's side, who once again stared at the mallgoers who were too embarrassed to look inside of Talbots.

"Yeah?"

"You need to leave a quarter inch of spacing between the hanger's clips and the edge, like this, see? It's kind of the unsaid tenant of Hanger Integrity. And your section…well, I figured it actually needed to be said."

～

Elliot couldn't really afford to be eating out during lunch, both from financial and caloric intake standpoints. The mall trafficked in over-indulgence, from Sbarro's to Cinnabon to bastardized Chinese to lamb-everything (somehow qualifying as Greek), and Elliot vowed not to succumb to said indulgence, to become Minnesotan, which is to say paunchy-to-fat, so she packed turkey sandwiches, sometimes salad, carrots, a light yogurt, and often, a package of Jacob's Dora the Explorer fruit snacks. The break room in the back of Talbots depressed the hell out of her with its posters of Minnesotan minimum wage and metal folding chairs, so she took her lunch out into the mall. The food court smelled like BO and yeast (Taco Bell and Subway, respectively), a combination that reminded Elliot of awkward teenage sex, a smell she wasn't trying to perpetrate in the fishbowl of Talbots or at her parents' dinner table, so she usually ate by the fountain in the mall's south end. The fountain wasn't great, a copper phallus maybe five feet tall, the water dribbling more than shooting, with its base full of change and usually a Doritos wrapper or two. But it would do. The sound was almost soothing.

She ate baby lettuce and red peppers with a dusting of balsamic. She drank a Diet Snapple peach iced tea. Her right bunion ached, but she would not be that woman, the one who rubs her disgusting growth while shoveling in forks of arugula. There was a loud noise over to her left, not unlike a beaver slapping its tail against the water. A teenager rode a skateboard in front of Zumiez. Elliot thought this was annoying. But she kept watching, and he was pretty good, spinning the board this way and that, his highest jump a good two feet off the ground. His buddies cheered and said things like *fuck yeah, bro*, and it was then she noticed the boy on the skateboard wasn't just attractive, but beautiful. He wore the skinny pants of his generation, black jeans feeding into the mouths of his high-tops, and a crisp white V-neck hugging his fatless body, dark hair, teeth still yet to be stained by coffee and neglect.

He gave two succinct pushes on his board. He was coming toward Elliot, and this made her nervous, because a) he was beautiful, and b) he was coming in her direction at a steady clip, and he veered a little, jumping, the board somehow attached to his feet, and landed on the two-foot-wide ledge of the fountain, which he rode around for half of its diameter, before slipping, the board shooting off toward Elliot, the boy tumbling to the fake marble flooring. Elliot feared broken bones, arms or maybe a neck, at least a clavicle. The boy got up and he was all smiles and it was then Elliot realized the board was at her feet and he was walking over with his swagger underneath the wrapping of false humility. He smiled. His beauty was real, so fucking real, dimples (a self-admitted weakness of Elliot's) and parents that stopped at no orthodontic expense, and an Adam's apple that for some reason made her imagine his penis, which she assumed would match in the surprisingly sexy combination of youth and masculinity.

"Sorry," he said. He pointed to the board.

"Are you...okay?"

"Yeah, fine, all good."

"Sure?" She pointed to his left elbow, which was bleeding. He turned his arm around, exposing a two-inch flap of skin that moved like a freshly hung nylon flag. He said, "Fuck." He pushed his elbow against his shirt. The white became a blotch of sloppy tie-dye. He was dumb to ruin his shirt, dumb to be skateboarding in the mall, to skateboard at all, to be all *fuck yeah* with his boys, but he was also about the most attractive person she'd seen since arriving back in Minnesota a month prior. Elliot's legs were pressed together. There was movement going on down there, something like the first drops of water from a green hose down a yellow Slip-N-Slide.

"Do you need, like, I mean, first aid or Band-Aids or a...hospital?"

His laugh was slightly effeminate, impressive in its tonal range. Elliot clenched her slacks (Talbot's black flat-front) closer together. She feared lettuce in her teeth.

"I'm good. It's nothing."

He was dumb. He was a dumb kid who probably thought the wounds of *extreme* anything were cool, badges of courage, something to be filmed and uploaded to YouTube and watched with his friends while they smoked cheap Mexican weed from Coke cans in their suburban subdivisions. He was dumb. And young. Maybe not as young as she'd first thought (something about that Mount Blanc of an Adam's apple), probably college-aged, maybe a sophomore, still using a fake to buy Coors Light, but still young, a good decade younger than Elliot, and he was bleeding, staring down at her, his eyes a touch of green, his dumb grin the sole reason he'd have a good life, successful in whatever he stumbled into.

"Thought I had it," he said.

"Huh?"

"Trying to ride around the whole fountain. Caught the trucks and, well…" He held up his arm, which caused a rapid change in stream flow, two braids of red gliding across his biceps, which Elliot noted was an impressive slab of muscle, natural, an athlete turned skateboarder.

"Here," Elliot said. She handed over a Chipotle napkin she'd taken from the food court.

"Thanks, sister."

He was dumb because he said things like *sister*, which meant he probably thought he was Black, or at least one of the lucky few accepted as somehow cool enough for hip hop culture, which he wasn't, no way, not a white kid from the suburbs of St. Paul.

"You work here? Like the mall or whatever?"

Elliot wanted to say no. No, she did not work in the Roseville mall. No, she was not employed by the thirty-seventh highest-grossing Talbots in the country. And fuck no, she was never lectured on Hanger Integrity, and no, that bit of excitement she'd felt at selling the fat woman the two long sleeve shirts with hideously clashing blouses, that wasn't about *competition* but *commission*, and had nothing to do with Carolyn.

"Yes."

"Right on. Which store?"

Say anything but Talbots, anything but Talbots. "Talbots."

The beautiful boy's smile faded and he was dumb for this too, his inability to maintain a smile while thinking, and then it was back, his grin, his teeth a perfect half-moon. "Oh yeah," he said. "My mom loves that store."

And there it was, the truth Elliot was trying to protect her fantasy from: she was in the category of *mother*, both literally and figuratively, had the ant colony of stretch marks along her hip flexors to prove it.

The boy pressed his foot against the tail of his skateboard. The bottom of the board was the cartoon from the second Guns N' Roses album, the girl lying against a fence, breasts exposed, panties ripped around her ankle, the robot stalking away, an album Elliot's older cousin had brought over when she was still in grade school. Even though she hadn't known what rape was at that age, the picture had frightened her, something about danger and helplessness and the sudden awareness of her own vagina, which her mother had instructed her to keep hidden.

"*Appetite for Destruction*," she said.

The boy smiled, this one like he was pleasantly surprised.

"You skate?"

"No."

"But you knew the name of the deck."

Elliot let herself laugh. He was dumb because he was young. They all were. She'd been dumb; the students her husband slept with were dumb. They were dumb because they didn't know enough not to be. And maybe that was why people championed their thirties. They'd tried and failed, and the resulting consequence was a Pavlovian response to things that caused less pain, and maybe there was something less bad about knowing how not to be hurt and embarrassed, which is to say, learning to give up.

"Lucky guess," she said.

He stood there looking down at her and then his board and then back at her. "Maddie," he said.

"Elliot."

"Well…"

"Yeah."

"Elliot from Talbots."

Elliot nodded. That was the summation of her being, her cliff-noted moniker, an epitaph, *Elliot from Talbots*. The beautiful boy said his goodbyes and skated back to Zumiez where his friends waited, eager to examine his gouged elbow, and then after a moment of hushed conversation, they all turned, three of these clones, and Maddie too—still fucking beautiful, still fucking dumb—and looked directly at Elliot, seemingly giving some sort of approval with their nodding heads, and the faucet sprouted back into action with a tickling of her inner belly-button as Elliot allowed herself the briefest of fantasies of them saying she was cute, Maddie telling them he would hit it, no question.

The pay structure was this: $9.75 an hour, and if Elliot's biweekly sales goals were met (an average of $89.78 per hour, a prorated amount for all Seasonals), she received a 1.75% cut of everything rung up under her employee number. After two weeks on the job—the first of which was spent going over three-ring binders of HR protocol and watching VHS movies with titles like *The Talbots Way* and *Accessorizing the Outfit: Capitalizing on Units Per Transaction*, the second week was her basically standing there while her superiors lectured on Hanger Integrity—Elliot knew she was nowhere near commission.

Her first paycheck confirmed this knowledge.

After taxes, she was taking home $544.67.

She wanted to ask her boss if she was kidding. If there'd been a mistake. How the hell was she supposed to make commission while being stuck in the break room watching videos? Shouldn't there be some sort of training bonus to offset the time off the floor? But of course she didn't say anything, both because Elliot wasn't usually that kind of person, the one to complain to people in roles of power, and because it was still $544.67 she hadn't had two weeks before, and with her overhead being practically nothing since moving back to Minnesota and in with her parents, she could squirrel away the majority of it for presents for Jacob and a future first-and-last deposit for an apartment in Minneapolis or at least St. Paul.

And really, there was something else there too, a sense of accomplishment, of earning, the proverbial getting your hands dirty with the sun beating down your neck and the exhaustion of a laborer's day, pride or at least fortitude, though she wouldn't admit this to herself, nor to anyone else. She hadn't worked over the past three years, not since Jacob was born. She'd spent time at parks, playgrounds, science museums, children's museums, art museums, Cherry Creek Mall, fake-as-fuck brunches with other faculty wives, day hikes up the foothills of the Rocky Mountains with her Bob jogging stroller and Patagonia soft-shell jackets. Most of these activities were done alone with her son, and looking back, they were done as a way to kill time while giving the appearance of being productive. *What were you two up to today? We saw the new Van Gogh exhibit at the Denver Art Museum, then took a five mile walk on Flatiron Trail. Sounds great. It was. It really was.* Here she would smile, give Devon a flirty-yet-serious look, one daring him to question how she spent her time, while also praying for him not to dig any deeper. It had been as if each meal were a test, each interaction a perverse playing out of father-daughter power dynamic (not so much in a sexual way, that had dried up over the last year, but in a financial way, as if each bite of salmon was packed with the subtext of value and subsidy, her being the government-sponsored overindulgence trying to keep her enterprise afloat.)

Elliot lined up the creases of all the folded cotton Ts. She size-ran her double-pleat slacks. She made sure the Talbots logos all faced the window for the wrinkle-resistant poly-cotton button-downs. She spread her fingers through the hanging cords because she knew Carolyn would be on her shit about spacing.

The assistant manager, Mrs. Williams (she insisted on the awkward title formality, more than likely an idea stolen from some "effective management" book she read on her lunch breaks in Borders), gave a quick sweep of the section. She sported the look of eccentric art teacher, or rather, a boring woman trying to pull off that look—dyed red hair cut short with wispy, forward-swooping sideburns, thick glasses in turquoise or purple, shirts that were made for the verb *flow*.

"Looks good, really good," Mrs. Williams said.

Elliot told herself not to smile, but she did. Praise was praise.

"You should try it more," Mrs. Williams said.

"What's that?"

"Smiling."

❧

Later that night, Elliot stood outside of Rosedale Mall. It was dark and almost cold and the south end of the mall was crowded with moviegoers. Wreaths hung on each lamppost. It was a week before Thanksgiving, and as people walked from their cars, they seemed happy, or at least not dour, no, happy, excited, friends and family and dates and groups of teenage girls with baby-sized T-shirts, imagining their braces snagging the pubic hair of whichever Twilight team they batted for. Elliot walked to the employee lot. She had the longing to be going to the mall instead of leaving. To have friends. To be amazed at The Cheesecake Factory's breadth of selection instead of repulsed. She wanted the simplicity of a night out, the momentary lapse of critical judgment that placed everything suburban and Minnesotan in the category of Kohl's compared to Denver's Nordstrom's. Just to not be herself for two fucking hours.

Elliot got to her father's Tacoma. He let her borrow it most days because he drove his van with *Svendson Plumbing: Getting Dirty Since '81* decaled in Clementine orange along both sides. The Tacoma made Elliot feel more like a lesbian than one of those rare hot girls in a pickup. The door opened with its usual creak and sudden two-inch drop, which always prompted Elliot to fear it was going to fling itself off its hinges. The seats were blue and cracked, the once-white stuffing poking through a dishwater gray.

She was about to venture the Herculean step into the truck, but stopped, sniffing the air like a dog catching the first scent of ignited charcoal. Skunk. There was a skunk, and it'd be her luck, for sure it'd be her luck to be dosed in yellow anal spit, and she wouldn't be able to return to work because it was hard enough to coax people into Talbots, but smelling like hell? Forget it.

Elliot heard laughing. She peered over the bed of the truck. A group of boys stood around smoking. Oh. Oh yeah. Weed. Elliot rolled her eyes at herself, embarrassed, ashamed even, and gave a quick look around to see if anybody had *what? Seen her think weed was a skunk?*

And it was on her hard—age, her life, divorce, Jacob, the Tacoma, Talbots and Carolyn, and the smile she couldn't contain from Mrs. Williams's compliments—juxtaposed to average Minnesotans living better lives, going to movies, eating saturated fats, smoking weed, laughing, and it didn't seem fair. Her whole life she'd wanted out. She'd felt better than. She'd done well enough in school to get a scholarship to good-enough UC Boulder, and there, she'd done well enough to get into graduate school, a TA, a stipend, a concentration on Thomas Middleton's notion of women as *leaky vessels*, the role of wine in early Elizabethan theater, highlighted peer-reviewed articles, memorization of feminist literary critic's work like de Beauvoir and Showalter, and she'd received acclaim from department chairs and jealous scorn from her fellow mousy grad students, and it'd felt good, better than good, like she belonged, so close to the card-carrying elite shuffling around college campuses and drinking hard liquor in hotel lobbies at the annual MLA conference, like she'd finally distanced herself from Roseville, Minnesota.

And then there was an elective, an undergrad creative writing course with then-youngish writer-in-residence, Devon Hester.

And then there was a pregnancy and Devon's offer for tenure contingent upon marrying his student and then four years of pretending a mistake was a blessing, that she was happy to put her thesis on hold, nobody read the plays of Thomas Middleton anyway, a child is such a precious thing, this is everything I've ever wanted, a somewhat cultured life in the shadows of 14,000-foot peaks and her author husband.

And then there were the jiggling thighs of a coed suffocating her husband's face, knelt as if in communion at the foot of his desk, the walls covered in rows of his three books, and Elliot had known the intoxicating feeling of those hardbound spines staring back like a promise of somehow being made famous.

"Hey, hey, um, *Ellen.*"

Elliot realized they were talking to her, and the *they* was really the skater from lunch, Maddie. They stood around a green Civic. She made him out after a second, all gusto and charm, smiles, his eyes a bit hooded from the weed.

"Come over here a sec," he said.

Elliot thought about shaking her head, telling them she had places to be, a child to raise, a *family meal* of hotdish to attend to, bath time and bedtime and then alone time (if she was lucky) in the family room watching reruns of *Everybody Loves Raymond.* That sounded about as fun as chemo. People filed into the theater. It was all she'd wanted, communication with somebody she wasn't related to or employed by, what she'd been wishing for not two seconds prior. He'd been close with her name. Maybe that meant something. She closed the truck's door. The thirty feet of pavement felt like a football field, and she was a cheerleader as the boys in the stands sized her up and mentally checked the box of *I would* and she wished she wasn't dressed as a home ec teacher and there Maddie was, now in a hooded sweatshirt, a joint between his lips, its corners pulled to a grin.

"Ellen, what's good?" Maddie said.

"Hey."

"This is Ellen, guys, the girl I was telling you about."

Telling them about? Elliot raised her hand in half a wave. She didn't listen as Maddie rattled off their anonymous sounding names, matching their anonymous looking faces caught in the awkward transitions from Clear-X to Neutrogena.

"You smoke?"

Elliot didn't, hadn't in years, not since undergrad.

"Yeah."

She took the joint. It was loosely rolled with a swatch of tar seared into the top third of the paper. She hit it, willed herself not to cough, felt one coming, willed herself even harder, experienced an explosion of tears pushing against her eyes like South American soccer fans against chain-link fences, thought about her thesis, women as *leaky vessels* unable to contain emotions or sexual urges without the gushing of some bodily fluid, willed herself not to cry or cough, and then exhaled. It was obvious Maddie expected her to take another hit. She did, this time careful on the intake. She exhaled, feeling a slight shifting in her eardrums, a barometric pressure reader indicating an upcoming storm, her shoulders loosening, and she realized she was high, had to be, but did it really happen that fast? It must have, because she didn't feel as nervous, and found herself asking about Maddie's elbow.

"It's all good. Nothing a little head adjustment can't remedy."

Elliot thought it was stupid that he called getting high a *head adjustment*, and she was back compiling reasons he was dumb, why it wouldn't work between the two of them, thinking about the inverse relationship between beauty and brains, which, she theorized, was precisely the reason places like Roseville, Minnesota, was chock-fucking-full of pretty people—they were too dumb not to knock up their high school sweethearts, thus perpetuating the cycle.

Elliot realized she was talking about herself.

"What's that?" Maddie said.

"Huh?"

"You just said something."

Elliot shook her head, suddenly paranoid she may have been theorizing out loud.

The boys laughed. Maddie took the joint from her hand and their fingers touched. His skin was soft. His contact was more than a mere grazing on exchange, had to be more, a gliding touch, purposeful.

"Ellen here thought my arm was broken," Maddie said, pointing to his elbow.

"Elliot."

"Huh?"

"My name. Elliot. Elliot's my name."

"Oh, my bad," Maddie said. "For real, my bad."

"That's fine."

Elliot couldn't tell if things were awkward or not as the joint made its way around the four others. She took two more hits when it was her turn. Things felt pretty and okay and not as cold. Maddie was talking about a party he was having that Saturday and his boys were nodding and he was their leader, Elliot understood this, felt it, his charisma, his ability to make you feel like you're the only person in the circle through a simple glance.

"You should come," he said.

Flattery. It'd been a while since she'd felt genuinely flattered, maybe years, maybe back to Devon's comments on her first short story—a melodramatic more-true-than-not story about a family's (hers) misadventures around seeing fireworks on the Fourth of July, where the mother (hers) drops the bombshell of ovarian cancer sitting on White Bear Lake beach—and he'd told her it showed real promise, real *pathos*, that he'd love to conference with her to discuss it further. And like then, it felt good. It was affirmation. Inclusion. Acceptance. Maddie with his emerald eyes and fist of an Adam's apple, him with his near-remembrance of her name, he was inviting her to his party.

"Yeah, I'll see if I can make it."

"Yeah?" He pulled out his phone and asked for her number. She gave it to him. One of the boys was laughing. Elliot wasn't sure if this was *exchanging digits*, or a friendly invite, but standing there high among the warmth of an enclosed circle, she realized it didn't matter, not in the slightest, because she'd passed for young enough, cool enough, to be included, and just like fifteen years before standing outside of the same mall (still with its old parking lot lamps then) playfully touching the chests of boys she wanted to date, she was part of something, and again she was back to the proclamation of the superiority of one's thirties, and maybe all those motherfuckers were right, but not because of growing families and fortified homes two turns off the highway, but because she was getting a chance to do something over again, (smoke weed in mall parking lots, fraternize with college boys), this time with the knowledge that happily ever after was a myth perpetrated by companies like Talbots.

"Cool," she said.

"Cool."

"Okay."

"All right."

"Bye."

"Peace."

❧

What to say about home life?

One would first need to get a better feeling of Roseville, Minnesota. It was the first suburb of St. Paul, both in proximity and founding date, a hundred-thousand person sprawling of single-story ramblers and strip malls, Snelling Avenue its throughway. Built on the GI Bill and the Greatest Generation's desire to claim what was rightfully theirs in payment for bayoneting Japanese and Germans, Roseville encapsulated the dichotomous relationship of people wanting privacy and people not ready to be completely sequestered inside of curtain-drawn living rooms. It was common to look out of a bedroom into your neighbor's bathroom. Brick was the material of choice. Windows faced twenty-yard driveways and swaths of grass were rented out for parking during the State Fair. It was a working-class suburb, then and now, blue-collar down to the calloused hands, and even though the color of skin had darkened in the last decade as Hmong people sought refuge from the mountains of Laos, the central *essence* of Roseville stayed the same—people proud of their half-lot of the American Dream.

The Svendsons fit this mold: Terry, mother, fifty-eight, cancer survivor, a school nurse for Martin Luther King, Jr. Elementary School (threatening retirement for the past nine Mays), big breasted and bigger boned, a kind woman whose statements sounded like questions, a weekly customer of Jenna's Beauty Parlor for a curl and dye, adult child of a mostly-silent Swedish alcoholic, fearful and loving, a pusher of baked goods; Edwin, father, fifty-seven, a lifelong plumber, wearer of white undershirts as regular shirts, forearms abnormally muscled from the gripping of tools, bald with the remnants of soft fuzz on the patch of skin behind his left ear down to his neck, a Minnesota Twins enthusiast (bragged to have at least seen/heard an inning of every game since '67), a phone bank volunteer for the Democratic Party, a fan of late night stand-up on HBO and Showtime (his self-proclaimed vice, premium cable). They'd been married for thirty-nine years, birthed one daughter, lost another three months after conception, decided Elliot was a blessing enough, and lived in one house their entire adult lives.

Their house stood along Oak Street. It was indistinguishable from those around it, a rectangle of brick and window, white Christmas lights looped around the base and first branches of the overgrown maple taking up the entire yard, white shutters, nothing chipped. The inside was a love affair with the wonders of the color brown—mud shag carpet,

wooden-paneled walls, couches the color of fresh mulch, a kitchen/
dining room table stained two shades darker than natural oak. The front
of the house was basically a single room from kitchen (brown cabinets)
to dining room to family room (new flat screen resting on top of a mahogany console). The walls were covered in pictures, most of which, for
some reason, were of Elliot eating throughout her life, and of course
Twins pennants and framed stubs to the '87 and '91 World Series. The
bedrooms were down the single hallway, a master that barely fit the
recent purchase of a king bed, and Elliot's, stripped of its teenage angst
into a sexless guestroom. The basement, which had been redone once
Elliot reached high school, was carpeted, dark and moist, never without
the hint of budding spores, a *lair* as her father had taken to calling it
during those hormone-filled years.

Elliot wanted to get to the basement, her room since moving back
home, as soon as possible. She prayed Jacob was asleep, her mother busy
with a Sudoku, her father laughing at comedians, dinner finished and
leftovers placed in Tupperware, the lights dark. She couldn't remember
weed ever working like this, not distorting the lights of every passing
car into tractor beams of energy, not making her a complete idiot. She
wanted seclusion and sleep, a futile wish, she knew as she opened the
front door, the lights on, TV cranked to retirement community volume,
Jacob sitting in her father's lap, his face lifting when he saw Elliot, a look
that meant love and excitement and maybe fear at still being awake way
past his bedtime.

The comedian on TV said, "The thing about bitches is they always
be calling each other bitches, but a brother like me says one thing, and
they're all *nigger, no you didn't.*"

"Nice, Dad."

"Ellie," her mom said, "have you a plate of mac 'n' cheese in the
microwave. The Velveeta kind you love with bits of hot dogs."

Her mom sat at the kitchen table wrapped in her housecoat/robe/
moo-moo with an open book of Sudokus.

"Bedtime," Elliot said. She beckoned with her hand to Jacob, who
gripped the jeans of his grandfather, and gave his *I-understand-what-the-
grown-ups-are-laughing-at* laugh.

The comedian on TV said, "A bitch is a bitch is a bitch, am I right?"

"I'll warm it up," her mother said.

"Jacob, say goodnight."

"Let the boy finish the bit," her father said.

"Are you serious?"

"How was work?" her mother asked.

The comedian said, "Just like a ho is a ho is a ho."

"Ho ho ho," Jacob mimicked.

"Jesus Christ," Elliot said.

"*Jesus Christ*," Jacob echoed.

Her mother said, "Eat, eat, eat."

Elliot held a steaming plate of processed cheese and noodles and quarter-inch chunks of Oscar Myers's finest, indecisive as hell about what to do, the choices either sitting with her mother at the table while struggling to make conversation or sitting in the brown La-Z-Boy with her three-year-old watching an HBO comedian talk about bitches and hos, and for some reason the latter seemed like the better choice. She sat. Her mom stood behind her and touched her hair. Her son squeezed his penis through his navy-blue cotton Batman pajamas. Her father laughed his gravelly grunt. Her mom was doing what she always did, talk in an almost indiscernible volume, an adaptation after forty years of marriage, a way to get her words in underneath the audience laughter of her husband's TV. She asked about work and about sales and about S-A-N-T-A being at the mall, and didn't she think it'd be nice to bring J-A-C-O-B in to sit on his lap? Maybe tomorrow before work? At least by this weekend? The mac 'n' cheese tasted like an orgasm, and although the bits of hotdog were like fireballs down her throat, Elliot didn't slow down, no, she couldn't, not when it was the best thing she'd ever tasted.

The TV: "The hood ain't dangerous because of niggers with guns, no-sir-y, but because bitches with jeans wedged up their fire-hot-Cheetos asses."

Her father: "They do love spicy chips."

Jacob: "Chips."

Her mother: "He certainly does like to touch his thingy."

Elliot: "Is this really appropriate?"

Her mother: "It's probably nothing to worry about, boys love their things."

The TV: "Like nature how you never get between a mother bear and her cub, shit, in the hood, never get between a bitch and her bag of flaming Doritos."

Her father: "So true."

Jacob: "Roarrrr!"

Her father: "Exactly, kiddo."

The three-person serving size (one Minnesotan) was gone. Elliot sucked the liquid-y cheese from her fork. Yes, she was still starving, and, yes, still high. Her mother was halfway through a Laura Ingalls Wilder braid of Elliot's hair. Her father was finishing off what he would claim was his third Bud (really sixth or seventh, no, it was Thursday, so probably eighth). Jacob was going to rip his penis clean off. And this was her life, whereas a month before, she would've been returning from a graduate reading, one of Devon's MFA students, some overly serious boy who thought subtlety was the same as nothing happening, and it would've been boring, but cultured, at least culture-ish, dinner afterward, salmon and goblets of red wine, the faculty jealous of her husband's fame, his ease with the students, his persona of cool confidence, and they would talk about the looming fiscal cliff or how Carver was nothing but weakly disguised sentimentality, and it would've been tedious and superficial and bullshit, that's what she would've thought—this is bullshit and these people don't like me because I'm a stay-at-home mother who busies herself with errands and exercise to fight off the hydra of loneliness and worthlessness—but it would've been hers, or at least partially hers, or maybe not hers at all, but Devon's, all of it, Elliot the accessory, the under-the-table deal to ensure tenure, her the faculty's bastard child, the butt of the joke that she had any claim on her husband's pussy-eating lips.

Elliot laughed.

She laughed because she was so close to thirty. Because she made less than she had in high school as a bank teller. Because she had just eaten thirteen hundred calories and still wanted more. Because she was high. Because her mother was braiding her hair. Because she was living at home. Because she had a crush on a dumb college boy. Because she knew the four tenants of Hanger Integrity backward and forward. Because the comedian was talking about how skinny jeans should've skipped the hood. Because she had a son who drew her as the monster who wrecked his family.

Jacob saw her laughing and started with his fake one, and she kept going, tears coming, these ones falling, her father looking over and grinning and then grunting and then gurgling his chuckles, Jacob's turning real, him finally letting go of his dick and scampering over to her lap, Elliot holding him tight and laughing and him laughing and her mother braiding and everything brown and warm and smelling like melted Velveeta.

II

I Love You This Much—A Party's Epicenter—
This Isn't Going to Happen

Every article of clothing Elliot owned was fucking stupid. This was Saturday night in the basement of her parents' home, clothes everywhere—sweaters and flannels and slutty camies and even a black dress that had been billed as *sportswear*, sweat-wicking and everything—but it was stupid, they all were stupid, not right for a college house party, not when she was old enough to be their professor or at least TA. She needed something sexy but effortless, a thrown-together number that conveyed not giving a fuck, apathy, youth, but still looked slamming. She settled on a pair of dark skinny jeans. And her go-to Frye boots (knee-high, pull-on, a real problem when her calves had swollen with pregnancy misery during Jacob's final trimester). Her top, her top, her top. Sweaters made her feel fat. Any sort of button-down made her feel like she worked at Talbots. It was too damn cold for a cami or tank, and she wanted her breasts to be, if not the *main* focal point, *a* focal point, something to lead with like a speedy shortstop batting first. She came across a somewhat ratty long underwear top, navy, three small green snap buttons, jammed into the side pocket of her still packed suitcase. An interesting choice for sure, but something about it felt right, the way it was both form-fitting and loose, suggestive, real suggestive with the top two buttons unclasped. Good enough.

Elliot made her way upstairs and down the hallway to her old bedroom. The door was cracked, a nightlight in the shape of a turtle shining over Jacob. He was so peaceful with one hand balled to his face, his legs spread-eagled underneath the sheets. Elliot was struck with the thought of *what the fuck am I doing?*, an urge to crawl in bed next to her son, to brush his caramel bangs (a little effeminate, should probably get those cut) out of his eyes, listen to his breathing, lost in the milky aromas of his exhales.

"Mom?"

"Yeah, honey?"

"What are you doing?"

"Watching you sleep."

"Don't."

Elliot laughed and crossed the threshold into his room and sat on the edge of his bed. She placed her hand on his chest. He wrapped his little fingers around her thumb and pinky and then he said it again, "Don't," and Elliot realized this may be about more than him wanting another story or the back-of-the-mind security that comes from knowing your loved ones are safe inside for the night, but about abandonment, about loss, about moving to Minnesota, a drive straight through the night, about not seeing his father, about a little boy trying to create order out of a family that imploded in the five seconds it took for Elliot to put the image of Devon on his knees with the coed on his desk into the context of *my husband is giving oral sex to a woman other than me.*

"I love you so much. You know that, don't you?"

Jacob nodded.

"How much do I love you?"

"This much," Jacob said, stretching his arms out to the side as far as he could.

"More."

Jacob strained to stretch farther.

"More."

"This whole room."

"More."

"The house."

"More."

"The world."

"More."

Jacob seemed puzzled. He let his arms fall to the bed, opting not to bring them back to Elliot's hand still on his chest. He said, "But Dad doesn't?"

Elliot felt something like an icicle being jammed through her belly-button. She'd tiptoed around this subject over the last month, made up lies about his father not feeling well, a vacation, and when these failed, she tried a hint of honesty—Mommy and Daddy are having a little argument, maybe we'll live with Grandma and Grandpa while Daddy lives back home—and she'd felt this was good enough, as close to true as a three year old would understand. The last thing she wanted was for Jacob to feel unloved by his father, because Devon was nothing, if not a good father, so happy to read story after story to their drowsy son. Yet here Jacob was internalizing his father's infidelities as a lack of love. But how could he not? It was a choice on Devon's part, his flicking tongue saying I choose her over you and your mother, my family, that life, I don't want it, and he probably didn't, never had, his hand forced by his sperm's vigor in bursting through Elliot's egg. But love? He still loved Jacob, and this was what Elliot said as she rubbed a circle into his chest.

"I know."

"You do?"

"Yes."

"Then why did you ask?"

Jacob turned his head away from Elliot and sighed (a dramatic gesture he'd started to employ over the last couple of weeks).

"What is it? Jacob? You can tell me."

More shaking of his head.

"Jacob?"

"I asked why he doesn't love *you*?"

Again with the icicles searing her innards, again with the shortness of breath. Jacob's powers of perception and intuition never ceased to amaze her. He watched her from the very bottom corner of his eyes. Elliot forced her face into a smile. She would tell him mommies and daddies don't always get along and it had nothing to do with him, nothing at all, they loved him more than anything, but he already understood this, as he'd just said, and she believed he really did. He was asking a simple question, one she wouldn't allow herself to actually articulate: why wasn't she good enough?

"I don't know," she said.

Jacob turned back to his mother. He took her pinky and thumb again. Elliot felt like the worst parent being consoled by her toddler.

"I love you," she said.

"I know."

ॐ

Maddie had sent his address via text, along with a semicolon wink face, which Elliot thought was about the stupidest thing ever, but also kind of sweet, innocent, or maybe an inside joke, a subtle jab at their age discrepancy. And now Elliot followed the directions on Google Maps on her phone, and she was confused because it was nowhere near the St. Paul or Minneapolis campuses of the U, but farther into the suburbs, the outskirts of Roseville, even past Costco and Sam's Club, Highway

36 dropping from four stop-lit lanes to two continuous ones, and then she was in a subdivision like an energy-efficient Oz. *What the fuck?* Cul-de-sacs and street names of famous authors (Fitzgerald, Joyce, Yates). Houses either garage front-left or front-right, synthetic paneling made to look like wood, bay windows framing the golden hue of Christmas trees. Cars lined the road and she slowed down and there it was, 1789 Beckett, a three-hundred thousand dollar interpretation of Home. Perhaps it could be the recession, an upside-down home foreclosed and rented to Maddie and his boys? Elliot checked her nostrils for boogers. It wasn't too late to turn around and head home and kiss Jacob's sleeping eyes and sit in the basement watching the ancient TV/VCR and get a good night's sleep because tomorrow was Sunday and the Talbots faithful loved to shop on Sundays. A single drink. A hello and nice place and an air of being too cool for a college party and then she could leave. Elliot thought about Maddie's Adam's apple and college abs and she thought about the white of Devon's knuckles as he clenched his desk as if the pussy he was devouring was painful in the deliciousness of its tang.

There were two inflatable snowmen in the yard. A lush wreath hung on the red front door. She stood on a bristly mat that screamed *Merry Christmas.* She was about to ring the doorbell, but what kind of person rang the doorbell besides a bitch who was weeks away from thirty? She opened the door. There were sneakers everywhere, the retro hi-tops of hipsters and skaters, and boots, all of them Uggs lined with fur. Rap played. People yelled from the kitchen. Two girls stared down at her from the carpeted stairway. They held the accessory of choice for parties, red plastic cups, both blond and judgmental and not hiding their visual appraising and apparent disapproval of Elliot. Elliot smiled and stepped into the foyer. A couple came in the door, not stopping to ask for pardon, brushing her shoulder, the girl with her arms raised in the air giving white-person whoops of party-joy. The room to her right was nice with its cream couches and electric fireplace and a couple made out (no shame in the over-the-sweatshirt rounding of second base). The room was too nice. This house was too nice. She felt as if in a dream, a bad one with nakedness and embarrassment and sludge-like footing.

The kitchen was the party's epicenter: rows of plastic bottles of cheap vodka, a keg, girls sitting on counters (even more Uggs), boys with flat-brim hats and skinny jeans and acne, a game of quarters around a tasteful kitchen island, rap with sixteenth notes, a boy working with an amateur's dexterity on the rolling of a blunt, citrus shampoo like a Floridian wet dream, screams and loud stories and the jockeying for attention and the general merriment/desperation of youngish people trying to get fucked.

They seemed so young.

The kitchen was so nice, what with its full set of burnt orange Cuisinart hanging above the four-burner stove.

And there was a lot of maroon and navy blue (beanies, sweatshirts), and just as Elliot made eyes with Maddie (leaky vessel for sure), she put it all together: maroon and navy were Roseville North's colors; this house was nice because it belonged to Maddie's folks; she was at a high school party, not a college party.

"Elliot, what's up?" Maddie gave her his beautiful-person smile and he held out a red cup. Elliot felt herself flush, her cheeks straight down to the pinpricks of sweat along the ridgeline of her low-rise jeans. Maddie seemed a little drunk, the happy amount of added warmth and confidence. He hugged Elliot. He told her how rad it was she made it out, can I get you something, you look great.

"I should go."

"You just got here."

"Right. But I should go."

"One drink."

"Sorry."

"One drink," Maddie said. He grinned the grin of the rarely turned down, holding out his cup, and Elliot thought about Rohypnol and about date rape and statutory rape and about sinking to a whole new level of sad, her the subject instead of the verb.

"Your parents have a lovely home," she said.

"What?" Somebody had turned the music up, and now people were rapping along with the chorus, all hand waves and flashed gang signs seen from TV.

"Nothing." Elliot looked around the kitchen, at a generation three or four removed from hers, one still yet to live away from home and be brokenhearted and develop eating disorders and fall into jobs that became careers, still believing the only reason for contraception was to protect against pregnancy.

"Have a good night," she said.

She turned and walked away, and he was calling out to her and she felt like crying and the girls on the stairs were still there with their insecure bitchy staring and she was outside with the wind and temperature so close to freezing and then she felt like laughing because it was all so fucking stupid—her life, herself.

"Elliot, Elliot."

Maddie was at her side, a tiny bit out of breath. He was smiling, and when he saw that she wasn't, his face changed toward concern, a slight pouting of lips and arching of eyebrows.

"What's up?"

Elliot shook her head. She wanted to lie, to tell him it wasn't her scene, something that shielded herself from the embarrassing truth of not knowing he was a high school boy, but just like her conversation with Jacob, it felt futile, immature, a pathetic attempt to save face in front of people who probably knew better.

"I thought…fuck, I thought you were older."

Maddie smiled like this was a compliment.

"Can't be here, you know?"

Maddie shivered in his black T-shirt. He rubbed his arms. Elliot forced herself to look away from his biceps.

"Just a drink, we can, like, go to the porch where it's quiet," he said. "Sorry."

"I'm eighteen."

Elliot laughed. Maddie did too. She said, "And I'm older."

"Twenty?"

"Flattery will get you everywhere."

"Twenty-two?"

"Going to get pneumonia standing out here."

"Twenty-three tops."

"Bye."

Elliot turned around and started back down the driveway, her mind a buffering clip of the last ten seconds of conversation, giving herself a passing grade, maybe even in the B range, flirty and ego saving, Maddie left in the position of being let down, of wanting.

She felt a pulling at the back of her elbow, and she turned around, and Maddie was right there, a foot away, closer, coming even closer, and it was his Adam's apple she stared up at, and she knew what was happening but made herself a hapless victim of a teenager's impulse, and his lips were on hers and his hands around the back of her head and she knew she should be pulling away with an *I can't* or maybe even *how could you*, but his tongue found hers and they pressed bodies and he kissed with the skill of a man twice his age and he'd said eighteen and it wasn't illegal and it was back to that dream-sequence feeling, her still naked, the world still goo, only she was the one providing the sticky substance, and maybe Thomas Middleton had been right about women being nothing but pissing and shitting and coming and crying creatures, and maybe that had been the real reason she'd quit with her thesis, her subconscious agreement with her sex's pathetic depictions.

Elliot finally pushed him away. Maddie still had his eyes closed. She had her hand on his chest, and he reached for it, held it, mostly her pinky and thumb, pressing it against his body, and the symmetry of Jacob was too much, too fucking weird, and she said, "This isn't going to happen. Goodnight, Maddie."

III

The Talbot's Guaranty—Christmas Party at Chili's—Glob on the Floor—Rookie of the Year

Talbot's had a policy about returns, a *philosophy*, as Mrs. Williams, the assistant manager, schooled Elliot during her first day of training, which basically allowed customers to return any item for any reason after any amount of time or wear. Cleverly, this practice was titled *The Talbots Guaranty*. The idea was something about a happy customer maybe affecting ten other people, while an unhappy customer poisoned the well of one hundred potential shoppers. Therefore, the cost-benefit of taking back a blouse with a slight stitch unraveling and giving the custie a new one or store credit far outweighed the potential loss of one hundred future customers. Sure, there were bound to be a few abusers of *The Talbots Guaranty*, but the store's demographic was middle-class women, Caucasian, aged thirty-seven to fifty-eight, which Mrs. Williams claimed (oblivious to any ageism-sexism-racism-classism), were not the most notorious of scammers.

However, for the sales associates at Talbots, there were problems with this *philosophy*:

Since Talbots merchandise was released on a quarterly calendar, switching over inventory every four months, sending out the previous season's styles to outlets in freeway strip malls, they rarely had the same item a customer was returning, so an even exchange was damn near impossible (calling all the outlets for the item was a miserable waste of everybody's time), and the customers were issued gift cards.

They never used the gift cards the same day, or maybe at all.

Each return underneath *The Talbots Guaranty* fell under the sales associate's number who originally sold the item, and if there was no record of this (rare in the age of electronic receipts and rewards members), the hit was divided evenly under the numbers of all staff working that day. Every cent of returned items went against a sales associate's expected numbers, against their commission. Therefore, Talbots, as a company, may have benefited from their lenient/irresponsible return policy, but the sales associates got fisted on the whole thing.

The returned items needed to be logged into both the computer and by hand, then snipped, and individually bagged, then shrink-wrapped, a duty that usually fell to the lowest woman on the tenure chain. This was done in a room the size of a basement bomb shelter, about as inviting too, all cinderblock and fluorescent light. There was fear of bed bugs being brought in from a customer's return infesting the entire store. Therefore, the bagger of returned items became the sacrificial lamb.

Certain women abused the system. They wore a sweater until they became too fat, then complained about it pilling. They purchased jackets with shoulder pads for a one-day marketing conference, then said the merino-blend caused rashes. They used the store as a trade-in program. And it got old, as does any time you know you're being used, yet are completely helpless in the situation, having to take it with a smile, an *apology*, a sorry that didn't work out for you, how can we make that right?

When it was brought to management's attention, as Elliot mentioned in the break room one day to Mrs. Williams, she was given a formulaic answer about a long-term approach, not necessarily commission on this paycheck, but down the road, the more people ecstatic about the customer service and policies at Talbots, the more people shopping there, and then look out for your commission!

Elliot said, "But my contract is up on January 6th."

"Well, I'm not supposed to say anything, but word from above is they are looking to keep one Seasonal on as a Part-Time! Just keep doing what you're doing, and you may have a shot!"

So that's what Elliot did. She fluffed her assigned section, returning from the folding table with a stack of cashmere cardigans, only to find the stack she'd finished making perfect was utterly destroyed. She internalized the tenants of Hanger Integrity. And she smiled when chubby ladies made up lies about why a three-year-old sweater was no longer holding up, dividing that hit against all their chances at commission. She did this because it was her job. Because she didn't have much of a choice. Because she needed the money, however little, to get presents for Jacob, to get rent for an apartment, to get away from her parents' looming bodies, which hovered over Elliot as she pretended to sleep, as if they preferred their daughter unconscious, safe and secure, dormant in their moist basement. And because her Seasonal contract was up in a month, and although being a Part-Time employee of Talbots sounded as fun as a pap smear, it was currently the only option partially on the table.

It wasn't so much a case of Elliot drinking the corporate Kool-Aid (Lord knows she hated everything about Talbots), but more of an understanding of what was needed to get by. She had to feign excitement at the redressing of the window mannequins, fawn over the softness of the 80-20 merino-to-poly blend of their new Christmas-themed scarves, use words like *dashing* and *definitely* and *super cute*. She had to play the game. And so, when Mrs. Williams asked if she would be attending the Christmas party (Mrs. Williams refused to pollute Jesus's birthday with the term *holiday*), Elliot swallowed, as she'd taken to doing since working at Talbots, a physical response to keep her from saying the first response that came to mind, and said, "Of course, wouldn't miss it."

That Monday after work, Elliot walked the five hundred yards from the mall exit to the adjacent restaurant. It smelled like fajitas, thick grease that practically ruins an outfit with its mysterious *is-it-onion-or-BO* aroma. The cliché irony of having a Christmas party for a mall store at Chili's seemed lost on the rest of the ladies at Talbots, but not Elliot, who, by the time she had helped close, fluff, and bag all the used returns, would rather have slid splinters underneath her toenails than pretend to be happy amongst coworkers in a restaurant connected to the mall. The rest of the ladies were well on their way to buzzed merriment. The Talbots staff with their paunchy spouses huddled together in the far corner of the restaurant. It wasn't really a private room, more like a grouping of heavy tables pushed to the windowed wall, covered in plates of picked-over fried appetizers. There were a lot of colorful drinks. The whole scene struck Elliot as a particular hue of sad she'd never imagined herself a part of. A few of the husbands nodded their heads to their blabbering wives while stealing glances at the football game being shown in the bar. Elliot ordered a vodka tonic. She placed the scraps of a blooming onion on an almost-clean plate and tried to inconspicuously edge her way into a grouping of coworkers who, as it turned out, were complaining about *The Talbots Guaranty*.

Jan, one of the Full-Time, non-floor leads, probably fifty, a cute butt-chin nestled into a turkey gobble of second and third chins, was holding court: "I'll tell you what. I know for a fact, an absolute certainty, that some employees are taking back *their* returns under the group code."

"Who?" another coworker asked.

"Not my style to throw people under the bus, but (looking over both shoulders, leaning forward), let's just say they *lead*."

"What?"

"*Lead*," Jan said again.

"Lead what?" the other woman asked.

"The floor. Floor-*lead*."

"No."

"Believe you me, hon, know for a fact."

Elliot pretended to be outraged, even allowing her mouth to drop open a fraction. She didn't care about store politics, but maybe she did, because the more she thought about it, the more she listened to triple-chin Jan talk about a coworker in a position of power (however slight) abusing said power, the madder she got, realizing it wasn't about some petty competition among the sales associates, but about money, about taking her money, about shirking blame, about deceit, but, no, mostly about money. The women had made a little more room for her in their circle. She realized the building of rapport through the justified anger toward others was as much a part of working retail as Hanger Integrity, and that this was her chance, both to vent some frustration and to ally herself with these women, and when a lull fell over the conversation, Elliot seized the opportunity. She said, "If you ask me, the whole concept of *The Talbots Guaranty* is ridiculous. A complete joke. Everything about it."

Elliot felt like she was on a bit of a roll, the first tingles of her vodka tonic warming her throat. "I don't even blame the people who bring back the clothes because it's management's fault. Just asking for it."

The ladies weren't nodding their heads. Some of them were looking out of the window. Jan was suddenly interested in her gaudy press-on nails. *What the fuck?* Elliot said something about the real bullshit being management putting the hit on them instead of eating it themselves, and just as she was about to launch into it probably being somehow illegal, she saw the wispy hair of Mrs. Williams, who'd evidently cozied herself into the circle.

Elliot quit talking.

"No, no, keep going," Mrs. Williams said.

"I'm sorry."

"Nothing to be sorry about. I think it's healthy to air one's grievances. However, at a Christmas party, well, that's a little..."

"Tacky," Jan said.

"You said it, sister."

The women laughed. Elliot made herself join in as if it was all so funny, her lack of tact, her being the firecracker of the group. Jan could eat a bag of dicks. Mrs. Williams said something about them making sure to grab another drink before the awards started. She reached across the circle and took Elliot's arm. She said, "Maybe not you, hate to see that mouth once it gets fully lubricated."

More laughs.

Elliot excused herself, citing the need for the restroom. Just as she turned around, she was greeted by Carolyn, her puffer-fish-faced seasonal nemesis, who wore a hideous mock turtleneck that caused her golden hoop earrings to rest at awkward angles An insurance salesman type stood by her side, all gelled hair spiked to cover up its apparent thinning. Carolyn slid her arm around his. She said, "Elliot, this is Randal, my *husband.*"

Elliot noted the emphasis on *husband,* or maybe it was on *my,* she wasn't sure, but either way, it was a dig, a not-so-subtle fuck you, this is how you keep a man, and what a man he is!

"Nice to meet you," she said.

"Wasn't sure you were going to make it," Carolyn said. "It doesn't really seem like your thing, and you being Seasonal and all."

"Well, what can I say?"

"Never pass up an offer on free booze," Randal said with a spastic wink.

Elliot had the feeling she could fuck Randal in the bathroom if she wanted to. Carolyn must have sensed the same thing because she pulled Randal's arm tighter, climbing to her tiptoes to put her heavily lipsticked lips on his cheek. Randal took the marking of territory because that's the kind of man he was, Elliot knew, the kind who showed up when he was supposed to, kept quiet when given one of many learned cues to shut up, and acted as a probably once-attractive accessory to Carolyn's need for control, all the while emptying a small fortune into webcam shows from Mexican girls in South Los Angeles.

"If you'll excuse me," Elliot said.

"Oh, before you leave," Carolyn said, touching Elliot's elbow, "Jan mentioned something yesterday about you ringing back returns from the guaranty under the store's number rather than your own. I know you're new, and *Seasonal,* but that's kind of a no-no, okay?"

And then there were tears.

This was walking away from Carolyn and her stupid adulterous husband, away from two-faced and three-chinned Jan, away from Mrs. Williams with her eccentric wisps of hair and false acceptance of aired grievances, away from the picked over apps, from Talbots, from the mall, Chili's, her bullshit life in a bullshit suburb. Elliot dabbed at her eyes, bit the hell out of the inside of her cheek. Families shoveled burgers and fries and mozzarella sticks into their pasty mouths. Everything was a replicated version of clay-red and green tile, hung Christmas lights, and laminated menus stained with barbeque sauce, multiplied by every grouping of twenty-thousand people in America, Chili's an institution, more recognizable than the Lincoln Memorial. She felt a pang of jealousy toward these people, the simplicity of it all, their lives, or at least the ease in which they consumed four thousand calories before their entrees arrived. She walked through the bar, which housed a slightly younger crowd, or at least patrons sans obese children. Her vision was cloudy with tears, and when she heard somebody calling her name, she didn't look, wouldn't look, because she couldn't think of a single person she actually wanted to see, not then, covered in flushed skin and cloudy eyes, not ever.

She made her way into the T in the back of the bar with restrooms on either end.

"Elliot."

She knew the voice, knew it was Maddie, and she kept going, pushing open the heavy wooden door. Some slutty girl Elliot recognized from working at Victoria's Secret applied mascara in the mirror. The door opened behind Elliot, and she saw Maddie through the mirror, cute as hell in his hooded sweatshirt, so young, but *God*. The Victoria's Secret girl turned, half appalled, half excited thinking this boy was for her.

"Always walking away from me," Maddie said. He had his grin, his Adam's apple, his confidence at always getting what he wanted. "Starting to wonder if you're trying to tell me something."

"You can't be in here," Victoria's Secret said, her voice suggesting otherwise.

Maddie didn't pay her any attention, but stared at Elliot, the mess of her puffy eyes and blotched skin, and he took two steps forward letting the door close behind him. "Are you okay?"

"Serious, man," the girl said. "Your girl doesn't want you in here." She gave Elliot a look of solidarity with her overly made-up face flattening, steeling-over, hardening, and Elliot felt a swell of gratitude for this girl, as if the entire female gender wasn't waiting to fuck over their sisters.

"I'm just seeing if she's okay."

"She's fine."

"I'm fine."

"See?" Victoria's Secret said.

"It's cool," Elliot said.

"Yeah?"

Elliot nodded.

The girl rolled her eyes, slipping her mascara back into her gaudy Coach purse. She said, "Whatever," and then walked past Maddie, placing her hand on the small of his back as she opened the door, leaving it there for a solid second just to make sure he understood she was DTF if the crying old bitch stayed pissy.

Elliot gave an unattractively aggressive sniffle. She felt like shit; she knew she looked like more of the same. But maybe she didn't care. Maybe she'd cared too much over the course of her life about appearances, about seeming okay, mentally together, smart, a good mother, dutiful wife, better than Minnesota, and what had it gotten her? Separated and living in her parents' basement, accepting consolation from her three-year-old son, working in the cesspool of menopausal cattiness that was Talbots.

"Listen," Maddie said, "about the other night. I'm sorry if I moved too fast, you know, like it's just…"

Elliot knew asking *just what* would be a mistake, a desperate trolling for compliments, but she needed it, and maybe deserved it, because why the fuck not?

"Just *what*?"

"I don't know what it is about you, you know? Like you're different."

"Old."

"Not even. I mean, like what, twenty-four?"

"Twenty-five," Elliot lied.

"It's like six years, seven. But that's not even it. I don't know, like you *know* shit, understand it, I can tell."

Elliot was about to launch into a faux-bashful *oh-stop-it*, but Maddie kept talking, saying things about her seeming like a cool person to hang out with, just to get to know, and Elliot realized it all might have been a miscalculation on her part, a drunken kiss representative of nothing more than retarding brain chemistry. And him following her into the bathroom? An apology in the form of an explanation. Friends. That what he was saying, repeating—*friends, hang out, rad*—and she'd never been in this position before, the often-satirized fault line between romantic interest and companionship. Even in high school, if she'd liked a boy, she'd fucked him. And in college? Same. And with Devon and his attention over cups of coffee, his comments about her showing brilliance on the sentence level, a subtle understanding of the *human condition*, she'd made the same leap, this one bridging what should've been a gulf between the sanctity of student and professor.

Oh, the horror.

The horror of the entire night. Of perverting a crush. Of Talbots. Of seeing your husband make another girl come.

"What's funny?" Maddie asked.

Everything was funny. Elliot realized this like an anvil being dropped from her neck, and it felt good, both the metaphoric rope burn and the eventual lifting of said burden. It was all funny. She'd tried to control things, tried her best through manipulation of people and events, sometimes the smiling employee/wife, sometimes the downcast martyr, all of it reeking of fear and the need for acceptance, and it'd netted her nothing. She looked like a maniac smiling in the mirror. What if she started taking what she wanted? What if she quit caring about other's opinions—Devon and the creative writing faculty at DU, mothers as she handed over non-organic juice boxes, Mrs. Williams and Jan and Carolyn, her mother and father, the two-faced bitch from Victoria's Secret—and started doing exactly as she wanted, striving for those things that may or may not make her happy, but that she *wanted*, desired, felt an irrational need to experience and possess?

"You're in the women's bathroom," she said.

"Can you blame me? Keep running away."

"Should probably go back out to the bar and talk to Miss Mascara."

"Don't want to."

"Why?"

"Because."

"Not good enough."

Maddie shook his head and let his grin come and it was a move stolen from a movie, the *I-can't-believe-you-don't-see-how-amazing-you-are* moment, and it looked both good and ridiculous, genuine and completely false.

"I want to get to know you. Hang out. See where it leads."

Elliot nodded. She rubbed the back of her thumbs from the bridge of her nose across the underbellies of her eyes. This was stepping into her thirties, the quitting with giving a fuck about people's opinions.

"That's not good enough," Elliot said.

"What? I mean, like I'm curious to see where—"

"That's not what I mean," Elliot said. She took a step closer to Maddie. She felt as if she was growing, her back straightening, pops of vertebra stretching to their rightful height.

The self-doubt was back on Maddie's face, something about his grin actually opening a half-inch without the white of his teeth pressing to be seen. Power. That's what she felt. It was a foreign sensation, yet intoxicating, an aphrodisiac, her a vessel of leaky proportions, but not helpless as Middleton had portrayed, which, Elliot realized, was the reason he was the discarded tampon to Shakespeare's rightful throne on top of the English canon, who in play after play, demonstrated the fact that a woman's gushing of fluids was not a symptom of weakness, but a tool to be employed in a quest for complete and utter dominance.

Elliot kissed Maddie. The kiss was not like their first, curious and embarrassed of itself, but forceful, aged, confident. Her hands found his stomach, and it was as hard as she'd imagined, its surface like running one's fingers over the contours of an ice tray. She pressed him against the door. His head knocked against the wood. Bing Crosby faded into a track from *Glee Christmas* from hidden speakers. Maddie's dick was a battering ram through the fly of his skinny jeans, well-manicured, the north side of six. Elliot switched positions so it was her against the door, her pencil skirt bunched around her waist, Maddie fumbling with long fingers. It didn't surprise her that a boy as beautiful as Maddie had a rubber in his pocket. She was soaking and it hurt a tiny bit because it'd been a while and Maddie cupped her ass and thrust. She thought about Devon's knuckles and Jacob repeating *a bitch is a bitch is a bitch* and about *The Talbots Guaranty* and about *the human condition* being a bullshit phrase of an excuse for doing shitty things to people. Maddie thrust harder and faster. Somebody was pushing against the door trying to get in. Maddie started making whimpering noises. She wasn't going to come, but maybe she was, yup, a surprise of warmth radiating outward, her toes flexing, Maddie's Adam's apple, the taboo deliciousness of him still eligible for varsity sports, power, the soft skin of his testicles against the soft skin of her upper-inner, her face over his shoulder staring back through the mirror, her coming while staring at herself, the spectacle, the woman who did things like have sex in the bathroom at Chili's.

A minute or two later, Maddie flung his filled rubber into the trash can (spilling a glob on the floor, which made them both laugh), and then took Elliot's hand, gave it a squeeze, told her that was amazing, and Elliot believed him, kissing his cheek, told him the same. She asked what his plans were for the rest of the night. He rolled his eyes.

"Right, a school night."

"Fuck you."

They laughed.

"Tomorrow?" Maddie said.

"Tomorrow."

"Thank you."

"Don't fucking thank me," Elliot said.

"Sorry."

"Don't apologize either."

Maddie leaned in for a kiss and they both were smiling so their teeth scraped and it wasn't a pleasant sensation, but it kind of was. Elliot opened the bathroom door, and there stood Carolyn, all indignation and cowl neck, ready to give Elliot shit about keeping the door closed, but upon seeing Maddie, she stopped, completely at a loss for words, even a choice facial expression, and Elliot said, "Excuse me," walking past, brushing shoulders, her fingers interlocked with Maddie's as she led him through the T.

Things were better after that.

Mrs. Williams had evidently caved and ordered another round of appetizers, saying it was only Christmas once a year, why spare any expense? Elliot drank two more vodka tonics. Word must've spread about what had transpired in the bathroom, because every time Elliot glanced around, a group of employees were staring. Carolyn's husband, Randal, tried to make small talk with her as they loaded up their miniature plates with chicken wings (his efforts were cut short by Carolyn's beckoning from across the room). Elliot said, "The bell tolls." Randal attempted his spastic wink one more time.

Mrs. Williams eventually took center stage (the back of Chili's with the red EXIT sign her spotlight) and launched into a speech about how proud she was to be a small part of the thirty-seventh highest grossing Talbots in the world, how even during an economic recession—*no, I'll go ahead and say it, put the big D on it, call it what it is, Depression*—they were able to not only stay afloat, but meet budget, and this, she said, almost to the point of tears, was a testament to the wonderful ladies copiloting her ship.

Mrs. Williams glanced down to the red table to her right. There were three identical glass paperweights. She held up the first, the Most Improved Player Award, which sounded like a backhanded compliment at best. The honors went to Evelyn, a nondescript woman who'd evidently accomplished a heap of nondescript achievements over the last fiscal year. People clapped. Elliot drank the last of her fourth vodka tonic, and although they were watered-down Chili's versions of a mixed drink, she felt good, more than a touch tipsy, maybe simply post-coital and relaxed, everything, even her eyebrows which were so quick to furrow. Next was the Rookie of the Year Award. Mrs. Williams talked about a newcomer with a fierce streak, a woman who she'd had to lobby to corporate on behalf of due to her age, somebody who embodied a can-do attitude, a new attitude, a Y2K Talbots attitude (Elliot laughed at Mrs. Williams's oh-so-clever fifteen-year-old allusion). Carolyn dabbed her mouth with a cocktail napkin. She handed over her drink to dutiful-and-adulterous Randal. Elliot watched this primping, not unlike a batter's routine stepping into the box with the tightening of gloves and taping of cleats. She imagined the glass paperweight going on a mantel, one that was really particleboard shelving, no fireplace, and it being a centerpiece, an achievement, a conversation starter. She felt bad for Carolyn. She wasn't sure if it was pity or empathy, but something strong born from a rush of alcohol and a skin-blotching orgasm, something that allowed her to see Carolyn's cuntiness as the result of a woman with nothing, trying to gain enough esteem to not eat herself to death.

Mrs. Williams was still blabbing on about Carolyn, about her addition to the work environment, about an energy, undeniable, even commented-upon by customers writing into the store in emailed compliments. Then she paused, holding the paperweight, and said, "Without further ado, I'd like to present the Rookie of the Year Award to newcomer, Elliot Svendson."

It was strange how people's first glance wasn't at Elliot, but Carolyn, who was caught in the awkward position of half-rising from her booth, legs flexed, puffy face doing its best to smile. Elliot walked to the back of Chili's. Jan gave her a big hug. Her breath was Caribbean jerk wings in Elliot's ear: "We're all expecting big things from you."

What little applause there'd been faded. Elliot wasn't sure what to say, how to act, if she should laugh, thank them, tell them it was all bullshit and she hated retail and Talbots and Rosedale Mall and Minnesota—I fucking hate this state, my past here, my coming back, your fatness, your acceptance of mediocrity—the fact that they were in Chili's, that Chili's was kind of good, the Awesome Blossom crack cocaine, that it was all familiar and comforting and sometimes that's all she wanted, to be comforted. She looked past her coworkers and their boring husbands. Maddie stood by the front door. He held up his fist like a Black Power salute (Elliot wasn't even sure he knew the reference). He was adorable, perfect. Elliot laughed. She started talking, but her voice was a funnel of phlegm, which tended to be her precursor to tears, something she was surprised by. There was a tightness in her chest. She was more touched than she was willing to admit to herself by the award and the notion of being of value.

She cleared her throat. She stared at Maddie as she spoke: "Thank you for this, for everything. Life's funny sometimes; it just takes a while to see it."

IV

WHAT IF SANTA IS A PEDO?—TOUR OF ITALY—SUITABLE
YOUNG MEN—ELLIOT GOES ON A PROPER DATE—THE
REMNANTS OF ICE PALACES

The last thing Elliot wanted to do was go to Rosedale Mall on her day off, but that was the plan, a family outing, a visit to Santa parlayed into a dinner at her mother's favorite restaurant, Olive Garden, and Elliot agreed because Jacob had never sat on Santa's lap, and what little kid should be denied this American fetishism?

The only car that could fit the four of them was her father's rapist van, so there they were, three generations cruising down Highway 36, *Svendson Plumbing: Getting Dirty Since '81* accosting any car they passed. Jacob seemed a little nervous to meet the mythical Santa (pulling his penis through his corduroys). Her mother was in a heated verbal debate with herself between the safer Tour of Italy or the vodka-sauce shrimp pasta dish her friend, Laurena, had recently raved about. Elliot, herself, felt a bit nervous about the evening's festivities, mainly seeing Maddie (or one of his Zumiez cohorts). They'd seen each other once since that Monday night Chili's bathroom session, a quick post-work rendezvous, which ended up in a smoked joint and cramped sex in his Civic. He had midterms to study for, but assured her he wanted to hang out, would like nothing more, two weeks of winter break where he never wanted to leave her side, to which Elliot played it cool, said something like, "Not sure that offer was on the table." Being that it was Thursday, a day she'd never seen Maddie at the mall, she felt okay about her chances of getting in and out without being spotted. But she was still nervous, caught between the mortification of her parents, and the fact she was a parent herself.

The mall was a hemorrhage of people who'd evidently skipped out on work to eat Cinnabons and Christmas shop. Jacob reached up with his non-penis-squeezing hand to Elliot's, which she thought was sweet. They walked past the kiosks full of Middle Eastern men selling collectable Lego figurines and bejeweled iPhone cases and vibrators disguised as neck massagers. Her mother waddled more than walked. Her father's jeans were worn completely white from where his Velcro tri-fold wallet rubbed against his butt. Jacob was asking about Santa, if he was real, if he was nice, how he really watched him all the time, was he the same as God (*yes, yes, we help him watch, I'm not sure*).

Each store vomited their own music to match whatever cliental they were trying to attract: Abercrombie Euro body-shot techno; Journey's gentrified hip-hop; Express (men and women) synthesized transgender pop with peppy BPM; Anthropology melancholy-yet-triumphant elf-in folk. The mall also had its own soundtrack piped in from vent-like speakers, which of course consisted of nothing but Christmas carols from October 27th through January 1st (Jews and Muslims be damned). Two grand pianos played more of the same outside of Nordstrom's and Macy's at the east and west ends. The combined auditory experience was schizophrenic, yet effective, a constant stimulus, its inflection subtly matching the mood of each store, spurring the shifting of customers' minds and their resulting purchases.

The North Pole had a soundtrack of its own (children singing the happier, nonreligious Christmas songs). Elliot stood in a twenty-person line with her son and parents. Kids cried and kids screamed and kids ran around while mothers with hairsprayed bangs took desperate swipes at their offspring's Columbia knock-off parkas. It was madness, miserable and manufactured, tired-looking teenage girls in inappropriately slutty elf costumes (red fishnets underneath green felt miniskirts) ushering kids along a white pathway to Santa's workshop/and or/crack house (gray and dilapidated), where he sat in a golden throne, all red satin and fat and beard.

Elliot watched a little boy climb onto Santa's lap. He was taking his sweet damn time listing off presents. Elliot tried to get the attention of one of the elf sluts to hurry him along, but they had the glassed-over look of PTSD soldiers amidst the swirling aftermath of a roadside IED. Santa placed his white-gloved hand on the little boy's chest; only it wasn't his chest, more like his stomach, Santa's finger extended in a flirty tickle. *What the fuck?*

Something deep inside Elliot stirred, a radar that all women have about the appropriateness of touches, and this here, that bellybutton tickle, it was the first Wednesday of the month noon tornado siren of bad touches.

"You see that?" Elliot said.

"I know, so cute," her mom responded.

"What? He's practically molesting him."

The woman in front of them in line turned, her face a pinched angle of disgust.

Her mom rubbed Jacob's hair as if to erase the last five seconds. She turned back to Elliot, whispering, "What is wrong with you?"

The kid finally got off Santa's lap.

Elliot wasn't sure what was wrong with her. The bratty boy looked happy and relatively unmolested. Everybody else was taking minuscule sideways steps to mimic movement while in line. People shopped and ate and texted and flirted with boys from their eighth grade home-room, and she was thinking horrible things about a slit ripped in Santa's trousers, a game of peek-a-boo, because…because…because like her mother had just implied, there was something *wrong* with Elliot, and in that moment, she connected this fear of sexual abuse in a position of power with the two times she'd had sex with a high school boy that week, as well as the fact that the first time her creative writing instructor ever touched her was on the bellybutton of her wool sweater, them walking through the quad, what few imported maple trees the campus had shedding their leaves as the sun got lazy, one of these red leaves sticking to her sweater, him pulling it away, his hand lingering, warmth through wool and warmth through attention and warmth through the juvenile thought of being special.

Ten minutes stretched to twenty, twenty to thirty, and finally, finally, thank God, they were making progress, two shitty kids away from sitting on Santa's lap (maybe Jacob could opt out of *sitting*, and merely *stand* to tell Santa what he wanted).

"Mommy?"

"Yes?"

"Can you stay here when I talk to Santa?" Jacob stared up at her with his father's expression—a condescending sincerity sprinkled with a touch of *it's-for-your-own-good*—and Elliot told herself it didn't matter, him wanting to be alone, him not wanting her to share this experience, his first communion with the God of American Consumerism, but maybe it did matter, because all the other mothers were right close to their sniveling offspring, coaxing them to speak, taking self-portraits (prohibited, so people purchased the digital printouts for $4.99).

"But don't you think I should introduce you? I know Santa pretty well."

Jacob weighed this bit of new information. They were one person away. He shook his head. He had the gift of deducing desperation.

"What if I walked you to his workshop? Can I at least do that?"

He sighed in consolation. "Fine."

"Okay."

She squeezed his hand. She felt like a bad mother, or at least a mother who wasn't sure what the hell she was doing, or at least a mother who was doing the best she could with a husband who indulged in extramarital oral sex like an all-you-can-eat Boston clam bar. A girl of seven whom more than likely thought she was cuter than she really was climbed off of Santa's lap (unmolested), and then it was their turn, the sluttiest of elves giving a FML jerking of her head as a beckoning to follow, rattling off monotone verbiage about a minute being the max, no pictures, but they are available for $4.99 with your choice of Christmas-themed borders, and Jacob shuffled his miniature Velcro boots, was scared, no doubt, needed his mother, and this apprehension made Elliot grateful.

They approached Santa. He was on the realer side of the spectrum of Santas—actual fat, his beard glued to his face instead of those crappy ones that strapped around the ears, his suit with real buttons sewn in and everything. He gave a toothy grin at Jacob. Elliot thought of Marlon Brando from *Apocalypse Now*.

And just then, Elliot looked over to her left, over the fake snowdrifts and candy cane fence, and saw the Adam's apple of Maddie walking by. *Fuck*. Her initial instinct was to duck, which she did, fumbling around for a lace to tie of her non-laced boots. Jacob took this moment to summon up his courage and break away from his mother and grandparents. Elliot reached out, but it was too late, her son walking the loneliest five feet, him walking to a stranger's outstretched arms, a possible pedo, a possible father figure, Jacob about to bear his most pressing wants to a man he feared.

"Get over there," Elliot's mother said.

"He doesn't want me to," Elliot hissed back.

"He's terrified, for heaven's sake."

Elliot could see the top of Maddie's head. He'd stopped in front of the Gadavia store. She could hear his laugh, so confident. Santa wrapped up her boy in his arms. Jacob was seconds away from tears, and there Elliot crouched, running her hands up and down her boots, searching for an explanation for her hidden state, no, for herself, for her fucking self, for the reason she wasn't at her son's side, his instructions be damned.

"What are you doing down there?" her mother said.

"He's losing it," her father said.

And Jacob was losing it, his jaw a sewing machine needle, his eyes glazed, her son needing her. Maddie laughed twenty feet away. The slutty elf told her son to look at her, to smile. The tears started. He brought his little hands all balled up to his eyes. And yet she couldn't move. She couldn't rescue her son from fear, from loneliness, from his desire to be independent and push his parents away because they'd failed him, which he understood, internalized, and there he was trying his best to trudge on with a jaded worldview that was thrust upon him. She couldn't because Maddie would see she had a son. That she was a mother. That she wasn't twenty-five. That she was pathetic, old, a dark horse to become Part-Time at the thirty-seventh highest grossing Talbots in America.

Elliot felt a pressure against her tailbone and turned around just in time to see her mother's foot giving her a not-so-gentle shove toward Santa's throne. Elliot fought to keep her balance, trying to right herself, stand, but the momentum was too great, and she took three awkward waddles forward before her hands hit the ground and then her body, then a rolling over, a crash, pulling the candy cane banister with her.

Elliot opened her eyes. She stared at the black Harley Davidson boots of Santa. She was covered in broken plastic candy canes and green streamers. Jacob stared down at her. He made the face of when he was interrupted sneaking a number two behind the couch. He said, "I told you to wait."

The slutty elf said, "Say cheese."

The entire mall stared. She wanted to die. To curl up and fucking die.

"Elliot?"

This voice really made her want to die, Maddie's.

"Is that your mother?" Santa asked.

"For heaven's sake," Elliot's mother said.

"Elliot?"

"What is it you want for Christmas?" Santa said.

"Get up," her father said.

"For my parents to be together," Jacob whispered.

Santa gave a fake laugh, and said some comment about that being out of his jurisdiction, but *what presents do you want, little buddy?*

Elliot pretended not to hear her son's heartbreaking wish because pity from a fat part-time Santa would be a look she couldn't stomach, shouldn't have to stomach, and standing up, brushing off the green streamers and broken Styrofoam candy canes, she felt a pang of anger toward Jacob (unfounded she knew, but *still*) because he dreamed of things that couldn't happen and blamed her and because he was… *hers*…her responsibility, Devon taking the role of nighttime caller…*I love you so much, wish I was there to tuck you in,* and because she wanted to forget this fact for one fucking second, maybe a night, a day, a holiday season, Maddie there as the perfect distraction, a beautiful quick-coming affirmation that she still had it, and if things had been different…

Maddie had hopped the North Pole's divider, and now was at Elliot's side, trying not to smile. He asked if she was okay.

"Fine."

Santa lowered Jacob to the floor, all the while staring at Elliot in an accusatory way. Elliot wasn't sure if this was because of what Jacob had muttered in his ear or because she'd wrecked his workshop. Jacob stared up at Maddie. Elliot felt her mother's hand on her back, heard her apologize, saying she hadn't meant to actually kick her over. There was no way out. No way of pretending she was anybody other than a mother so close to thirty ushering her son to Santa's lap with parents like cringe-worthy clichés as an entourage. Maddie seemed to be putting things together (maybe he wasn't as dumb as she'd suspected). He looked down at Jacob, who had taken an aggressive stance with his miniature arms crossed and head tilted.

"What's up, little man?"

Jacob shrugged.

"Sorry, listen, I have to get going," Elliot said.

Maddie gave no hint of having heard her. He stuck out his hand for a low-five. Jacob didn't budge. Maddie switched his hand to a fist (a favorite of Devon's, who took to the *pound* with the pathetic excitement of all aging white men who thought they were ahead of some Black-to-white cultural adaptation), and Jacob's quizzical-if-not-defiant exterior melted, his little fist extended as, touching knuckles, he made the explosion sound.

"There it is," Maddie said.

"So, great seeing you, but—"

"Aren't you going to introduce us?" Elliot's mother was no longer in the background, but front and center, her dry-yet-always-lotioned hand extended for a shake.

"There's a line, and we need to get—"

"Maddie. Madison Johnson."

"Hope that first name doesn't mean you're a Badger fan," her father said.

"The only varmint I cheer for is a gopher, sir."

"Good answer."

Her parents shook Maddie's hand (her father even slapping his shoulder), and Elliot needed out of this situation, not so much for the sake of saving whatever the hell was left of her sexual escapades with Maddie, but from her parents putting two and two together, realizing their daughter was having relations with a boy still woken by his mother. She finally was able to catch Maddie's stare, and she gave what she hoped was a *don't say anything, I'll talk to you later, sorry I wasn't completely honest, it's complicated.*

Maddie smiled his beautiful smile, and answered the question posed by her father about how they knew one another with a surprising amount of tact—*friends of friends, us retail employees need to look out for one another during the holiday season*—while somehow managing to bend over and give one more pound to Jacob, who for whatever reason seemed to have taken a real liking to Maddie (Elliot assumed it was a proximity of age). The slutty elf told them they needed to move. Her mother was busy buying the picture of Elliot sprawled out at the feet of Santa, Jacob whispering his Christmas miracle of a reunited family into the creepy ear of a predatory fat man.

And Elliot was doing what she normally did in times of great emotional distress: dissociate. She only caught snippets of conversation, Maddie's intuitive lies—*going to the U, studying film, yeah, little man, there's another pound*—and it wasn't so much a feeling of hovering or floating, but of being a hologram, transparent, lacking substance, being a presence only at first glance. It was the same feeling as walking into Devon's office. She was there, but she wasn't. She was seen but lacked the impact of a physical body to retard her husband's frenzied slurping. And maybe it was the same as pissing on a plastic stick in her one-bedroom efficiency, the blue plus sign a hologram in itself, meta to the core of her personal Lifetime movie, the pregnancy test dropping to the tile floor, the sound way less dramatic than the circumstances called for. In each of these circumstances, the overriding feeling was the same refrain of *this is not my life*, but the only thought was a repetition of the word *no*.

No, no, no.

No to Maddie speaking with her parents.

No to Jacob wanting his mother and father to pretend it was all a misunderstanding.

No to Devon's adultery.

No to Jacob's burrowing inside her uterine walls.

And fuck *no, no, no,* to her mother's insistence on Maddie joining them for some fine dining at Olive Garden, and *no* to his half-shielded wink at Elliot, his response of it being his pleasure, would never pass up a chance for a Tour of Italy (her mother exclaiming, "That's it, you're right, I can't veer away from my favorite!"), and *no* to the melding of two aspects of her life that were never supposed to merge, all five of them walking through the mall, Jacob refusing to hold Elliot's hand, him stumbling over his own feet as he fawned over the hip stranger who had suddenly become something more.

They made their way to Olive Garden, which was connected to the east entrance of the mall. Elliot needed a moment to speak with Maddie, to apologize, to get their stories straight, yet the only chance she had was in the foyer of the restaurant, the smell of over-cooked marinara and butter like her mother's dying wish, the wait staff in white and black, which only made the whole thing somehow less formal but more sad, when her parents spoke to the hostess about procuring their favorite seat in the corner with two walls of windows (the view of the parking lot apparently a must-see attraction). Elliot turned to Maddie. She didn't know where to start, what to say, how to save face. She said, "Sorry."

"About what?"

She motioned her head to Jacob and her parents a few feet away.

"I love kids."

"Maddie, stop, it's cool, fine. I can tell them you had to get going—"

"I don't."

"You should."

"It's cool."

"It's not fucking cool. Have a kid, have tons of shit—"

"We all do."

"But I have a lot."

"So do I."

"Maddie, fuck, leave."

"Not going to scare me away," he said. He gave his grin and headed toward her parents who were following the hostess toward the back of the restaurant.

They sat. Jacob insisted his booster be set up next to Maddie. They ordered drinks (Maddie a Coke). Less than three minutes went by before they were inundated with bowls of garlicky salad and salt-smothered breadsticks. Jacob attacked his salad with the force of a twister through a rural Missourian town, and Elliot felt embarrassed, both about his eating habits and his being hers, not to mention embarrassment about her lies (omission and flat-out), and about Maddie being sweet, placating her fears with his declaration of loving kids and having issues of his own, and embarrassed of her father, who had managed to steer the conversation to stand-up comedy, comparing favorites (disagreed with Maddie on several, but bonded over the love of early Richard Pryor), and who was just then launching into his theory of African Americans being funnier than Caucasians, which, he told Maddie, had everything to do with *community*, lack of isolating resources like single rooms and computers, and the survival mechanism of needing to make light of oppression (Elliot wasn't sure how her father didn't see this as at least slightly racist).

But Maddie kept nodding, agreeing, saying things like *great point* and *interesting*. He spoke like an older man; one who'd mastered the art of flattery. It was obvious Elliot's parents adored him. They vied for his attention. They flagged the waiter down to get him a refill on his soda. They were like the teenage girls at his house party, all pay-me-attention, direct that grin my way. Elliot realized Maddie's charisma wasn't simply a matter of attraction, but bigger, grander, all-encompassing, a ten on a universal scale of charisma, everybody wanting to be part of his world. For some reason, this made her feel better, as if some of the blame for her irresponsibility could be deflected away from her neediness to not feel like a victim of Devon's oral obsessions (which excluded their shared bedroom), but instead, could be attributed to a boy who was a man who was a beacon of good feeling. She found herself loosening up, if only a little in her shoulders. She joined in with smiles and laughter. She saw her son become more animated than he'd been since leaving Colorado, him misconstruing *Maddie* for *Mister* (*mister, give me a pound; mister, look at my drawing*). And when she felt Maddie's hand on her knee, then her thigh, where it respectfully halted its advance, she didn't flinch, didn't brush it off, but scooted forward, causing his hand to creep up an extra two inches, and took a sip of her cheap house red. She allowed herself to contemplate dangerous thoughts: What if he really does love children? What if it's more than physical attraction? What if I was supposed to meet him? If I was supposed to catch Devon cheating? What if he goes to the U of M, and I resume my graduate work there, and we take it slow, or slow-ish, me renting an apartment near campus, Maddie sleeping over only a few nights a week, us studying together in maroon and gold Gopher sweatshirts?

But of course, like any time Elliot allowed herself to daydream, to partake in a game of *what if?*, the world or circumstance or her mother brought her clamoring back down to its frozen-ass surface. This time, it came from her mother, the blunt-force trauma of Elliot's recent past, her mother touching Maddie's hand (they'd become even closer over their revelry in the carbs of the Tour of Italy), saying something that sounded like an apology for their daughter, an excuse about living at home, it being temporary, just until the divorce was settled.

"Mom, Jesus."

"Terry, that's enough," her father said.

"I'm simply saying Elliot's in a bit of a rough patch right now, but it's only *temporary*."

"Thanks for that," Elliot said. "Anything else you feel like the entirety of Olive Garden needs to know about me?"

"Elliot, now that's enough out of you," her father said.

Maddie's grin was caught somewhere between the processing of new information and running for the door, and just like that, Elliot felt her shoulders tighten, her body retract, her mind a sprung bear trap around this being anything other than fucking.

"I thought you would have told him," her mom said. "I mean, why you're living with us and working retail—"

"Not something I normally lead with," Elliot said.

"I was *explaining* that this isn't really you…"

"Terry," her father said.

Maddie cleared his throat. He said, "My parents divorced when I was eight. It was hard, for sure, but you know, you get used to it." Maddie paused, once again accepting Elliot's mother's hand over his. "My mom sacrificed everything for me, did what she had to, even if that was staying up late watching the same Richard Pryor routine night after night."

Her parents laughed like they'd never heard anything funnier (actual table slaps from her father, napkin over the mouth from her mother), and Jacob would not be outdone by the adults, so he started in too, mimicking them both, and Elliot realized the outburst of emotion wasn't so much a result of what Maddie said being funny, but that there'd been no harm done to their daughter's chances with this charming young man, and she saw it all too clearly, the reason for her mother's *explanations* for her retail job and residing in mildewy basements, the reason her daughter was an old loser, and the same with her father's good-old-boy acceptance of a young man whose penis might house itself inside his offspring—it was because they were imaging a future where their damaged-goods daughter was happy and married and out of their house.

In the midst of the laughter, Maddie put his hand back on her knee. He leaned over, whispering, "I'm serious, can't push me away."

A moment later, her father pulled out his Velcro wallet, telling Maddie he was crazy if he thought he was going to make a college student chip in so much as a dime, and looked at Elliot. He seemed to be sizing her up, for what, exactly, Elliot wasn't sure. He said, "Why don't you two get out of here, go have some fun. We can put the little man down. Want to watch some stand-up, Jacob?"

"Bitch is bitch is bitch."

Laughter.

"I'm sure he's got exams or whatever," Elliot said.

"Finished my last one today."

"You've spent more than enough time with us Svendsons for one day," she said.

"Mr. Svendson—"

"Ed."

"Sorry, *Ed*. I would love the chance to take your daughter out, if that's okay with you?"

Elliot felt the familiar camouflage of the easily embarrassed erupt in rose patches along her neck. Her mother, honest to God, had clasped her hands over her heart, let an audible *ahh* escape her marinara-slicked mouth.

"Can't think of a more suitable young man to have that honor."

Here's what Elliot wanted to say:

Run.

Leave.

I'm old and soon-to-be divorced and a mother and probably make less money than you and my family's a motherfucking shit show.

Thank you for lying.

You did your good deed for the year.

I'm sorry.

Who the fuck are you?

You'll make some girl so fucking happy.

But she didn't say these things, didn't have the chance, at least not initially, walking out of Olive Garden back through the cacophony of canned music and fruity aromas of Rosedale Mall, not once Maddie took her hand and she allowed herself to be one of those people—the boastful girl who kissed with tongue and pressed bodies amidst swirls of holiday shoppers. She allowed herself to believe she hadn't been aware of Carolyn staring out from the Talbots window. She allowed herself to forget Jacob's Christmas wish to Santa. She allowed herself to believe everything was real.

They smoked a joint, as was quickly becoming their custom. They rode in Maddie's Civic, which was a smorgasbord of Red Bull cans and skateboard decks and stickers plastered to the dash, and he wouldn't tell her where he was headed, only saying it was a date, a *proper* date. One joint became two. Elliot finally got around to thanking him for his behavior during dinner, the humoring of her parents and son, the lying.

"Wasn't lying."

"You're a senior at the U?"

"Senior at Roseville."

"Fuck my life."

"Don't."

"Don't *what*?"

"Get all weird about age and everything."

"Right," Elliot said. She hit the joint. Darkness had come in the span of her previous exhale, and she felt tired, but good tired, cozy tired. "But thank you anyway," she said.

They made their way to the east side of St. Paul. Elliot realized they were headed to Como Lake, to the Winter Carnival, a Minnesota tradition, a castle built out of blocks of ice, livable, a mansion, rooms and spires, freezing to the touch. The yearly trek to the Winter Carnival had been a mainstay of her childhood, the Svendsons bundled up in down and Sorrel boots, Elliot pretending the castle was her own, Rapunzel and Cinderella and Belle, running from room to room laying claim over a fairy tale, her mother always saying, "Might be a bit chilly," this causing laughter because Elliot didn't know any better. "Used to love this place," Elliot said.

"*Used to?* I mean, it's a *palace*, made out of *ice*, what's not to love?"

"The sheer practicality of it is astounding," Elliot said.

"Practice for the ice age."

"Something like that."

They parked the car along Como. Families filed past and everyone seemed happy and she wrapped her arm through Maddie's and they started toward the lights, reds and greens and blues illuminating the cloudy ice walls, the dark sky being dissected by booming spotlights. The Winter Carnival had evidently grown, now encompassing aspects of an actual carnival (Ferris wheel, merry-go-round, vendors selling steaming something or other on a stick). A static-y rendition of "Joy to the World" played from somewhere.

Maddie paid for their admission into the ice castle.

She allowed him to do this, because it was his *proper date*, his taking her out, even asking permission from her father, and they started toward the mammoth gauntlet of an entrance, arm in arm, giggles and stoned eyes, the walls morphing hues as spotlights swept by. Kids ran and parents chased and angels sang. The foyer of the castle was lined with freestanding ice sculptures, each partitioned off with a red sash, and they were beautiful, stunningly intricate faces carved into an unstable substance, smiling children sledding, Santa, Nordic gods with ice braids and snarls that might be grins. Elliot reached over the sash to trace the face of one of the ice sculpture goddesses.

"Looks like you," Maddie said.

"Because I'm three feet tall and made of ice?"

"Because it's beautiful."

"You're so full of shit."

"You're so cynical."

"A gift of age."

"Here we go again."

"Shut it," Elliot said.

They continued farther into the ice palace, past the sculptures and the bustling children, past the overhead lights, and into the drafty shadows of the palace's dead space. They found a nook of a room, apparently an oversight or miscalculation on behalf of the builders, a pantry closet really. Maddie leaned his back against the wall. He looked up the three stories of ice and said, "Jesus, you have to see this." Elliot joined him. She pressed her back to the ice and she was instantly cold or at least chilled, a tingling from where her bare neck rubbed against frozen water, her toes tingling too. The spectacle was amazing, as in actually inspiring awe, lack of words, wonder—fifty feet of curving ice loomed overhead, a rip curl building and building before crashing, which it hinted at doing, tons of glowing ice tumbling down upon their delicate heads.

"Kind of freaky," Elliot said.

"Like it's going to crash down?"

"Yeah."

"It won't."

"It will eventually."

"Not exactly the optimist, are you?" Maddie said.

Elliot was ready with some sort of snarky answer, but she paused, let his words sink in, followed by the glassed-over words from her mother in Santa's line (*What is wrong with you?*), and Maddie's two declarations about not letting her push him away, and she felt a moment of clarity about herself, though she couldn't necessarily verbalize this realization, just a glimpse of understanding, a hologram itself, something about being on her way to a bitter woman, to becoming Jan with her chins or Carolyn with her puffy face.

"Hasn't been the best of years," she said.

"Husband?"

"Yeah."

"What happened?"

"He cheated."

"Sucks. Sorry."

"Happens, I guess," Elliot said.

"Can still suck."

"You think everything's supposed to go a certain way, and, well…"

"You realize that shit's not your fault, don't you?" Maddie said.

"And you know this *how?*"

"Because I saw it with my mom. Straight beat herself up for years thinking all of it was on her, my dad's stepping out. Not her fault, highly doubt it's yours."

The wall became a menacing red before transitioning to a docile green. Elliot's sense of balance was becoming skewed, as if her world was inverting upon itself, the ceiling now the floor, her somehow perpendicular, a mind-trip she only kind of hated.

"Sorry about not, you know, being completely honest with you and everything," Elliot said.

"Not worried about it."

"Jacob really liked you."

"Rad kid, for sure."

"Probably a shock, huh?"

"Figured you weren't really the type to have let yourself go…"

"That supposed to mean?"

"A couple of…" Maddie rubbed at the side of his coat along his waist, and Elliot realized he was referring to her stretch marks, which made her want to die for the umpteenth time that day, and the tidal wave of ice was now a soft purple, and she thought about Maddie being too smart for high school, too smart for his twenties, him being a version of perfect she'd never before considered.

"Asshole," she said.

"Please, your body's amazing."

"Covered in spider webs of stretch marks."

"Shut up, already."

"This ceiling is kind of making me want to puke," Elliot said.

"It could work."

"Like vertigo or something."

"Us," Maddie said.

"Jacob would love it here."

"Just need to give it a shot."

"I need to take him here on my next day off."

"Us, you know what I'm saying?"

"No, I'm sorry, what? I wasn't listening."

"Asked if you wanted to hit up the Ferris wheel."

"And you know this, man."

"Huh?"

"*Friday*, Chris Tucker."

"Oh."

"Before your time."

"Fucking dinosaurs roaming the earth and shit."

Elliot play-hit Maddie, and he caught her punch, pulling her in for a kiss, partially missing her mouth, settling on her upper lip and cheek.

"Lucky you're handsome," Elliot said.

"Why's that?"

"Because your aim is fucking awful."

They walked out of the ice castle and made their way to the parking lot turned carnival. Floodlights were set up on the edge of the frozen lake where couples skated. The air held a cinnamon flavor, roasted nuts probably. The atmosphere changed from winter family fun to something closer to an actual carnival with bearded men in Carhart coveralls operating the few rides, spitting arcs of brown chew juice onto patches of dirty snow.

"Can't imagine these machines were built to operate in twenty degrees," Elliot said.

"Worst case scenario we get stuck going two miles per hour."

"And freeze to death."

Maddie pointed to the fire truck at the far end of the parking lot. Little kids climbed in and out of the cab, and again, Elliot was struck with the fact that Jacob should be at her side, not Maddie, that she was failing in some monumental way she'd only understand eighteen years in the future during some intervention for her son, his meth-picked face accusatory, his tone even more so, *Why didn't you take me to the Winter Carnival?*

They climbed the three slick metal steps, Maddie handing over five dollars, the man with an icicle of dip spit on his chin creaking the metal door closed behind them. The seat was the kind of cold where tongues stick, and Elliot gasped, and Maddie pulled her onto his lap and wrapped his arms around her waist and she didn't feel protected per say, but *comforted*, at least less cold, Maddie's chin tucked over her shoulder and his breath like chicken parm (the western portion of the Tour of Italy). The wheel rotated and they started climbing and the machine had music of its own, The Velvet Underground, "Sweet Jane," and Elliot thought about *Natural Born Killers* and about high school and about elementary school and about Denver and a life spent attempting to appear busy and about *leaky vessels* and then they were rounding the very pinnacle of the ride—fifty, sixty, seventy feet above the ground, people skating and kids running and lights making ice magical, Lou Reed professing his love to a girl named Jane—and Maddie wasn't kissing her neck or forcing a finger fuck like she'd half-expected, but instead holding her, warming her, *comforting* her. It was here where she thought of the word *love*, not that she was experiencing it, but that this would be a moment when a woman could experience such a thing, or at least convince herself of it, tell people years later about their first *proper date* resulting in a marrow-deep *knowing*.

"Your ass is kind of bony," Maddie said.

"Is that supposed to be a compliment?"

"An observation."

"Your dick's kind of hard."

"Compliment?"

"Observation."

And down they went, slow and methodical, Elliot no longer hiding her smile into the fur-lined neck of her coat but flashing it for all to see. It was as if she were suddenly an embodiment of the ageless joys of the Winter Carnival, for Minnesota, for a simple life of learning to live with mediocrity and cold, a picture worthy of being plastered on the front page of The Pioneer Press (WOMAN ON FERRIS WHEEL HAS FUN DESPITE HERSELF).

On the way back up, Maddie said, "I like you."

"Like you too."

"A lot."

"Yeah, me too."

"Like *a lot*, a lot."

Elliot's smile flattened, still facing away from Maddie, because she knew where this was headed—a confession, a declaration, something Maddie didn't know the first thing about—and Elliot didn't want this moment ruined with irretraceable words. She said, "Don't."

"Don't *what?*"

"*You* don't."

"What don't I do?"

Elliot felt a wave of steaming embarrassment at realizing she may have misunderstood what he'd been inferring. She said, "Never mind."

"No, what?"

"Your dick's still hard."

"You thought I was going to say *I love you*."

"Shut the fuck up."

Maddie laughed and she could feel his stomach muscles constricting against her spine and the fur-lined collar she'd always loved all of a sudden felt like an eighties turtleneck and her saliva turned to bathwater.

He said, "Is there something you're trying to tell me?"

"Get me off of this thing."

"A little fast for me, but…"

"Such a dick."

Maddie squeezed her even tighter. His laugh turned to a giggle. He said, "I guess it makes sense. Did stage that shit at the North Pole so I'd meet your parents. Kind of elaborate, but sweet."

"Are you going to fuck me on this thing or not?"

"Love? Already? This is our first date."

Elliot reached behind her and fumbled with Maddie's zipper. She could feel his dick pressing against his jeans. He kept laughing and saying things about older girls moving fast, that he was flattered, but *love?* She felt stupid and she needed him to shut up and the easiest way for that to happen was for the warmth of her vagina to leak onto his bare lap and they'd stopped at the pinnacle as the carts below emptied one by one and she told herself that sex in public was for him, some fantasy he could bring back to the hallway filled with Roseville Red lockers, and she guided his dick inside of her, her jeans pulled down just in the back, and Maddie kept making fun of her, obviously thrilled about the reversal in the power dynamic, that of need and desire, and she stared out at a state she'd sworn off, a life she'd convinced herself was beneath her, and she realized this had been a fantasy of hers since Marky Mark fingered Reese Witherspoon on the rollercoaster, and maybe it was for her, not just to deflect embarrassment, but to fulfill some sense of regret from high school and maybe the last ten years too.

Maddie pulled her down against his pelvis, thus preventing her from any further riding. He spoke into her ear: "I do, you know."

"No, you don't."

"I do. And you're a motherfucking liar if you say you don't feel it too."

"Sweet Jane" was coming to a climax, the baritone instruments and yelling of the refrain. Elliot felt a heartbeat between her legs and wondered if it was Maddie's pulse or her own. She let herself think about love, about maybe never knowing it, not the kind that came from an overflowing of emotion, from sweet things, from admiration, from a boy who cared enough not to thrust while his penis was submerged inside of her, but instead talk, become vulnerable, and maybe the kind of love she knew came from the result of consequences and adaptation. And maybe age didn't matter. Maybe her baggage didn't matter. And here the most charismatic boy she'd ever met was telling her what she felt was love. And maybe it was being hurt and being broken and a loss of trust that clouded this obvious truth from Elliot, whereas Maddie could see it for what it was: love. Elliot tried it out inside her head: I'm in love; I'm in love with a man other than Devon; I'm in love with a man who's a boy; I'm in love with a boy in high school.

"We can play your game," Maddie said, "about not saying shit, because I know you need time and everything, which is totally cool, but fuck, you won't tell me you don't feel the same thing."

Maddie slipped his penis out of Elliot and helped her pull her jeans back up. She looked at the ice castle with its morphing color and kitschy charm and remembered seeing the remnants of the same palace when she was a kid come March, how all that was left was a three-foot wall of the slickest ice she'd ever witnessed, Pepsi cups and cigarette butts melted into its base like a petrified packrat nest, how the juxtaposition between that sight and the Disney palace she'd claimed as her own had been all sorts of sad. She tried to remember her train of thought from a moment before, that thing about her being too damaged to see love when it presented itself.

V

A Cosmic Ease—A Blueberry Muffin at Perkins—Tell
Me I'm a Good Person—A Conversation with Mom

There were times in life when Elliot felt a certain ease about her actions, her mindset, the proverbial *go with the flow*, as if she no longer was fighting Hanger Integrity and her parents and her penis-pulling son, but accepting things as they came, copacetic if not a touch jolly. The following week was one of those times. She killed it at work, ensuring all four tenants of H.I., fluffing with a craftsman's precision, doling out compliments to tree-trunk-ankled women, not even caring about *The Talbot's Guaranty* eroding her steadily building commission. Mrs. Williams noticed, pulling her aside, squeezing her elbow, saying something about her never having seen a Seasonal tackle the *Christmas Crunch* (here Mrs. Williams smiled at her own clever alliteration) with such tact and style.

Yes, her actions were being noticed, and this felt good, very good, embarrassingly so.

At home, Elliot experienced more of the same cosmic ease. Her parents seemed to be cutting her some slack and her mother helped with her laundry and her father poured her a stiff drink when she came through the door after what he would assume was a grueling day of retail sales, extending his arm, motioning to the empty seat next to him on the couch, Comedy Central blaring, her nestling into his flannel smell, Daddy's Girl once again. Even Jacob, bless his heart, appeared to be giving her a break. He quit with the too-smart comments about love and reunited families and even with the drawings of Evil Mommy Godzilla-big. He let her read him stories, kiss his heavy eyelids, tell him how much she loved him.

And of course, there was Maddie.

Elliot was vaguely aware that her turn in attitude and ease with which she navigated the equivalent of retail and marital hell was due to a crush (a term she'd taken to calling what was going on with Maddie to both her parents and Carolyn who accosted her with bitchy comments about her Chili's bathroom rendezvous), but she tried not to think too deeply on the subject, tried not to bog herself down with habitually masturbatory self-analysis. It was good (whatever *it* was). They hung out more days than not. One night they met up with some of his friends at Martin Luther King Jr. Park and smoked joints while sitting on snow-covered swings until they wanted beer and she relented…just a few cans a piece and there had to be a DD. She liked that night, how they seemed to accept her as their own. They laughed and talked about girls and parents and Elliot felt privy to a group consciousness—*I want somebody to love; I want to be away from my parents; I'm scared of my future*—and she realized it wasn't unique to their generation or her own, but the same sentiment of every age, the same sentiment Thomas Middleton conveyed in his unheralded plays, universal.

And Maddie was sweet. During the days they both worked, he'd meet her by the fountain where she'd first seen him as a beautiful dumb boy with a bleeding elbow. He'd often bring her a gift, something small but thoughtful, skater socks from Zumiez or salted peanut butter chocolates from one of three specialty stores in the mall. They'd compare horror stories of shoplifters and sketchy returns and product chases to outlets in Newport Beach. He made her laugh. He made her feel better about her circumstances and maybe herself. At the end of every shared meal, they hugged, kissed, sometimes with tongue. Elliot always walked away with a smile she couldn't help but let escape.

Yes, things were good, better than she could remember for quite some time, and the Elliot of a month prior would have seen this as somehow a bad thing, a peak before a crash, an imbalance. She would have guarded herself against this change in perception, seeking out the faults of work (*fucking retail with old ladies, working for less than I made as an undergrad checking out books at the circulation desk*), and her family (*my parents are the epitome of Midwestern, which is to say overweight and undereducated, ignorant of any sense of culture, okay with the* Tour of Italy *as their reference point for fine Italian dining*), and Maddie (*a high school boy whose infatuation is with the exotic, the other, the apple he's yet to bite from, rather than with me as a person*).

Elliot would have been less surprised on Saturday evening, fresh from a post-work shower and tucking-in of Jacob and a kiss on both her parents' cheeks, keys in hand, walking to the Tacoma, when from across the street she saw the dome light of a generic-looking sedan flicker off with the soft thumping of a door, and a man coming toward her, his gait the familiar straddling of jock-turned-academic.

No, no, no.

"Elle."

Fuck, no, God no.

Devon stood at the edge of the fifty-foot driveway, which sloped upward, so he looked small, pathetic in his navy pea coat three years out of style and wool beanie pushed back to his hairline as if to imitate the next generation of Brooklyn writers he always ridiculed if only because he wasn't one of them. He was employing his sheepish face (normally adorable with his naturally hooded eyelids), but Elliot wasn't thinking about forgiveness or penance or his tracking her down being romantic-and-or-creepy, only a repetition of *no's*. That and disbelief.

"You look great."

"Don't."

"I'm sorry."

"What the fuck…how did you even…*why?*"

"Because you weren't taking my calls, and I wanted to see Jacob… and you, Elle, I wanted to see—"

"Shut the fuck up."

"You have every right to be mad."

"Thanks for your permission."

"Can we talk for a minute, somewhere not freezing cold?"

Elliot held the slender key for the truck between her knuckles like a single talon, which Devon saw, sighing, telling her it wasn't like that— *Jesus, who do you think I am?*—and Elliot wasn't sure who he was or what was happening, only that she didn't like it, not in the slightest. She'd wanted away from this man. She'd seen him eating the pussy of a girl less than half her age. She'd seen the way he gripped his desk like it was a granite ledge to a five-hundred-foot cliff, his body dangling, his life dependent upon his purchase of said ledge. And it had shattered her. And it was still there, the anger bubbling over a caldron of hurt. But she'd made her decision and driven home with three suitcases and a child in hand, and she'd accepted a fate she could only kind of pretend was temporary and she'd built something over the last two months, and maybe it wasn't much, but it was hers, the antithesis of everything Devon, and it made her happy. Or maybe content. Or maybe just apathetic to what she'd lost.

"You need to get the fuck out of here, like, I can't believe you're here."

"Five minutes, that's all I'm asking."

"Space, that's all I'm asking."

"Which I've granted you."

"Fuck you and your need for control," Elliot said.

"I need to see my son."

"Don't make this about him."

"Of which it primarily is."

For some reason, this stung Elliot. Devon must have seen the quick aversion of her eyes, the righting of her shoulders.

"It's about both of you. I fucked up. I fucked up so badly, and I can't begin to tell you how sorry I am. Truly sorry. Willing to do whatever I have to—no, *can*—whatever I *can* do, in order to…"

Elliot sighed and the wind pulled her breath back over her shoulder. She knew he wouldn't stop. He'd drag this out until he made his pitch, until he was granted at least an afternoon with Jacob, during which he'd turn him against his mother by planting delusions about all of them returning to Denver and his preschool friends and movie night as a family. Elliot said, "Five minutes. Follow me to Perkins."

On the way to the restaurant, Elliot called Maddie. She told him she was running a little late and he told her it was no problem, and Elliot didn't know what else to say but stayed on the line. Maddie asked if everything was cool. Elliot had the urge to tell him it wasn't cool, Devon was back, and they were going for coffee, and it'd get complicated from here on out with lawyers and custody and tears and testimonies, but she felt like this could be too much for Maddie, a burden he didn't need to saddle himself with. Here was a separation of church and state that she wanted to keep compartmentalized, if only for ease of Maddie's mind; yes, it was for him.

"See you in a bit," she said.

"Cool."

"Bye."

"I don't you," Maddie said.

"I don't you, either."

☙

They sat in a red booth that had obviously once been the smoking section with its unmistakable stink coating the vinyl upholstery. A tired-looking waitress with crow's feet for miles asked what they wanted and Devon spoke for them both—two coffees, black, a blueberry muffin to split—and this pissed Elliot off, her lack of voice, him tracking her down, him not understanding he had no power in this situation and needed to stay away and him being controlling and him being a dick and him fucking up something of her own.

"So how have you been?" Devon said.

"Not doing that."

"How's Jacob?"

"Good."

"Does he…"

"Nope."

"Ask about me."

"Nope."

"Elle, I know you're ma—"

"Not mad, Devon, not mad. I get it."

The waitress set the coffees down, not caring about splashing Devon's. She gave Elliot a look like *men are such assholes*, and this solidarity was like a booster of B12 as it quickened Elliot's pulse, her resolve to attack.

Devon waited for the waitress to leave. He leaned forward. "You get *what?*"

"That you need to feel sought-after. Lusted-after."

"Elle, that's not—"

"That you're a narcissistic man, scared, insecure. And what better way to cover up those blemishes than making a coed come all over your stupid face?"

"Okay, I deserve that. I do. But you have to know it was only that once…"

"Which makes it okay?"

"Which doesn't pardon my actions, no, but—"

"But it's excusable. Because it was only once. So if I went out and killed somebody, but only *one* person, then it would be fine, right?"

"That's not the same thing."

"No shit. But your logic's the same."

Devon caught his next words before they breached the surface of his lips. He sipped his coffee, then broke off a dainty corner of the square-top blueberry muffin. Elliot knew how his mind worked, how at this very moment he was changing tactics, knowing he'd been backed into a corner of guilt, no way out, so he'd change strategies, fight dirty through their son. But he didn't. He said, "I love you so fucking much. I will do whatever I can to make this right with you. However long it takes…I fucked up. I completely fucked up. But I love you."

How desperately she'd longed to hear these words over the last four years. An unguarded admission, a display of vulnerability, a leveling of power.

"Should have thought of that before," she said.

"I know."

"And we're done."

"That's fair."

"Say that one more time I'm going to leave."

"What?"

"About whatever I'm doing being *fair* or *understandable*."

"Sorry."

"Again," Elliot said.

"What?"

"Apologize."

Devon scooted the muffin to his left and let his hairy-knuckle hands rest over the invisible divider of Elliot's half of the table. His voice was lower: "I'm sorry, Elle, for all of this."

Elliot tilted her head as if in contemplation, a feigned affect, but maybe it wasn't, because her mind betrayed her, spinning versions of reconciliation and forgiveness and things being better, a newfound emotional depth, a newfound person, Devon different, changed, grown up from the insecure man who slunk through life as if eternally misunderstood and judged by people who didn't know he existed, Devon becoming grateful for what he had, their family, her. She could see it on Devon's face, hope, in his inching fingers too. She allowed herself to imagine lying beside him. She imagined walks they'd take through falling snow. She imagined sitting around their quaint kitchen, the discussion turned to her dormant thesis, Devon supportive and interested. And then with a crushing weight, these images morphed into the scratched disk of her mind, and he was crouching between the legs of another woman, a girl. Elliot straightened her head. She said, "Nope, still don't give a fuck."

"Please give me a chance."

Elliot forced a laugh.

"To make it up to you, to show you that I've changed."

"Why?"

"Because I love you. Because we have a son together."

"No, why are you trying to do this?"

"I just told you."

"You didn't give a fuck before. You *tolerated* me, tolerated being home—"

"That's unfair."

"You got me pregnant doing what you evidently always do, fuck your students, a—"

"I did not have intercourse with—"

"*Face* fuck, excuse me."

"Elle—"

"And you were pretty much forced to marry me, but I'm telling you that you're free. Done. Your penance is up, Devon, you're off the chain. Go fuck whomever you want."

"Stop."

"Don't tell me to stop."

"It's not like that."

Elliot smiled. Her body hummed with a sort of heated electricity, a power born from self-righteous anger, a tad intoxicating, so much better than the vulnerability of hope, so she kept going, kept jabbing at him through permission to do vulgar acts with coeds, and he took these comments because he had no choice, not if he was trying to be Groveling Shameful Husband. She kept attacking, getting down to his penis, it being thin if not a touch small, asking him if this was the reason he'd opted to use his tongue.

Devon pulled out his wallet, setting a ten on the table. He wasn't supposed to be the one leaving, Elliot was supposed to be storming off while he sat there alone in a Perkins with nobody to turn to. Devon put his wool beanie back on his head, giving a quick glance at his reflection in the darkened window. He stood. He said, "I love you. I love Jacob. I'm going to be here for the next month, maybe longer if need be. I expect to see Jacob at least twice a week, which I think is more than reasonable. All I ask from you is a chance, which I'm not asking for right away, but maybe later, in the future, a chance, at least the possibility of a chance."

❧

Elliot sat in the Perkins parking lot crying and then hit her thigh twice with a closed fist, and sniffling, pressing the soft sides of her fingers against the swollen skin underneath her eyes, she told herself it could've been worse. Devon wanted to see his son. That was it. That was fine. She could allow him this, because it was for Jacob, and Jacob deserved to see his father. And in a few weeks, once Christmas break was over and the spring semester started back up, Devon would be gone, regardless of what he said.

But she didn't really believe that.

She'd spent years with Devon, and if she knew anything, it was his persistence, his propensity to come out on top. He controlled the world through charm or self-pity, or seductive stares and he got what he wanted, girls or book deals or tenure track positions, always. And this was where the fear lay for Elliot—she would somehow again lose, return to Denver with its sprawling downtown against the backdrop of snowcapped mountains, return to a daily routine of exercise and Whole Foods and reading novels in bed while Devon jerked off in the shower.

She thought of the coed's moans with Devon between her legs.

She thought of Maddie and his otherworldly understanding of pretty much everything, his charisma, his Adam's apple like an ice sculpture.

She thought of Talbots and her Rookie of the Year award and her fantasy of resuming graduate studies at the University of Minnesota with Maddie and about her new life, which was really an old life, but it'd be better, it had to be better than what it'd been.

She forced any thoughts about a changed Devon out of her mind through the repetition of seeing him commit adultery, over and over again, her imagination adding details, admissions of love, of this student being so much better than Elliot, Devon telling this coed he felt trapped by his wife and son, that it'd all been a mistake.

And she knew it was fucked up, the calling of Devon, him answering on the first ring, her saying it wasn't going to happen, him seeing Jacob or him having a chance, to stay the fuck away, filing for divorce in the morning, you fucked up and I swear to fucking God if I see you at my house I'll call the cops and tell them you threatened my life, and Elliot hung up without waiting for a response. She thought about Jacob's wish to Santa, him wanting everything to go back to how it was. His crayon drawings of her all big and ruining his life. And she realized maybe there was truth to that, a kernel at least, but fuck that, it wasn't her fault, but Devon's, Devon with his stupid fucking affected persona and Devon whose actions were forcing her own hand were the reason she had to keep Jacob from his father. It was an act of love, going against her instincts, keeping her boy from his father, a hardship, for sure, but it was for Jacob's own good. What kind of boy would Jacob be with a cheating manipulative fuck like Devon showing him how to be a man? Jacob would grow up perpetuating the same cycle, ruining marriages and lives in the process, which would cause pain, lots of it, immense amounts, ungodly amounts. And by shielding him from this threat? Yes, it was good parenting; her actions were love.

She told Maddie to go to Roseville North. They met in the parking lot and she went to his car and knocked on the window and told him to get out. He was nothing but smiles and then he was nothing but concern and he took her arms and kept saying, "What's wrong? What's wrong?"

"Am I a good person?"

"What?"

"Am. I. A. Good. Person?"

"Yeah, yeah, totally. What's going on?"

"A good mom?"

"The fucking best."

"Why are you hanging out with me?"

"Because I fucking…love you."

"How do you know?"

"Feel it," Maddie said.

"I lied to you."

Maddie tilted his head.

"I'm about to be thirty, in less than a week."

Maddie grinned and then did his high-pitched giggle and then a real laugh and Elliot wondered if he'd expected worse from her preface of a lie and if that undercut everything he'd said about her being a good person and then about him having no idea what made up a good person in the first place. She play-hit his chest, and he caught her by her wrist, pulled her close, and she looked up to his face and caught a glimpse of his nostrils with their dusting of flaky snot, and he didn't care about her age, about Jacob, about the lies, and it was acceptance of her insecurities and it was love.

"Fucking MILF," he said.

"Little boy."

"Love you."

"Tell me again," Elliot said.

"Love you."

"No, about being a good person."

"The best fucking person I've ever met."

"And mom."

"Jacob's the luckiest kid in the world."

"And how I'm sexy."

"Can you not feel this wood?"

"And how Talbots isn't a career."

"Fuck Talbots."

"And you've never had better."

"Well, there was this one girl…"

"Fuck you."

"The best ever. Like a…"

"Cougar."

"Your words," Maddie said through a grin.

"And you're going to the U of M, and we can like…"

"Hang out?"

"Hang out," Elliot said.

"Is that what you want?"

Elliot nodded. Maddie dropped her wrists and wrapped his arms around her shoulders, resting his chin on top of her head. She stared out past the tennis courts covered in snow to the football field, to the bleachers, the scoreboard (the same one from more than a decade before with its burned-out bulbs), and she remembered being a scared teenager trying to fit in through cheers for a game she didn't understand, how she always waited for her classmates to clap first, this being safer. She wasn't sure what exactly about this memory felt important, only that it did. Elliot pulled herself tighter to Maddie's body. He was telling her how she was perfect, a good person, a great mother, funny as shit, gave head like a champ, beautiful, kind, and Elliot was a tabby slurping up the leftover cereal milk of these affirmations, fearful of the rare delicacy being ripped away.

Elliot's mom was the only person up when she got home. She sat on the brown couch, a Sudoku in her lap, Comedy Central playing on the TV. Elliot sat down in what was normally her father's spot, the cushions devastated from the nightly abuse of his weight. She asked where her dad was. Her mom told her he hadn't been feeling great, something about a case of heartburn, but, as her mom suspected, was actually a *case* of *the trots*. "Thirty-seven years," her mom said, "and he's still too embarrassed to tell me he has diarrhea."

Elliot laughed.

Her mom said, "He's a gentleman in his own way."

"Right."

"Speaking of which…"

"What?"

"How was your evening?"

Elliot was too small for her father's grooves worn into the cushions, and suddenly felt a bit uncomfortable, a tad flushed, and adjusting her weight, she realized she'd never really had this conversation with her mom—boys and crushes and loves—and she was struck by the opposing forces of wanting to share and wanting to hide, or maybe she was simply reverting back to being sixteen. "You don't have to watch this stand-up. Dad's sleeping or going to the bathroom or whatever."

"I like it."

"No, you don't."

"If you're exposed to something for as long as I've been, you get to like it. Reminds me of him."

"Talking like he's dead."

"Don't say that," her mom said.

"No, I meant like you were being dramatic."

"Aren't you the little critic?"

"Never mind," Elliot said.

They sat there for a moment, her mother erasing an error in her Sudoku. The comedian talked about baby shit. Elliot said, "I'm applying to the graduate program at the U for spring semester."

Her mom didn't look up from her puzzle, but nodded, causing her tacky Christmas tree earrings to jangle. This wasn't exactly the response Elliot had expected (she'd imagined a tearing-up or at least a hug, a comment about Minnesota being her home, a mother's dream coming true to be so close to her beautiful daughter and amazing grandson), and Elliot felt a bit hurt at the nodding of her mom's head, so she went on the offensive, saying, "That's it? That's all you have to say?"

Her mom counted on her fingers, then wrote something down in her book. "He's young, Elliot, really young."

Elliot said *what* even though she knew perfectly well whom her mother was referring to.

"Don't get me wrong, sweetie. He's smart, funny, gorgeous, we both really like him, but…"

"But what?"

"He's young."

"And I'm old?"

"You're married with a child."

"That's great. Really nice of you."

"I just don't want to see you get hurt again."

"Because I'm old and damaged and not good enough, right?"

"Keep your voice down. You'll wake up Jacob."

"And I'm a bad mom too. Is that what you're hinting at?"

Her mom finally closed her book, looking over, extending her hand to Elliot's lap, and Elliot wanted to brush off her fingers that were nothing but knuckles, but her touch was soothing, a sedative. Her mother said, "I think you're a great mother, doing the absolute best you can with the shit deal you were handed. I think it's a great idea to finish up your degree. I think Maddie is a sweet boy. I just wish you'd give yourself the gift of some time to heal."

"And find somebody my own age."

"No, time to heal. I'm not sure you could handle another heartbreak at this time. I mentioned his age because boys will be boys, even your father."

"What's that supposed to mean?" Elliot asked.

"They need to mature."

"No, about Dad?"

Her mom sighed her sigh that preceded any explanation she didn't want to give. It'd been a staple growing up—Mom, where do babies come from? (Exaggerated sigh); Mom, is Santa real? (exhausted sigh)—and it was a trait Elliot had learned to associate with news she wasn't going to like.

"It was a different time then," her mom said. "Your father was a different man."

"What are you saying?"

"Different expectations."

"He cheated?"

"That was who he was then, not the man he is now. Not the father you love."

"You're fucking kidding me."

"He was young and stupid and immature—"

"But he cheated? Dad? Dad fucking cheated?"

"Your voice."

Elliot felt a little like crying, a little like laughing, a little like going into her parent's bathroom and seeing her dad sweating on the toilet and slapping him hard across the face while she debased him—*fucking hypocrite, all hateful of Devon when you did the same shit*—but she didn't do any of these things, just sat there while her mother stroked her leg and then the split ends of her hair.

"But the important thing is that he grew up and realized what was important," her mom said. "Which is what the good ones do. They grow up. They learn they're damn lucky to have what they have. But it's a process."

"Dad cheated—"

"He wasn't your dad yet."

"And you didn't leave?"

"Don't sit there judging me," her mom said. "I knew, just like all women do, which ones are capable of changing."

Elliot had the feeling the conversation was turning away from Maddie and her father and embarking upon territory she never in a hundred years would think her mother would be broaching—her choice to pack up and leave Devon—but how could she not see the not-so-subtle transition?

"You think it was a mistake?" Elliot said.

"No, like I said, he was young and—"

"No, with Devon. That's what you're saying, right? That I left too early, should have stuck it out and *straightened* him out because that's what women do, right? Sit by while they're shit all over."

"Honey, I said I knew your father was one of the good ones, open to change. But Devon—"

"Is a piece of shit."

"Is a piece of shit," her mom echoed.

The stroking of her hair continued. Her mom opened her Sudoku back up with her non-petting hand. She said, "I love you so much. I love Jacob so much. I just get protective, I guess."

"I can't believe Dad cheated."

"Time has a way of glossing over knots and fissures."

"What does that even mean?"

"It made more sense when Dr. Phil said it this afternoon."

Elliot laughed. She asked what the episode was about.

Her mom gave her exhausted sigh. She said, "Forgiving unfaithfulness."

VI

THIS IS THIRTY—FOLLOWING MRS. JOHNSON—A PARTY OF
SIX—SOME UNTIL-DEATH-DO-US-PART SHIT

On December 21st, the budget for the thirty-seventh highest grossing Talbots in America was just south of forty thousand, which was obtainable, Mrs. Williams assured the staff in a pre-opening meeting with a box of stale glazed doughnuts from Sam's Club because of three things: 1) the extended *Christmas* hours; 2) the incredible array of product they had both merchandized and back-stocked; 3) the dedicated and talented group of ladies on the front lines of the sale's floor. She spoke to her charges like they were going into battle, which they were, according to Mrs. Williams, the battle of the *Christmas Crunch*, a time which separated the ladies from the girls; a time where the cream of the crop rose; a time when the going gets tough…

The women ate up the clichéd pep talk. Bloated Carolyn rolled her head, and then arched her back, causing two vertebrae to pop. Jan kept fussing with the hem of her slacks, obviously not realizing the tightness was due to kankles rather than static cling. Elliot wanted an accomplice in the sarcastic comments she held on her tongue, but all the women were serious, excited, called-upon. Mrs. Williams made them put their hands in the middle. The smell was Powder Fresh Sure and Obsession and stale coffee.

"And one more thing," Mrs. Williams said. "It's our baby's birthday. Elliot joins the thirties today. So let's welcome her to the first decade of womanhood!"

The ladies sang "Happy Birthday," and it was uncomfortable because of the proximity and touching hands, and what had started as a touch of stale coffee breath was now a church reception parlor, strong enough to force Elliot to breathe through her mouth. She told herself this was thirty.

"Talbots on three," Mrs. Williams said.

One, two, three, TALBOTS.

The ladies were assigned sections of the store where they were to help customers and ensure Hanger Integrity and fluff and smile—*smile today, ladies; many of you have already broken into commission territory for the month, and today is literally money in your pocket*—and of course Elliot was paired with Carolyn because life had a way of putting the emphasis on the *un* in unbearable. It didn't take long before Carolyn floated over to the row of cashmere cardigans Elliot was size-running. Carolyn placed her fingers between the hangers. She smiled, saying, "We'll get you spacing these hangers perfectly if it's the last thing we do."

"Who's *we*?"

Carolyn ignored the comment. She made a big show of looking over both of her shoulders (a considerable effort considering the girth of her cheeks in her peripheral). She said, "So how's your *boy*?"

"Jacob's good."

"So, how is it you two even met?"

"Jacob is my son."

"That's not who I was talking about."

"No, *really*?"

"People don't say that anymore," Carolyn said.

"No, they don't say *no duh*, but I'm pretty sure *no really* is still in circulation."

Elliot turned her back on Carolyn, walking to the far white wall, bending down to straighten a stack of white organic cotton long-sleeved T-shirts. It didn't take but three seconds for the clomping of Carolyn's heels to make their way over. "It's just a little…*weird*," Carolyn said.

Elliot didn't respond, didn't turn around.

"That you think it's normal to sleep with a high school boy. But hey, more power to you. Guess you've still got it, even if you're starting your fourth decade."

Elliot wouldn't take the bait. She wouldn't turn around and poke Carolyn's chest and tell her she was a pathetic and insecure woman, a girl having long-since peaked, a rule Nazi for a bullshit job, that she was fat—*your face, Carolyn, what the fuck is going on? Is it like from some medication, the water retention? Tell me, because I can't for the life of me figure out how the hell this happens*—but she wouldn't give the satisfaction of a reaction, the validation of caring about Talbots or other people's opinions.

Carolyn inched closer. Elliot could feel the heat from her coworker's legs or maybe crotch. "Is it legal, though, I mean, him being so young?"

"Thirty seconds till opening, ladies, get your smiles on!" Mrs. Williams yelled.

"I went down there, to Zumiez, because Randal loves those sweat-shirts because they're a little longer, and he's all torso, and I met him, your *Maddie*. We got to talking about styles and ages and everything, and he told me he was in *high school*."

Elliot quit rearranging shirts. She had no doubt Carolyn would be just the kind of cunt to go *investigate* her life.

"I'm not one to pry into other people's business," Carolyn said, leaning forward, practically breathing into Elliot's ear, "but is that even legal?"

Elliot stood up with a jolt, bumping into Carolyn's hovering chin, which caused a clacking sound of her teeth clamping, but Elliot didn't give a fuck, not when Carolyn had crossed all sorts of lines—hell, lines weren't even an issue, weren't on Carolyn's radar, and this was…was something like slitting the screens to her bedroom window and staring at her while she slept, an invasion of privacy of her life, a threat—and Elliot wasn't about to take it.

"Open sesame!" Mrs. Williams yelled, unlatching the French doors.

Carolyn rubbed her jaw. Elliot said, "You need to stay the fuck out of my life. Period. Whatever you *think* you know, I promise, you don't. So back. The fuck. Off."

Those were the last words spoken between the two women for the rest of the day. The purposeful ignoring was mutual. Elliot figured it was an act of grace by the world or God or maybe it was Carolyn's fear, and really, Elliot didn't care about the reason, only that it was over with (both the criticism of her lack of Hanger Integrity and the bitchy meddling in her love life). Anyway, she didn't have time to be thinking about Carolyn, nor about her cheating father at twenty years old, nor Devon's white-knuckled pussy eating and their ominous conversation at Perkins two days prior, because it was madness, sheer madness in-side the store. Women and more women. Women buying outfits for Christmas parties. Women buying sisters sweaters. Thirty-somethings purchasing merino-poly blended scarves for Minnesota moms. It was all Elliot could do to greet the women who ventured into her section, let alone find them sizes in the stacks or in the back. Hanger Integrity be damned; there simply wasn't time. Her feet felt like the worst flare-up of gout; her lower back felt like she may be coming down with a case of spinal meningitis.

But the day passed.

Elliot kept a mental tally of items sold, or rather, a running total of dollars coming in, and she hit her monthly goals after two hours, and then kept adding—$89.99 for a pair of double-pleat khakis, $174.99 for a floral print silk blouse, $159.99 for a hideous lambswool full-zip cardigan—and she wasn't great at math, couldn't figure out her commission of each purchase, but it was looking good, very good. She'd buy Jacob presents. Yes, this needed to happen after work, and she'd get him enough plastic toys to melt a glacier, enough to make him forget about his wish to Santa. The fake silver tree next to her parents' fireplace would overflow with wrapped gifts of every size, and Jacob would squeal on Christmas morning (might even drop his penis for a second), running to the gifts, to the shrine for Jesus and Santa and parental bribes, tear into paper they'd stuff into more plastic bags, all of it for him.

On her way to the break room for lunch, Mrs. Williams stopped Elliot. Her face was a landslide of sweating makeup. She said something about it being busy, really busy, would you mind taking a ten-minute lunch? Elliot minded. But she understood the not-so-quiet desperation on Mrs. Williams's mess of a face, how this day meant everything to her, and maybe it was all Mrs. Williams had, the store, its reputation, it being so close to becoming the thirty-*sixth* highest grossing Talbots in America. Elliot told her she'd grab a few bites and head back to the floor. Mrs. Williams grinned (an unfortunate choice because it cracked what little foundation was still holding on to her left cheek). She said, "That's real Part-Time mentality."

Elliot ate an apple and then an orange. She checked her phone. She'd received a call from Maddie, and he was sweet in his message, saying he'd always wanted to have sex with an old lady, that he loved her, couldn't wait for dinner that night. And then there was a message from Jacob singing happy birthday. And then one from Devon. He said, "Elle, happy birthday. Crazy how much you've grown up. I enjoyed seeing you the other night, even considering the circumstances. Welcome to your thirties. Love you."

Women and more women.

They never let up.

Christmas music and fake cheer and running to and from the inventory room and *you look amazing in that blouse, really slimming,* and then Elliot rang up a lady for black leggings (Talbots' one attempt at appealing to a younger demographic) and while taking the women's credit card, she noticed the last name Johnson, and although it was anything but a unique last name, especially in a state as homogenous with Viking bloodlines as Minnesota, it gave Elliot pause. She looked at the lady for the first time. She was an attractive shade of mid-forty, all jaw and cheekbone as if her face was a hurried marble statue. Elliot tried to place a protruding Adam's apple on this woman, and kind of could see it, Maddie in this woman's reflection, and then the woman grinned, saying something about the mall being an absolute circus, and there was no mistaking in Elliot's mind that the woman in front of her was Maddie's mother.

Elliot couldn't think of anything to say, or do, or even if she'd run the credit card or not. She fumbled through an awkward attempt at gift-wrapping—*oh, honey, they're for me, don't bother*—and then the woman grinned again, and it was so Maddie with the dimples and teeth and she was pretty if not beautiful, and watching her walk out of the store, Elliot felt it of utmost importance to follow this woman, if only to see her navigate the crowds.

Elliot found Mrs. Williams standing by the front door, her mascara having now succumbed to the combined effects of perspiration and gravity. Elliot said, "Mrs. Williams, is it okay if I take a quick break?"

"Elliot."

"To use the lady's room?"

"Don't have to ask me that. Just hop in back."

"It's…"

"What?"

"Kind of an emergency."

"Yeah, yeah, steal a minute."

"I'd feel more comfortable using the public restrooms."

"Why?"

"*Number three*," Elliot whispered.

"Huh?"

"Diarrhea."

"Gross. God, I don't want to hear about…*number three*. Christ, child. Go."

"Thank you, thank you."

"Wash your hands."

Elliot found the maraschino cherry red of Maddie's mother's down coat, and started walking through the crowds, the smells, the heat of gathered bodies. *What the hell am I doing?* Mrs. Johnson veered into GameStop. Elliot pressed her body against the wall, finding a little eddy in the current of foot traffic. She watched this woman walk to the counter and start speaking to some fat kid about a game, and then he smiled, turning around to grab a copy of an Xbox game with a solider on its front. Elliot imagined Maddie at home sitting in his room on a beanbag or something (she'd never stepped foot in his room) with a controller in his hand and a headset wrapped around his ear, him orchestrating missions and talking trash. There'd be band posters on the wall, rappers with gold mouths and tattoos on their necks. And semen-crusted socks growing colonies of bacteria underneath a bed—no, *futon*—and empty cans of Mountain Dew, for sure there would be those. It would be a room from a movie, one about a beautiful teenage boy growing up in a divorced household and isolation and an illicit love affair with an old bitch with a kid. Was it really illegal? She thought about jail and lawsuits and the entering of her name on a national database of sex offenders.

He's eighteen, Elliot told herself. A summer birthday. Eighteen and legal and he's about to be done with school and age is a stupid measurement of maturity anyway. Look at Devon. He's twice Maddie's age and look at him—lusting after every girl still young enough to never have had an abortion, writing about zombies and sex-addicted men—and Maddie was wise beyond his years, sweet, gentle, beautiful, and was good with Jacob...

Mrs. Johnson was on the move again. She navigated the crowded walkways like she knew her way around the mall, and when she merged from left lane to right by the coin-filled fountain, Elliot realized she really was Maddie's mother, heading to see her son at Zumiez.

Elliot was correct.

There was a hug (Maddie was confident enough in himself to give affection to his mother in front of his boys, a trait Elliot loved), and then there were introductions and smiles, Maddie proud of his mother. Elliot couldn't help but imagine her own life in fifteen years, her going to see Jacob at his first job, him giving her this kind of attention and love among his peers. She told herself it would happen, but she didn't believe it, not even a little bit. No, instead she saw her son shunning her, his cheeks Alabamian Crimson Tide red, his energy turning both frantic and inward. And this image of her grown son kept escalating, kept getting worse—Jacob at thirteen declaring that he wanted to live with his father in Denver, Elliot having no say, Jacob becoming a stranger she saw once a month for weekends spent at Holiday Inns, resentment festering like the acne on his pubescent shoulder blades. She heard future confrontations, screams about her ruining the family, keeping father and son apart because of petty jealousies.

And on and on.

Her mind was a semi they'd seen descending Independence Pass, nothing but the flashing of dirty white siding and the blaring of its air horn, breaks failed, terror all around, the semi veering to the right and literally leaving the ground going over the first bump on the run-away-truck embankment.

Jacob losing faith in Santa, then God, then her.

Jacob becoming mute.

Jacob discovering online forums with other devastated boys searching for reasons for their misery.

Jacob's entire worldview hardening with hurt and isolation and blame (righteous blame) and fuck, Elliot thought, what if he becomes one of those kids stalking the high school hallway dressed in a black trench coat with a gun only partially shielded?

"Hey, you're Maddie's girl, right? Elliot or something?"

Elliot snapped to her left, to a boy she'd met, she was pretty sure, when smoking a joint in the parking lot. He wore the Zumiez unofficial uniform of skinny black jeans and a T-Shirt with hi-tops.

"Umm."

"He's right there. Come on."

Elliot now stood a few feet from the black doors of the shop (she'd evidently been drifting while locked inside nightmares of Jacob's future), and the boy motioned with his head, and all Elliot could do is mutter *no*. *No* to Jacob blaming her. *No* to knowing there was actually blame on her side. *No* to being Maddie's girl. *No* to Maddie's mom with her identical grin. And *no, God no*, to Maddie's friend motioning back to where she stood, Maddie's gaze searching for Elliot, his mother's too. She didn't want to do this. *Couldn't* do this. Couldn't be introduced to his mother. Couldn't pretend she wasn't fucking her son. Couldn't pretend this was normal. So she turned and took a series of five quick steps, merging back into the foot traffic of the *Christmas Crunch*, back into anonymity.

❧

Growing up, the Svendsons subscribed to the binary notions of their daughter's birthday being a tremendous occasion and that they wanted as little part of the preparation/cleanup as possible. The result was every birthday being hosted by Chuck-E-Cheese, a staple of the fabric of

'90s suburban life, what with its arcade games and grotesque life-sized puppets singing happy birthday, not to mention grease-soaked cheese pizza and staff ready to clean up spilled pitchers of Orange Sunkist. Elliot had often complained about the lack of variance in her parties, maybe they could do a princess-themed party at Jumpers like Missy Davis had done? "Sure," her mom had said. "I'll get some *Little Mermaid* paper plates. To be used at Chuck-E-Cheese."

Fast-forward thirty years, and a Chuck-E-Cheese birthday party became a ball of irony and nostalgia, one Elliot couldn't help but enjoy. Her mother purchased princess-themed paper hats with strangling cords, matching plates, even napkins. She'd reserved the party room (eight o'clock on a Thursday night was evidently not peak hours), so that's where they sat, Elliot and her parents, Jacob and Maddie, at a too-big table in a room painted in off-yellows and reds (pizza themed). The four-person band of monsters had already sung an uninspired rendition of The Beatles' "You Say It's Your Birthday," during which Jacob stood and danced, doing his best Michael Jackson impersonation, crotch grab and all. They ate two pizzas, which were ten varieties of delicious, grease slicking their lips and chins.

And things felt okay.

Maddie hadn't asked about possibly seeing her standing outside of Zumiez like a moron. Hadn't even brought it up. And he was being sweet to Jacob, helping him re-sod the layers of cheese that slid off his pizza. Elliot's feet hurt, and her head, and her back, and her entire damn body from nine hours spent slinging sweatshop-stitched clothes in modest three-inch heels, but something felt good or at least okay. Her mother was telling the story of her birth. She thought it had been some indigestion, maybe a kidney stone. Her father chimed in about being all the way out in Plymouth trying to snake a drain of the hairiest woman in the world, bar none. It'd been before cell phones, and then her water broke (*I honestly thought I'd peed myself!*), and there wasn't even time to leave a note, her mom hopping in the car and driving herself to St. Joe's. Her father said Elliot's birth was like throwing a hotdog down a hallway. Maddie laughed. Her mom told the table that Ed showed up just as Elliot was crowning. She reached out and took her husband's hand. She said, "At that moment, I knew everything was going to be okay."

"Mom, do me, do me," Jacob said.

"It's not your birthday, monster."

"Do it. *Please*."

The four of them looked at Elliot, who dabbed at her chin with a scratchy napkin. She explained how she was home alone trying to finish up the nursery. How she was struggling with leveling and hanging pictures of zoo animals. "What kind?" Jacob asked.

"Lions. Bears. A monkey."

"A *monkey!*"

"Like you," Elliot said. Jacob beamed. Elliot said, "My back hurt so bad. And then it was like…"

Elliot's mom nodded.

"I called…" Elliot paused, looking down at her son. He was all smiles and then she could see his little mind work, could see him fill in the blank of whom she called, Devon, his father, and just like that, his smile was a shaken Etch-a-Sketch, everything erased. She put her hand on his back and rubbed the little diamonds of his vertebrae. "You took almost a full day to come out."

"From where?"

"My belly."

"Was Dad there?"

Elliot nodded, still looking down at her son. She knew her parents were staring at her, Maddie too, knew that they were thinking about it being sad having a broken family, a boy needing his father, and Elliot thought about Maddie's mom being beautiful and her blaming herself for the divorce like Maddie had said and then about Maddie being Jacob and him stuck with the opposing feelings of extreme protection and resentment toward the woman who was supposed to insist everything was going to work out.

Jacob looked up at her. He wasn't smiling, but serious, his little eyebrows weighted on their outside edges. He said, "Don't be sad."

"I'm not, honey."

"Yes, you are."

"Love you."

"I want to play games."

Her father laughed, and then Maddie, then all of them except Jacob, who stuck out his two cupped hands like a beggar off the highway.

"Want me to play with you?" Elliot asked.

"No."

"What about me, little man?" Maddie said.

"I'm not little."

"My bad."

"Okay."

"Okay I can come?"

Jacob shrugged.

"And your mom? It's her birthday, after all."

"Fine," Jacob said.

The three of them walked out of the party room. The rest of Chuck-E-Cheese was more empty than not, small pockets of preteens playing first-person shooters. Elliot remembered the video game Maddie's mother had purchased. She cashed a few dollars for tokens. She found Maddie and Jacob around the corner at the whack-a-mole game and Jacob was all beaming smiles and they each held a club clothed in thick padding. "Put in the money, Mom."

Elliot laughed, slipping in two tokens. The machine lit up and then started with an asthmatic carnival tune. Jacob stood on his tiptoes, mallet cocked, and when the first mole poked its head up, he screamed, smashing down his club, which caused the lights circling the game's scoreboard to erupt in an epileptic flash. The next one came and he smashed it down. Then the moles started to come a little quicker, and Jacob's squeals faded, his face a mix of anxiety and apprehension, and before long, the moles were coming too quickly, Jacob's whole body now panicked. Maddie seemed to sense this and swooped in at the exact moment Jacob was about to give up with a flood of tears. Maddie whacked the moles, and seeing the help, Jacob became reinvigorated, his giggles returning as he realized he had support and it was a game and it was supposed to be fun, and soon, they weren't even hitting the rubber moles anymore, but everything—the scoreboard, one another—and it was beautiful, Maddie and her son, beautiful and maybe real.

The game ended. Jacob reached up to Maddie for a pound. Then they turned around, Maddie with his grin, her son his smile, them a team (Elliot could see it, knew she wasn't crazy, there was something there, a bond).

"What's next?"

"The balls," Jacob said.

"Okay."

They made their way over to the pit of plastic balls. Jacob asked Maddie to come play, to which Maddie replied that he was too big but would be right there watching. Jacob processed this information, the fact he'd have to go in alone (scary) versus the fifty-foot tub of balls (fun), and then crawled through the black mesh. He took a tentative step in like he was testing lake water, then jumped forward, landing on his stomach, writhing around and laughing.

"Thank you," Elliot said. She slid her arm around Maddie's skinny waist.

"For what?"

"Being you."

"Kind of cheesy," Maddie said.

"Getting sentimental in my old age."

"My sugar mama."

"Right, *sugar mama* making minimum wage with the chance of commission."

"But you make the store look so good."

"You don't have to lay it on so thick. Going to get laid regardless."

"Is that a promise?"

"A fact."

Jacob was doing a version of the breaststroke through the primary colored balls. Every so often, he'd look back, maybe more toward Maddie than Elliot. Elliot thought about him wanting independence and him wanting protection and how these were two opposing desires every person possessed. "He's so fucking great," Maddie said.

"Yeah."

"A good mom taking him here on your birthday."

"Don't know what you're talking about, did this shit for me."

"Serious," Maddie said.

Elliot fought the urge to tell him otherwise, the fact she was messing Jacob up in more ways than she could count, that this fear/knowledge was the humming constant of her life. She wondered if Maddie's mom took him places like this. Probably. Probably places like this, gifts and parties on tap. It was this train of thought that made Elliot realize she had to say something, so she did: "I saw your mom today."

"Was wondering if we were going to talk about that."

"You saw me, huh?"

"Your back outside of the store, yeah."

"Sorry."

"Nothing to be sorry about."

"I just…I don't know. Like what would I have said? Hey, Mrs. Johnson, I'm sleeping with your boy."

"Don't always have to minimize it."

"That's not what I mean," Elliot said.

"Really?"

"Yeah, *really*."

"If you say so," Maddie said.

Jacob was throwing balls against the mesh wall. He threw like a girl or maybe like a three-year-old.

"It's fine," Maddie said.

"You know I love you."

"I mean about not saying hi to my moms."

"Yeah?"

"She's...protective, I guess you could say."

"Protective against all girls or from somebody like me?"

"Protective. You know how it is."

Elliot thought she knew *how it was*—a single mother's bond with her son, fortified through hardships and betrayal—but she couldn't help but take offense at what Maddie was saying, and told him she wasn't sure what he was talking about.

"Just with the age and everything."

"Because I'm a predator?"

"Alien vs. Predator," Maddie said.

"No, serious, is that what you're saying? That I'm a predator?"

"You know that's not what I mean."

"Then what?"

Maddie studied her face to see if she was serious, if this was really the germination of a fight, and Elliot stared back, not sure herself. She had the notion of being childish, of being needy in her desire for pardon in the form of affirmations and placating comments about nothing ever being her fault, yet she couldn't help it.

Maddie said, "Okay, let me ask you why you didn't come say hello."

"Because I had to get back to work."

"Because you love your job so much?"

"Because it was busy as fuck."

"And that's your final answer?" Maddie's lips slid into their grin, obviously realizing he had her backed into a corner.

"I don't know," Elliot said.

"Because you felt like she might not understand, might be weird about the age difference or whatever."

"Maybe."

"Because she's *protective*, just like you are over Jacob."

"Because I'm robbing the cradle."

"Please," Maddie said. "I pursued you."

"Whatever you need to tell yourself, *stud.*"

"Can't resist this," Maddie said.

Jacob had evidently grown bored jumping and throwing, and now was stuffing the plastic balls down his pants.

"Listen," Maddie said. "I love you. Know you love me. And I've dated my fair share of girls—"

"Hashtag humble brag."

"Hear me out. I've been in relationships and all of that, and never, never once have I felt like this."

"Like what?"

"Like this could be some till-death-do-us-part shit."

And then their lips pressed and Elliot thought about her fantasy of second chances and colligate careers being within grasp and it being better this time, a choice instead of a pregnancy, mutual feelings of that heady intoxication of another's smell, perfectly timed comments straight from the truest of romantic comedies, and as they kissed, she heard Jacob yelling, *Daddy,* which caused the emotional cousins of euphoria and guilt to ripple through her brain, Elliot thinking her son's mind equated a kiss to fatherhood. But Jacob kept yelling it, and Elliot stopped kissing Maddie, seeing her son struggle through the pit of balls, running his hardest to the mesh opening, arms outstretched. Elliot turned around. Devon stood there in his stupid wool beanie, his face revealing the same disdain as when he received a bad review for his writing.

Jacob crawled through the mesh divider, red and blue balls spilling to the linoleum floor. Devon scooped him up, cupping the back of his son's head. Jacob's little Sorel boots fought for traction against Devon's stupid pea coat. Elliot couldn't think of anything to say, only to drop Maddie's hand and take a step away, distance herself from infidelity that wasn't infidelity, no way it was, not after what Devon had done, not when they were separated. But she couldn't deny a sense of guilt, of embarrassment, a defensive heat setting her cheeks aflame, and before she could utter a *what the fuck are you doing here?* she realized this defensive posturing was born from Maddie's age, or lack thereof.

Devon looked over Jacob's head straight at Elliot. He said, "Happy birthday."

"What? How are you even— What the hell are you doing here?"

"You'd always told me about your Chuck-E-Cheese parties. Wasn't very difficult to know this was where you'd be."

Elliot knew he was right about her blabbering about past birthdays, but this knowledge didn't make her feel any less violated. Maddie's Adam's apple chugged up and down as he swallowed.

"You need to leave," Elliot said.

"No!" Jacob yelled. He whirled his head around and stuck out his tongue.

"Yes, your father needs to leave. Now. This is unacceptable."

"No!" Jacob yelled again.

"Swear to God if my dad sees you…"

"I'm Maddie, I don't think we've been introduced."

Devon looked at Maddie's extended hand and let it hang there for an awkward second before smiling, adjusting the weight of Jacob to his left arm, and then shaking Maddie's hand.

"Of course you are," Devon said.

"And you're…"

"Devon. Elliot's husband."

"Ex," Elliot said.

"And Jacob's father."

"Daddy, a bitch is a bitch is a bitch."

"What's that, buddy?"

"A ho is a ho is a ho."

"Is that right?" Devon said.

"Yup. Grandpa's show said so."

"That's great, buddy."

"Leave, now," Elliot said.

"Thirty years old, wow. Crazy."

"I'm not joking. This is…is…"

"Don't look a day over twenty-one," Devon said.

"You'd know," Elliot said.

"Honestly, I was thinking that the other night over coffee. You haven't aged a day, or no, you've aged, matured, but grown more beautiful."

Elliot stole a glance at Maddie, who'd evidently heard what Devon had said, and was trying to put it together—*coffee, the other day*—and in his mind this probably meant a hidden date and continued contact and his grin was gone, his energy pulled inward, him retreating, and fuck, Devon wouldn't do this, come in like a motherfucking hero to Jacob, make Elliot's birthday about himself, trample the fragile grass of the life Elliot was tending to.

"Coffee?" Maddie said.

Devon smiled. "What, she didn't tell you, bud? We met up for some dessert the other night. It was—"

"Shut the fuck up," Elliot said.

"Bad word!" Jacob screamed.

"Leave us alone," Elliot said.

Devon looked at Maddie, who'd taken a step back from Elliot. Devon laughed. He gave Jacob an Eskimo kiss. He wrapped his hand around Jacob's head, shielding his ears under the guise of an embrace. "That's the thing with this one, pal: she's not always forthcoming with information."

"Stop," Elliot said. She reached to take Jacob, who kicked at her hands with his winter boots. Elliot felt a jolt of pain not unlike a sliver and knew instantly her son had just kicked and broken the nail of her index finger. Elliot cussed, squeezing her nail. The injury seemed to diffuse the situation, at least the insults and insinuated threats, and the three boys stared at Elliot, who stared at her finger and then her son and then back at her nail, which had a fault line running through it in a southeast diagonal zigzag. Blood grew around her cuticle.

"Why don't I get out of here," Devon said, "and take Jacob with me. Would you like that, bud? Come hang out at Daddy's hotel?"

Jacob quit looking at his mother's bleeding finger, smiled, nodded, and started jiggling around. He started saying *yep, yep, yep*. Elliot realized she had no power. At least not the kind of power she'd thought she possessed, the kind she wanted, the kind which offered independence and protection, the kind she could wield like the most wronged of victims. She said, "Fuck you," but it came out more defeated than angry.

"Think you should leave," Maddie said.

"I am, *champ*. With my son." Jacob pushed his father's wool beanie off his head exposing a hairline on Jenny Craig, the sides speckled like dirty snow. Devon said, "I like the tenacity, kid, but honestly, if you think you're anything other than a revenge fuck, I feel sorry for you."

"Grow the fuck up," Elliot said.

Devon still covered Jacob's ears. He started with a comment, but stopped, shaking his head, letting a hint of a smile creep across his lips. "Elle, happy birthday. Kid, nice to meet you. I wish you luck on finding your *own* family when you hit puberty. I'll bring *my son* back around dinner tomorrow."

"Fuck you, man," Maddie said.

"Bad word, Maddie!" Jacob yelled.

"If you'd refrain from cursing around my son, that'd be greatly appreciated," Devon said. He winked at Maddie.

Elliot was shaking her head and there were tears and hot spits and she was thinking about Devon always getting his way and her having no choice or power and walking into an office and seeing another girl's hands running through Devon's slightly curled hair. Jacob wiggled out of his covered ears. He was repeating *Daddy Daddy Daddy* with increasing volume. Elliot knew letting her son spend the night with his father was the right thing to do (she hadn't seen him this excited in over two months), but letting Devon carry him away felt like a failure she'd vowed never to experience again.

"I'm at the Marriott, if you need me for any reason." Devon hoisted a squealing Jacob over his head. "Ready to have some fun? Go swimming? Watch cartoons? Eat Milk Duds?"

Daddy Daddy Daddy.

And then Devon walked away, Jacob slung over his shoulder, Jacob kicking and laughing uncontrollably, his laughs being swallowed by the electronic beeps of arcade games. Elliot turned back to Maddie, who stood with his arms crossed. He seemed young at that moment, wounded, immature. She put her fingers through his belt loops. She could tell he was hurt, which was stupid as hell considering Elliot's situation. The placating kiss she gave his cheek felt like a consolation she shouldn't have to be making. She wrapped her arms around his shoulders and she asked if he was okay and he gave a sullen head nod and she thought about taking whatever she wanted, as Devon did to her—as everyone did, all day, every day, take and take, other people be damned—and about getting older and about being trapped as both a stay-at-home mother and as a thirty-year-old retail employee. She pressed her mouth to Maddie's. She told herself if it was met by tongue, things would work out, with him and with Devon, with her thirties, with her life, finally.

Maddie's mouth was motionless.

Kids screamed and games blared.

Then his tongue found hers, and she wasn't filled with a sense that things were going to be okay, but rather power, her finally figuring out how the fuck to exercise it.

VII

My Son

The next day at work, Elliot experienced a floating sensation, dream-like, drug-like, everything foggy with a touch of falsity. She couldn't get out of her head. She replayed Devon showing up and Jacob squealing in delight and Maddie trying to be protective and maybe this was sweet or maybe it was annoying and then the car ride home, her father angry to the point of silence, him not even turning on stand-up when he got home, just sitting in the parked van as coldness seeped through its closed windows. She had two main tracts of thought: one being the victim of infidelity, of broken vows, of being voiceless, powerless, a woman who had to retreat home in order to *cool off*, at least until her knight in black armor showed back up in order to rectify the sanctity of Family; the other train of thought was about her son, about him having to experience the world as Mommy or Daddy time, about his God-like innocence freezing into a colder form of analytics, him just wanting to see his father.

At certain times, say when Elliot refolded a stack of retro khaki chinos, she almost understood what Devon was doing. Maybe it wasn't so much about her, but Jacob, about Christmas being four days away, the first one where Jacob nervously weighed his good deeds versus sins as if he were Santa, and Devon wanted to be part of that memory.

Other times, like when Carolyn stormed over to Elliot's section, not saying anything (they still hadn't exchanged a word since their confrontation the previous afternoon), abruptly changing the direction of the hanger on the face-out so it aligned with H.I., Elliot's mind experienced a storm-front shifting of barometric pressure, and with it, a sense of fury at Devon, at everything he represented, at the role he insisted on carving out of her life from his first comments on her short story some six years prior.

By three-thirty that afternoon, Elliot no longer felt this push and pull of mentalities, only a fear in the form of mutating cells, and when four o'clock hit, these cells had formed a tumor, Elliot avoiding every fat woman who waddled into the store, her unable to greet those needy eyes with so much as a plastered smile, and at a quarter to five, fifteen minutes before she was officially done (she'd been scheduled as one of four coveted openers that morning), Eliot felt as if her entire body had metastasized, fear making every movement near impossible. She spoke to Mrs. Williams, citing something about her stomach acting up again, was it okay to duck out fifteen minutes early?

Elliot sped home.

All she could think about was seeing Jacob. She needed to feel his body against hers, even if he was fighting to free himself from what he felt as too-needy embraces. She'd order kung-pao chicken, his favorite. She'd rent every Pixar film created over the past decade. And she'd go through the recycling to get the Toys-R-Us glossy insert from the paper and give him a red pen to mark the presents he coveted the most, hell, not even the most, *at all*, circle any toy that looks even remotely fun.

Neither her mother nor father was home when she arrived. It was dark inside and out, late December doing its damnedest to coat its inhabitants with seasonal depression. Jacob wasn't there either. Elliot turned on the TV, which was tuned to Comedy Central and was hearing-aid loud, but she didn't notice. She told herself she'd wait a half hour, because dinner time could be six, might be six, was probably closer to six when they'd lived together in Colorado.

Some fifteen minutes later, headlights lit up the dim family room. Elliot rushed to the door, and paused, not wanting to appear desperate or crazy, but opened the door anyway. Her father was slamming the van door shut. And it was here Elliot allowed herself to think the unthinkable for the first time—*Devon's taken my son*—and her father must've seen this internalized terror on his daughter's face, because he said, "It's early yet," as he steered her back inside, his freezing and callused hands clasped around hers. He got each of them a Bud. The carbonation burned Elliot's throat. Her father pretended to pay attention to the comedian, but it was a woman, and Elliot knew he hated women stand-ups, and then her father was telling her about work, which he never did, talking about a drain with the better part of a plastic toy soldier ground in the disposal, and something wasn't right because he was trying so hard to be kind, to be distracting, and he must've feared the same thing, a missing grandson, 911, Amber alert, because he probably understood the protectiveness a father felt over a child, and maybe he would've done the same thing with Elliot had his affair happened a few years later.

Six o'clock.

Six-fifteen.

Six-thirty.

Another set of lights illuminated the room (her father had turned on a few lights, but something about the room still felt ill-lit). Her father told her this must be them because her mom was at bridge group, which never let out before nine-thirty. Elliot was at the door. She didn't mess around with feigning composure. She was outside on the two steps, shielding her eyes from the headlights, and when they finally cut, she saw her mother's Pontiac, her mother's outline, both hands gripping the wheel as if she were pushing ninety on an icy road.

Elliot pulled out her phone and called Devon. It went straight to voicemail. She tried again. Voicemail. Her mother still sat in her car. The wind blew crystals of snow against Elliot's face. And how the fuck could she have been so stupid? Devon didn't care about getting Elliot back, or rather, if he did, it was more due to the fact of him losing—both to Elliot and Maddie—and Devon was nothing if not competitive with an unhealthy amount of vindictiveness. He cared about winning in every aspect of his life. He motherfucked bad reviews and every rejected short story. And last night? It must've done horrible things to his fragile little ego to see Elliot with another man, to see Jacob bonding with a stranger. This would've caused the audible in Devon's plan. His trip no longer was about fighting off the loneliness of solitary Christmases, but revenge, righteous anger, and reversal of victim roles, and they'd be in western Nebraska by now, Jacob trying to sleep in a strange car with no blanket, the roads dark and the mountains still yet to be seen.

The detached sensation was back, molesting Elliot's sense of reality. Her mother had ushered her inside and her father was standing and there was lots of rubbing of shoulders and *let's not panic just yet*. Elliot redialed as soon as the baritone of Devon's voice started on the recording; she imagined Devon coming unhinged, him saying fuck it—the state university, his middling career, a woman he never loved—and maybe he'd be driving north through towns that were nothing but a gas pump/grocery, until snow-covered pine trees were the only witnesses, and then there'd be a checkpoint, a customs agent who would see a father and son from his warm booth and not even bother checking passports.

Eight o'clock.

Eight-fifteen.

Another set of lights from the street. Elliot's father was the first one out of the door. Elliot said a silent prayer, her mother squeezing her shoulders. Maddie's voice drifted in through the door. And then it was her father with a pained look of pretend, Maddie standing there seeing Elliot's puffy eyes, Maddie absorbing the tension in the room, him asking what was wrong. He sat next to Elliot on the couch. She told him about Jacob not being home, and he told her it was fine, probably just lost track of time, had she tried the hotel?

Her mother called the Marriott, asking to be connected to Devon Hester's room. The clerk told her he had checked out the previous evening, and it was with this news that the fear in the room reached a boiling point of sorts, Terry crying, Ed slamming his fist against the round oak table, Elliot letting a choke of a sob escape from her mouth. She punched 911 for the second time in her life. She remembered the first time after she'd found Jacob chewing those gel packets of dishwashing detergent, and she felt the same refrain of thought sitting at the kitchen table as she felt a year prior wiping green and blue poisonous gel from Jacob's mouth: *I'm a horrible mother; I can't live without my son; I'll do anything in this fucking world to make sure he's okay.*

She was asked about her emergency and she tried to be rational and clear the mucus from her throat, but it wouldn't stop, the tears and snot, Elliot a leaky fucking vessel with no power. Maddie was rubbing her shoulder, and this soothing made her feel pathetic, barbless in a world of sharp points, ill-equipped, a failure. She managed to tell the operator her address and then he was telling her to calm down, to breathe—everybody was telling her to calm down and fucking breathe—and he asked if she was in immediate danger, was she safe?

"My son, he took my son."

WE, ADULTS

(Excerpts from Devon Hester's unpublished memoir, *We, Adults*)

I

Make the most of your regrets; never smother your sorrow, but tend and cherish it till it comes to have a separate and integral interest. To regret deeply is to live afresh.

-Henry David Thoreau

My father was an alcoholic. Don't worry, this isn't one of those kinds of memoirs. He didn't beat me with bibles and he didn't fiddle my penis with vomit-covered hands. He was a good man, or what I believe a good man looks like after two years spent in Vietnam. I know there were things inside of him, those incongruent flashes of memory where everything was saturated with too much light, which fundamentally changed the person he had once been. My earliest memories of him are of sitting on his lap in his green chair. I remember the musty-sour smell of his chewing tobacco. I remember being uncomfortable by his silent stillness. I remember how I cringed when his mutilated right hand from a friendly fire M-16 round (missing his pinky and ring finger, the rough edges of where they'd been like the weathered Appalachian Mountains) would come in direct contact with any part of my skin. I remember having some sense of him being a fixture in the house, rather than an actual person, nonetheless my father, as if he was wooden, vacant.

I blame nothing on my father.

I'm a big boy, past the age of pointed fingers and couches meant for crying.

I bring him up because of a story he told me in the seventh grade. I'd been sent to the principal's office for teasing a classmate, Madeline. She was a heavy girl with the wrong kind of freckles who always wore collared polo shirts tucked into a pair of brown corduroys with an elastic waist. She'd recently returned from a two-week absence, only to have a colostomy bag taped to her right side (we were given a very rough sketch by our homeroom teacher of what this contraption "helped" Madeline accomplish). I sat behind her in French. I heard a crinkling noise like somebody was sneaking a handful of potato chips. Then I saw her white polo shirt expand out a few inches. I said, Gross, Poop Bag Madeline is taking a shit!

The principal had phoned my mother, who told me to go to my room and wait for my father (her usual disciplinary action). My father came home. I was expecting a spanking or the loss of allowance or maybe a battery of screams. But he just sat on my bed. He loosened his tie. He started to speak but stopped. He rubbed his baby-carrot nubs of fingers. He said, When you're about to die, you don't think about the things you have. Not your parents. Your girlfriends. Kids. None of that. You think about the people you've been cruel to. The mistakes you've made. The times you were a complete asshole. It is these regrets you die lamenting.

I'd be lying to you if I claimed to have known the importance his words would have on me over the course of my life, if I said I was touched by my father's opening up, becoming vulnerable through his first words to me about Vietnam. I felt nothing but gratitude for his lack of punishment. I felt as if I'd dodged a bullet. I felt as if I'd escaped.

I can honestly say I didn't think about this conversation for twenty-seven years. Don't get me wrong, I had plenty of opportunities to contemplate mistakes I'd made, small cruelties I dished out with the cold indifference of adolescence and then young adulthood—unreturned phone calls, gossip, theft, sleeping with Peter Mantel's girlfriend freshmen year at Northwestern, offering no assistance to my mother as cancer eroded my father's jaw and then bone marrow (the list is infinite)—yet for some reason, my father's words were trapped, along with the rest of my father, in some dead bolted door of my mind.

Then I hit forty.

Then I made a lot of small choices, which seemed harmless at the time.

And, of course, there were reasons, as there always are.

Then I was alone in a five hundred thousand dollar bungalow in northern Denver, drunk, feeling sorry for myself on my son's bed as I thumbed through a children's book about a zombie family. It was December. I felt a tightness in my chest that was either cardiac arrest or a panic attack, neither of which I'd ever experienced, both of which I was terrified of, my father struggling with the latter his whole life. It was probably this thought of my father, plus the fact I was sitting on my son's bed, plus the fact the tightness in my chest had started to radiate through my left shoulder, that jogged this three-decade-old memory. I felt my father's presence. I heard his words. And I understood that if I were really dying, the only thing accompanying me would be the memories of the pinched faces of those I'd wronged.

II

AN EXCERPT FROM *WE, ADULTS*: "A PTERODACTYL IS
HATCHED"

Elliot and I didn't read books about how to raise a child. We figured there was no point. The books were for stupid people or people who needed to feel some sense of control over their growing bellies and wife's hormonal slamming of doors. We understood the need for love. For calm. For colors in the nursery. For story time spanning an hour a night. For snuggling and for organic baby food after at least six months of breastfeeding. We knew the shortcomings of our own parents, and we'd do better because our lives hadn't been shaped by years spent trying not to be killed in mountainous jungles, and Elliot and I were equals, something the women in our parents' generation only made a show of pageantry toward achieving.

I pictured parenthood as something that would suit me well, my son a new cashmere scarf, the perfect accessory. I had an open work schedule (wrote for two hours in the morning and taught two workshops over the course of the week). I pictured myself pushing a stroller through Denver with the leaves changing and a slight nip to the air, the promise of snow with no actual threat. I'd stop by the coffee shop and smile at baristas as they studied my offspring, but really they'd be studying me, the hip dad, the man about whom they muttered, *Why can't he be mine?* when they slipped into bed after another disastrous date. And maybe I'd go to a DU sporting event. It would be my first in seven years at the school, but I'd go, something outside, maybe lacrosse. My son would be a little older then, able to eat puffy cereal without my help, and he'd sit in my lap, more interested in the clapping and cold bleachers than the boys running on the field. The whole thing would be a pastoral rite of passage (for whom, I wasn't sure). I was ready for that change. I was ready for the next phase of my life.

Elliot would take a semester off but then would resume her thesis work on Thomas Middleton. I'd have to be a tiny bit flexible, but there was something romantic about the notion of juggling and sacrificing myself for the betterment of our family. I found the whole thing appealing in a *something-to-complain-about-with-the-fraternity-members-of-fatherhood* sort of way. We'd make it work. We'd persevere. We'd trudge. And we'd hold hands in autumn clothing as we did so.

Labor came with a snake-like blood clot floating in our toilet. Elliot had evidently been doing *some* reading because she said this was her *mucus plug*. We called the doctor. He told us otherwise, to let him know if there was any more bleeding. Then there was back pain. Then there were contractions (*I think they're Braxton Hicks; who the fuck is Braxton Hicks?*). A warm bath and tea and it will pass by the morning and then cries and the stopwatch application on my phone reading ten minutes apart and oh my fucking god it hurts and isn't your water supposed to break and contractions five minutes apart and we need to go and I'm scared and it's okay, baby, it's all going to be okay.

Things were better after the epidural.

We watched *Hoarders: Buried Alive* from the small hanging TV as we waited for her cervix to dilate. I ate a Snickers. I fetched ice chips. A TV antenna-like instrument was used to break Elliot's water. Only it wasn't water, but blood, lots of it, the white crinkling bed sheets greedy in their absorption.

And then things weren't better.

The doctor looked like a *Meet the Parents* De Niro. He told me to put on some relaxing music. I had no idea what this would be—my music collection was mostly depressing male-led vocals. I put on an album I'd listened to once before. It was soft and gentle, if not a touch inspirational. The doctor kept saying *capiche*. There was no way a baby was going to fit through the tiny hairless opening I stared down at.

Push.

Beeping heart monitors.

Blood covering the doctor's blue gloves.

Push, two, three, four, five, six, seven, eight.

I watched the doctor. He kept glancing between Elliot's vagina and the monitor along the wall and then he said something about getting the vacuum and he started to work faster, him not even mentioning the generous cut he was giving the base of her vagina, more blood, more plummeting heart rates, the doctor yelling that they needed to get the baby out now, my stupid acoustic song the exact musical choice for a bad Lifetime movie montage about stillborn babies and the ensuing deterioration of a marriage.

A nurse guided me to a chair.

Everything was the *wha-wha* echoes of nitrous oxide.

I thought about a dead son and about taking down the zoo alphabet in the nursery while Elliot cried herself to sleep and about months filled with conversation about what Jacob would've been like, and then Jacob reverting to a pronoun, he, and then nothing, silence, no mention, it never happened.

I realized I needed to get my shit together and be there for Elliot. She cried. Snot bubbled at her nose while she pushed. Blood. Beeping. A hair-covered head. A white-goop covered body. Little tiny feet. All of them unmoving.

And then there was a cry.

It was the most beautiful fucking sound in the world. Prehistoric. A pterodactyl.

Jacob was placed on Elliot's chest. He screamed with his eyes open. I knew he couldn't actually see me, but it seemed that way, him all cold and shivering and beautiful staring at his father.

It took all of one night at home with our baby to realize my views of parenthood were so fucking far from realistic.

Enter colic.

Enter postpartum depression.

Enter exhaustion so utter and complete NoDoz didn't begin to scratch the surface of it.

And cue that melodramatic music, because nothing, and I mean absolutely nothing, compared to his giggle at three months when I shook my head in front of his face as I made farting sounds.

We started reading books about how to be decent parents. We started complaining about our perpetual tiredness. We broke our own rules and put him in our bed so we didn't have to deal with the crying. And when eight o'clock (on a good night) rolled around, and he was out, so were we, not even bothering to turn on our bedside lamps to read, us barely able to mutter a mechanical *I love you*.

I suppose it was here when we actually became parents.

III

Elliot Svendsen wasn't a universally beautiful girl. Her hair was a blond close to brown, her body molded in Midwestern practicality, as if her ancestrally high-wear areas (ankles, shoulders, hips) were reinforced through generations of crop harvesting. She had the habit of thinking with the end of her pen pressed to her left front tooth. More often than not, it seemed as if she dressed with no concern for creating a cohesive whole, colors or fabrics be damned.

Yet it worked, all of it.

She possessed the self-assuredness of a woman twice her age—no, strike that—the confidence of the beautiful and charismatic, those rare demigods who hit sevens on the genetic slot machine, and float through life with an unapologetic notion of *isn't it this easy for everyone?* Yet she was neither overly beautiful nor charismatic. Elliot was shy, more than a smidgen awkward. She was sweet. Yet, there was something there in her pale blue eyes that forced me to question the sincerity of her learned bashfulness. More than once while I was lecturing and caught her eye, I was struck with the notion that she didn't give two shits about what I was saying. Something about her stare was challenging. There was a hint of *I could do your job better*. It was as if she knew something the rest of us didn't.

Or maybe this speculation is the result of retrospect and regret. Maybe I was simply drawn to a girl who let her intention be known by refusing to avert her gaze when eye contact exceeded the acceptable half-second time frame.

I found myself thinking about her with alarming regularity.

I'd be in the shower and I'd be preparing for lessons and I'd be stuck in the horrendous traffic south of Denver. I'd envision conferences where our knees brushed against each other. Maybe our hands would graze while handing in assignments. I pictured her room, the books she'd have (definitely not a *Jane Eyre* type of girl, maybe the Russians?), the sweet smell of her sweat and Dove coating the comforter she'd purchased at Target. And in October, as she sat at her desk in a black cotton skirt, unabashedly exposing a chink of her cream-colored panties through her slightly separated legs, my thoughts turned from the infatuated curious to the sexualized hypothetical.

❧

So much of life is the drawing of lines, the setting of boundaries. *I won't do this, but I'll do that. Maybe I'll say this, but for sure I won't say that.* It's a game, really, a way to wrestle control over our desires. We are constantly in a sterile conference room of mediation. We are lawyers with bitter clients trying their best to keep up the appearance of steely resolve. We're passing offers scrawled on legal pads back and forth, claiming this is the furthest we'll go, absolutely no wiggle room in this offer, I walk after this. Yet we receive those counter offers in the form of *maybe this once, what would it really hurt, I've already done x, y, and z.*

I watched my parents keep a running scorecard to their lives as if it were nothing but a game of bridge. My father's unsaid trump was always Vietnam. My mother's was my father's alcoholism, followed closely by his lack of success at Sears, and her resulting cashier job at CVS. I watched my father ignore my mother my entire childhood because he felt entitled to the inebriation of drink. I watched my mother's transition into the type of woman who *deserved* to have a string of affairs—bangs, expenditures on shoulder-pad jackets, going out with coworkers on Friday nights—all over the simmering resentment of crushing loneliness and perceived injustice. For each of them, I'm sure they made lists of actions they'd never allow, followed by actions they'd *really* never take.

The first personal line I can remember breaking was shoplifting.

I was in the sixth grade. Everybody was coming to school with base-ball cards. My friends were assembling complete decks with the ease of the rich, and it didn't make sense because I knew what they were taking in on Sundays for allowance. Eventually, I figured out what *five-finger discount* meant (after somebody explicitly informed me), and I shook my head, disgusted or at least afraid, vowing I'd never steal.

But everybody's card collections kept growing at astonishing rates, while mine grew by eleven cards a week. Soon, I was the only one without a Ryne Sandberg rookie. I'd sit there at the rectangular lunch table, my cards sweaty in my hands, my peers' cards spread out before them for the world to admire. And I *did* admire the collections. The joy they must be feeling being in possession of the entire Topps set. The stories they traded about their petty acts of rebellion. The inclusiveness of it all.

My rule—one I'd never even had to verbalize because the chance of committing it was so much of an impossibility—was broken a week after the term *five-finger discount* became commonplace in the cafeteria I didn't steal baseball cards. I stole a plastic dinosaur, a stegosaurus I believe. This was from The Red Balloon, a children's bookshop I passed on my way home. I made up an extravagant lie about needing a book for my fictitious baby sister, one that let her understand how much I loved her. The overweight clerk gave me a smile like pure love, then waddled out from behind her counter to point out *just the one*. I used this moment to slip the plastic dinosaur into my tighty-whities. On the way home, I felt sick. I pictured an angry God and an angry father and I imagined being arrested and I imagined living in the streets with cardboard signs begging for food. My Poe moment came in the woods a few hundred yards from my house. I buried the stegosaurus. I vowed never again. I vowed to take that secret to my grave.

Three days later, I stole my first pack of Topps baseball cards.

We covet.

We covet people and things and feelings and security and danger and we covet love, esteem, and validation in every conceivable form of measurement. We covet these things because of the nagging voice inside of our heads that whispers a thousand variations of the same message: *you're not good enough*. This is why we make easily breakable rules. This is why we compromise morals. This is why *just this once* and *never again* roll so effortlessly off our tongues.

My *just this once* came in the form of agreeing to meet my student, Elliot Svendsen, for coffee to discuss the story she'd handed in. She asked me after class. Normally, this wouldn't even be a question—*by all means, my office is your office, we can meet right now*—but it was different with Elliot for two reasons: she asked to grab a cup of coffee at The Little Owl, which was a ten minute walk from campus; it was Elliot, a girl who showed an unabashed interest in me, and conversely, a student whom I'd spent hours outside of the classroom thinking—no, *fantasizing*—about.

Just this once. Talking isn't intercourse. She only wants feedback on her story. Flirtation isn't intercourse. She's a graduate student taking an undergraduate course;

not an undergraduate. Playful brushing of leaves from the belly of her sweater is not intercourse. You're one published story away from tenure track assistant professorship, don't fuck this up. She's twenty-four, almost twenty-five. She wouldn't tell. Her hand on your knee isn't intercourse...

The Little Owl was about as hip a place as Denver had to offer. This was the year when skinny jeans started showing up in *US Weekly*, but still a good eighteen months before they made their way to the masses in the American West, that is except for the patrons of The Little Owl. I was confused and then I felt old and then I looked up from Elliot's story and she had her blue Bic pen pushed against her tooth and I let myself be a creep and imagined the pen as something else and she didn't look away, and neither did I, because it was *just this once* and because I liked the melodic vocals over electronic beats playing from dangling speakers and because she'd flattered everything about me (my published work, my teaching style, the fact that I scored a 9.8 on professorhotornot.com) and because the last woman I'd slept with had been an overly serious Korean lit agent at a writer's conference the previous summer and because the soles of our shoes were touching and here it comes, the crux of every rationalization, the assigning of merit, the notion of *deserving*, and hell, I did, why not, why the fuck didn't I deserve attention from a sometimes-beautiful grad student?

A decision was made at that very moment.

Hell, it was probably made weeks before, but I distinctly remember allowing myself this small pleasure as I sat in a too-hip coffee shop with a student thirteen years my junior. The next three weeks were some of the best of my life. I was intoxicated with the game of *this isn't happening*. Elliot did her part to pretend the same. We were connected by the feigned awe of our mutual attraction, how we *couldn't help it*. The thrill of *accidental* physical contact was irresistible. Everything was unspoken; everything was implied. I found myself giddy the nights before my Tuesday-Thursday class. I'd imagine the looks she'd give me, the pressure our shins would apply underneath the wooden table at The Little Owl. I'd be a touch bolder in my passes. I'd let my eyes linger a beat longer. I'd dig deeper into her past—*how'd you end up interested in an unheralded playwright? How'd you decide on Colorado? Why isn't a beautiful* (I'd convinced myself she was by this point) *girl like you dating anyone?*

When everything is still yet to happen, there is no right or wrong, or rather, there's the trying on of guilt for hypothetical actions weighed against the desire to commit said actions. Only this equation is bullshit—in this instance and probably all others involving sex—because even the administered guilt takes on the erotic pleasure of shame.

Our game of pretend reached a sort of critical mass the day before Halloween. We sat in the coffee shop, both complaining of hunger. Dinner was suggested. Elliot told me she had no money. I offered to pay. She stared with her marble eyes. She said, I'm a big fan of breakfast for dinner. You have eggs at your house?

I beat her to my house. I brushed my teeth and took a damp washcloth to my groin and I smoothed my hair in the mirror, never allowing myself to meet my own stare. Elliot arrived ten minutes later. She wore a cheap knee-length coat with fake fur around the edges. She ran her hand over my leather couch. I imagined it as my spine. She said my place was cute. She looked at my books. I told myself it was a bad idea and that she was a student and that I was close to tenure and I'd feel the same if I sent her on her way and viewed my rapidly growing cache of pornography clips resembling Elliot, only minus the intoxicating guilt of *only this once.*

Our fingers touched on the spine of Durrell's *Justine.*

She turned away from my bookcase and her mouth was slightly open and I noticed a blotch of discoloration on her left-front tooth and I wondered how I'd never seen this blemish before and then our stomachs were touching and hers had the slightest give, which I thought was both repulsive and amazing. Her taste was the bitter of recently drank espresso.

A kiss isn't intercourse.

Just this once.

The sex was neither sensual nor erotic. It was rather perfunctory, timid even. There was a silence afterward which was the closest thing to awful I'd ever experienced. We made eggs and toast. We ate in front of a rerun of *The Simpsons.* I wanted her to leave. I wanted the last half hour back. The last month. I'd insist on meeting with her in my office to discuss her story. I'd leave the door open. I'd see her exposed underwear in class as an accident, or at the very least, as the actions of a girl who'd watched too many movies.

I needed to be tactful in my exit from the situation. I needed to let her down slowly, tell her mistakes had been made—no, not mistakes, but rules, rules were in place by the university prohibiting such interactions—and it was a matter of my career, and maybe in the future, once she was done with her thesis, it could be different.

But once *Everybody Loves Raymond* started, Elliot leaned her head into my lap. Her shirt rode up exposing a tiny pillow of back fat. She unzipped my pants. She put me in her mouth. Raymond complained about Debora. I got hard. *Never again* became *one more time*.

IV

When I was seventeen, my father was arrested. He'd discovered my mother's infidelities. He'd been informed of his cancer. His drinking had steadily crept its way to his ten o'clock break at Sears. Things weren't great for him, I understood this, even then. This was the only night I remember him raising his voice. He yelled, or maybe they were closer to screams. He punched the wall. He smashed the TV.

I watched from the doorway of the dining room.

I was obviously scared, but more sad because everybody was going to leave him and he was crying and snot dripped across his lips and because it was pathetic. His life was pathetic. He was pathetic. Everything he'd ever done was for naught, a futile exercise in trying to build some semblance of the Greatest Generation's American Dream, only in the wrong era of post-Vietnam. And he'd failed. And when the TV crashed down, and with it my father, his head pressed against our vinyl siding, I think he fully accepted this failure.

The cops came.

He didn't fight.

They put him in handcuffs right there in our kitchen. My mother wasn't saying anything, just smoking cigarette after cigarette, her hairsprayed bangs having flattened hours before. The two officers ushered my father out of our house. I'll never forget how gentle the Black cop was as he cradled my father's head, guiding it underneath the squad car's roof.

&

I've never raised my voice at a woman.

I've never broken something out of anger. I've never called a woman a cunt to her face and I've never allowed my drinking to interfere with my life. I've strived hard to accumulate the luxuries of the upper-middle class—a full-ride to Northwestern, fully funded graduate school at Michigan, adjunct work until tenure track, paid for my house in full with my saved book advances. I am a willing participant in the daily rituals of life. I tell my son I love him at least twice a day.

In these ways, I accomplished the one goal I set out to: I am not my father.

But Jacob has seen me being ushered away by policemen. I saw his face pressed to the Svendsons' kitchen window. The Christmas tree lights gave him a halo, or maybe that's simply how I remember it.

We've gone over the misunderstanding on several different occasions. He understands I didn't do anything wrong. He understands Mommy was confused and scared, that the whole thing was a misunderstanding, like how sometimes he runs from his room to watch Saturday morning cartoons when it's only Friday.

But I wonder.

I wonder what role this memory will have throughout his life. I wonder if he'll remember me shaking my head, me spitting, me putting my hands up like I meant no harm and was leaving. I wonder if later in his life, he'll reverse blame, somehow spin the situation into me being in the wrong. If he'll connect the dots between motivations. And maybe he'll make a list of *nevers*—I'll never be arrested in front of my children; I'll never marry; I'll never procreate.

In this way, I am my father, as he was his own. We go through life promising to do better, to *be* better, to love, to provide, to cherish, to exercise gratitude, to guide. But more specifically, we hold on to a set of rules of *nevers*. And if we're lucky, we succeed in not repeating the same sins. My father, unlike his own, never hit my mother or me. I'm sure there were times when that was all he wanted to do. I'm sure he fought against a thousand grainy memories of his father's bony knuckles tattooing his back. I'm sure my father breathed, drank, rubbed the nubs of his missing fingers, and told himself he wasn't that man. But in accomplishing this feat, he unearthed a whole other mess of faults I would internalize as neglect. He isolated himself in alcohol and television. He became a ghost. He became a threat I subconsciously rebelled against in hopes of having his attention turned my way.

And really, had I not fucked everything up so badly with Elliot, I wouldn't have felt the need to make things so right with Jacob. But I did. So showing up in Minnesota, surprising my wife at her thirtieth birthday party, and seeing my son for the first time in close to two months, I wanted to make him happy. Driving back to the Marriott with my son in his seat in the middle back of the rented Taurus, I thought about the hotel pool being rather pathetic. It couldn't have spanned more than fifty feet and the florescent lights made the whole thing feel sterile without actually being clean. I thought about Wisconsin Dells only being a three-hour drive east. Jacob would fall asleep in a matter of minutes. I had a full tank of gas, wouldn't even have to stop. I'd carry my sleeping child into an indoor water resort of a hotel and I'd cover him in blankets and he'd wake up, excited at the thought of the crappy Marriott pool, only to be informed of the sixty-plus slides waiting for us both.

So that's what I did.

I arrived at the Kalahari Water Park Resort close to midnight. I was able to carry Jacob inside without him so much as exercising his startle reflex. I set him down in a queen bed and turned on the TV. I watched a rerun of *Seinfeld*. But really I watched my child. He seemed both bigger and frailer since I'd seen him last. His fists were clenched as he slept. This was new. I wondered if it was a result of anxiety and if it was irreversible damage or if he was simply having a bad dream. I thought about calling Elliot and letting her know there'd been a slight audible, nothing serious, would still have him home by dinner. This didn't need to happen. I thought about Elliot yelling at me over the phone and then Jacob sensing some emotional change in the room and waking, crying, the surprise being ruined. I thought about the boy Elliot was with. If she was fucking him. If he was better. If she realized it was all so cliché, both of us needing to fight against our accumulated years through the flesh of the youth.

I eventually crawled over to Jacob's queen. I held my son. I tried to pry apart his hands, but they weren't budging. I fell asleep with my shoes on.

Everything went as planned—Jacob confused, Jacob ecstatic, continental breakfast with as many doughnuts as we could muster, purchased swimsuits for twice their value at the gift shop, then the indoor water park, screams and shrieks and my son trying to act so brave as he shivered in line three stories above the pool, our backs rubbed raw from the ridges connecting each slide. We ate pizza for lunch in our room, took a short nap, and then hit the park for an afternoon session. And it is here that I struggle not to dip into melodrama, but I must run the risk. We were on the lazy river (admittedly, this one was for me, and Jacob was obediently humoring his old man). We approached a small waterfall to our left. I told Jacob he was going to get wet and he smiled and then we were under the waterfall and he screamed the androgynous scream of adolescence, his eyes wide in shock from the cold, him lunging away from the waterfall and out of his tube to my lap, his arms clasping around my neck, me returning with a bear hug. And then his whole body went limp. My immediate thought was something had broken inside of him, an aneurism or heart attack, because that was how lifeless his body became. But then I realized he was hugging me. His ear pressed against my chest. He lay like that for close to a minute. I'd never experienced a better feeling.

We didn't take off from the Dells until five. I knew I'd be a little late, but I'd call from the road. I realized my phone was dead. I didn't think much about it. No, instead I was lost inside my head with thoughts about making things right. Maybe that would be with Elliot, maybe it wouldn't. But it had to be right for Jacob. Worst-case scenario, I could take a leave of absence from teaching and relocate to Minnesota. I could get away with this for at least a semester. I could watch Jacob during the day when Elliot was at work. Maybe I could take the weekends too. And maybe, just fucking maybe, there'd be a night when I dropped off Jacob, and Elliot's Hitler father was already asleep, when she'd ask if I wanted a cup of coffee. We'd sit around the kitchen table. I'd be holding Jacob, who'd be fast asleep. I'd ask her about work. She'd make her usual witty and self-deprecating comments about being thirty and working at a geriatric clothing store. She'd ask how I liked Minnesota in January with its negative-thirty windchill. I'd tell her it was growing on me. There'd be silence. We'd look at our cups of Folgers. We'd be thinking of things to say. She'd be fighting the thought of things being easier if we were together. She'd be forcing herself to remember the sight of me committing adultery. I'd be trying to come up with a way to bridge the foot gap between our resting hands, for there to be some small intimate contact. Maybe the silence would stretch toward uncomfortable, and it'd be becoming clear that the cup of coffee was a moment of weakness on Elliot's behalf. We'd both sense this. And there'd be no *angle* or *strategy* for me to play to extend the handoff of our child, only honesty, and I'd say it—*Elliot, I just want you to know I am so fucking sorry for everything. I'm sorry I wasn't a better husband when you were dealing with your postpartum depression. I'm sorry I withdrew under the bullshit rationale of being a strong father for Jacob. I'm sorry I didn't make more of an effort to understand your*

pain. I'm sorry I left you alone with him all day. I'm sorry I went on building my life, one where you were a compartmentalized home furnishing. And I'm so fucking sorry for the other stuff. I can't imagine what it was like for you to see that. I can say all the bullshit about it only being once and it not meaning anything, but I know that's unfair, because it did mean something; it meant immense hurt for you and Jacob. And for this, I beg your forgiveness. No, I take that back, you don't owe me that. I just want you to know that although our relationship was far from perfect, you were and are the only woman I've ever loved. There's not a minute that goes by where I don't think about how badly I've fucked up by hurting you.

Here Elliot would be crying. She'd make a motion with her hands that I would mistake as her beckoning me over, but really it'd be for our son. She'd take him in her arms and he'd stir and she'd kiss his hairline. She'd huff in the boy smell of his neck. She'd look at me. She'd say, I'm trying, Devon. I'm really fucking trying.

I'd nod. I'd stand. I'd tell her I knew she was, and I was grateful beyond words. I'd bend over and mimic the action she'd done to Jacob. I'd kiss the crown of her head. I'd know I wasn't deserving of this second chance. I'd tell her to get some sleep.

I pulled into the Svendsons' driveway at nine-eighteen. The front door swung open before I noticed the parked cop car. Elliot was at my back door yanking it open, ripping out a just-woken Jacob. His cries started instantly. Elliot was yelling at me and so was her father and her fucking boyfriend and there was a policeman standing between us and I understood she'd called 911 because she thought I had kidnapped my child and fat Mr. Svendson's fingers were waving in my face and my son was wailing and Elliot kept yelling that I'd never fucking see Jacob again, and it was freezing cold, but all I could think about was the naivety of my stupid fucking fantasy. Elliot believed me capable of abduction. Elliot believed me capable of ruining her life twice.

Something snapped with this realization and Mr. Svendson's meaty fingers making contact with my chest. I swung. It was the first time I'd ever punched another person in the face. It felt like hitting a bowling ball. Then I was being shoved against my rented Taurus and everybody's screams became muted and this was when I looked to the kitchen window and saw Jacob illuminated by the Christmas tree lights and this was when I thought of my father and this was when a *never* became a laughable joke with every fucking mistake I'd ever made being the punch line.

V

I sat in jail for a total of seven hours. It was a communal room capable of housing twenty, but it was just an older guy with a frostbit nose and me. The room wasn't a barred cage like on TV; it was white cinderblock with Plexiglas windows and two tables fastened to the cement floor with a single rack of bunks inexplicably pushed adjacent to the chrome toilet. I tried to sleep but couldn't. I pissed sitting down for some reason. I didn't ask for a phone call or for a lawyer or for a meal or anything else I knew from movies. I sat there at a table trying my best to avoid eye contact with the bum with the black-tipped nose. I rubbed my sore knuckles. I remembered my father doing the same thing to his nubs.

At five the next morning, a policeman said I was free to go. I asked him about bail and court and he rolled his eyes and said, No charges filed. I thanked him. He didn't respond. He walked me to another room where I gathered my wallet and phone and keys and belt and then he told me the car was around the back, to give the attendant this ticket stub (connected to a $250 towing charge), and to be on my way.

I had nowhere to go.

I checked back in at the Marriott and tried to sleep, but couldn't, my mind a reel of *you're never going to see Jacob again* and the crushing hardness of Mr. Svendsons' skull against my fist and my son seeing me shoved against a car as I was cuffed. Every show on TV was a Christmas special. I left and drove to a nearby Buffalo Wild Wings and ate a chicken sandwich while Verizon kiosk salesmen types yelled at the hanging televisions. I got kind of drunk. The waitress reminded me of a girl I slept with my junior year at Northwestern because both of their eyebrows came to a sharp peak three-quarters of the way toward the outsides. I tried to force myself to pay attention to a meaningless bowl game. I ate chips and salsa. I drank more. One of the teams won with a late field goal.

I left BW3. It was dark out, which didn't make sense, but maybe it did, my phone still dead so I hadn't checked the time all afternoon, my head sloshy with shitty beer. I dreaded the thought of going back to the Marriott and trying to convince myself things would work out so I'd be able to sleep. I drove toward the Svendsons' house. I parked two blocks away and turned off the car and the coldness was instant in its permeating of the car's windows and I told myself I liked it. I drank two single-serving bottles of gin I'd taken from the hotel mini refrigerator. I wasn't sure what I was waiting for. To see Jacob? To see Elliot? That prick Mr. Svendson?

But I knew when a Civic pulled up and that cocky kid jumped out and jogged to the door, his hooded down coat pulled around his baseball cap. I imagined him fucking Elliot and then him tucking in my boy. I imagined Elliot talking shit about me, saying it'd been a mistake from the very onset, how she'd been relieved when I'd finally cheated because she had an out. The alcohol helped my righteous indignation. *You'll never see Jacob again.* Some idiot kid eating my wife's pussy. Like I'd done. Maybe she wanted me to walk in, to see him between her legs, to reverse the situation, to feel the crushing weight of infidelity, to know what it was like to know some stranger was more important than your family.

I told myself it wasn't like that.

It was, but it wasn't.

We didn't have sex for twenty months after Jacob was born. I told her she was beautiful and a good mother and everything was okay and I called doctors and tried to remind her to take her combination of benzos and SSRI inhibitors, which she always yelled at me for doing—*fuck you for thinking I'm crazy; you're not crazy, baby, it's completely out of your control, a hormonal imbalance; fuck you*—and then there'd been a night when she told me she wanted to have sex, and we did, the act rehearsed at best, Elliot climbing off of me after I'd finished, her saying, You feel like a man again?

I could deal without sex. The internet was invented for such a purpose. But the emotional coldness was another thing. For two years, her attitude toward me, on a good day, was complete indifference. Most every other day it was a tense civility not even coming close to covering seething resentment. It was as if she blamed me for how she felt. I kept trying to get her back into her graduate program. I even went so far as to have her advisor, a fellow colleague, over for dinner. I thought the evening went well. Our conversation was good, and by dessert, I'd bowed out of the conversation completely, and sat there drinking coffee, watching my wife speak with more animation than I'd seen in close to two years as she talked about long-forgotten plays and their unsaid power in shaping our modern literary canon. But after Dr. Rich left, Elliot looked me in the eye, the joy and color of her checks completely drained. She said, That was the most humiliating experience of my life. Fuck you for trying to play the hero. You're not my goddamn father.

I read *The Postpartum Husband: How to Help Your Suffering Wife*. I complimented her whenever possible. I started all my comments with *I understand how you're feeling*. I bought her things. I woke up twice a night to feed Jacob bottles. I planned vacations that we never took. I tried.

And then I didn't.

At a certain point, it became easier to accept the role of dutiful husband and overtaxed father. I embraced this role. I wouldn't consciously view myself as a martyr, but that was the general mindset. I told myself things would get better, and even if they didn't, there was a certain comfort and self-congratulating that went along with caring for a newborn and then toddler and a suffering wife. Something about it seemed strangely heroic.

In an odd way, over those two years, I carved Elliot out of my life. I'm sure there was a level of emotional self-preservation at play on my part, the hardening against her hormonal, and later, chemical, and even later, emotional resentment toward me. There was also an issue of time: I simply didn't have enough of it—between work and Jacob—to spend it trying to extricate a coherent sentence from Elliot's lips. But if I were to be completely honest, the emotional separation from my wife was simply easier than the alternative. Like any species, I adapted. I found the path of least resistance. I quit trying to make Elliot better. I quit trying to make her laugh. I quit suggesting date nights. I masturbated in my home office and kissed her forehead when she'd let me.

At around the twenty-four-month postpartum mark, Elliot snapped back to herself. The transformation, like the one preceding it, was drastic. One afternoon she was lying in bed, the next she was crashing two of Jacob's trucks together, the both of them laughing uncontrollably on the light blue carpet of his room. Things were better after that. The resentment underneath each held word dissipated. We made love. We kissed with tongue. We talked. We smiled.

Yet there was still something different from how it'd been before the two-year plague of depression. I spent a lot of time trying to figure out exactly what it was. My best hypothesis was a level of trust had been broken; I was constantly waiting for the other shoe to drop, for her to return to the catatonic version of wife and mother, for her hatred toward me to be evident in every silent meal.

But maybe that's bullshit.

I could have simply learned how to live a somewhat productive, albeit unfulfilling, life without her. And if I were completely honest, some part of me liked this life. I liked the freedom of isolation and compartmentalization, of my familiar duties ending at seven-thirty when Jacob went down.

It can't be a coincidence that my one and only affair started at twenty-five months into Jacob's life. Sure, I rationalized it by the memories of Elliot's coldness and neglect, but really, that wasn't it. It was the return to our relationship's near-normalcy, and the nagging feeling that it wasn't enough.

Forty-five minutes later, when the kid jogged out of the Svendsons' house to his shitty car and backed out of the driveway, I started mine. My fingers were completely numb from the cold or maybe the drink. I did my best to stay a few car lengths back. I wasn't sure what I was doing. I wanted to see his house. A dorm room, I'd figured. He probably went to the U and lived with his *boys* and he'd run back and brag about the MILF he was pounding, let his friends smell his fingers. I drove faster. I'd didn't give a fuck if I was right behind him, because who, besides people in movies, really notices if they are being tailed? I thought about Elliot calling the cops and her doing everything in her power to keep me from Jacob—it was here I realized she really would, her brain chemistry faulty, prone to distorted thinking.

The kid drove up a driveway to a house that was Minnesota nice with its fake accents of projected wealth. The kid was out of his car and walking toward the front door by the time I pulled into the driveway. He turned when my lights lit him up. I got out of the car and slipped a little bit because of the ice. He'd opened the red door to his house but stopped as I approached.

The fuck you doing here?

Listen, kid, you can drop the tough guy shit. Not here to fight.

Dude, I don't know what your trip is, but telling you straight up, you need to get the fuck off my property.

Says the guy sleeping with my wife.

Not your wife.

I stuck out my left hand and wiggled my ring finger. I said, Beg to differ.

I could hear a voice calling out from inside the house.

He squared up his body to face me. He stood on two brick steps and looked down at me. He said, Bet you're not trying to go back to jail, so I suggest you get the fuck out of here. As in right fucking now.

She's using you, kid. That's why I'm here. The only fucking reason. Consider this your public service announcement.

Okay. Thanks, buddy.

I smiled. I looked up toward the sky. Jacob had the same stars stuck to the ceiling of his room in Colorado. I said, I fucked a younger girl, so she's fucking a younger boy. That's all you are. You're her little boy revenge fuck. Thought I'd let you know before you got hurt.

Maddie, who is this?

I looked back from the sky and felt dizzy from the sudden movement and the door was open and a stern-looking shade of middle-aged woman stood there with one hand on her hip.

Nobody, just some asshole.

Who the hell are you and what do you want with my son?

I laughed. The loser still lived with his mom. I said, I'm the husband of the wife your son's fucking.

I turned around and walked to my car and his mom was calling out to me and I could hear him protesting and reassuring and lying and I climbed into my car and backed down the slanted driveway and nothing about my life felt better or even that much different.

VI

Jacob sleeps in my bed. He's four, going on both six months and thirty years. He can't sleep alone. I know about sleep training, about independence, about the "strength" and "self-esteem" of a "well-adjusted, self-soothing" child; but I also know that he wakes up screaming the cries of the abandoned, sometimes yelling for his mom, sometimes for me.

Each morning, he wakes me up by rubbing his fingers against my back. More specifically, across the twin patches of hair along my shoulder blades. This is at five-thirty, without fail. I roll over and he tells me I have dragon breath and I tell him it smells like he ate a bag of dog poop. We say this joke every morning. He starts laughing before the short exchange is even half over. He clings to predictability.

I don't believe in God, so our routine of stating the one thing we're grateful for isn't a religious thing, more of a how-not-to-be-a-prick thing. Depending on his mood, Jacob tells me he's grateful either for a specific toy or day of the week or for me. My answer is the same every morning: you, buddy.

We eat organic cereal for breakfast. I let him watch cartoons. I pretend to read the paper, but really end up watching animations kill one another. I make him eat fruit. He hates bananas. He says he doesn't like the strings of "yarn."

He also hates showering, but I make him every morning. I'm not trying to have him be the smelly kid at preschool, which is where he goes for six hours three days a week. I drop him off and most of the time he doesn't even turn around and wave, just walks with his short little steps, his head slightly lowered, his shoulders slouched. I'm always struck with the comical notion of him headed to the salt mines. This notion turns from humorous to oddly tragic in the span of a second.

I work thirty hours a week. I don't really need the money (I'm not rich by any stretch of the imagination, but I rent a two-bedroom apartment in Roseville, Minnesota, pretty much the affordable cost-of-living capital of the country), but I need adult conversation. I need to be around people who wait until they're in the privacy of locked rooms to put their hands down their pants. I need companionship. So I work at The Hungry Mind, a bookstore in St. Paul near Macalester College. It's an eccentric shop with two cats and pun-laden mugs and booksellers who are either college kids or retired teachers with a few workers stuck somewhere in the middle. My favorite coworker is Cheryl because she's still all Gen-X, even though it's at least twenty years past the point of working. She's crude in a way that's endearing rather than projected. I appreciate the way her skin has started to sag around her eyes and ears. It makes me feel good about myself. Sometimes I imagine sleeping with her, if it would be fun, fulfilling, if it would change anything.

After work, I drive back to Roseville. I listen to NPR and sometimes the classic rock station. It's the middle of winter and freezing and everything is gray, which is more tiring than depressing. I drive to my wife's parents' house. It's exactly what you would picture a house of a plumber in a suburb of St. Paul, Minnesota, would look like. Her parents don't like me. I can't blame them. Good old Edwin and Terry. Jacob's always sitting on the couch with Ed watching inappropriate stand-up comedians. He always says, Hey, Dad, in a voice too flat to make a father feel good about anything. I normally stand there in the doorway. Ed never takes his eyes off the TV. They never offer me something to drink. They never ask how things are going.

I try to cook dinner at least four nights a week. My repertoire is pathetic: Anne's Organic seashell pasta; salmon with wild rice; broiled chicken with green beans; fajitas. The other nights we go out to eat at the fine establishments surrounding our apartment complex. We prefer TGIFs. I always get the Asian chicken salad. Jacob always gets a children's sized malt and a bowl of New England clam chowder. Sometimes he tells me about his day. Sometimes he colors. Sometimes he looks at me with his head tilted and I know he's trying to figure out a way to make me smile or maybe he's simply wondering what the hell is going on.

At night, we climb into my bed. I read him stories about trains that need to get home, and then I read him some of whatever novel I'm reading. He falls asleep. Sometimes I continue reading; sometimes I put on the TV. I try my hardest not to watch my son sleep; it's such a violent process, I can't help but feel guilty about whatever horrible visions are terrorizing his REM.

This is my life.

I suppose this is trudging.

It's not bad and it's what's necessary and it's okay because I spend it with my son. But I'm forty-one years old. I haven't touched a woman in close to three months. I make $7.45 an hour. I've destroyed my marriage. I can't stop thinking about my deceased father. My son lives in constant fear of being left alone. Nancy Grace spent a full week blasting my wife on national television. Sometimes I want to leave work and drive south instead of north—fuck Roseville, fuck Minnesota—and I'd keep driving, not caring, Jacob better off with his grandparents anyway. My favorite part of the day is when I catch my son looking at me with a smile rather than his constant furrowed expression of anxiety. The only people I really know in this state are my in-laws, who won't exchange words with me that aren't about the logistics of childcare. The excuse of *Mommy's gone getting help* was good enough until the other day when Jacob lay silent on my bed. He said, Why is Mom in jail? Sometimes I cry in the shower. Sometimes Jacob cries in the shower. I'm four years away from how old my father was when he died, and this realization steals hours of sleep a night. There are no books about how to explain to your child that Mommy is in jail for statutory rape. I obsess over single choices I've made that set everything in motion. These obsessions are so far past the point of regrets. I pray there's a way Jacob transforms into a loving, well-adjusted human being. I want him to know he's the most important thing in my life. That the love I feel for him is greater than anything he will ever know until he has a son of his own. I leaned over the other night, staring down at Jacob. He wouldn't look at me. I asked him where he'd heard that. He didn't say anything, but he blinked twice, very forcibly, a new habit I'm worried is a distressed tic. I told him I loved him. That his mom loved him. That we'd each made mistakes, and sometimes, like when he gets a timeout, we had to experience consequences for our mistakes. I find myself thinking about Cheryl from work, wondering if it'd be different, exciting, better. My wife cries when I visit her on Sundays. She just fucking cries and the guards won't let me hug her, not even touch her hand. Jacob finally said, Is Mom bad? I wanted to tell him that given enough time on this earth, we all expose ourselves to be bad. I must've taken too long to respond, because Jacob turned over onto his side, his back facing me. I lay there trying to think of something to say, anything. Then Jacob's little legs started to shake. His fists were balled up. Sleep had come, and with it the violence of trying to make sense of his parents' fuck ups.

VII

Nobody would've given a shit about a boy six months away from being old enough to die for his country and a woman in her first week of her thirties sleeping with one another if it wasn't for Talbots. People would've maybe seen a two-sentence blurb in the back of the local paper—nothing about statutory rape because it would've been pleaded down to reckless endangerment, not to mention Mrs. Johnson wouldn't have pressed charges without the public outcry—and that'd be it, game over, let's move on.

But some petty, anonymous Talbots solider (later revealed to be Carolyn Sheppard, a bowling-ball faced woman who embraced the adjective *frigid*) leaked the store security footage to Channel 9, accompanied with an explanation of why two ladies were fighting in a mall on December 23rd, and Channel 9, being somewhat professional, contacted the attacker, Mrs. Patricia Johnson, and she confirmed the story, telling them yes, the woman she had confronted had raped her son.

At six o'clock the following night, and again at ten, Minnesotans sat on their couches wrapping last-minute Christmas presents. They watched the news. They watched a black-and-white security feed of an attractive woman with man-length strides storm into Talbots. There was no sound, but they could tell the tall woman was yelling, looking frantically around the store. The astute observer could tell the ladies in Talbots turned toward the far right of the screen, directly toward a blond woman who looked a little too young to be in the store in the first place. This woman had her hands raised in a *calm-down* manner. The taller woman did not calm down. No, instead she strode across the screen, her finger an accusatory exclamation point. The first woman was obviously yelling. The second woman was obviously trying to usher the woman outside of the store. The woman being accosted placed her hand on the first lady's arm in a nonthreatening way, to which she reacted wildly, flailing her arm, then rearing back and swinging with an open fist. The second lady staggered backward. She held her cheek. The first woman came toward her, and swung once more, the blond lady raising her left arm as protection. She then simultaneously moved to her right while deflecting the second swing, while also kind of pulling on the attacking woman's coat. The first woman lost her balance, and tumbled forward, lunging headfirst into the metal corner of an outward facing four-way rack of slacks. She crumpled to the floor. That same astute Minnesotan sitting on his couch could see a puddle of dark growing along the floor before the camera feed switched to a female anchor shaking her head.

Forty-seven stitches and a concussion later, Mrs. Johnson spoke from her hospital room about statutory rape.

By the 26th, her verbiage had changed. Americans watched Nancy Grace conduct a video interview. She used words phrases like *child molestation* and *adult predators*. She dropped *statutory* from her vocabulary. Between Mrs. Johnson and Nancy Grace, they used the word *rape* eleven times in a three-minute interview.

On the 27th, my wife was arrested on charges of criminal sexual conduct and assault. I drained our bank account and paid the fifty-thousand-dollar bail. I picked her up and there were news crews everywhere and she draped a coat over her head and I felt like security detail hopelessly shielding a doomed president. We drove away. Elliot couldn't speak, or wouldn't speak, or maybe there was nothing to say. The sun was out even though it was only eleven degrees. Everything felt broken. I wanted to ask what her what the fuck she'd been thinking, first about the kid, then about shoving the mom into the metal rack, then about needing revenge against me so badly she ruined her whole life, but I drove. I used my blinkers. Elliot smelled a bit like laundry that had been left for too long in the washing machine. I started toward her parents' house, but she told me no, she couldn't.

Then where?

Your hotel. I need to sleep.

I turned around and headed toward the Marriott. I needed her to think about lawyers. I needed her to think about the boy falsifying his age, first to her, then to her parents, and how the fuck could she have known? It wouldn't even be a case. It'd be over with. Her little romp with youth would be a blip on the national news, then recede into oblivion, child molesters with basements full of Amber alert little boys once again taking the nation's morbid hatred.

But I didn't say these things.

I parked near the side entrance. I led Elliot to my room. She crumpled on the bed. I took off her shoes and pulled the scratchy comforter around her and she was crying and I told her it was okay and she told me she needed noise so I turned on the TV. She cried harder. Then she was sobbing. I sat on the bed and rubbed her shoulder and I wanted to yell, to tell her she'd fucked everything up—*what the hell is Jacob going to say when he's old enough to understand?*—and I wanted to complain about our savings being wiped out and about the public disgrace of having a rapist as a wife, but she beat me to the punch: I fucked up. I fucked up. I fucked up.

Then I was hugging her, holding her, petting her greasy hair.

I fucked up.

Shh.

I fucked up.

It'll be fine.

I fucked up.

Everything's okay.

Fuck me.

Her kiss was wet with the extra saliva from the crying.

Her hands were frantic tools of erasure.

And as she pinned me down, tearing my T-shirt over my head, thrusting me into her dry vagina, I couldn't help but feel like a scene from a B movie meant to illustrate *rock bottom*. The red hotel comforter. The watercolor painting of loons bobbing on a lake. The bailed wife fucking her frustration and fear out on the cheating husband. I kept telling myself to stop. I was the rational adult in the situation. I was the one who should be strong and levelheaded and I was the one who needed her to lawyer up and put this whole thing behind us. She wouldn't meet my eyes. I wasn't sure if she was panting or crying. Maybe *rock bottom* was a good thing? Maybe it was a chiming elevator door, us finally deciding to quit going down and step off the elevator, and yeah, we were basement low, hurt and with legal troubles, and God only knew what damage we'd done to Jacob, but we were together. I grabbed her head, trying to steady her gaze on mine. She bucked. I felt like the worst kind of person. *Harder.* I was close, and so was she, her tell the biting of her tongue on the left side of her teeth, and I pulled her hair, pulled it tight so she was forced to look at me. Her eyes were oil spills. I told her I loved her. She closed her eyes and I pulled her hair tighter and then she opened up and it was the stare of a girl in my class who didn't know enough to turn away and it was the look of a girl so swallowed by postpartum that she didn't see the point in caring for her son's screams, and then it was a different look, this one animalistic, cornered, this one willing to do whatever was necessary in order to stay alive.

She brought her mouth to mine and I breathed in her words: I can't do this.

꙳

There was no trial.

Unknown to me, on the first of the year, Elliot drove herself to the Dakota County Police Department. She confessed to sleeping with a minor. She told them she knew he was under eighteen. She said she supplied him alcohol and marijuana in order for him to consent. These were lies. Lies I was absolutely furious about when I read them in the police report, lies I stayed up countless hours trying to understand. But maybe that's a lie in and of itself, because part of me got it, both then and now, the perverse need for blame and guilt, the public flogging for internal turmoil. And even that's not it. No, it's probably closer to what she told me in the hotel room—*I can't do this*—and the "this" being the life we'd created, the one that felt more confining than a jail cell.

She was convicted of fifth-degree criminal sexual conduct and third-degree assault. She was sentenced to seven months in a minimum-security jail in Shakopee, Minnesota. She didn't say goodbye to me. She didn't say goodbye to her parents. She'd told Jacob that she was going to work, that she couldn't wait to see him that night, maybe they'd stay up late watching *Toy Story 3*.

VIII

I write letters to my wife. I try to write at least three a week. She usually writes one or two. Sometimes my letters are long. Sometimes they're short. Sometimes they are lists of things I did with Jacob and funny stories about him being too smart for his own good. Sometimes I talk about movies we watched. Sometimes I tell her plans I have for our future—we leave Minnesota, forget Colorado, let's go to Washington, to some tiny town on the Olympic Peninsula, and it won't matter what we do for work, just so long as we have enough money for food and shelter, and it will be perfect, the three of us in a small bungalow, evergreens like relics from the Jurassic period, Jacob between us, holding our hands, all of us splashing puddles and laughing. Sometimes I tell her what I bought at the grocery store. Sometimes I tell her about work, how it's all kinds of tedious to spend half my day searching for misplaced books. And sometimes the letters are a bit deeper. Sometimes they are about mistakes and regrets. Sometimes they are apologies. Sometimes they're overly intellectualized lamentations on the nature of self-sabotage. Sometimes they are simple pleas that she allow me to make it up to her.

Her letters span a similar gamut. There's a lot of her daily life. There's talk about boredom. About the Black girls monopolizing the TV, *Family Feud* the program of choice. About the food. About the fungus she's grown on her feet. About prayer groups she's constantly being shamed into attending. She talks about regret too. She tells me she regrets what happened to us. She says she knows it couldn't have been easy for me during the first two years of Jacob's life. She says it was still completely wrong of me to cheat, but she understands and is working toward forgiveness. She talks about our futures. She never comes up with ideas of her own, but instead will comment on suggestions I've put forth in previous letters. She uses exclamation points. And when her letters turn deeper, she talks about love. She says she loves me. She says she wants to do better. She questions what the fuck happened. She tells me we can fix our relationship. She's started telling me that things happen for a reason. She says she's sorry. She signs her letters with *love*.

She never asks about Jacob.

I guess this makes sense: some things are just too hard to bring up.

That was until the beginning of March. She wrote a letter about a leak in her cell from the thawing snow. She said there was a puddle next to her cot. She said she couldn't imagine the mold growing in the walls being good for my daughter. *Oh yeah*, she wrote, *Jacob's going to have a baby sister. Congrats, Papa!*

Love,

Elle

IX

I baby-proofed a home with no baby. I nested with no pregnant woman barking out instructions. I purchased a tasteful crib at Babies-R-Us, solid oak painted white. I picked out brown sheets with pink and green and light blue polka dots, and although the combination sounds hideous, it worked and was cute, everything coming together with the white bumper with a thin band of pink. I fastened a white mobile with soft felt birds to the crib. I bought one of those cube shelves at IKEA, also white. I put green and pink baskets in the bottom row. I stacked blocks and books and arranged miniature Toms and Mary Janes in the other cubbies. Cheryl, from work, didn't have children, but had a changing table/dresser, and let me borrow that. I purchased frames from a store by work, and then cut out the covers of children's books—*Madeline, Amelia Bedelia, Babar*—and did my best to hang them evenly spaced and level.

But something was still missing. The obvious answer was a baby, or at least a pregnant partner, but that wasn't it. I brought Jacob in there. We lay on the floor. He suggested the glow-in-the-dark stars he'd had in Colorado. I didn't think this was the right touch, so I asked him if he really wanted to share this motif with his sister. He shook his head. I asked what else. He told me the carpet was scratchy and we should get a rug. So the next day we bought a white shag rug at Pottery Barn.

It still wasn't good enough.

I spent every night cruising through Etsy. I looked at handmade decorations and contraptions designed to make your baby a genius. Posters and prints and handcrafted outlet protectors. Hours of this. Days of this. I realized it was bordering on obsession, but I couldn't stop: I needed her room to be perfect. I needed Elliot to get out and come to this apartment and not see it as a shitty shade of mediocrity. I needed it to feel inviting. To have a certain amount of charm. To feel, if only temporarily, like home, or at least *a* home. We were stuck in Minnesota for the foreseeable future (she'd have at least two years of probation, the first of which couldn't be transferred to another state). I'd contacted

University of Denver, told them I needed a sabbatical, to which they reminded me I wasn't due until year ten, but I pleaded, begged, and it was agreed upon to have a year off, a leave of absence, no pay, but keeping of position and our benefits. So, Minnesota would be our home for at least a year. And this apartment didn't need any sense of permanence, but it needed to be good enough to make my wife smile and nestle into the nook of my arm, her bringing my hand to her stomach, our baby weeks away from being born kicking and kicking.

I purchased a thousand-dollar glider from an upscale baby boutique in the suburb of Edina. It was somehow both sleek and modern and incredibly comfortable. It was white, which seemed like a horrible idea with a projecting baby, but it was beautiful. I put the whole thing on credit. Then I purchased a small nightstand and a two-hundred-dollar lamp at Pottery Barn Kids. And the room was ready, sans any sign of a baby.

Each Sunday, I saw the progress of my child in my wife's belly.

She started to fill out her orange jumpsuit. Her upper neck started to swell. She wasn't glowing, per se, but she looked healthy, content. She promised me they were taking care of her and she saw a doctor once a week and they gave her extra portions plus prenatal vitamins. She told me our daughter was beautiful, she could tell from the ultrasound pictures, had my nose but her head shape. The guards became more lenient on me touching Elliot's hands as she grew. Same with our good-bye hugs. Toward May, the one skinny Black guard even averted his eyes when Elliot pulled her orange jumpsuit down from her shoulders. I bent over and kissed her bellybutton, which she'd said had recently popped. I thought I felt a kick, but I wasn't sure.

And things went on.

I read books to Jacob about what it meant to be a good big brother. We talked about sharing. About being gentle. About being helpful. When I asked if he was nervous about meeting his sister, he said he was more nervous about seeing his mom.

৵

They threw me a baby shower at work. This was in early June, a month before Elliot got out. Stan and Judy organized the whole thing. They were old hippies, retired teachers (Stan high school English, Judy a community college civics professor). They understood my situation was anything but normal, therefore the shower should be anything but typical.

They held the gathering at The Nook, a tiny bar/restaurant sandwiched between a 1920s bowling alley and a dry cleaners. Everyone from work came. We were given a back room, which really wasn't a separate room, just the far end of the narrow bar next to three electronic dartboards. We got drunk on cheap draft beer. Stan shook his head when I was getting ready to order food. He told me my selection had been called in ahead of time. My food eventually came out. I had a plate of six sliders. I started to protest that I couldn't possibly eat that much, but Stan was laughing, shaking his head, and I asked him what was so funny.

You can't look, he said, but you have to guess the special sauce on each burger.

The first bite tasted like some sort of earthy shit. I spit it out. Everybody laughed. Judy yelled for me to guess the baby food.

Cat vomit?

Laughter.

Yams?

Nope.

Beets?

Bingo, Stan yelled, giving me a high five.

I guessed four out of six. The worst was mango and acacia berry. I dry heaved three times into a paper-thin napkin.

They gave me gifts. Most of the presents were my coworker's favorite novels with a gift card to Target or Babies-R-Us as a bookmark. I got a little drunker than I'd expected, but Jacob was having a sleepover at his grandparents, so it wasn't the end of the world. Everything felt okay that night. We laughed. We debated the merits or lack thereof of confessional memoirs. We talked shit about publishing mergers. They always deferred to me because I'd written books for the Big Six. We compared horror stories of early parenthood. We complained about homeless customers who bombed out our bathrooms. We slapped one another on the backs. We didn't care that our clothes and pores smelled like burgers.

Sometime around eleven, people started to leave. I felt like I should be a good sport and stick it out until the end. Or maybe I was drunk and didn't give it two thoughts. Or maybe I wanted to be left alone with Cheryl, which it turned out I was, just the two of us sitting across from one another in a huge booth. I was slouched toward one side. I rolled the base of my glass in a circle.

Cheryl said, You realize you can't drive home, don't you?

Am an excellent drunk driver, have you know.

Just what Jacob needs, Cheryl said.

Two parents in jail?

Bingo.

Lucky I like you, I said.

Or else what? You'd take offense?

Bingo.

You're lucky I like you, she said.

Or else?

I'd tell you what I really thought.

I laughed. Cheryl poured the last of the pitcher into her cup. The way she was sitting made her black cami pull downward. I stared at three quarters of her C cup. The late spring sun had caused an eruption of freckles on her cleavage.

What's going on there?

I looked up from her breasts. I said, Huh?

Lose something down there?

I laughed. Sorry.

Free country. May be a feminist, but know damn well what I'm doing rocking this top.

Which is?

Letting these things breathe.

We laughed and drank and looked around the bar before returning to one another. I asked what she was talking about.

My tits? You try carrying two—

No, about what you really thought.

Fuck it. I'm drunk.

No, I want to hear.

Cheryl leaned back against the maroon booth cushion. She pulled the front of her cami up a bit. She said, What's changed?

With what?

You? Her?

Everything.

Like?

The old adage *don't know what you have until it's gone*.

Ah, right, Cheryl said. Predicating a future relationship based on the fear of being alone.

Fuck you.

See, you didn't really want me to be honest.

I shook my head. I was smiling the drunk smile of the insulted. I told her it wasn't like that.

Then what's it like?

It's like that moment when all you want in the world is to be able to take back your actions. Like that's it. Not a million dollars or eternal life or the happiness of your loved ones; just to take back what you've done.

A second chance.

A second chance, I said.

You realize that's a fallacy, right? There are no second chances. In anything. Doesn't exist.

Bullshit.

Take, I don't know, a video game or something. You play a level of Super Mario Brothers and you get real far and then get hit and shrink and then you die.

And then you get a second chance, I said.

Okay, yes, a *second* chance, yes, but not a redo of your first.

I used my best Gatsby voice: What do you mean you can't repeat the past? Of course you can.

Accent is fucking horrible, Cheryl said. We smiled and then we didn't. She said, It's not the same thing, and you know it.

You start again and beat the level. Case in point, I said.

Cheryl shook her head. She brushed her flat red bangs off her greasy forehead. She said, You get that second life knowing what lies ahead. You know about the attacking birds. You know what pipes to go down. You're not the same player you were the first time.

Which is exactly my point, I said. It's a *second chance* with the memory of the first to improve upon.

Cheryl said, You're fundamentally changed by your first time. That's the only pure one you get. Everything else is clouded.

So you're saying there's never room for making mistakes, and learning from those mistakes?

I'm saying it's not the same. You're a different person the second time.

Me or Mario?

I'm fucking serious, Cheryl said. You think Elliot won't think about you fucking other students? You think she'll handle postpartum any differently?

That's not fair—

And more to my point, you think you won't tiptoe around those same pitfalls with the knowledge of their impending doom, which only serves to strengthen their presence in your lives? I'm saying there are no *redoes*. Only a simulacrum of your first attempt.

Yeah, I read Baudrillard in undergrad too.

Should have kept my mouth shut, Cheryl said.

It's fine. I just think you're wrong.

Okay.

In your worldview, there is only failure, with no possibility of redemption, I said.

More or less.

Kind of depressing.

Look around you, Cheryl said. These dudes here, think they're getting lots of *redemption*? Think they haven't been coming in here for the past fifteen years, trying to recreate the first Thanksgiving back from college with all their friends, which, when you think about it, was initially an attempt to recreate their high school experience in the first place. Think that *second chance* is working well for them? Think there's a lot of happiness and redemption going on?

People can change, I said.

People can't change. They think they can.

I have.

Maybe matured, but *changed*?

Yeah.

If I offered to suck your dick right here and now, what would you say?

I laughed.

Serious. I'll suck your dick. You don't even have to move. Just sit there drinking your beer and I'll crawl under the table and do my thing.

Sounds great, but no.

Really?

Really.

Cheryl raised her eyebrows as an exaggerated challenge. She shrugged. She said, We'll see. She ducked under the table. I felt her knee knock against my knee and then heard her laughing and her hands were on my thighs and then my dick and I ducked under the table and asked her if she had any idea how much bacteria she was rooting around in down there. I helped her up on my side of the booth. There was a smashed french fry stuck to her knee. She flicked it back underneath the table.

I said, Did I dispel your theory?

The night's young.

Cheryl looked for her beer, and saw that mine was closer and finished the two inches in a single gulp. There was a spec of something on her lips, probably some crumb from the floor. Something about it seemed pretty.

She asked what I was staring at.

You.

This girl's a straight-up barstool philosopher.

Bar *floor* philosopher.

We laughed. I thought about running my hand up her legs and feeling the warmth of a day's work and a night's drink between her thighs and I imagined the musty taste on my tongue and I thought about her being right—not completely, but I understood what she was getting at about trying to recreate naivety—and how stupid all of us were trying to find redemption between the legs of others.

Cheryl rested her left elbow on the table, cradling her head in her hand. This angle, like the one across the table, made everything but her nipple visible. She said, So, if you're so much of a *changed* man, why are you thinking about fucking me right now?

I coughed and tried to make it into a laugh. I motioned to her chest and said, What guy wouldn't be thinking the same thing with your full frontal?

Matured, Cheryl said. That's what you've done. A matured man has mastered the art of projected self-control. But really, with all that shit, he's gained an hour or two of self-restraint.

I quit staring at her tits. I leaned back in my booth and rested my head on the cushion. I said, Did you ever question if this little theory of yours is a form of protection?

Oh, do tell me, Dr. Freud.

If a person is unable to change, and there are no second chances, then what the fuck is the point to doing anything? You are doomed to failure. There's no responsibility to your actions. There's no regret.

You say that like it's a bad thing, Cheryl said.

You put yourself in a god-like role. If you hurt someone, fuck it, can't do anything about it. Not your problem, because even if you wanted to make amends, you couldn't. One chance only. Game over.

Cheryl opened her mouth to counter but stopped. She started laughing. She said, Guess that about sums up my life. Would explain why every guy I've ever dated fucking hates me.

❧

We eventually made our way out of the bar. I searched for a cab. Cheryl told me not to be stupid; it would be fifty dollars at least to my shitty suburb; I could crash on her couch; she promised not to give me head. I laughed and hugged her. It was strange pressing my body against another woman. She was shorter than Elliot. Her shoulder blades were the prominent feature I felt with my hands. It could be as easy as not saying anything. Elliot would never know. But it was never that easy; they always knew.

Cheryl spoke into my sweatshirt: You're one of the good ones, Devon Hester.

Do what I can.

It may have been right the first time, but it's not the second time.

Okay.

Is the baby even yours?

Goodnight.

Sorry.

You don't get to do that, I said.

Devon, I'm sorry.

It's fine, I said. I let my hand slip from hers as I walked toward the corner to catch a cab. I turned. I said, See that? That's redemption. You apologized and I forgave you. Easy as that.

Cheryl flicked me off and I smiled and walked away thinking about Elliot growing the raped boy's baby in her stomach and about Cheryl being a bitch for reinforcing this fear and about Cheryl spreadeagled with her trembling hamstrings between my grasp and about Monica States doing the same thing on my desk and about my future—at its very fucking best—being a shitty simulacrum of our life in Colorado, this time in a tiny apartment I'd overspent to decorate.

X

There was only one photographer at the south entrance of Shakopee County Jail. He snapped stills of a pregnant Elliot, who pretended he wasn't there, waddling toward me in her best attempt to appear carefree, her arms outstretched, her bloated face caught somewhere between a smile and a grimace. I guessed the rest of the country had lost its appetite for justice once Elliot had turned herself in. I walked on the right side of my wife, attempting to block the photographer's view.

During the drive, I had to remind myself to take it slow. Even though she'd only been in there for eight months, it was still eight months. If she didn't want to talk, so be it. The sun was out and it was ten in the morning and we passed cows and youthful sprouts of corn and the road was mostly flat and deserted. After nearly twenty minutes of silence, Elliot reached over and took my right hand. She brought it to her side of the car and placed it on her stomach. My hand wasn't directly on her skin, but I could still feel the sporadic movement of the confined. I told myself it was my daughter underneath there, end of fucking story. I was more than man enough to squash out the kernel of doubt for the betterment of my family.

We returned to an empty apartment. Jacob was at her parents' house, where we'd head later that afternoon. I kept telling her our place was temporary, just something for the time being until our house in Colorado sold, until we knew for sure what we wanted to do. I wanted her to be holding my hand, but she wasn't. I saw the apartment through her eyes—walls a horrible shade of white, a couch with too much wear, the TV the obvious focal point of the main room, a kitchen too small to both prep and cook in, a bedroom that did everything in its power to cover up the fact it'd been home for two boys for almost a year—and then I led her to the nursery. I watched Elliot's hand go to her mouth. She looked at the crib and the glider and the hanging books and the shelves. Her left hand rubbed her belly. She wasn't crying with gratitude, but her lips were shaking ever so slightly, and something about this felt like a victory. I put my arm around her. She rested her head on my shoulder. We both stared at an empty crib with the perfect matching bumper.

Elliot said, What are we doing?

I said, The best we can.

I love you.

Love you too.

❦

I have only one conscious memory of my mother and father expressing their love verbally to one another. I'm sure there were other times, me too young or self-absorbed to notice, or maybe they held these affirmative endearments for behind closed doors. Regardless of the reality of the situation, I have one memory of such a moment, and like all children, my perception of this has solidified into fact—my parents only said they loved one another once—and this moment has become a touchstone to my life.

My father had won a contest at work, something about selling the most ice chest-style freezers for the month of July. I was probably ten. I remember that month, how my father was more animated around the house, actually speaking to us about work, about sales that he made, how he convinced a woman that a combined refrigerator-freezer was a poor choice compared to two separate appliances, the ice chest in the garage stock-full of ready-to-heat soups and hot dishes. I'm not sure if I thought this at the time, but I realize now this was one of the rare moments when my father was proud. I think about his life being different if he'd experienced this emotion more often, and in turn, my own.

The prize for the contest was a weekend stay at a cabin two hours north on Lake Michigan. We loaded the station wagon with enough stuff for a month—coolers, the miniature Weber, baseball gloves (we'd never once played catch), inflatable rafts my mother purchased from work. My father made a big deal about getting Coke in individual bottles instead of cans, and gave me one in the car, which felt antiquated and queer, but also like I was being let in on some part of him as a boy, the mystery he never spoke of.

The cabin was rather dilapidated. The screens were all broken and the buzzing of mosquitos was incessant. The yellow paint was more chipped than not. The toilet ran constantly. There was a foldout couch where I slept, my parents in the tiny closet of a bedroom. I convinced myself the nightlong scratching of wood wasn't mice sharpening their nails.

There wasn't much to do, either. The water was freezing, too deep to actually warm. We had no boat and no fish were biting from the shore. I felt bored, anxious at the thought of having to spend so much time alone with my parents. Or maybe I felt anxiousness at the thought of my parents having to spend so much time together, no TV or going out with coworkers as alternatives.

But it was nice.

Better than nice.

They applied sunscreen to each other's backs. They read magazines and the paper, their feet submerged in the dark water. We cooked burgers and roasted marshmallows. They drank together, neither of them to excess. And suddenly I wasn't anxious, wasn't worried about having to kill another two days in this prison.

On the last night, we sat on the shore of the lake. We had a small fire going. My father had given me a single beer, what he thought was my first. I wasn't drunk, but rather warm, content. My father was trying to paint my mother's toenails, getting polish everywhere, my mother shrieking with laughter, my father blaming the sloppy job on her constant movement and his missing fingers. And it was here when he stopped, holding the feet of my mother by the fire, and looked her in the eye. He said, I love you, you know that?

My mother stared back, caught in the act of ashing her cigarette, which just dangled there like a firefly. Her smile faded into a look I'll forever equate with seeing the goodness in people. She said, I love you too.

I didn't love Elliot the first time we slept together. I didn't love her the second or third or tenth. But contrary to what she's always believed, I loved her before she became pregnant with Jacob. I realized it with all the clichéd clarity of a romantic comedy one evening in early December. We'd been together, more or less, for two months. I'd gotten free hockey tickets, and although I'm not one for sport, we figured it'd be fun. While we walked downtown, a man stood on a portable wooden box with a megaphone. He yelled about God and about the Devil and about eternal salvation. The light was taking forever to change, and when the man started in about the sanctimony of marriage, about man and woman, about the *gay agenda*, Elliot looked up at him. As soon as she made eye contact, he stopped talking. Elliot said, Jesus would be so fucking proud of you. The man smiled, and then realized she wasn't giving him a compliment. His speechlessness only lasted a moment, but in that moment, I knew he felt the weight of her words, her presence, her ability to cut through whatever firewall he'd created around himself and his viewpoints, and he saw himself through her eyes as a man standing on a corner preaching hate under the guise of religion.

It's a stupid example, one that doesn't have much to do with anything, but when the light turned green and Elliot took my arm, I distinctly remember thinking *I love this girl.* I love this girl because she's real and because she's different and because she has a power that is completely unexplainable, completely unknowable, but real, some penetrating magnetism that makes you feel vulnerable. I thought about our relationship being more than a crush with sex. I felt proud to be with her. I felt like a better version of myself. I felt in love.

And thinking about it now, I wonder what the look on my face was as we crossed Speer Avenue toward the arena. I wonder if it was the same contemplative softness of my mother's as she stared at her husband by the fire. I wonder if it was the same look as Elliot, who, turning around in my arms in our unborn daughter's nursery, stared up at me with a sincerity that bordered on sublime. I wonder if we all three thought the same things—*I love this person more than anybody else in my life*—and if this thought is the same as seeing their inherent goodness.

XI

Things took some getting used to. For starters, Jacob seemed terrified of his mother. The first time he hugged her, he looked over her shoulder at me. I nodded and smiled. I could see that his hands were limp around Elliot's neck. I felt him watching me throughout that first week as if for guidance about how to behave around his mother. I tried to smile and to plan fun activities and to be the cheering mascot for our displaced family. Jacob still slept in our bed. When he'd finally fall asleep, Elliot would get her fill of mother-son physical contact that was being withheld from her during Jacob's waking hours. She'd rub the hair from his eyes. She'd trace the bridge of his nose. She'd circle his lips with the tip of her finger. She'd nestle into the nook of his neck.

It was weird with us too.

We were too polite. We were too courteous. We had trouble making decisions, even the simple ones about TGIFs or Chili's. We'd hold our bowel movements until it was time for our showers. We'd promptly place our dirty clothes in a new wicker hamper I'd purchased at Target. We'd pick television shows we knew the other liked. We'd thank one another for the smallest acts of thoughtfulness.

The whole thing felt sophomoric, as if we'd transported twenty years to our past and we were pimply teenage versions of ourselves, nervous with insecurities about smells and penis size, yet somehow forced to cohabitate, to act as adults, to raise children.

The first time we had sex, we were timid. I worried about killing my daughter and Elliot worried about being too loud on the carpeted floor as Jacob slept in our bed. We kissed mostly without tongue. I sucked her breasts until I tasted the sweet-sour of her colostrum. I kept wondering if she was thinking about the teenager. I kept wondering if it was his baby.

❧

We lost our ability for awkwardness on October 3rd.

Violent contractions in the middle of the night and Jacob crying and me getting our hospital bag ready and calling the Svendsons, telling them they needed to come over this instant to watch Jacob. We made it to the hospital with the contractions still seven minutes apart, but by the time Elliot was admitted, it was too late for an epidural, the contractions a constant flexed excruciation, a cervix dilated to ten.

The doctor didn't ask me to play music this time.

He told me to hold a leg. He told me to count out loud for my wife. And I did.

It was the first time since Elliot had been released that we actually made sustained eye contact. It had the feeling of being back when we first met. When she was a graduate student taking a creative writing elective. When she didn't seem to give a fuck about anything. When she knew what she wanted—or rather, she *didn't* know what she wanted, and was desperate in her need to ingest as many experiences as she could in attempts to figure out exactly what was missing. I stared at my wife without blinking. I counted to ten. She'd stopped screaming, and now just stared at me, spittle thick on the right side of her mouth. We stared at one another for fifteen minutes. I imagined she was telling me everything was going to be okay and she was sorry and she forgave me and we'd both fucked up so badly, but it didn't matter because we had one another, our children there to keep us honest. I don't believe in souls, but maybe I do, because that's what I was seeing: a terrified girl who just wanted to be okay and have people love her enough so she loved herself. I imagined she was seeing the exact same thing through my eyes.

They placed my daughter on Elliot's chest.

She didn't cry like Jacob had. She just stared up at me. She had my exact eyes, the hooded brow, the gravity-pulling weights on each outside making it seem like she was lost inside of a depressingly morbid day-dream. She was mine, no doubt.

I know they say children can't fix relationships, but maybe they're wrong, because from the moment we brought Netta-Mae home, things were better. The stilted tiptoeing vanished. The practiced civility too. We fell into routine. Elliot nursed and I changed diapers and Jacob seemed like Jesus with his gentle whispers to his baby sister. We slept in two-hour shifts. We burped and washed miniature outfits with Downy. We read stories. We snapped at one another when sleep deprivation made itself known. We supported limp necks. We took pictures with our phones. Jacob continued going to preschool. I worked two shifts a week. We made bastardized versions of recipes from the *Joy of Cooking*. We applied diaper rash cream to red genitals. We watched the Travel Channel and imagined living in Vietnam. We had family meals with her parents, the tension still there between myself and them, but bearable with Netta-Mae as a buffer, a hatred that was close to morphing into a simple dislike. We walked around Roseville dressed in autumn clothes, me pushing the stroller, Elliot holding Jacob's hand. We kissed foreheads and lips, even each other's.

XII

The first night we were without our children was six weeks after Netta-Mae was born. Stan, the old retired teacher from work, was re-upping on his wedding vows, forty years together with the same woman, and had invited everybody he'd known for what he called *a blowout to welcome us to the next forty.* The ceremony was held at Como Park in a white gazebo. There were geese milling about, seemingly confused about when to head south. Stan wore a navy blazer and slacks; his wife, a stocky woman with a plethora of chins, wore an unfortunate pantsuit of a reddish hue. Elliot leaned over and whispered that the suit was from Talbots.

The reception was at The University Club on Summit Avenue. It was an old building, a castle really, all rock and spires overlooking the west ghetto of St. Paul. There were framed pictures of F. Scott and Zelda sitting in that very dining room all over the walls. They'd hired an oldies band. There was an endless procession of served appetizers, which turned out to be dinner, Stan telling me people could *fuck right off if they thought they were getting a filet on his dollar.*

There was a lot of laughter as old people drank more than they probably should have and attempted dance moves that would've been hard to pull off forty years before. Elliot was taking a mild benzo as an agreed-upon safeguard against any possible postpartum depression, and two drinks in, she was tipsy or maybe drunk, her lips no longer abashed at finding mine in public. I introduced Elliot to my coworkers. They were polite and she was the perfect amount of self-deprecating (I'm his jailbird wife; the prodigal wife returns), which was always met with a nervous laughter preceding a nice enough conversation. When I introduced her to Cheryl, I worried she'd detect some unspoken chemistry between us. But Elliot didn't. She said, Jesus, I'm glad there's at least one person he works with who isn't collecting social security. Great to meet you. And that was that.

At one point, we were slow dancing to "What a Wonderful World," and she placed her now shoeless feet on the tops of mine like a little girl might to her father. I thought about dancing with Netta-Mae during her wedding. I thought about giving away those I loved. I wondered if Jacob would marry. For some reason, I doubted it. I worried about him, the fact he'd been there through everything we had to mess up before getting it right.

Elliot's face was pressed to my chest. She spoke without lifting her head: You know what the worst part about jail was?

I momentarily stopped dancing. She never spoke about jail, not once she was out, always telling me it was over with, and that's how she wanted to leave it. I imagined her about to confess to rape by inmates and guards, daily sodomy by black wooden batons.

Probably everything, I said.

No, Elliot said.

She was silent. I wondered if she was building up the courage to tell me some horrible transgression or experience or maybe she simply had forgotten what she was about to divulge, the chemicals and drink leaving a foggy residue on her abilities of recollection. But she eventually spoke. She said, Wondering which girl would be next.

I pretended to have no idea what she was talking about.

I'd lay there all day, all night, and think about who it'd be. Nothing but time, you know? Envision a thousand different girls, scenarios—

Elliot, stop, baby.

Have to admit, I never pictured it being her.

Who? What are you even talking about?

The redhead. She's cute.

Who? What? Please stop.

It makes sense. You've gone young, and that didn't turn out too well, so now—

Cheryl is a *friend*. A *coworker*. That's it. I swear to fucking God—

You don't believe in God.

I swear on our children's life that—

Calm down, Devon, Jesus Christ. I'm not saying you *did* anything. I really doubt you did. I just know that's who it would've been. She was your backup plan.

Elliot placed her head back against my chest. I felt sweat around the nape of my neck. I moved my feet in a simple two-step pattern, each shuffle made difficult by Elliot's weight. Toward the song's climax, I put my lips to Elliot's ear and told her I loved her more than anything.

I know you do, Elliot said. I know you do.

XIV

It's very rare in one's life to actually understand a moment for what it is. On the one hand, we're too close, too fearful to admit what one's actions actually indicate. We'll make up a thousand self-aggrandizing rationales for those actions, excuses on top of excuses, our last line of defense a turning of one's gaze as if it were the sun, our vision already blurred white from staring too intently. The other reason, of course, is that we need retrospect to contextualize these actions. This is only natural; we're not psychics.

But there are those rare moments when we experience something and know it has far more significance than it should. It's as if this action somehow crystallizes the unspoken momentum of events and attitudes into a singular moment. This forms the smallest of epiphanies. They are rare and often unheeded. They are the moments art traffics in.

There's a moment I remember with my parents. I was thirteen. My father was sitting in his chair, as he did every night after dinner. He drank. He wore his white Sears Polo shirt still tucked into his navy blue pants. My mother came into the family room/kitchen. She was trying hard not to smile, which I found odd and slightly annoying. She walked over to my father and sat on the couch. This was a rare enough occurrence for me to quit doing the dishes and watch. She crossed her leg and bounced her ankle. My father glanced over at her. I couldn't see his face, only my mother's, which was smiling. My father turned back to the news. My mother sat there for a few more minutes. She switched her crossed legs. She commented on the news, something about the gas prices being outrageous. I went back to doing the dishes.

After fifteen minutes, my mother stood up and walked in front of my father. She said something about the lawn looking very nice as of late. My father muttered a response. My mom stood there looking down at her husband. Then she kind of bit her tongue and walked toward the kitchen side of the room. She stood by my side, kind of sticking out her chest. She asked how the dishes were going. I told her fine. Then I noticed a small golden pin fastened to her sweatshirt. It was an inch-long bird of some sort, a sparrow maybe. I told her I liked it. She beamed. It was one of the few memories of my mother where she's smiling as a means of happiness rather than a tool to mask other emotions. She told me it was from work, a *token of appreciation* for her excellence, an indication of *soaring above and beyond*, real gold on the outside and everything.

I understood at that very moment she'd wanted my father to notice it. She'd wanted to share her success, however trivial. She'd wanted to be congratulated or maybe simply seen.

My mom kissed my temple and left the room, not before turning around to check back on my father to see if he'd overheard our conversation and was about to take an interest in his wife. He stared at the TV. My mom walked out. And I knew at that very moment, nothing between them would be the same.

I experienced the same sensation two days after Stan's wedding.

I'd opened the bookstore and returned home at four. I walked into the apartment. I could hear Netta-Mae screaming and the television turned to a migraine-inducing volume. I rounded the white hallway and saw Jacob sitting a foot away from the TV, one hand down his pants, one petting the cream carpet. Elliot sat on the couch. Netta also lay on the couch, but on the opposite end, a good three feet away from her mother. My daughter's face was crimson from screaming. Her left hand shook in the air. But Elliot didn't notice. Or maybe she did notice, just didn't care. She stared at the TV.

I was about to ask what the fuck was going on, but I couldn't. I knew. I understood. I'd researched and read since the last time. I knew the glassed-over look of Elliot's eyes. I recognized this image as a textbook example of being *unable to care for one's children.* And I knew it was a shitty metaphor—even then, honest to God—but I couldn't help imagining her postpartum depression as a tsunami, water that was stories tall and so blue it was black, everyone standing there like complete idiots marveling at its enormity, knowing nothing would spare the devastation.

Enter the devastation.

But maybe my initial metaphor was poor, because Elliot's postpartum didn't have a violent or even forceful bone in its body. It was apathy—a complete and utter lack of interest or concern—and it crept into every facet of our lives. It was Stephen King's *fog*. It was the colonizer's malaria. It was a burst appendix. It was heroin hitting the heart and being pumped to every recess of the body in less than a second. It was my past, our past, our two years of hell, of monosyllabic communication, of single fatherhood, of wondering what I could do to help, if only I made the perfect dinner and gave the perfect foot massage, if only then she'd smile or at least blink in regular intervals.

She agreed to see a doctor.

The doctor upped her benzo dose and added an SSRI inhibitor, which only seemed to make her all the more tired.

Showers became a once-a-week occurrence. Her breast milk dried up. Jacob watched hours of television a day. The doctor ordered us to take a daily walk. These walks started out as mile-long jaunts, but within three days, became the hurried square block shuffle of those forcing their dogs to urinate. Netta-Mae's diaper rash grew between her soft folds. Specs of granular formula coated every surface of the kitchen. Our sheets smelled like unwashed hair. Elliot's body found its pre-baby form, and then shrunk from there. I stopped by the Svendsons' home without Elliot knowing. I sat at their kitchen table explaining what was going on. Terry cried. Ed shook his head. They insisted on taking Jacob until their daughter's meds started taking hold, until things were *back on track*. I told them that wasn't necessary. Four days later, when I returned from half a shift (I'd informed my employer that I could open and close the store, but had to leave shortly thereafter), to see Jacob holding his baby sister in his lap on the couch, Elliot sleeping, I took the Svendsons up on their offer. Elliot wouldn't stop watching *Factory Girl* on Netflix. I'd talk to her. Tell her everything in our lives that was good. I'd talk about our children's health. The fact that we had money to get by. That her family loved her. That *I* loved her. I'd talk about the worst being over with, and now we simply had to jump through a few hoops before we could live the rest of our lives however the hell we wanted. I hired a nurse to help twice a week while I had to work. Elliot would close the bedroom door when Yolanda would arrive, never once venturing outside of her lair to check on her daughter or the stranger taking care of her.

I kept waiting for the proverbial lifting of the clouds.

I kept being the dutiful husband and father, only this time there was nothing romantic about any of it.

I kept reminding myself that Elliot's actions, or lack of actions, were the result of a hormonal imbalance. It was a sickness, not the revealing of her true character.

❧

Things came to a boiling point on Netta-Mae's three-month birthday. We lay in bed watching Edie Sedgwick run around New York all junked out for the umpteenth time. Andy Warhol had already turned on her. The movie was nearing its climax. Elliot placed her hand on mine. She said, You're Andy Warhol to my Edie Sedgwick.

I laughed. I was thrilled about the body contact, plus the initiation of conversation. Maybe the meds were finally helping? Maybe this was the first moment of dawn. I said, Because I'm a homosexual artist with a love of pop culture?

Because you're a smug prick.

I inhaled a little too deeply. I remembered Elliot's depression before, how in its boredom it became beyond cutting.

You're right, I said.

See, right there. That's you being a smug prick.

Sorry. You want to watch something else?

Think about it, Elliot said. Edie was happy. Excited. About everything. And then she met Andy. And everything turned to shit.

You're right, baby.

Don't patronize me.

Then you're not right.

Elliot laughed. I glanced to my left to see if the whole thing had been a joke. Elliot's eyes were little marbles in cavernous eye sockets. She wasn't joking; she was just getting started. She said, The thing is, Edie wasn't blameless. She embraced the lifestyle. She gave herself over to a person completely incapable of any real emotion.

I told myself to let it pass. She was trying to pick a fight. She was bored and miserable and it wasn't her fault, but her wiring, her hormones, and it'd pass, and it'd be better, us together, our family reunited, it finally getting better.

I fucked a kid, she said. That's my fault, I guess.

We've made mistakes, I said.

You fucked a kid, Elliot said.

I didn't fu— We both messed up, babe, but it's over with now.

I think about him sometimes.

Okay.

He was gorgeous.

Let's go to bed.

His stomach was all muscle. Not like yours.

Why are you doing this?

That's an age thing, isn't it? Tightness. *Tautness*. No, tightness. That's right, isn't it Professor Hester?

I stared at our ceiling. I imagined the overhead fan derailing and spinning at us both, slicing through our throats, silence, a fitting end to our conversation.

That's why you were with little Monica States, right? Because it was tight? Because everything about her was tight?

Please, for the love of God, stop.

I'm not judging you. I get it. There's something there I understand.

Elliot kind of laughed to herself and rolled over to face the wall. I prayed it was over with. I reminded myself to breathe.

It's like becoming immortal, she said.

I love you.

I love you, Elliot mimicked.

Goodnight.

Elliot was silent for a minute. I switched the television from Netflix to regular cable and put on Bravo because it'd been Elliot's favorite before.

I still fantasize about him, she said.

I watched grown women act like insecure middle schoolers. It was a reunion show, all of the housewives sitting on two white couches around Andy Cohen. They were arguing about something somebody had said.

He was a great lover, Elliot said.

The fattest woman stood. She waved her pink nails in the direction of a girl across from her.

I think I loved him, Elliot said.

That's great, I said.

Oh, the smug prick can talk. Praise the lord, he's saved.

Bouncers from offstage rushed to the couches and separated the women.

Is that what you pray for me? Elliot said. That I'm *saved*? That I become the loving mother and wife you so desperately want me to be? She chuckled and said, The mighty Devon Hester praying to God for his wife to become a housewife. Maybe I could try out for *The Real Housewives of Roseville*. Hi, I'm Elliot, I'm a convicted sex offender and my last job was at Talbots, where I showed great promise.

On the TV, everybody was seated back on the two white couches. There was a lot of smoothing of dresses and hair.

You know what the funny thing is? Elliot said.

The camera zoomed in on Andy Cohen. He smiled. He liked it when they fought.

I wanted you to fuck me. That's it. That was the only reason I came over to your shitty house after those boring coffee sessions at The Little Owl. I wanted you to fuck me good, which you didn't, not like Maddie did. I didn't ask you to fall in love with me. I didn't ask for Jacob. I sure as shit didn't ask for Netta. I didn't want this life. I never came close to loving you.

∾

An hour later, Cheryl answered the door in a men's sized flannel shirt. I wasn't sure if it was covering up panties or not. She'd been sleeping, her face puffy, her red hair frizzy on the right side.

Devon, what the fuck? Everything okay? Is it the kids?

I asked if I could come in.

Cheryl moved to the side. She kept talking. She was asking what I was doing and what I needed and then she tried humor, telling me that offer from this spring was more of a joke than anything serious. Her house was a tiny bungalow, basically the same layout as my apartment with its connected kitchen and family room and then two small bedrooms. The only difference was hers had a sense of charm, everything salvaged, furniture that made up a cozy, cohesive whole. I made my way to her bedroom. It wasn't the '90s shrine I expected it to be, but instead clean and tidy, a wall of books and a white nightstand the only things other than a low-lying bed.

I motioned for her to lie down.

She tilted her head.

Just do it, I said.

Cheryl sat on the bed and looked at me for guidance. I told her to scoot back. She told me I was kind of freaking her out. She laughed. I didn't. She sat against the back wall with her legs pulled underneath her Indian style, the ends of her red flannel shirt tucked to cover her vagina. I told her to spread her legs.

Dude, what's up? Let's talk. Something obviously went the fuck down, and I'm here for you, like whatever you need, this too, she said, motioning to her body, but let's talk about it first so you're not fucking something up beyond repair.

I unzipped my pants.

I was already hard.

Cheryl sat there looking at me touch myself. I felt like a fucking rapist. A freak. A failure. I closed my eyes. I thought about trying to explain that my wife hated me and always had. That like alcohol, the postpartum granted her the freedom to actually speak her mind, and she had, clear as fucking day. I thought about Elliot sleeping with that kid. I thought about her ignoring my screaming daughter. I thought about choosing prison instead of my bed, which in that moment, made so much fucking sense. I thought about Jacob living with his grandparents. I thought about second chances. About hitting *redo*. About Cheryl being right. About people never changing. About me running to the arms of any willing participant when I was faced with the failure of making another person love me.

Cheryl's cries cut through. I opened my eyes. She'd pulled her legs inward, shielding as much as her body with her oversized flannel as she could. I told her I was sorry, so fucking sorry.

Leave.

Cheryl, please, I—

Get the fuck out.

XII

Yeah, I arrived there at forty-one.

Things settled down. After a horrible month, Elliot seemed to rebound as if her maternal care were an elastic band reaching its breaking point. She started holding Netta-Mae. She read to Jacob, who moved back in with us after three weeks of improvement. She fed them both, sometimes even me, the four of us around a table meant for two, a semblance of a family. She quit watching *Factory Girl*. We resumed our talks about our futures, even if it was more along the lines of the practical (*I need to find work, wish we were hiring at the bookstore, can see about Talbots, forget Talbots*). We even made love one night. It was nothing exceptional, but it was nice. She used a towel to clean the semen off my thigh hair. We never spoke of the fated night of our fight and my disappearing for forty-five minutes.

I allowed myself to think about things being on the mend. I would get carried away picturing these steps as the initial crawl toward improvement, and then things brightening from there exponentially.

The autumn gave way to Halloween. We walked around the Svendsons' neighborhood as a group of six, Jacob in a muscled-up Superman costume, Netta-Mae as a fluffy bunny with floppy ears. Then it was Thanksgiving and I pretended to like football while sitting on Ed's couch with him not talking, but *warming*, offering me chips and dip. Snow wouldn't stop falling. We decorated the best we could with a three-foot plastic tree already strung with lights purchased from Home Depot.

And this was life.

It wasn't great, but it wasn't horrible. Or maybe it was actually great. Or maybe it was actually fucking horrible.

We settled into routine, into tedium, into bedtimes and family photos and debates over whether or not to open up a new credit card. We were anonymous, which at first was a godsend considering what Elliot's brush with fame had been, but then it became a little disconcerting. I imagined the apartment being something other than temporary. And of course, I thought about my parents. I saw our routine as theirs, me a mixture of them both—on the one hand silent and resentful in front of the television, on the other pining for attention.

Often, I'd lay awake at night. I'd catalog every mistake I'd ever made. I'd think about people I'd harmed. I'd imagine Poop Bag Madeline crying in some forgotten apartment littered with wet cat food cans. I'd imagine speaking to my dead father. I'd ask him the questions I never could muster the courage to ask when he was alive. I'd ask how it felt to fear for your life. What it was like taking somebody else's life. If any part of the war was fun. If he wished he'd died over there instead of coming back. If he knew his wife was cheating on him the entire time, and if so, why didn't he care? Was it his consolation for not being able to give her everything she wanted? I'd ask my mom why she put up with my father for so long. Was it for me? Was it because she was scared? What was it like living your home life with the curse of invisibility? Was she happy when he died? Did it feel like the gift of freedom? Did she remember that moment at the cabin when he was painting her nails and she stared at him as if he was the only man in the world and declared her love? And what were her exact thoughts when she said this?

I'd replay the small cruelties of my life: times I stared at a person's acne across their forehead, times I hadn't held the door, unreturned phone calls, gossip I'd propagated that found its way back to the target. The list was endless, and regardless of how hard I thought of these instances, there were always more. I'd remember the look of complete shock and then resolve that coated Elliot's face when she walked into my office while I was having an affair. I'd imagine her in jail crying in a communal shower. I'd see Cheryl curled up in her bed as I masturbated like a rapist fiend, seeing clearly the tears I'd made myself believe were moans of pleasure. I'd think about ruined lives. About my children. About Jacob. About Netta-Mae and the fact that she'd missed the bond a newborn child needs with her mother. How all of this, regardless of how I rationalized my actions, was my fault.

And without fail, I heard my father telling me these were the most important moments of my life. They were the sum of my experiences. That when I left this world, these images would be my swan song, a cacophony of hurt eyes and quivering lips.

I suppose, like Jane Smiley, this was my father's attempt to explain *the age of grief.* It was the same thing, really: a sauce of hurt and pity over a bed of regret.

My *age of grief* lasted until the night Elliot turned thirty-one.

Or maybe that's when it really began.

I sat in Chuck-E-Cheese with the Svendsons and my two children. We eventually ate. Jacob kept spilling his root beer. Netta-Mae wouldn't stop fussing. Elliot was late. Her phone kept going straight to voicemail.

It wasn't until I stood watching my son jump into a pit of plastic balls that I fully admitted to myself that the last month had been a mirage instead of improvement. The symmetry of time and event seemed like a cruel joke. I knew she was gone. I knew it wasn't to the Wisconsin Dells, as it had been for me a year ago to the day. It was *gone* gone. This was her Edie Sedgwick moment of running through the streets of New York. This was her taking action for everything she'd told me during our fight. This was her attempt at hitting *redo* for a second chance.

STATUTORY

Written by Madison Johnson

Based on a True Story

From: Madison Johnson
Minnesota Correctional Facility - Stillwater 970 Pickett Street
Bayport, MN 55003
651-779-2700

EXT. COMO LAKE - EARLY MORNING

The CAMERA pans across a frozen lake. It looks desolate, barren.
The sun is close to rising but isn't quiet there.

                    MADDIE (V.O.)
Every story has a beginning. The thing is, if somebody tells you he
knows it, he's lying. Nobody knows that shit. We're too simple and
too fucked up. And really, if you're thinking about beginnings,
     it's only because everything's real bad at the present.

CLOSE UP of Maddie's face. He's young, late teens or early twenties, attractive in a delicate way. He's obviously distressed,
               sweaty, his bottom lip split.

                    MADDIE (V.O.)
Me, I'm holding a gun. I've never fired one, but it's probably as
          simple as point and pull and repeat.

The CAMERA pans out. Maddie holds a snub-nosed revolver with his
right hand. He nervously taps the tip against his thigh.

                    MADDIE (V.O.)
And I'm thinking about beginnings. I'm thinking about absent fa-
thers and overbearing mothers and being a celebrity for being
raped and nothing as pure as a boy and girl in love.

                    CUT TO:
          INT. INSIDE OF ICE PALACE - NIGHT

We see a slightly younger Maddie leaning against an iridescent
ice wall, his arm around Elliot, a blond girl on the border of
womanhood, sharp featured, stunning but not conventionally pretty.
          They're smiling into one another's mouths.

                    CUT TO:
           EXT. COMO LAKE - CONTINUOUS

                    MADDIE (V.O.)
I'm thinking about daughters and affairs and dying in prison.

INT. HONDA CIVIC - CONTINUOUS

The CAMERA shows Netta-Mae, a three-month-old girl, sitting awkwardly in the driver's seat. Her purple pajamas show from underneath a man's parka wrapped around her body. She's crying.

EXT. COMO LAKE - CONTINUOUS

We follow Maddie's range of vision to his left. We see Devon, a
forty-something type, his face covered in three-days' worth of
beard, and Elliot. They are on their knees, both crying.

We hear the approaching of sirens, first a distant buzz, now becoming a constant wailing.

                        MADDIE (V.O.)
Maybe the only time we ever think about beginnings is at the end.
Like a prayer. Like if we conjure up the exact moment everything
started, we'll be transported back in time, able to cherish every
                    pointless conversation.

Maddie rubs the back of his hand holding the pistol across his
        mouth, smearing snot and blood and saliva.

                        MADDIE (V.O.)
Or maybe our search for the beginning is an attempt to find the
            exact moment we should've walked away.

The CAMERA pans across the frozen lake, focusing on the snow. We
                hear three gun shots.

                        FADE TO WHITE:
                EXT. BASEBALL FIELD - MORNING

A six-year-old Maddie is dressed in a baseball uniform and oversized helmet. He holds a metal baseball bat that looks too heavy.

                        MADDIE (V.O.)
            I had the all-American Childhood.

He swings at a black tee holding an oversized softball. He misses
    the ball but makes contact with the tee, knocking it over.

                        T-ball...

                        MADDIE (V.O.)

CUT TO:

EXT. STATE PARK - DUSK

A seven-year-old Maddie sits with his mother and father around a campfire. They're roasting marshmallows. They look more bored than happy.

MADDIE (V.O.)
Camping...

CUT TO:

INT. DINING ROOM - NIGHT

An eight-year-old Maddie sits at a rectangular dining table. He plays with his peas.

MADDIE (V.O.)
Family dinners...

The CAMERA pans out to show the full table. His parents sit on opposite ends. They're screaming. His father throws his plate against the wall. His mother, a blond woman who appears attractive if not a bit timid, covers her mouth with a cloth napkin.

CUT TO:

EXT. FRONT DOOR - NIGHT

Nine-year-old Maddie stands in front of a red door to a prefabricated suburban home. His mother stands to his side, her arm slung over his shoulder.

MADDIE (V.O.)
Divorce...

Mr. Johnson's face is visible through the windshield of a black Acura. He backs out of the driveway.

CUT TO:

INT. MADDIE'S ROOM - NIGHT

A twelve-year-old Maddie sits at the foot of his bed. He's dressed in jeans and a T-shirt. He's wearing a headset and holding an Xbox controller. The CAMERA zooms in on his face, which reflects back the light from the video game. We can hear the noise of gunfighting.

MADDIE (V.O.)
Vids...

CUT TO:
INT. FRIEND'S ROOM - NIGHT

A group of thirteen-year-old boys stand around in a circle. The
CAMERA moves over Maddie's shoulder to show that they're looking
at internet pornography.

MADDIE (V.O.)
Sleepovers...

CUT TO:
EXT. OUTSIDE OF GIRL'S WINDOW - NIGHT

The bedroom window opens. An awkwardly attractive blond girl with
braces beckons a fourteen-year-old Maddie over with nervous
excitement.

MADDIE (V.O.)
More sleepovers.

Maddie dives through the open window.

CUT TO:
EXT. BEHIND A BURGER KING DUMPSTER - DAY

A fifteen-year-old Maddie passes a forty between himself and two
friends.

MADDIE (V.O.)
Drinking...

CUT TO:
INT. KITCHEN OF PARTY - NIGHT

Maddie at sixteen sits amongst a crowded table of high school
peers. Rap plays in the background. The drunken cheers of youth
echo. The girl sitting on his lap squeezes his cheeks until he
opens his mouth and sticks out his tongue.

MADDIE (V.O.)
Drugs...

She sticks out her own tongue, rolling two hits of ecstasy from
her mouth to his own.

CUT TO:

INT. GIRL'S BEDROOM - NIGHT

A CLOSE UP of Maddie's face. He's speaking directly to the camera.

> MADDIE (V.O.)
> For all intents and purposes, I was the poster child for the Millennial Generation. I was white and lived in the suburbs and listened to rap and smiled around adults and worked a shitty retail job in order to pay for drugs and got decent grades and was planning on going to the state university and was disenfranchised with pretty much everything, including this.

The CAMERA pulls back, showing a shirtless Maddie thrusting. The sound of slapping becomes louder and louder.

> GIRL (O.C.)
> Oh God!

CUT TO:

INT - ROSEVILLE MALL - DAY

Maddie walks through the mall traffic with calm ease and self-assurance, as if he knows he's better than the fat masses around him, while not coming across as conceited. He wears skinny jeans and a white T-shirt.

> MADDIE (V.O.)
> So maybe that's my beginning - bored with everything and everyone.

Beat.

> MADDIE (CONT'D)
> Enter Elliot.

Maddie pauses in front of Talbots. Elliot stands near the entrance folding turtlenecks. She sees Maddie through the glass of the storefront. It's unclear if she's staring at Maddie or simply spaced out.

> MADDIE (CONT'D)
> It wasn't like she was even overly beautiful — a little old, a little too much nose — but there was something about her I couldn't get enough of.

CUT TO:
INT. - ROSEVILLE MALL - FOUNTAIN - DAY

Elliot sits at a two-person table picking at a salad. Water from a dilapidated fountain sprinkles. We follow her gaze to Zumiez, to Maddie, who stares back.

MADDIE (V.O.)
It was probably the fact that she wouldn't stop staring at me.

EXT. - PARKING LOT - NIGHT

Maddie and two friends huddle outside of his Civic passing around a joint. It's obviously cold, all of them dressed in hooded sweat-shirts, blowing on their hands for warmth.
They're joking around, slapping nuts, and talking shit.

Elliot walks across the parking lot with her knee-length sweater coat held closed by her arms clasped around her stomach.

She doesn't look altogether comfortable walking in heels, which becomes all the more apparent when one breaks, causing her to stumble, arms outstretched, finally tipping over.

Maddie's two friends burst out laughing. Maddie starts, but then stops, the joint in his mouth, peering. He breaks away from his friends and jogs toward Elliot.

MADDIE
You Okay?

ELLIOT
Besides wanting to die?

MADDIE
Wasn't all bad. (laughing)
Graceful almost.

ELLIOT
Like a fucking train wreck. (taking her broken shoe
from Maddie) Payless.

MADDIE
Two-for-one?

                         ELLIOT
                         Bingo.

                         MADDIE
                   And the other pair?

                         ELLIOT
                         Broken.

They laugh. Elliot's obviously embarrassed, flushed, with her blond
hair pulled out from her ponytail. But it's in this moment where
she seems to first notice Maddie. The slightest dimple grows on her
              left cheek as she bites its inside.

                         MADDIE
                (extending his hand) Maddie.

                         ELLIOT
                         Elliot.
           (shakes his hand) Your name's kind of girly.

                         MADDIE
                        (laughing)
               And your name's kind of masculine.

                         ELLIOT
                       Could trade.

                         MADDIE
                         Could.

                         ELLIOT
           Your Adam's apple is too big for an Elliot.

                         MADDIE
                         Your...

              CLOSE UP of Elliot's nose.

                         ELLIOT
             Can say it, dick. Staring right at my nose.
                (feigns anger and turns around)

                         MADDIE
   (grabs her arm, laughing) Girl can dish it out, but can't take it?

ELLIOT
Oh, I can take it.

MADDIE
Yeah?

ELLIOT
(staring directly at him) Nice to meet you, Maddie.

MADDIE
Wait, wait. What are you up to Saturday?

ELLIOT
An invigorating evening of returning these broke-ass shoes to
Payless.

MADDIE
Give me your phone.

ELLIOT
Aren't you the confident boy?

MADDIE
A party. I'm having a party. You should come.
(MORE)

MADDIE (CONT'D)
Rock some of that Talbots gear like it's going out of style.

ELLIOT
How do you know where I work?

MADDIE
(taking her phone) A brother has eyes.

ELLIOT
Maybe I should go pick up some teenybopper tube-tops at Zumiez?

MADDIE
How do you know where I work?

ELLIOT
(grinning)
A sister has eyes.

INT. THE JOHNSON'S KITCHEN - MORNING

Maddie sits at a breakfast island eating Lucky Charms. The kitchen is a modest stab at opulence — fake mahogany and granite, pans strung from a wrought-iron hanging wrack above the stove. Mrs. Johnson, 46, attractive for a mother, her jeans doing their best to hold back the slight pouch of middle-age, rubs Maddie's back.

                    MRS. JOHNSON
So you'll go directly to Jared's after school. I'll be back Sunday. Obviously call if you need me.

                    MADDIE
                Yup. Love you.

                    MRS. JOHNSON
                Love you too.

                    MRS. JOHNSON
                And no parties.

                    MADDIE
                No parties.

                MONTAGE - VARIOUS
        (A$AP ROCKY's Wild For The Night plays)

A) EXT. THE JOHNSON'S FRONT YARD - NIGHT - The yard is swarmed with cars and teenagers filing toward the red front door. One boy kicks the head of a plastic Frosty the Snowman decoration.

B) INT. THE JOHNSON'S FOYER - NIGHT - Teenagers dance seductively. A couple on the stairs forcefully kisses. They bump into a picture of Maddie and his mom, which falls and breaks.

C) INT. THE JOHNSON'S KITCHEN - NIGHT - High school girls scream as a ping-pong ball lands in a red cup. They all raise their cups to do shots.

D) EXT. OUTSIDE OF ELLIOT'S TRUCK - Maddie chases Elliot.

E) INT. THE JOHNSON'S FOYER - NIGHT - Two girls grind one another. Their gyrations alternate between slow-motion and regular speed.

F) INT. MRS. JOHNSON'S BEDROOM - NIGHT - A teenage couple lay on the red comforter. A CLOSE UP of hands rubbing over exposed skin.

G) EXT. THE JOHNSON'S BACK PATIO - NIGHT - A group of boys sit around smoking blunts.

H) EXT. OUTSIDE OF ELLIOT'S TRUCK - NIGHT - Elliot has her hand on the truck's handle. Maddie is two feet away. He smiles.

> MADDIE
> Hey.

I) INT. THE JOHNSON'S FOYER - NIGHT - The same two girls grind. Elliot stares at the dancing girls. Then the couple making out on the stairs. She's obviously a little disturbed.

J) INT. THE JOHNSON'S KITCHEN - NIGHT - Maddie checks his phone. He's distracted, alone in a crowd of a hundred.

K) EXT. OUTSIDE OF ELLIOT'S TRUCK - NIGHT - Elliot holds her keys.

> ELLIOT
> It's just...fuck...I thought you were older.

> MADDIE
> I'm eighteen.

> ELLIOT
> And I'm older.

> MADDIE
> Twenty-one?

> ELLIOT
> Boy's flush with charm.

> MADDIE
> Twenty-three tops.

> ELLIOT
> Closer.

> MADDIE
> (stepping closer) One drink.

L) INT. THE JOHNSON's FOYER - NIGHT - One of the grinding girl's reaches out and takes Elliot's hand. The girl brings Elliot's hand to her own small breasts. Elliot shakes her head and turns to leave. Maddie rushes from the end of the foyer toward the front door.

M) INT. THE JOHNSON'S BATHROOM - NIGHT - A girl is on her hands and knees vomiting into the toilet. Two boys are laughing behind her. They are snapping pictures of her ass crack, fully exposed, as she gets sick.

N) EXT. OUTSIDE OF ELLIOT'S TRUCK - NIGHT - Maddie's inches away from Elliot. She's shaking her head, but he's smiling.

                    ELLIOT
This isn't going to happen, little boy. Goodnight.

She runs her hand across his chest in a way that would suggest otherwise. She gets into the truck. It takes two attempts before the engine catches. The lights blind Maddie.

                 END OF MONTAGE

                 FADE TO WHITE:

            INT. ROSEVILLE MALL - DUSK

Maddie's standing behind the counter at Zumiez. Shoppers walk around the store, destroying stacks of folded T-Shirts. A four-teen-year-old girl slips a beanie from the bin into her purse. Maddie is texting on his phone.

CLOSE UP of his phone. He's in the text message screen. The contact says "Elliot". He's written: What you up to 2night?

The typing icon fills the screen, then Elliot's message: Shouldn't you be playing WOW or something?

Maddie laughs. He types: Serious.

The typing icon shows. Elliot's response: Some bullshit work thing at Chili's. Kill me.

              INT. CHILI'S - NIGHT

Maddie stamps the snow off his feet and rubs his hands together as he enters Chili's. He's greeted by a twenty-something hostess, who's obviously attracted to him. She puts her hand on his back as she guides him to the bar.

As they're walking, Maddie cranes his neck to see the back of the restaurant. Elliot stands in a cluster of older women.

Maddie slows, causing the hostess to turn, reaching out with her hand as if he were a child in need of coaxing. It's obvious Maddie wants Elliot to see him, but she doesn't look over.

From Elliot's POV, we see the profile of Maddie as he walks around the corner.

Elliot smiles into her drink. She excuses herself from the women.

From Elliot's POV, we pass by fat families devouring Blooming Onions. Sleazy thirty-something mall salesmen give her the up and down. She rounds the corner into the bar. Maddie looks up from a two-person booth. He gives us a true smile, this one all emotion, without trying to be sexy or cool.

INT. WOMEN'S BATHROOM AT CHILI'S - CONTINUOUS

A slutty-yet-attractive twenty-five-year-old applies eyeliner at the mirror. Elliot tentatively positions herself next to the girl. She pretends to look through her purse, but really stares at herself compared to the girl next to her. Their difference in sex appeal is evident. Elliot pulls the skin underneath her eyes back for a few seconds.
The door opens. Maddie slips in.

> ATTRACTIVE/SLUTTY GIRL
> You can't be in here.

> MADDIE
> Hey.

> ATTRACTIVE/SLUTTY GIRL
> (noticing Maddie, grinning slightly)

> ELLIOT
> What are you doing here?

> MADDIE
> I wanted to talk about the other night...

> ATTRACTIVE/SLUTTY GIRL
> (realizing Maddie had come in for Elliot)
> This is the women's bathroom. As in, you can't be here.

                    ELLIOT
          (turning to girl) It's fine.

              ATTRACTIVE/SLUTTY GIRL
                   For who?

                    ELLIOT
                    Whom.

              ATTRACTIVE/SLUTTY GIRL
                    What?

                    ELLIOT
                  For whom?

              ATTRACTIVE/SLUTTY GIRL
                   Bitch.

                    ELLIOT
       Always appreciate female solidarity.

The girl tosses her eyeliner in her Michael Kors clutch. She walks
toward the bathroom exit. Maddie steps to the side, but she still
places her hand on the small of his back as if she were barely
                able to squeeze by.

                    MADDIE
I'm sorry about the party. Shouldn't have tried to kiss you. Was
               a little drunk and...

                    ELLIOT
                  And what?

                    MADDIE
          Scared to say anything more.

                    ELLIOT
                    Why?

                    MADDIE
        Because you'll correct my grammar.

The both laugh. Maddie walks to the edge of the green sink and
       leans against it before straightening back up.

                 MADDIE (CONT'D)
                  It's just...

                    ELLIOT
          The fact you're a baby.

                    MADDIE
               Eighteen.

                    ELLIOT
             In high school.

                    MADDIE
          Old enough to buy porno—

                    ELLIOT
        Then maybe that's what you should do.

                    MADDIE
     Or maybe you should believe what I'm telling you.

                    ELLIOT
                Which is?

Maddie seems a tiny bit flustered, his fingers rubbing against the
green counter, his gaze ducking to the sink for a second.

                    MADDIE
             That I really...

                    ELLIOT
                 What?

                    MADDIE
          Want to get to know you.

                    ELLIOT
        That's not what you were going to say?

                    MADDIE
     I don't know, there's something about you...

                    ELLIOT
                (laughing)
          The fact I'm old as fuck.

                    MADDIE
          The fact you're...like...

ELLIOT
Ready for assisted living?

MADDIE
(laughing) I don't know.

ELLIOT
That's not good enough.

MADDIE
Different.

ELLIOT
That's not good enough.

MADDIE
Good different. Like the best fucking different.

Elliot rolls her eyes and walks past Maddie. She reaches the door.
Maddie starts toward her.

MADDIE (CONT'D)
Hold up.

Elliot stops, leaning her head against the wooden bathroom door.
CLOSE UP of her arching neck.

ELLIOT
Not good enough.

MADDIE
(walking toward her)
I can't stop thinking about you.

ELLIOT
Not good enough.

MADDIE
I keep volunteering to go on Jamba Juice runs at the store so I
can walk by Talbots.

ELLIOT
(her voice softer) Not good enough.

MADDIE
I couldn't sleep Saturday night thinking I'd messed everything up.

They are a foot apart by this point. Elliot kind of rolls the back
of her head against the wall.

ELLIOT
(whispering) Not good enough.

MADDIE
I like you.

Elliot laughs. Maddie seems instantly embarrassed.

MADDIE (CONT'D) (CONT'D)
What?

ELLIOT
Life.

Elliot reaches toward Maddie's face. She pulls at the back of his
neck and then they're kissing. Elliot appears to be the aggressor,
lifting her leg, fumbling with Maddie's belt.
Maddie fishes a condom out of his wallet and hurriedly puts it on.
Elliot moans when he enters her. Somebody tries to push open the
bathroom door from the other side. Both Maddie and Elliot laugh
and continue having sex.

CUT TO:
INT. PSYCHOLOGIST'S OFFICE - MORNING

Maddie sits in a leather chair. He's dressed in a sweater with
a collared shirt. The psychologist sitting across from him is
attractive in a frigid way, a gray skirt-suit, black hair pulled
back in a severe manner.

PSYCHOLOGIST
And this was the first time Mrs. Svendson had intercourse with you?

MADDIE
The first time we had intercourse, yes.

PSYCHOLOGIST
Was this the first time you'd had intercourse in a public location?

Maddie shakes his head. The psychologist jots a note.

PSYCHOLOGIST (CONT'D)
How old did you believe Mrs. Svendson to be at that time?

                         MADDIE
          Twenty-four. Twenty-five at the oldest.

                      PSYCHOLOGIST
            And she believed you to be...

                         MADDIE
                        Eighteen.

                      PSYCHOLOGIST
                        (pausing)
    What was your intention when following Mrs. Svendson into the
                        restroom?

                         MADDIE
                      To apologize.

                      PSYCHOLOGIST
          What was your reaction when she kissed you?

                         MADDIE
                    To kiss her back.

                      PSYCHOLOGIST
        (giving a curt smile) Emotionally speaking?

                         MADDIE
              Surprised, I guess. (pausing)
                    A little confused.

                      PSYCHOLOGIST
                      Why is that?

                          Beat.

                         MADDIE
          Because she'd been telling me no.

                    MADDIE (CONT'D)
            Never knew what she was thinking.

                        CUT TO:
        INT. YOUTH PSYCHOLOGIST'S OFFICE - MORNING

An eight-year-old Maddie sits on an oversized leather chair. He
sits with his fists jammed underneath his knees. He looks uncom-

fortable. The youth psychologist is a moderately attractive blond in a floral patterned blazer with ugly shoulder pads.

                    YOUTH PSYCHOLOGIST
How does it make you feel when you don't know what she's thinking?

                    EIGHT-YEAR-OLD MADDIE
                           Bad.

                    YOUTH PSYCHOLOGIST
                  Tell me more about that.

                    EIGHT-YEAR-OLD MADDIE
                         (shrugging)
                   Like she's mad. Or sad.

                    YOUTH PSYCHOLOGIST
          Are you only happy if your mother is happy?

            Eight-year-old Maddie nods.

                 YOUTH PSYCHOLOGIST (CONT'D)
              That's a lot of pressure for you, isn't it?

            Eight-year-old Maddie continues nodding.

                 YOUTH PSYCHOLOGIST (CONT'D)
        Does it feel like it's your job to make your mother happy?

                    EIGHT-YEAR-OLD MADDIE
                          It is.

                    YOUTH PSYCHOLOGIST
                (nodding in a sympathetic way)
              What do you do if you fail at this?

            Eight-year-old Maddie looks down at his lap.

                 YOUTH PSYCHOLOGIST (CONT'D)
                 What do you do, Madison?

                    EIGHT-YEAR-OLD MADDIE
                    It was only once.

                    YOUTH PSYCHOLOGIST
                      May I see them?

Eight-year-old Maddie nods. He bunches up his navy-blue T-shirt and pulls its bottom up toward his chin. There are a series of small cuts along his prepubescent pectorals.

YOUTH PSYCHOLOGIST (CONT'D)
Can you tell me exactly what you were thinking when you hurt yourself?

EIGHT-YEAR-OLD MADDIE
I needed to be better at making my mom happy.

The psychologist has moved her chair closer to Maddie. She's studying the small cuts. She extends her hand, letting her fingers trace the two-inch marks.

From eight-year-old Maddie's POV, we are in a CLOSE UP of her hand, wrist, floral blazer, her cleavage (which has grown since the scene started, and now seems wildly inappropriate), then her neck and clavicles, then her mouth, then her nose, and it's here both the audience and Maddie seem to realize it's a different lady, now Elliot dressed as the youth psychologist, her rubbing of his chest turning sexual.

YOUTH PSYCHOLOGIST
Does that feel good?

CUT TO:
INT. WOMEN'S BATHROOM AT CHILI'S - CONTINUOUS

MADDIE
Yes.

ELLIOT
That makes me happy.

MADDIE
It feels so fucking good.

FADE OUT.

INT. MADDIE'S CAR - NIGHT

Maddie and Elliot sit in his handed-down Civic. It's full of sweat-shirts and crushed Monster cans and skateboard decks.
They're at a park. The headlights shine on swings and a slide covered in snow.

                    MADDIE
             Still kind of cool.

Elliot holds up a small glass paperweight. Rookie of The Year is
etched into its surface. She raises her eyebrows.

                    ELLIOT
              Pretty big deal.

                    MADDIE
               Obviously.

                    ELLIOT
        Might have a future at Talbots.

                    MADDIE
        Daring to aim for the stars, huh?

                    ELLIOT
             Fuck that place.

                    MADDIE
               Fuck retail.

                    ELLIOT
             Fuck Minnesota.

                    MADDIE
          Don't forget high school.

                    ELLIOT
     (shaking her head) Can't believe you're in high school.

                    MADDIE
                  (smiling)
    Can't believe I'm in high school or the fact you slept with a high
                school boy?

Elliot play hits Maddie's shoulder. He catches her punch. They
hold hands for a few seconds before Elliot brings her hand back to
her body as if suddenly self-conscious.

                    ELLIOT
      You realize it's the best time of your life.

                    MADDIE
       What is? Right now? Pretty damn close—

                    ELLIOT
                 High school.

                    MADDIE
                  Shut up.

                    ELLIOT
                  Serious.

                    MADDIE
Living at home? Doing homework? Sitting in a building designed by
the same company that made the female prison down in Shakopee? If
that's as good as my life's going to get, might as well slit my
                 wrist right now.

                    ELLIOT
         Not responsible for a single thing.

                    MADDIE
              Exactly my point.

                    ELLIOT
                  You'll see.

                    MADDIE
               Enlighten me.

Maddie lights a joint and hits it twice before passing it to El-
     liot. She speaks with her lungs full of smoke.

                    ELLIOT
What you're feeling now — that anxious, almost humming sensation
of being trapped — that's because you're busy imagining what it
               will be like next year.

                    MADDIE
           Because high school sucks.

                    ELLIOT
      Once college ends, you feel that same sensation.

                    MADDIE
   And here's where you tell me the difference, right?

ELLIOT
Smart ass.

MADDIE
But you kind of love it.

ELLIOT
Whatever.

MADDIE
Continue.

ELLIOT
No, forget it.

MADDIE
(feigning seriousness) Please.

ELLIOT
Only it's different when you're older. Every year you lose more options. Pretty soon you're trapped, only it's the real kind, the forever kind, the kind that seems worse than any shitty circumstance you can imagine.

Maddie takes the joint back. He hits it, thinks about saying something, leans his head against the window, then hits it again.

MADDIE
You talking about your kid?

CLOSE UP of Elliot. Her face is caught between horror and the masking smile of denial.

ELLIOT
What are you talking about?

MADDIE
It's cool. I like kids.

ELLIOT
I don't have—

MADDIE
My mom has the same stretch marks that aren't from a kid.

                    ELLIOT
                  Oh my god.

Maddie turns toward Elliot. She's obviously flustered, her energy
pulled inward, her relaxed and high demeanor of a moment before
completely gone. Maddie takes her hands. He moves his head down
           and to the left so he's in her line of vision.

                    MADDIE
                  It's cool.

                    ELLIOT
                  I should go.

                    MADDIE
                  Shut up.

                    ELLIOT
              This was a mistake.

                    MADDIE
                  I like kids.

                    ELLIOT
           (gathering her purse) Sorry.

                    MADDIE
                    Stop.

Maddie grabs her wrist. The sudden movement seems to startle them
                     both.

                MADDIE (CONT'D)
Here's what we're going to do: we're going to trust each other.

                    ELLIOT
                  Oh Jesus...

                    MADDIE
I'll trust that this is the best time of my life. And you'll trust
me that once you hit a certain hazily defined age, you're not out
                   of options.

                    ELLIOT
        That's the cheesiest thing I've ever heard.

> MADDIE

Then why don't you just let yourself have fun with a boy in his peak physical condition and let everything else fall where it may.

CLOSE UP of Elliot. She rolls her eyes, but her mouth is smiling. It appears like she wants to protest, either like she really thinks it's a horrible idea or she wants to be complimented and reassured some more.

She takes the joint from Maddie's fingers and exits the car.

EXT. MLK PARK - CONTINUOUS

Elliot walks through the snow toward the swings. She's mostly a shadow with a glowing ember. The dome light from Maddie's car comes on as he opens and closes the door. Elliot brushes off a swing and sits.

From Elliot's POV, we see Maddie walking toward her.

> ELLIOT

So you're okay with being a teenage fuck toy?

> MADDIE
> (laughing)

If you're okay with being a twenty-something MILF.

> ELLIOT

But not a cougar?

> MADDIE

Most definitely a cougar.

Maddie sits on the swing next to Elliot.

> MADDIE (CONT'D)
> Freezing.

> ELLIOT
> Pussy.

> MADDIE

If I'm such a pussy, why can I swing higher than you?

Maddie starts to pump his legs. Elliot laughs. Maddie taunts her. She's shaking her head, trying to catch up. Soon, both are pumping their legs, swinging almost perpendicular to the top of the swing, laughing and screaming like children.

INT. ROSEVILLE MALL - SANTA'S WORKSHOP - DAY

Children are running around screaming and laughing. Plastic candy canes line the little path from the mass of people waiting. Christmas music plays. A child picks his nose. A little girl pulls her green and red dress over her head.

Elliot stands in line with Ed and Terry Svendson behind her, and Jacob, her dark-haired and serious three-year-old, in front of her. She bends over and whispers something and he looks up, then over at Santa, and in a resigned way, shuffles over toward Santa's throne.

From Jacob's POV, we walk toward Santa, who appears somewhat terrifying, more old than jolly, his felt suit thread-worn and speckled with facial dander.

Jacob sits on Santa's lap.

SANTA
What is your name, little boy?

Jacob stares up at Santa. He looks back at Elliot, who appears to be flustered. She's kneeling over, glancing up over the candy-cane wreaths surrounding Santa's Workshop.

Maddie walks by.

SANTA (CONT'D)
What do you want for Christmas?

Jacob's bottom lip is quivering. His right hand tightens its grip on the crotch of his corduroys.

Terry Svendson, seeing her grandson about to lose it, nudges a crouching Elliot to go help her son. Elliot loses her balance, making several desperate crab-like crawls forward until she completely loses her balance and topples over. She knocks down a section of the candy-cane fencing. Everybody looks.

From Maddie's POV, we see Elliot sprawled out across Santa's Workshop.

MADDIE
Elliot?

ELLIOT
Busted.

Jacob gets off Santa's lap. He seems to have composed himself, and maybe is even embarrassed for his mother. He stands looking over her. Terry and Ed have joined the standing and staring as well.

JACOB
Mom, get up.

TERRY
Cheese and crackers, Elle, get off the floor.

Maddie helps Elliot off the floor. She's mortified. Maddie's all politeness and stifled smiles.

JACOB
Who are you?

MADDIE
Maddie. Who are you?

JACOB
Jacob.

MADDIE
Pretty cool name.
Jacob shrugs.

ELLIOT
Why don't you go with Grandma and Grandpa and I'll catch up with—

ED
(extending his hand to Maddie)
Ed Svendson.

MADDIE
Madison Johnson.

TERRY
Ahh, Maddie. Yes, we were starting to suspect you weren't real.

ELLIOT
Oh my God, kill me.

MADDIE

And likewise to the three of you. It's a pleasure.

TERRY

See, Elle, he wanted to meet us.

JACOB

A bitch is a bitch is a bitch.

ELLIOT

Jacob.

MADDIE

Is that so, little man?

ED

So what is it you do?

MADDIE

I work at a store here. But I'm in school, at the U, studying film.

ED

A Gopher, huh?

MADDIE

Bleed maroon and gold.

ELLIOT

All right, we should be going.

Terry mouths, "He's cute," to Elliot.

JACOB

I'm going to be a stand-up comedian when I'm your age.

MADDIE

Rad. Let's hear a joke.

JACOB

Knock-knock.

MADDIE

Who's there?

JACOB

Queen.

                    MADDIE
                  Queen who?

                    JACOB
              Queen my dishes, please.

                    MADDIE
              (laughing) Clever, my man.

Jacob smiles and looks up at Elliot, who, for the first time during
the interaction, appears not to be in the midst of a panic attack.

                     ED
                 Play any sports?

                    MADDIE
         All-State third baseman in high school.

                     ED
             (whistling) Bat right or left?

                    MADDIE
      Right, thus the reason I'm not playing in college.

                     ED
         Still, All-State is nothing to sneeze at.

                    TERRY
      You should join us for dinner at Olive Garden.

                    MADDIE
           You going for a Tour of Italy?

Terry slaps Ed's arm in disbelief.

                    TERRY
            My all-time favorite dish.

                    MADDIE
              Tell me about it.

                    ELLIOT
               He's busy, Mom.

                    JACOB
        Why'd the chicken cross the road?

                    ELLIOT
              That's enough, honey.

                    MADDIE
                     Why?

                    JACOB
        To get a boneless eight-pack at KFC.

           Maddie laughs, this one real.

                     ED
Come on, Terry, he doesn't want to be eating with us. Why don't
                 you two go out?

                    JACOB
How many Wisconsin people does it take to change a light bulb?

                    TERRY
       You're right, go you two, get out of here.

                    ELLIOT
              I'm sure he's busy —

                    MADDIE
I'd love to. What time would you like your beautiful daughter home?

                     ED
           (smiling) Before midnight.

                    MADDIE
         (extending his hand again) Done.

Maddie sticks out his elbow for Elliot to take. She reluctantly
does. Terry takes Jacob's hand. They say their goodbyes and Maddie
and Elliot start in the opposite direction. Maddie stops.

                MADDIE (CONT'D)
               Hey, little man.

           Jacob turns, smiling.

                MADDIE (CONT'D)
You didn't finish your joke. How many does it take?

                         JACOB
                       (beaming)
        Zero. They wait for someone from Minnesota to do it for them.

                EXT. WINTER CARNIVAL - LATER

        Maddie and Elliot hold glove-covered hands as they walk toward an
                    enormous palace made out of ice.

        Families are everywhere. Kids in snowsuits play tag. Huge
        multi-colored spotlights illuminate the translucent walls of the
        ice palace. Vendors sell roasted nuts and hot chocolate.

                         MADDIE
        My mom used to take me here every year. Used to pretend it was
                          our palace.

                         ELLIOT
                         Palace?

                         MADDIE
                      Yeah, palace.

                         ELLIOT
                Most boys would say castle.

                         MADDIE
                Most boys aren't named Maddie.

                INT. ICE PALACE - CONTINUOUS

        Maddie and Elliot stand in the entryway of the palace. The walls
        are easily four stories tall. Voices of children echo off the cav-
        ernous structure. Rows of ice sculptures line the entrance hall.

        Elliot walks around a sculpture of an immaculately carved woman.
        The sculpture is naked, curled around a baby. Elliot takes off her
        glove. She runs her fingers over the sculpture's face, then the
                 forehead of the baby. Her fingers glisten.

                         MADDIE
                We'd pick out which rooms were ours.

                         ELLIOT
                   Like *The Mighty Ducks*.

>   MADDIE
>   What?

>   ELLIOT
>   They do that in the movie... Never mind.

>   MADDIE
>   No, they don't.

>   ELLIOT
>   They do.

>   MADDIE
> Listen, I know a thing or two about the flying V and the mighty
>   ducks man himself, and they don't do that shit in the movie.

Elliot gets on her tiptoes and kisses Maddie. She takes his arm.

>   ELLIOT
>   Show me around.

They walk away from the sculptures, away from the crowds. It gets
darker the farther they travel into one of the castle's wings. They
appear small compared to the walls. Soon they're alone, tucked
into a small room.

>   MADDIE
>   This is the help's quarters.

>   ELLIOT
>   Paid or indentured?

>   MADDIE
>   Slave, I think.

Elliot laughs. She sits down, leaning her head against the wall.

From Elliot's POV, we see the vastness of the vaulted ice ceiling.
Floodlights change the ice from black to pink to purple to green.
Still in her POV, we focus on Maddie. He's smiling. We see Elliot's
hand motion for him to join her, which he does.

We're back to seeing the wall of ice looming above us.

>   ELLIOT
>   Who are you, anyway?

MADDIE

What do you mean?

ELLIOT

All that about going to the U. The Tour of Italy. They love you.

MADDIE

All parents do.

ELLIOT

Was that directed at me?

MADDIE

(Beat)

He's a sweet kid. Smart as hell, can tell.

ELLIOT

The love of my life.

MADDIE

Not his father?

ELLIOT

Tried to convince myself, but no.

MADDIE

What happened?

ELLIOT

Caught him eating the pussy of one of his freshman students.

MADDIE

High school?

ELLIOT

College.

MADDIE

Still fucked up.

ELLIOT

Fuck him.

MADDIE

You're supposed to say that, but you don't have to. My mom was the

same way. Always fronting like she didn't care my dad slept with
every girl he saw. Nothing wrong with admitting hurt.

> ELLIOT
> Back to my original question: who
> are you?

An OVERHEAD view of the two of them lying on the ice floor. Elliot
has brought Maddie's hand to her chest. Maddie's smiling as if he
knows he's saying all the right things.

> MADDIE
> I'm not following.

> ELLIOT
> Bullshit, you're not.

> MADDIE
> (laughing) Serious.

> ELLIOT
> Want me to say it?

> MADDIE
> (grinning) Say what?

Elliot leans over and kisses Maddie forcefully.

> MADDIE (CONT'D)
> Still not following.

The CAMERA goes back to the view of the arching ice wall.

> ELLIOT
> Where were you five years ago?

> MADDIE
> In diapers.

> ELLIOT
> (laughing) Dick.

> MADDIE
> It's not too late, you know?

> ELLIOT
> What isn't?

MADDIE
Everything.

ELLIOT
Thanks, Socrates.

MADDIE
Life. Family. Love.

ELLIOT
Hold the phone, cowboy.

MADDIE
You mean my horse?

ELLIOT
Whatever.

MADDIE
Why?

ELLIOT
Can we not?

MADDIE
Tell me you don't feel it.

ELLIOT
I don't feel it.

MADDIE
I'm not going to cheat.

ELLIOT
So we're exclusive?

MADDIE
Fact.

ELLIOT
I can deal with that.

MADDIE
Because I lo —

ELLIOT
Don't say that.

                    MADDIE
                    I do.

                    ELLIOT
              Just don't say it.

                    MADDIE
              Fine. I don't you.

                    ELLIOT
                  (laughing)
              I don't you, either.

The CAMERA loses focus in the cascade of lights.

              FADE TO YELLOW:

                  MADDIE (V.O.)
Shit seemed infinite at that moment. Everything. Completely end-
                     less.

          INT. HOSPITAL ROOM - NIGHT

The CAMERA backs away from the multicolored lights, focusing on a
miniature Christmas tree. The beeping of hospital machines sounds
                  rhythmically.

                  MADDIE (V.O.)
That was before Elliot's dumb-fuck husband trailed me home from
                     work.

                    CUT TO:
          EXT. THE JOHNSON'S FRONT DOOR - NIGHT

Maddie stands next to his mother in front of their red door. Devon,
the forty-year-old, slightly chubby and lightly bearded husband of
Elliot, stands at the base of the three stone steps. He's pointing
                  a finger at Maddie.

                  MADDIE (V.O.)
                   And said:

                    DEVON
     (his mouth is moving, but it's Maddie's voice)
     I'm the husband of the wife your son's fucking.

                    CUT TO:

INT. HOSPITAL ROOM - CONTINUOUS

The CAMERA pans from Maddie sitting in an uncomfortable chair to
the small hanging television. The monitor shows black-and-white
footage of what appears to be a security tape from a clothing
store. There's no sound. A woman comes storming into the store and
starts screaming and waving her hand at another woman. The first
woman slaps her. Then there's a tussle, and the attacking woman
        falls headfirst into the metal edge of a clothing rack.

                          MADDIE (V.O.)
And before my mom flipped her shit and attacked Elliot at Talbots.

The CAMERA pans to the hospital bed. Mrs. Johnson is dressed in
a hospital gown. She has a bandage wrapped around the right side
of her forehead. A wispy man dressed in black applies makeup to
what little of her face isn't covered in gauze. There are three
spotlights set up around the bed. The man backs away, and motions
with his finger to Mrs. Johnson, who speaks into a rolling camera.

                          MADDIE (V.O.)
                Before my mom told the world that:

                          MRS. JOHNSON
                (moving her lips, but Maddie's voice)
                Elliot Svendson raped my son.

The CAMERA focuses on Maddie sitting in the chair. The news crew
        is gone and it's back to the beeping of monitors.

                          MADDIE (V.O.)
Before Elliot turned herself in. Before I called my mom a miserable
cunt. Before I was sent to Des Moines to finish my senior year with
                          my father.

                          CUT TO:
                INT. MR. JOHNSON'S TOYOTA - MORNING

Maddie sits shotgun, staring out of the window at snow-covered
                          cornfields.

                          CUT TO:
                EXT. COMO LAKE - MORNING

Maddie stands there with his busted lip. He's holding the revolver. Sirens can be heard in the background, as well as the cries
                          of a baby.

Beat.

ELLIOT (O.C.)
Maddie, please.

MADDIE (V.O.)
Before any of that shit.

MADDIE (V.O.)
It was a perfect moment.

CUT TO:

INT. ICE PALACE - NIGHT

CLOSE UP of Maddie and Elliot. They're both smiling as wide as possible.

MADDIE
I don't you.

ELLIOT
I don't you, either.

CUT TO:

EXT. COMO LAKE - CONTINUOUS

Maddie rubs his busted lip with the hand holding the revolver. We hear the sirens and cries and Elliot begging.

MADDIE (V.O.)
It was before I was even thinking about beginnings. Before I ever contemplated walking away.

INT. MR. JOHNSON'S KITCHEN - NIGHT

Mr. Johnson scoops store-bought mashed potatoes out of a plastic tray. He's an attractive man, or rather has the appearance of once having been attractive, now doughy around a strong jawline. He wears slacks with a polo shirt tucked in. He's tired but trying to be upbeat. He opens the plastic container for a whole rotisserie chicken and rips off a leg and thigh and places them on two separate plates.

Maddie stands across from the kitchen island. The condo kitchen has the feeling of being too small for both of them.

Mr. Johnson hands over a plate and motions with his head to the adjoining room.

INT. MR. JOHNSON'S TV ROOM - CONTINUOUS

The TV room is exactly that, a room with a sectional couch and a flat-screen TV. It feels sterile, inhabited but not stylized. Mr. Johnson turns on the TV. A college football game plays. They stare at the TV and eat from the plates on their laps.

> MR. JOHNSON
> Good, right?

> MADDIE
> Yeah, it's good.

They sit there eating and watching TV.

INT. MR. JOHNSON'S GUEST ROOM - LATER

Maddie moves aside golf clubs in the closet to hang a few shirts. He places his hi-tops next to the sliding closet door. The room, like the rest of the condo, lacks any sense of personality. The lamp light shines against the white walls making them an ugly yellowish cream.

Mr. Johnson knocks on the door frame.

> MADDIE
> Yeah.

> MR. JOHNSON
> You have enough space?

> MADDIE
> Yeah.

> MR. JOHNSON
> Bed seem okay? Used to be mine, good quality, a queen. You have a queen at your mom's?

> MADDIE
> A full.

> MR. JOHNSON
> Moving on up.

>   MADDIE
>   (nodding)
>   Yup.

Mr. Johnson looks around the room. He's smiling, but it's a bit
forced and pained.

>   MR. JOHNSON
> Feel free to decorate the walls. Posters, album covers...probably
> don't have those anymore, but you know what I mean.

>   MADDIE
>   Okay.

>   MR. JOHNSON
>   This will be good. A fresh start.

>   Beat.

>   MR. JOHNSON (CONT'D)
>   A couple of bachelors living the dream.

Mr. Johnson laughs. Maddie doesn't. Mr. Johnson taps the doorframe
again.

>   MR. JOHNSON (CONT'D)
>   Well...

>   MADDIE
>   Yeah, night.

Mr. Johnson hesitates, unsure if he should try to speak to his son
anymore. He waits an awkward moment before closing the door.

Maddie sits on his bed. He pulls his laptop out and opens it up.

CLOSE UP of computer. Maddie searches "Elliot Svendson." A long
list comes up. He scrolls through various "statutory rape" head-
lines. He clicks on a picture of Elliot. She's climbing into her
Tacoma outside of her parent's home. She wears her knee-length
coat with faux fur around the collar. The angle of her face makes
her seem older, weathered.

CLOSE UP of Maddie's face. His eyes are straining, fighting to
blink, then finally close.

>   CUT TO:
> INT. PSYCHOLOGIST'S OFFICE - MORNING

CLOSE UP of Maddie's face. He opens his eyes. His face is relaxed, maybe high. The CAMERA backs up, showing him sitting on a leather chair. He's wearing a thin gray cardigan, but dressing it down with black skinny jeans. He's giving off the the impression of aloofness but there's a hint of discomfort. The psychologist (same one from earlier) is wearing a gray skirt-suit. She crosses her legs. Her ankle bone rotates and then bounces.

> PSYCHOLOGIST
> How are you feeling about being here to see me?

> MADDIE
> Fine.

> PSYCHOLOGIST
> What does that feel like to you?

> MADDIE
> Okay. Not great but not horrible. I don't know. Fine.

> PSYCHOLOGIST
> How is the transition going for you?

> MADDIE
> From what to what?

> PSYCHOLOGIST
> The Twin Cities to Des Moines.

> MADDIE
> (smirking)
> Same city, really. Interstates and subdivisions. Malls with the same stores. Chili's and TGIFs and Olive Gardens.

> PSYCHOLOGIST
> That's an astute observation.

> MADDIE
> That's a bit of condescension.

> PSYCHOLOGIST
> (frowns)
> That wasn't my intention. In fact, I was giving you a compliment.

> MADDIE
> For an obvious observation, which you said was astute, thus coming across as condescending.

The psychologist nods her head, letting the phony frown dissipate. She jots a note.

                          PSYCHOLOGIST
           How does it feel being away from your friends?

                             MADDIE
                       (shrugs) Sucks, I guess.

                          PSYCHOLOGIST
         How does the idea of making new friends make you feel?

                             MADDIE
                Not much of anything. Annoyed, maybe.

                          PSYCHOLOGIST
                           Why's that?

                             MADDIE
     Because it's something I don't want to have to do. I mean, I know
                    it won't be hard, but still...

                          PSYCHOLOGIST
                           It's scary?

                             MADDIE
     No, not at all. I'm attractive and do drugs and make people laugh,
       which is all you need in high school, college too. Maybe life.
     People want to be around me. Not worried about "making friends."
     It's just annoying because this whole fucking thing's annoying. A
                       waste of time. Unnecessary.

                          PSYCHOLOGIST
                           Why's that?

                             MADDIE
     Because she's in fucking jail. Because I'm not some "rape victim."
     Because it's my mom's own fault she went and bashed her head into
     that metal pole. But I'm the one who has to move to the one state
                       shittier than Minnesota.

                          PSYCHOLOGIST
                  You're the one being punished.

                             MADDIE
                             Right.

> PSYCHOLOGIST
> Does living with your father feel like punishment?

> MADDIE
> You've talked to him, right?

> PSYCHOLOGIST
> Yes.

> MADDIE
> So yeah, you know.

The psychologist smiles. She makes direct eye contact with Maddie. She holds the smile for a beat longer than normal.

> MADDIE (CONT'D)
> The whole thing is like a sitcom. The bachelor gets his teenage son and hilarity ensues. But there's nothing funny about a man who has no idea how to be a father trying to be a father for the first time in ten years.

> PSYCHOLOGIST
> Like you're being punished all over again for the divorce?

> MADDIE
> No, we're not doing that.

> PSYCHOLOGIST
> What?

> MADDIE
> Connecting shaky Freudian dots.

EXT. WEST DES MOINES HIGH SCHOOL ENTRANCE - MORNING

The high school is a two-story brick rectangle. Windows are scarcely inserted at odd intervals. WILDCATS is painted in red above the glass doors of the entrance. A light snow falls. Students shuffle in. Maddie walks behind them, his hood up, backpack slung over his shoulder.

INT. SCHOOL HALLWAY - CONTINUOUS

From Maddie's POV, we walk down a linoleum hallway. The walls are lined with red lockers. It's crowded with the normal mix of

high school kids (jocks, skaters, sluts, nerds, prom queens). The
CAMERA is jostled every so often when somebody bumps into Maddie.

As we travel down the hallway, we notice more and more people dou-
ble-taking Maddie. A skater-hipster gives a head nod. A grouping
of three party girls give the CAMERA an up and down, the tallest
giving a suggestive smile.

INT. ROOM 113 - CONTINUOUS

Still from Maddie's first-person POV, we look at a printed schedule, then the green stenciled plate above the brick door.

We enter. The room is thirty-deep with students. They're sitting
in small desks, some of which have broken hinges on the fold-over
section of the desk. A male teacher, mid-forties, chubby, has his
back turned to Maddie as he tries to plug in the cord for his
projection screen connected to an ancient-looking Dell.

We walk down an aisle. Students stare, some smiling, some nodding,
some just dumbly blank. There's an empty desk next to a brunette,
dressed hip if not a touch slutty with a white cami and gray jeans,
black glasses with her bangs flat across her forehead.

Break from Maddie's POV to a shot of Maddie sitting in the desk
next to her. She's looking over at him.

MADDIE
Hey.

RACHEL
Hey.

MADDIE
Maddie.

RACHEL
Rachel.

MADDIE
I know.

RACHEL
(smiling) Huh?

MADDIE
The artsy hip girl sitting in the back sketching pictures of Midwestern mediocrity. Probably early decision to NYU.

Rachel laughs and shakes her head.

                    RACHEL
And you're the jock turned stoner who comes to a new school when
Mommy found your stash of custie-priced nuggets who thinks he's
                better than everyone else.

                    MADDIE
                More or less.

                    Beat.

                    RACHEL
            (laughing) Yeah, me too.

                RACHEL (CONT'D)
              But RISD, not NYU.

              MONTAGE - VARIOUS
        (Modest Mouse's "Custom Concern" plays)

A) INT. MAILBOXES ETC - DUSK - Maddie's at the Formica counter fill-
ing out a form for a PO box. A balding man, too young to be bald,
walks Maddie over to a wall of PO boxes. He demonstrates how to
        open the door, then hands over the little key.

B) INT - DES MOINES WEST MALL - DAY - Maddie walks through the mall.
He turns into Zumiez. He walks to the counter and hands over an
application to a twenty-five-year-old guy behind the counter. The
        guy looks it over, nodding, raising his eyebrows.

C) INT. MR. JOHNSON'S GUEST ROOM - NIGHT - Maddie sits on the bed.
He licks an envelope. He writes: ATTN: Elliot Svendson. Shakopee
                County Jail.

D) INT. HIGH SCHOOL CAFETERIA - DAY - The cafeteria is full of
students shouting and joking, the calls of the insecure as they
vie for attention. The CAMERA moves down the rows of rectangular
tables. Maddie sits among the hip/popular crowd. He's telling a
story, everyone laughing, hanging on his every word. He turns to
Rachel, who's sitting directly to his right. He says something and
            she explodes laughing and hits his arm.

E) INT. MR. JOHNSON's TV ROOM - NIGHT - Maddie and Mr. Johnson sit
there in a darkened room. They're both holding plates on their

laps. The TV casts blue light on their faces. Neither are talking or even making the effort to.

F) INT. ICE PALACE - NIGHT - An OVERHEAD shot of Maddie and Elliot's faces. Maddie's mouth says, "I don't you." Elliot's mouth says, "I don't you, either."

G) INT. PSYCHOLOGIST'S OFFICE - DAY - Maddie's talking on the leather chair. The psychologist is nodding emphatically.

H) EXT. PARKING LOT OF WEST DES MOINES MALL - NIGHT - A group of teenage boys skate underneath the parking lot lights.

They still wear sweatshirts and pants and beanies, but it's obvious the weather has changed, warmed, snow no longer covering the ground. A CLOSE SHOT of Maddie skating. He prepares for a trick, his face all concentration. He approaches a set of four stairs by the loading dock. He kick-flips off the stairs, landing with a slight wobble.

I) INT. MR. JOHNSON'S GUEST ROOM - NIGHT - Maddie writes a letter by hand to a dim light.

J) EXT. PARTY - NIGHT - Maddie sits in a lawn chair surrounded by his peers. They wear short sleeves. They pass pipes. Rachel saunters over, her red plastic cup raised above her head as she sits in Maddie's lap. She drunkenly whispers something in his ear.

K) INT. MAILBOXES ETC - DUSK - Maddie opens his PO box. It's empty. He slams it shut.

L) INT. PSYCHOLOGIST'S OFFICE - DAY - Maddie is speaking, using his hands to reiterate his points. The CAMERA switches to his POV, and we see the psychologist nodding in a manner that conveys empathy and maybe something more. She uncrosses her legs, pausing for the briefest of seconds with her black pencil skirt spread open, in which we see a flash of her vagina, then she crosses her other leg at the knee.

M) INT. MR. JOHNSON'S GUEST ROOM - NIGHT - Maddie reads old articles about Elliot.

N) INT. PARTY BEDROOM - NIGHT - Maddie and Rachel are kissing, Rachel walks backward toward a bed shaped like a race car. They fumble with shirts and belts. There's a yellow night light illuminating the toddler's room. Rachel has her legs spread, and guides Maddie into her.

O) INT. ICE PALACE - NIGHT - CLOSE UP of Elliot and Maddie. Elliot inches over and places her head on his chest. He puts his arm around her. He presses his face to her hat-covered head.

END OF MONTAGE

EXT. HIGH SCHOOL GRADUATION - MORNING

The West Des Moines High School football field is covered in folding chairs. A stage is set up at the fifty-yard line.
About five hundred students sit in the chairs dressed in black robes.

CLOSE UP of Maddie. He's high, smiling, the sun shining down on him. Something about him suggests freedom.

Beat.

COMMENCEMENT SPEAKER (O.C.)
Some of you will go on to have wildly successful careers. Some of you will become captains of industry. Some of you will help feed our nation. Others will invent new technology, create beautiful art, cure the sick, help the needy. Some of you will raise families.

COMMENCEMENT SPEAKER (CONT'D)
But all of you, and I mean every single one of you, will look back at your time spent in this high school and wish you'd done something differently. Taken a certain chance. Tried a little harder. Been kinder to a peer.

CLOSE UP of Maddie, who rolls his eyes.

COMMENCEMENT SPEAKER (CONT'D)
My challenge to all of you is to feel this regret — go ahead, really feel it right this instant — and now, go forward into your new lives with this memory of regret, let it shape you into a better person.

INT. THE CHEESECAKE FACTORY - LATER

Maddie, Mr. Johnson, and Mrs. Johnson sit around a table. They seem stiff, formal in their movements. Mrs. Johnson won't look at Mr. Johnson, but only at her food and Maddie. She keeps squeezing his arm like her pride is too much to contain.

MR. JOHNSON

Didn't think I'd ever see the day.

MRS. JOHNSON

Didn't think you would either.

Maddie shoots his mother a please stop look. She smiles. There's
a faint scar above her eye.

MR. JOHNSON

Proud of you.

MRS. JOHNSON

We both are.

MADDIE

Takes a bit of an idiot not to finish high school.

MRS. JOHNSON

But to get a 3.5 average? To get into the U? Especially with all
the other stuff —

MR. JOHNSON

Which is why your mother and I splurged and got you a present.

Maddie tries not to smile, but he can't help it.

MR. JOHNSON (CONT'D)

Now, it's not the most exciting of presents, but —

MRS. JOHNSON

It's a thousand times better.

MR. JOHNSON

The new American Dream.

MADDIE
(laughing)
Enough already, spit it out.

MRS. JOHNSON
(grinning)
Your father and I are going to pay for your entire college education. You won't have to take out a single cent of student loans.

Maddie shakes his head. It's unclear if he's extremely grateful or maybe disappointed. Maddie looks up from his steak, and he's not crying, but close, flushed around the cheeks, his eyes glassy.

> MADDIE
> You guys can't.

> MR. JOHNSON
> Shut up and say thank you.

> MADDIE
> (nodding) Thank you.

Maddie gets up from his chair and hugs his mother first, then his father. They all sit back down. The energy has changed.
The tension of marital failure and resentment has dissipated, if only temporarily. They eat. Maddie pauses, looks at his father, then his mother.

> MADDIE (CONT'D)
> This is nice.

> MR. JOHNSON
> Proud of you.

> MRS. JOHNSON
> So proud of you.

> MADDIE
> No; I mean this... Together.
> (motioning to the three of them eating at the same table)

Instantly, the body language of Mrs. Johnson jolts back to resentful rigidity. Mr. Johnson places his napkin on the table.

> MR. JOHNSON
> The guy giving the commencement speech, he wasn't all wrong, you know?

Maddie stares at his father. Mrs. Johnson arranges her fork and knife to three o'clock on her plate.

> MR. JOHNSON (CONT'D)
> Every life has one major regret.
> (looking across the table at Mrs. Johnson, then turning to Maddie)
> You'd be among the lucky few if that regret was already behind you.

EXT. CORN FIELD PARTY - DUSK

The CAMERA is at a BIRD'S-EYE view of squares of corn fields separated by straight roads. The occasional farmhouse register as a
blip. There's a change of color, green vegetation of trees next
to a circular lake/pond. There are close to a hundred cars parked
along the road. The moving bodies are like ants.

The CAMERA pans at GROUND LEVEL. The recent graduates are engaging
in all forms of debauchery. One drunken kid keeps ripping up his
graduation gown, flashing his stubby penis.

Couples make out. A girl pukes. Others shoot off bottle rockets.

EXT. THE HOOD OF MADDIE'S CIVIC - LATER

The party is still raging in the background. Maddie and Rachel sit
on the hood of his Civic. They pass a pipe back and forth.

                    RACHEL
          (speaking with smoke in her lungs)
    This will be the best moment of half of their lives.

                    MADDIE
              Depressing.

                    RACHEL
              It will.

                    MADDIE
              But not yours?

                    RACHEL
    Getting rejected everywhere but the shitty U of M, so maybe.

                    MADDIE
              (faking insult)
    How dare you talk about my future alma mater like that.

                    RACHEL
              Least it's out of Iowa.

                    MADDIE
              True.

                    RACHEL
    But I'll be motherfucked if this is the best night of my life.

MADDIE
Word.

RACHEL
FYI, you're not Black.

MADDIE
Have you seen the size of my dick?

RACHEL
(laughing)
Not only have I seen it, it's been inside of me, which makes my
statement about your race all the more true.

They laugh, then are silent. They stare out at the pond.

RACHEL (CONT'D)
What's your regret?

MADDIE
Why's everyone so into that speech?

RACHEL
What is it?

MADDIE
(shrugging) Have no idea.

RACHEL
That you're kind of a liar?

MADDIE
How do you figure?

RACHEL
Just don't know why you couldn't have told me.

MADDIE
Told you what?

RACHEL
Took me all of five minutes on Google to figure out you're the un-
named rape victim. Then I saw your mom today, and she matches the
thousand pictures online.

Maddie holds the glass pipe. He thinks, takes a hit, then another.

                    MADDIE
            What would that have done?

                    RACHEL
Telling me? Gee, I don't know, maybe it would've been the truth,
      which is usually how you engage with friends.

                    MADDIE
            I'm...sorry, I guess.

                    RACHEL
          (laughing) Sounds like it.

                    MADDIE
      Just wasn't trying to be that kid, you know?

                    RACHEL
            The raped one?

                    MADDIE
            (laughing) Yeah.

                    RACHEL
              Was it?

                    MADDIE
              Rape? No.

                    RACHEL
            Did you love her?

Maddie nods, not looking at Rachel.

                RACHEL (CONT'D)
            Explains so much.

                    MADDIE
              How so?

                    RACHEL
That you didn't fall all over this. (looks herself up and down)
Thought maybe you liked dick, which is totally cool if you do, but—

                    MADDIE
      We had sex. Did you forget that fact?

                              RACHEL
Once. And even a guy who loves getting pounded can convince himself
                   that a pussy is an asshole.

They laugh. Rachel knocks out the cashed bowl against the sole of
                        her Converse.

                        RACHEL (CONT'D)
                        How'd it end?

                              MADDIE
                        What's yours?

                              RACHEL
              She just went to jail, and it was over?

                              MADDIE
                       No, your turn.

                              RACHEL
                (pretending to be lost in thought)
Probably that Glee exists and completely ruined our actual glee
club with idiots thinking they could sing their way to stardom.

                              MADDIE
                        Serious.

                              RACHEL
                    (shaking her head)
Would you have done it differently, I mean like knowing what you do
                now, how it all turned out?

Maddie takes a second to respond.

                              MADDIE
                           No.

                              RACHEL
             I thought I would. But not anymore.

                              MADDIE
              Still talking about your glee club?

                              RACHEL
You know, when you first walked into English, I had this feeling.

MADDIE

Between your legs?

RACHEL

(ignoring him)

Like finally, fucking finally there was a guy I could relate to, you know.

(MORE)

RACHEL (CONT'D)

Like this vision of us together taking on the bullshit of high school in Iowa.

MADDIE

Rach, I'm sorry, I just wasn't ready for —

RACHEL

(shushing him with her hand)

Not looking for an apology. I think I realized it wasn't going to happen way before we ever slept together, but I thought maybe if we fucked, maybe if we hung out more, maybe if...

Maddie puts his arm around Rachel. She doesn't seem to register his touch, still staring straight ahead.

RACHEL (CONT'D)

But when I found out I was pregnant, I knew, I just fucking knew it was never going to be a thing.

MADDIE

(panic registering on his face)

Wait? What the fuck are you saying? Are you pregnant?

RACHEL

No.

MADDIE

Did you get an...

RACHEL

(shakes her head)

Chemical miscarriage like a week later.

MADDIE

Was it mine?

                         RACHEL
                          Yeah.

                         MADDIE
                       And you're...

                         RACHEL
                      Not pregnant.

                         MADDIE
              I had no... Why didn't you tell me?

                         RACHEL
                 That was it. My big regret.

                         MADDIE
                Why didn't you say anything?

                         RACHEL
         But maybe that guy giving the speech today was wrong.

Rachel slides off the hood of the car. She takes off her sweatshirt
and lets it fall to the dirt. She kicks off her shoes. She turns
back to Maddie. She's illuminated by a nearly full moon. She takes
               off her cami. Then her bra.

                      RACHEL (CONT'D)
It happened like it was supposed to. I'll always be connected to
you, but not part of your life in any meaningful way, which I'm
                   completely cool with.

                         MADDIE
                       Come here.

                         RACHEL
And that's the problem with regret: there's nothing you can do
differently, not in the past, not in the future. You don't learn
                  shit from it. It just is.

Rachel turns and walks into the pond, wadding up to her waist
                  before fully submerging.

                INT. PSYCHOLOGIST'S OFFICE - DAY

The psychologist absentmindedly taps the end of her pen against her
chest, which shows a questionably appropriate amount of cleavage.

PSYCHOLOGIST
How did this news make you feel?

MADDIE
I don't know. Horrible. Relieved. Guilty.

Beat.

MADDIE (CONT'D)
Angry for some reason.

PSYCHOLOGIST
That Rachel kept this news from you?

MADDIE
I guess.

PSYCHOLOGIST
Why is that?

MADDIE
Because...I don't know. I mean, I didn't want a kid, don't want a
kid, but it's like the girl holds all the power. I'm going about
my life and have no idea everything could change.

PSYCHOLOGIST
A sense of powerlessness.

MADDIE
Exactly.

PSYCHOLOGIST
Because she just as easily could've had the child.

MADDIE
Yeah.
(adjusting in the leather chair)
I mean, it worked itself out on its own with the whole miscarriage
thing, but yeah.

PSYCHOLOGIST
I'm sensing some hesitation on your part. Do you believe her?

MADDIE
About the pregnancy?

PSYCHOLOGIST

Sure, both about the pregnancy and the cause of its termination.

MADDIE

What? Yeah. I don't know. Yeah, Rachel won't lie about that.

The psychologist nods. She adjusts herself in her seat. A quick
CLOSE UP of her inner thigh from Maddie's POV.

PSYCHOLOGIST

You'd be amazed at what women are willing to lie about in order to
get what they think they want.

INT. MAILBOXES ECT. - NIGHT

Maddie opens up his PO box. There's a single letter in a white
envelope. He rips open the top. It's a handwritten note, and all
we see is "Dear Maddie" before Maddie closes the PO box and rushes
out to his car.

INT. MADDIE'S CAR - LATER

He's driving past strip malls. The lights of fast-food restaurants
and check-cashing depots cast neon on his face.

ELLIOT (V.O.)

There's really no words for this. It sounds cliche, but it's true.
There's not a single thing I can say that reiterates and conveys
exactly how I feel. But I'll try.

A light mist is falling. There's traffic. Maddie struggles to make
his way into a left turn lane, then runs a questionably yellow
light.

ELLIOT (V.O.)

I'm sorry. I'm so fucking sorry. I'm sorry like I've never been for
a single thing in my life and like you'll never know. I'm sorry I
did what I did. Even though I thought you were eighteen, my actions
were completely fucked. You were a kid in many ways, and I robbed
you of something you won't realize until you're older.

Maddie speeds along a two-lane road. Walls of corn form a darkened
tunnel around him.

ELLIOT (V.O.)

I'm sorry I didn't respond to a single letter until now. I'm sorry my refusal to do so probably kept a bit of hope for us alive.

Maddie enters a residential area. The houses are all replicas of one another, some with garage front-left, others with garage front-right.

> ELLIOT (V.O.)
> I'm sorry that you became tangled up in my messy marriage. That I had to use you, not intentionally, but still to the same effect, to figure out I love Devon.

Maddie parks in front of a two-story home in a cul-de-sac. He flips up his hood and hurries out of the car.

> ELLIOT (V.O.)
> Our marriage isn't perfect, far from it, but I love him. I love my son. I love Devon's baby girl I'm carrying inside me.

EXT. RACHEL'S FRONT DOOR - CONTINUOUS

Maddie rings the doorbell. An ascending chime progression can be heard inside the house, followed by footsteps coming downstairs.

> ELLIOT (V.O.)
> That night in the ice palace, I didn't want you to say "love." It wasn't because I didn't feel the same thing, but because I knew, at some level, that I had to return to my family.

The door opens. Rachel stands there in leggings and an oversized sweatshirt. She smiles but then sees Maddie, and her face instant-ly turns to concern.

> ELLIOT (V.O.)
> Be well, Maddie. You'll make some girl happy beyond her wildest dreams.

> MADDIE
> Did it really happen?

> RACHEL
> What?

> MADDIE
> The pregnancy?

Rachels shushes him and pushes him outside of the doorway, closing the door behind her.

                    RACHEL
            What the... Be quiet.

                    MADDIE
                    Did it?

                    RACHEL
        Yes. But whatever. It's over, done, just be quiet.

                    MADDIE
                Did you get an...

Rachel's shaking her head. Her cheek pulls inward as she bites it.
            She's trying not to cry.

                MADDIE (CONT'D)
                    Why?

                    RACHEL
            What do you want from me?

                    MADDIE
To be there. To fucking be there. To smell your stale breath in
the morning and to listen to you snore. To fucking, like, I don't
        know, to do this, you know? Like really do it.

                    RACHEL
                What about —

                    MADDIE
That's my regret. Chasing something that wasn't there. Never was.
                While you're —

Rachel leans forward and kisses Maddie tenderly on the lips. She
        backs away, wiping tears from her eyes.

                    RACHEL
    That was the cheesiest fucking thing since *Sixteen Candles*.

                    MADDIE
                Fuck off and die.

                    RACHEL
                But I loved it.

                    MADDIE
                  Love you.

                    RACHEL
                 Love you too.

INT. CLASSROOM - DAY

Maddie sits in a large, stadium-tiered lecture hall. He has a
laptop open taking notes. He seems interested, excited.

                   PROFESSOR
The outlines for your scripts are due on Monday, so remember that
when you're debating between your second and third keg stand this
                    weekend.

The students all laugh. Maddie slips his computer into his backpack and files out of the class.

              EXT. COURTYARD - CONTINUOUS

It's fall, the leaves have turned, sweatshirt weather, slightly
overcast. Maddie walks among hundreds of others.

CLOSE UP of Maddie. He reaches into his pocket and pulls out his
phone. CLOSE UP of phone. It's a text message from Rachel: Get me
a sandwich and I'll make it worth ur while.

                Maddie laughs.

            INT. JIMMY JOHN'S - CONTINUOUS

Maddie walks through the door. Reggae plays. There's a small line
of people. He's texting as he stands in line.

                    ELLIOT
                    Maddie?

Maddie looks up, then to his left. Elliot sits at a two-person
table. She's wearing jeans and a wrap-sweater, her hair a touch
longer, her eyes darkened with the lack of sleep. She holds a
sandwich in one hand.

Maddie stares at her, unsure what to say or do.

                ELLIOT (CONT'D)
            Jesus, man, it's been forever.

Elliot stands. Maddie still hasn't moved. His normal composure is
shot.

ELLIOT (CONT'D)
Come here.

Elliot bridges the four-foot gap between them with her arms outstretched. She hugs Maddie.

CUT TO:
INT. ICE PALACE - NIGHT

CLOSE UP of Elliot's face buried in the nook of Maddie's neck.

MADDIE
I don't you.

ELLIOT
I don't you, either.

CUT TO:
INT. JIMMY JOHN'S - CONTINUOUS

Elliot lets go of Maddie. He stares, blinks, a tiny bit of composure creeping across his face.

MADDIE
Hey.

ELLIOT
Is for horses. Shit, it's good to see you. What are you doing here?

MADDIE
Umm, eating after class.

ELLIOT
Going to the U? Good for you, that's really rad.

MADDIE
What are...when'd you..how's...

ELLIOT
Running errands. July. Things are good.

MADDIE
Good. That's good.

ELLIOT
Yeah, totally. And you?

MADDIE
Fine.

ELLIOT
You look good, happy.

Maddie nods.

CLOSE UP of Elliot. She maybe doesn't look all that good herself.
It's hard to tell if it's exhaustion or depression. Random strands
of her hair slip across her face. She has bangs now, short ones
resting a good three inches above her eyebrows. Something severe
has happened to the skin around her face; it's tighter, stretched
across her cheekbones.

ELLIOT (CONT'D)
Pull up a chair.

Maddie glances at his phone, which has chimed with a new text. He
looks at Elliot.

MADDIE
I should be...

ELLIOT
(nodding) Yeah, totally.

MADDIE
But it was good seeing you.

ELLIOT
Totally.

MADDIE
Okay.

ELLIOT
Okay.

They stand there for an awkward beat. Elliot smiles, then Maddie
does.

ELLIOT (CONT'D)
Come here.

She hugs Maddie once again. This time Maddie isn't as shocked and pulls her with some force. The hug lasts a smidgen longer than normal.

                    ELLIOT (CONT'D)
              Call me sometime? Catch up?

                    MADDIE
                 Yeah, for sure.

          INT. RACHEL'S DORM ROOM - LATER

It's a double room, tiny, half of the room a page straight from the Target catalog with its plastic organizers and matching comforter and throw pillows, the other half messy and dark, cut-out pictures and taped drawings. Rachel sits on the bed on the messy side with her laptop in her lap. There's no sound, but she smiles when Maddie enters. He walks over and sits on the edge of her bed. She crawls over on her knees and wraps her arms around Maddie's chest.

                    MADDIE (V.O.)
Just like that, it was different. I didn't care that I hadn't gotten Rachel a sandwich. I didn't care that she said it didn't matter, she'd still make it worth my while.

Rachel lays Maddie down and disappears below. The CAMERA slowly ZOOMS in on Maddie's face.

                    MADDIE (V.O.)
I didn't care that everything was great. School. Work. Our relationship. I didn't care that Rachel may or may not have aborted my baby.

                    CUT TO:
          INT. WOMEN'S BATHROOM AT CHILI'S - NIGHT

Maddie thrusts into Elliot, his hand cupping her bare ass, her thin blond hair stuck to his lips.

                    CUT TO:
          INT. RACHEL'S DORM ROOM - CONTINUOUS

CLOSE UP of Maddie's face. There's a soft sucking sound from below.

                    MADDIE (V.O.)
I didn't care that Elliot had bashed my mom's face into a metal

rack. That I had to leave the state because I became a rape victim. That she'd ignored me for close to a year before finally writing me, telling me it'd all been a mistake, one she had to make in order to remember she loved her husband.

Rachel comes back up into the frame. She's talking to him with her mouth full, threatening to spill his semen onto his face. Maddie doesn't flinch, still staring straight into the OVERHEAD CAMERA.

> MADDIE (V.O.)
> All I cared about was seeing Elliot again.

Rachel swallows with a grimace. She nestles into Maddie's neck.

> Beat.

> MADDIE (V.O.)
> All I cared about was having a second chance.

> MADDIE (V.O.)
> So maybe that was really where this story started.

EXT. THE CABOOZE ENTRANCE - NIGHT

The Cabooze is a small bar/venue, crumbling brick, barred windows. Seven or eight Harley's are parked out front. A few hipster types smoke cigarettes in a small group. Maddie walks toward the entrance.

> MADDIE (V.O.)
> I waited three weeks to finally text Elliot. I thought about what to say the entire time. I settled on making something up about having seen that bitch with the fat face who worked at Talbots.

> Beat.

> MADDIE (V.O.)
> She wrote back in ten minutes.

White lettering fills the foreground of the screen, the image of Maddie walking toward the Cabooze still in the background: What a bitch. Haven't thought about her in ages. Lol.
Light blue lettering: Face is even fatter.
White lettering: Puff fish.
Light blue lettering: Think it's called a blow fish.
White lettering: She recognize you?

Light blue lettering: Think so, unless she stares at everyone all
psycho-like.
White lettering: lol. U see her at mall? U still work at Zumiez.
Light blue lettering: No and no. Trying to never work retail again.
White lettering: Feel you. Light blue lettering: You?
White lettering: Would rather die. What u up to later? I want to
apologize in person.

INT. THE CABOOZE - CONTINUOUS

The bar is dark, smokey. A band plays in the far corner. There's
an island bar which two thirty-something women work behind. It's
not crowded but it's not deserted. There seems to be an even mix
between college hipsters and ridden-hard-put-up-wet bikers. Maddie
gives a fake ID to a bouncer who barely looks at it.

Light blue lettering: Nothing really.
White lettering: U want to grab a drink or something? Light blue
lettering: K. U know the Cabooze?
White lettering: U a biker now?
Light blue lettering: Hipster bar now, but maybe when you were
college-aged it was biker...
White lettering: Fuck off and die. See you there.

Maddie walks through the bar. He's looking around for Elliot,
while trying not to appear too eager. He eventually sees her toward
the back of the bar sitting at a two-person high-top.

MEDIUM SHOT of Elliot sitting at the table. She's dressed modestly
in tight jeans and a cardigan. She rests her fingers around a bottle
of a beer.

Maddie walks over. She smiles, makes half an effort to get up from
her stool to hug him. Maddie sits opposite her.

The band starts playing a soulful cover of The Velvet Underground's "Oh! Sweet Nothing."

ELLIOT
Still pretty biker heavy, fuck you very much.

MADDIE
(laughing)
See the number of ironic handlebar mustaches in here?

ELLIOT
Touché.

                    MADDIE
Although, to be fair, I passed at least three pair of leather chaps
                    on the way in.

                    ELLIOT
            Maybe those are just hip now?

                    MADDIE
             Beats the hell out of me.

                    ELLIOT
                    Yeah.

A waitress walks by, and Elliot motions for two more beers.

Maddie turns away from Elliot when she turns toward him. He looks
at the band. The singer is older than the rest of the band, probably forty, skinny like he collected every letter of hepatitis.
The one spotlight shines too brightly on him, making half his face
                    orange.

                ELLIOT (CONT'D)
      So how's college life? Everything you hoped for?

                    MADDIE
                  (shrugging)
             Guess so. Pretty much. Yeah.

                    ELLIOT
                    Good.

                    MADDIE
Not much into frat parties and date rape, so I try to do my own
                    thing.

                    ELLIOT
       What? Rohypnol's a rite of college passage.

                    MADDIE
                  (laughing)
Practically sell the two-for-one kit of roofies and Plan B outside
                 of every party.

Elliot laughs. The server brings over two bottles. Elliot raises
           hers. They clink necks.

                    MADDIE (CONT'D)
              And parenthood, round two?

                        ELLIOT
                    (rolling her eyes)
     Would kill for two hours of sleep, but it's good.

                        MADDIE
                        Nice.

                        ELLIOT
                        Yeah.

                        MADDIE
              And your lovely husband?

                        ELLIOT
                      Is lovely.

Maddie's smiling, expecting Elliot to, but she doesn't, looking
down, rolling her bottle around its circular edge.

                    ELLIOT (CONT'D)
                  And your love life?

                        MADDIE
                      It's okay.

                        ELLIOT
                (forced shock and interest)
                Is there a special somebody?

                        MADDIE
                  I don't know. Kind of.

                        ELLIOT
     (making a show of being interested and not jealous)
                    Give me the goods.

                        MADDIE
     Rachel. We went to high school together in Iowa.

                        ELLIOT
                      (nodding)
       High school sweetheart, cute. I like that.

                    MADDIE
                    Yeah.

                    ELLIOT
                You love her?

Maddie seems a bit uncomfortable by the question. He's looking at
the band. They're into the first chorus of the song. A few older
                  bikers slow dance.

                    MADDIE
            A little. Yeah. No. I don't know.

Elliot nods with an unnatural smile on her face. She takes a pull
                    of her beer.

                    ELLIOT
        (slightly melancholic) I'm happy for you.

There's an awkward silence. Maddie seems to sense the shift from
    flirty banter to resigned regret. He leans forward.

                    MADDIE
                  You okay?

                    ELLIOT
            You remember the swing set?

                    MADDIE
                    Yeah.

                    ELLIOT
For some reason, when I was...inside or whatever, I would think
about that night. Like everything about it. I'd be lying there on
that horrible mattress, and feel the cold of the swing seat, that
    butterfly sensation in my stomach from the motion.

                    MADDIE
                    Yeah.

                    Beat.

                    ELLIOT
That was the only way I'd be able to sleep, to think about that,
                  to recreate it.

                    ELLIOT (CONT'D)
                    Weird, right?

                    MADDIE
                (shaking his head)
        Did the same thing with the ice palace.

                    ELLIOT
                    (laughing)
            That's right, you called it a
            palace. So dainty of you.

                    MADDIE
                    Shut up.

Elliot's staring at Maddie. He smiles. Elliot doesn't.

                MADDIE (CONT'D)
                    What?

Elliot continues staring. She slowly shakes her head.

                    ELLIOT
(almost under her breath) Could have been different with you, boy.

Elliot stands. Maddie's face is nothing but confusion. She extends
her hand. Maddie understands she's asking him to dance, and he
            laughs, shaking his head.

                ELLIOT (CONT'D)
            Gonna make a girl beg?

Elliot leads Maddie past a few tables to the dance floor. Most people stand with drinks in their hands, slightly swaying. The older
biker couple still dances. Elliot turns, wraps her arms around
Maddie's neck. Maddie does the same to the small of her back. Elliot places her head against Maddie's chest/shoulder. The CAMERA
slowly starts circling the dancing couple. The band picks up their
    intensity, the singer bending as he belts out the refrain.

                ELLIOT (CONT'D)
                    I'm sorry.

                    MADDIE
                    Stop.

                              ELLIOT
Jacob still asks about you. He says, "Where'd that funny guy go?"

                  Maddie grins into Elliot's hair.

                              MADDIE
          He still talk about bitches being bitches?

                              ELLIOT
                     (ignoring his question)
    She reminds me of you. I know it's messed up, but she does.

                              MADDIE
                               Who?

                              ELLIOT
                            Netta-Mae.

                              MADDIE
                  That's your daughter's name?

                              ELLIOT
                              Our.

The CAMERA picks up its circular speed, now almost dizzying. The
song is at its climax. Maddie stops his shuffling slow dancing. He
stares down at Elliot, who stares back, completely unflinching,
serious. After a second, she gives the slightest of nods. The music
                 is at a deafening crescendo.

The CAMERA spins and spins. Maddie cups Elliot's face. He leans
down, kissing her softly, then harder, the CAMERA spinning faster
and the music louder, Maddie and Elliot kissing to the point of
                         bruised gums.

                          FADE TO BLACK.

                   INT. MADDIE'S CAR - LATER

Elliot reaches in the backseat to grab her sweater. Maddie zips up
his fly in the driver's seat. Elliot arches her back, so she's able
to button her pants back up. Maddie lights a joint. He passes it
                   to Elliot, who waves him off.

                              MADDIE
                     Don't smoke anymore?

                    ELLIOT
          Joys of being on probation.

Maddie pauses, either in thought or summoning up the correct words.

                    MADDIE
             So now what?

                    ELLIOT
            Now what what?

                    MADDIE
             I mean, with...

                    ELLIOT
        Easy there, tiger. We go slow.

                    MADDIE
     Slow like what just happened in the backseat?

                    ELLIOT
   Slow like we just see what happens. We hang out when we can. We
          don't do anything stupid.

                    MADDIE
        What does that even mean?

                    ELLIOT
   It means I was just released from jail for sleeping with you. It
   means I have no money, you have no money, so we sure as fuck don't
            want to be out on our own.

                    (MORE)

                 ELLIOT (CONT'D)
   It means we see each other a few times a week, enjoy one another's
               company, and —

                    MADDIE
             What about...

                    ELLIOT
              Netta?

                    MADDIE
              Netta.

                    ELLIOT
            All in good time, baby.

                    CUT TO:
            INT. RACHEL'S DORM ROOM - NIGHT

Maddie's kissing Rachel, laying on her bed. Her glasses are slightly askew from their pressing faces. She moves her mouth down to
                    his neck.

                  MATCH CUT TO:
            INT. MADDIE'S CAR - AFTERNOON

Elliot licks Maddie's Adam's apple. He slides his hand underneath
                the back of her shirt.

                  MADDIE (V.O.)
I started seeing Elliot three days a week when her husband was
                    working.

                  MATCH CUT TO:
            INT. MADDIE'S DORM ROOM - NIGHT

Maddie unhooks Rachel's bra. Her breasts are perky, her nipples
upturned and slightly puffy. He traces her left with his tongue.

                  MADDIE (V.O.)
        I hung out with Rachel the other days.

                  MATCH CUT TO:
            EXT. MLK PARK - DUSK

Maddie and Elliot stand underneath a wooden playground structure.
They're surrounded by wood and slides and monkey bars, partially
                hidden, as they kiss.

                  MADDIE (V.O.)
With Elliot, it was like being in junior high again. Like kids
desperate to explore one another's bodies without the safety of
                  private shelter.

                  MATCH CUT TO:
            INT. RACHEL'S DORM ROOM - NIGHT

Rachel's bare legs are spread around Maddie. His naked butt flexes
                  as he thrusts.

MADDIE (V.O.)

But with Rachel, it was different. There was something rehearsed and expected about everything from how I knew she'd answer the phone to the series of actions that led her to come. It was weird, almost like we were older.

MATCH CUT TO:

INT. MOVIE THEATER - NIGHT

The movie theater is deserted. Some horrible action movie blares from the screen. Elliot sits on Maddie's lap, her jeans pulled down to her knees. She braces herself against the seat in front of her.

MADDIE (V.O.)

But honestly, it wasn't even a question of who I wanted to be with.

MATCH CUT TO:

EXT. U OF M QUAD - AFTERNOON

Maddie and Rachel walk hand-in-hand. All the leaves have fallen. It's overcast and gray. CLOSE UP of Maddie. He seems distant, retreated.

MATCH CUT TO:

EXT. COMO LAKE - AFTERNOON

Maddie walks hand-in-hand with Elliot. It looks close to freezing, everything blowing and dark. But they're laughing. Maddie is telling some story, and he's animated and excited.

MADDIE (V.O.)

We just had to wait for the right moment. That's what Elliot kept telling me, the right moment, and I went along with it because why wouldn't I? I was so far past the point of being able to walk away.

The CAMERA shoots Maddie and Elliot from the front as they walk. They've quit laughing, and now just walk holding hands.

ELLIOT
He's cheating.

MADDIE
Who?

ELLIOT
Devon.

Maddie bites down on the tip of his tongue. He looks annoyed or maybe hurt at the mention of his name.

> MADDIE
> How do you know?

> ELLIOT
> I met her.

> MADDIE
> Who?

> ELLIOT
> This girl he works with.

They walk for a few steps in silence.

> MADDIE
> Is that why you're...

> ELLIOT
> This has nothing to do with that.

> MADDIE
> (nodding)
> You said that last time.

> ELLIOT
> (angry) You know...
> (shaking her head and breathing)
> Guess that's fair.

They walk some more, not talking. A flock of geese take off from the murky lake.

> ELLIOT (CONT'D)
> It's different.

> MADDIE
> How?

> ELLIOT
> Because I lo —

> MADDIE
> (smiling) What was that?

ELLIOT
Because we have a child together.

MADDIE
Who exists only in pictures.

ELLIOT
Because we have to wait for the right moment.

MADDIE
Right. Like you keep saying.

Elliot stops. Maddie takes another step forward. Elliot's still
holding his hand and pulls him backward.

ELLIOT
Before, when we first met, I did everything because I wanted it.
Because I thought I deserved it after what Devon had done.

Beat.

ELLIOT (CONT'D)
It was selfish. I'll be the first to admit it.

(MORE)

ELLIOT (CONT'D)
That's why I confessed. That's why I sat in jail for seven fucking
months. Because I hurt you. Your family. My own.

MADDIE
You don't have to —

ELLIOT
Just listen.

Maddie nods.

ELLIOT (CONT'D)
For once in my fucking life, I'm trying to think about other people. I'm thinking about you. I'm trying to warn you that when you
meet Netta, boom, it's different. You'll be different. This will be
different. Your entire fucking life will be different.

MADDIE
Which is what I want.

ELLIOT

Which is what you think you want. But really you have no idea.
Because there's no way you can.

MADDIE

I love you.

ELLIOT

Those choices and opportunities you still have...gone.

MADDIE

Say it.

ELLIOT

Parties and your artsy girlfriend and a future of living on food
stamps until you sell a screenplay.

MADDIE

Say it.

ELLIOT

It's gone. Your life as you know it, as you planned it, is gone.

MADDIE

You can't do it.

ELLIOT

I'm trying to protect you.

Maddie shakes his head. He's on the verge of tears. He turns and
starts walking away. The flock of geese fly in a V ahead of Maddie.

INT. ROOM 113 - DAY

Maddie sits in class. His phone vibrates. A picture text comes up.

CLOSE UP of picture. It's a photograph of Elliot holding a baby,
who's wearing a pink onesie, which reads Daddy's Girl. The photo
is accompanied with a short text: Mama and her baby love Daddy.

Maddie's smiling, studying the picture. Students are leaving their
desks. Maddie slips his phone into his pocket and gathers his
laptop and heads toward the stairs.

PROFESSOR

Maddie.

Maddie looks up at his professor, who's motioning with his hand for Maddie to come over.

Maddie walks over to the desk. The professor waits for a second as the last of the students leave the classroom. He's holding a stack of papers.

A quick CLOSE UP of the papers shows a title page for a screen play: Statutory: Written by Maddie Johnson, Based on a True Story.

PROFESSOR (CONT'D)
Listen, I just wanted to say, and this stays right here, okay?

MADDIE
Okay.

PROFESSOR
I've been teaching this course, in some form or another, for the better part of two decades. And in that time, I can remember two scripts that weren't completely horrible.

The professor taps the screenplay with his pen.

PROFESSOR (CONT'D)
Both of those scripts were eventually made into movies, one of them with Warner Brothers.

Maddie's nodding, trying not to smile.

PROFESSOR (CONT'D)
And this here, at least the pages I've seen, is right on track to not being completely unreadable.

MADDIE
(laughing) Thanks, I think?

Professor nods.

MADDIE (CONT'D)
See you on Wednesday.

PROFESSOR
No class for Thanksgiving break.

MADDIE
That's right.

                    PROFESSOR
                 Oh, and Maddie.

                     MADDIE
                     Yeah?

                    PROFESSOR
                  Be careful.

        INT. THE JOHNSON'S KITCHEN - AFTERNOON

Mrs. Johnson is mashing potatoes. Maddie sits at the island count-
     er looking at his phone and eating cashews.

                     MADDIE
        Are you absolutely sure I can't help?

                  MRS. JOHNSON
                     Sure.

                     MADDIE
                  You nervous?

                  MRS. JOHNSON
             Why should I be nervous?

                     MADDIE
        When's the last time Dad set foot in this house?

                  MRS. JOHNSON
          Slipped my mind that he was even coming.

                     MADDIE
                (laughing) Right.

                  MRS. JOHNSON
                We're all adults.

                     MADDIE
Which apparently is different at forty-eight than it was for the
                 past fifteen years?

                  MRS. JOHNSON
This whole I'm in college, I can poke fun at my mother thing is
                 slightly annoying.

                    MADDIE
Isn't it a rite of passage? Can't tell me you didn't do the same
                    thing.

                  MRS. JOHNSON
Worse. I started calling my parents by their first names.

                    MADDIE
              That's so Seventies of you.

Mrs. Johnson raises her eyebrows and turns toward the oven. She
        opens it up, checking on the turkey.

                 MADDIE (CONT'D)
You were in college when you got pregnant with me, right?

Mrs. Johnson pushes the oven closed with a little more force than
either of them expected. She turns around, wiping her hands on her
                 autumn-themed apron.

                  MRS. JOHNSON
            Rachel's not pregnant, is she?

                    MADDIE
               (smiling) No, chill.

Mrs. Johnson exhales, dramatically placing her hand over her chest.

                  MRS. JOHNSON
              Don't do that to me.

                    MADDIE
                 Anxious much?

                  MRS. JOHNSON
               (shaking her head)
Quick way to learn how difficult the world really is, that's all.

                    MADDIE
         Make me sound like such a blessing.

Mrs. Johnson walks over to the island. She reaches across the
         granite and clasps Maddie's hands.

                  MRS. JOHNSON
You are the best thing to ever happen to me. But your timing? Your
father? The entire trajectory your conception put my life on?

Beat.

                    MRS. JOHNSON (CONT'D)
You're the love of my life. Never forget that. But Lordy-be, child,
                    you came at a price.

            INT. THE JOHNSON'S DINING ROOM - LATER

Mr. and Mrs. Johnson sit at opposite ends of a rectangular din-
ing-room table. Maddie sits in the middle. The table is done up
in Midwestern kitsch, a tablecloth with gold and red leaves, a
few gourds as the centerpiece, and enough food to feed a family
                    of twenty.

Mrs. Johnson has her head bowed. Maddie and Mr. Johnson look at
                each other and smirk.

                    MRS. JOHNSON
I'm grateful for my son. How he's turned out. How well he's doing
    in college. Proud of him. Grateful for him.

            Mrs. Johnson opens her eyes.

                    MADDIE
                  Can we eat?

                    MRS. JOHNSON
Not until we all say what we're grateful for.

            Maddie rolls his eyes.

                    Beat.

                    MR. JOHNSON
                    I'll go.
                  (bowing head)
I, also, am grateful for my son. I'm thankful for this past year...
    Obviously not the circumstances, but the outcome.

                MR. JOHNSON (CONT'D)
        (slightly choked up but trying not to show it)
Sometimes you don't realize how badly you miss something until
            you're shown the alternative.

Mr. Johnson raises his head, and looks at Maddie, then Mrs. John-
                    son.

MADDIE

I'm grateful for second chances. And for the both of you.

They start eating. The energy is both familiar and awkward. It's unclear if the lack of speaking is due to the food being eaten or the uncertainty of what to say.

MR. JOHNSON

Too bad Rachel isn't here. Would've loved to see her again.

MRS. JOHNSON

It is.

MADDIE

Back in Iowa.

MRS. JOHNSON

She left this morning?

MADDIE

Yesterday.

MRS. JOHNSON

Thought you said you were hanging out with her last night?

MADDIE

(glancing upward) Umm...I don't think so.

MR. JOHNSON

Things are still going well with her?

MADDIE

Yeah, pretty much.

MR. JOHNSON

Pretty much?

MADDIE

They're good.

MRS. JOHNSON

Don't get me wrong, I love Rachel, absolutely love her, but remember that you're young, and —

MADDIE

Got it.

                    MRS. JOHNSON
            Have your whole life in front of you.

Mr. Johnson gives Mrs. Johnson a quick shaking of his head, to
which she rolls her eyes. Maddie sees the exchange.

                    MR. JOHNSON
                    And classes?

                    MADDIE
                    Going well.

                    MR. JOHNSON
                    Parties?

                    MADDIE
            Not really my scene anymore.

                    MR. JOHNSON
            And being back in the Twin Cities?

Mrs. Johnson freezes with her fork inches away from her mouth.
Maddie picks the skin off his turkey.

                    MR. JOHNSON (CONT'D)
            I mean, with everything that went on...

                    MRS. JOHNSON
            We don't speak about her.

                    MR. JOHNSON
I'm simply asking if it's difficult, or if you've happened to run
                    across each other.

                    MRS. JOHNSON
            Will you please drop it?

                    MR. JOHNSON
            I'm asking my son a question.

                    MRS. JOHNSON
            Which I've asked you not to do.

                    MR. JOHNSON
Better off pretending that she wasn't released from jail, and—

Mrs. Johnson drops her fork against her plate. She's shaking her head, staring at Mr. Johnson.

                    MR. JOHNSON (CONT'D)
Are you really that naïve to think he doesn't know she's out of jail?

CLOSE UP from Maddie's POV. He's staring at his plate of food. Everything is the same brownish color and runs together.

                         CUT TO:
INT. THE JOHNSON'S DINING ROOM - FIFTEEN YEARS BEFORE

Still from Maddie's POV, we see a younger Mr. Johnson throw a plate against the wall.

                         CUT TO:
INT. THE JOHNSON'S DINING ROOM - CONTINUOUS

                     MRS. JOHNSON
                You're unbelievable.

                      MR. JOHNSON
            Can go ahead and bury your head -

                        MADDIE
                  I know she's out.

Silence. Both parents stare at their son waiting for him to continue, but he doesn't, just looks down at his plate.

                     MRS. JOHNSON
                     Have you...

Maddie doesn't respond.

                 MRS. JOHNSON (CONT'D)
                Jesus, have you seen her?

                        MADDIE
                         No.

                     MRS. JOHNSON
            I swear to God, if you're seeing her —

                    MR. JOHNSON
                      Stop.

                   MRS. JOHNSON
        You can forget about us paying for college.

                    MR. JOHNSON
                      Stop!

                   MRS. JOHNSON
              Are you seeing her again?

Maddie shakes his head, his mouth open, as if he can't believe how
the dinner unfolded. He puts his matching cloth napkin down next
                    to his plate.

                     MADDIE
              Thank you for dinner.

                    MR. JOHNSON
                Maddie, sit down.

                     MADDIE
                (shaking his head)
        You guys haven't changed. Not one fucking bit.

                   MRS. JOHNSON
               Watch your language.

                      Beat.

                     MADDIE
And the funny thing is, you two deserve one another. You're the
same, and you don't see it. So miserable with your mistakes and
yourselves, that you're bound and determined not to have me turn
                   out the same.

                  MADDIE (CONT'D)
        But I guess you've done one thing right.

              Maddie pushes in his chair.

                  MADDIE (CONT'D)
I know exactly what a completely fucked-up relationship looks
            like. I know exactly what to avoid.

INT. MADDIE'S CAR - MOMENTS LATER

Maddie drives and calls Elliot. It rings once before going to voicemail. He tries again. This time, the phone goes directly to voicemail.

CLOSE UP of Maddie biting his bottom lip. His nostrils flare. He screams twice, smashing the palm of his hand against his steering wheel.

INT. MADDIE'S DORM ROOM - LATER

He lies in bed, smoking weed. He listens to The Velvet Underground's "Oh! Sweet Nothing." His phone vibrates with a text.

CLOSE UP of phone. The text is from Elliot: Devon's working Black Friday. Tomorrow is the right moment to meet your daughter.

EXT. COMO LAKE - AFTERNOON

It's a sunny day, obviously cold, but bright. There are couples and families walking around the lake. A multi-generational game of touch football is being played.

Maddie walks from his car. He's carrying a white plastic bag.

From Maddie's POV, we see Elliot sitting on a swing. The rest of the playground is deserted. She's holding a pink bundle of fleece in her arms. She gives an empathetic smile to Maddie.

Maddie stands a few feet away. He's nervous, maybe the first time we've really seen him this way ever. He looks between Elliot and the smushed face of Netta-Mae.

ELLIOT
It's okay to be scared.

Maddie doesn't respond. He stares at his daughter.

ELLIOT (CONT'D)
(speaking down toward her baby)
I want you to meet somebody.
CLOSE UP of Maddie swallowing hard.

ELLIOT (CONT'D)
You ready?

> MADDIE
> (staring dumbly) I got her a present.

Elliot gives the same smile as earlier, a mix between appreciating
fear and bestowing pity.

Maddie reaches into the bag. He pulls out a foot-long pink stuffed
monster. It's a cyclops with a crooked smile.

> MADDIE (CONT'D)
> They said these were all the rage.

> ELLIOT
> (grinning) It's perfect.

Maddie hands the stuffed monster over to Elliot, who nestles it
next to her baby. Netta-Mae makes a fussy sound, and Elliot laughs.

> ELLIOT (CONT'D)
> She loves it.

Maddie doesn't laugh at the sarcasm. He stares.

> ELLIOT (CONT'D)
> Ready?

Maddie nods. Elliot stands.

> ELLIOT (CONT'D)
> Just support her head and hold her like a football.

Maddie reaches out his arms. They're not shaking, but close.
Netta-Mae fusses during the exchange. Maddie holds her somewhat
awkwardly. The baby lets out a cry.

> ELLIOT (CONT'D)
> (soothing voice)
> Just relax. Everything's okay. You're doing well.

Maddie adjusts Netta-Mae into the crook of his left arm. She stares
up at him. Her eyes are blue orbs. She doesn't smile, just stares,
studying intently.

> ELLIOT (CONT'D)
> What's it feel like?

Maddie stares down at his daughter. He takes a moment to answer.

MADDIE

Like nothing else has ever mattered.

EXT. COMO PARK - LIFE GUARD TOWER - LATER

The sun sets across the lake, a brilliant mix of deep reds and pinks. Maddie and Elliot sit on a raised wooden lifeguard tower. They're bundled up against the cold. Maddie holds Netta-Mae in his arms.

MADDIE

(speaking while looking at the small waves)
It took like five minutes before they started fighting. Fifteen years, and in five minutes, they were screaming.

ELLIOT

(shaking her head) What about?

MADDIE

Doesn't matter. Same shit as always.

ELLIOT

Sorry.

MADDIE

Not your fault.

They stare out over the water.

ELLIOT

You go through life thinking a family looks a certain way, you know, like the nuclear family. And as much as you tell yourself that's a failed myth, it still sticks with you. Fucks up your view of any alternatives.

MADDIE

That why you went back to Devon?

ELLIOT

Probably.

Beat.

MADDIE

Why my parents got married in the first place.

ELLIOT

Why I got married.

MADDIE
Maybe it looks like this.

ELLIOT
Maybe.

MADDIE
Serious.

ELLIOT
(resting her head on his shoulder)
A sexual predator and her victim and their illegitimate offspring.

MADDIE
Don't.

ELLIOT
Sorry.

She reaches into the front pocket of Maddie's jeans. She takes out
his cell phone. CLOSE UP of the image of the three of them in the
camera. It freezes as the picture is taken.

MADDIE
Feels perfect.

ELLIOT
You're one of the good ones, Madison Johnson.

Maddie kisses the soft hair of Netta-Mae. He gently nestles his
chin behind her head. She holds her pink stuffed monster.

MADDIE
(possibly speaking to himself)
Nothing else matters.

ELLIOT
Love you.

MADDIE
Nothing.

FADE TO BLACK.

INT. RACHEL'S DORM ROOM - NIGHT

Rachel's standing, screaming, waving a phone in front of Maddie, who's propped up on her bed, his hands raised and upturned.

> RACHEL
>
> What the fuck is this? Huh?

> MADDIE
>
> Rach, please.

She's in hysterics, her face blotchy red, tears and snot.

> RACHEL
>
> Oh my fucking God. You're such a piece of shit. Oh my God. I can't believe you. I can't believe how stupid—

> MADDIE
>
> (reaching toward her wrists)
> Baby, please, just calm -

> RACHEL
>
> Get your fucking hands off me.

> MADDIE
>
> It's not what it looks like.

> RACHEL
>
> (snorts a laugh)
> Really? Really? Because it looks to me like you're playing family with that bitch who raped you. Did you forget that little fact? Raped you.

Maddie stands. He puts his hands on Rachel's arms. She shakes them off, stepping backward, and Maddie does it again.

> RACHEL (CONT'D)
>
> Are you fucking her? How long?

> MADDIE
>
> It's not like that.
> Rachel throws Maddie's cell phone against the wall.

CLOSE UP of the phone. The screen is cracked, a fissure running between Maddie holding Netta-Mae and Elliot.

> RACHEL
>
> Hate you.

>   MADDIE
>   It's complicated.

>   RACHEL
>   Get the fuck out.

Maddie grabs her wrists with a bit of aggressive force. He squeezes.

>   MADDIE
>   That's my daughter.

>   RACHEL
>   I don't give a fu — What?

>   MADDIE
>   My daughter.

All of the fight drains from Rachel. She's shaking her head, her jaw quivering. It's clear she's going through the thought process of having aborted their baby, Maddie cheating, Maddie being a father, Maddie ending up with Elliot.

She crumples to the floor, her back pressed against her roommate's bed. Rachel pulls her legs to her chest. Her tears change from outrage to absolutely broken sobs.

>   RACHEL
>   (whispering) Go.

>   CUT TO:
>   INT. PSYCHOLOGIST'S OFFICE - DAY

The light of the psychologist's office is fuzzy, indicating a fantasy. The psychologist crosses and uncrosses her legs. She leans forward.

>   MADDIE (V.O.)
> Part of me wished to be back in her office. I'd be sitting there looking at the clock, giving half-truths that maybe were more than halves. Just to have somebody to talk to.

The psychologist adjusts her legs.

>   MADDIE (V.O.)
> Rachel crumpled. She just fucking crumpled when I told her the baby was mine.

Beat.

                    MADDIE
          Like she was completely broken.

The psychologist rubs her hands over her skirt.

                  PSYCHOLOGIST
           How does that make you feel?

                    MADDIE
          Like a bag of fucking dicks.

                  PSYCHOLOGIST
           (aroused) Tell me more.

                    MADDIE
            Everything was perfect.

The psychologist shakes her head teasingly.

                  PSYCHOLOGIST
         That's not what you said, is it?

                    CUT TO:
     INT. YOUTH PSYCHOLOGIST'S OFFICE - DAY

Eight-year-old Maddie sits on a leather couch, the light still
hazy. The youth psychologist pouts her lips.

              EIGHT-YEAR-OLD MADDIE
                     No.

                YOUTH PSYCHOLOGIST
             What did you actually say?

              EIGHT-YEAR-OLD MADDIE
             That nothing else matters.

                    CUT TO:
     INT. PSYCHOLOGIST'S OFFICE - CONTINUOUS

The psychologist taps the end of her pen against her pouted bottom
lip.

                  PSYCHOLOGIST
        Nothing else matters when you have what?

CUT TO:

INT. ICE PALACE - NIGHT

OVERHEAD SHOT of Maddie and Elliot. Netta-Mae is between them holding her pink monster. They all stare up at the multi-colored wall of ice.

MADDIE
Family.

INT. MADDIE'S DORM ROOM - DUSK

CLOSE UP of Maddie and Elliot underneath a single blanket. The sun shines through the blanket, giving enough light to see their faces.

MADDIE
What if they're serious about college?

ELLIOT
They're not.

MADDIE
My mom's crazy.

ELLIOT
No parent willingly makes life harder for their kid.

MADDIE
Still weird to think about being a parent.

ELLIOT
Netta-Mae loves you.

MADDIE
But what if they really do cut me off?

ELLIOT
Then you get loans like every other kid.

Elliot traces her finger around Maddie's nipple, more as a form of doodling than anything sexual.

ELLIOT (CONT'D)
Or you sell your screenplay.

                    MADDIE
Or work my way up to assistant manager at Zumiez.

                    ELLIOT
Fuck that. Rob houses before I let you waste any more time there.

                    MADDIE
              (quoting *Pulp Fiction*)
All right, everybody be cool. This is a robbery.

                    ELLIOT
Any of you pricks move, I'll execute every last motherfucking one
                    of you.

They smile but don't laugh.

                    MADDIE
I knew this guy, a classmate. Really weird kid. Used to break into
houses all the time and steal random shit, like nothing worth
          money, just trinkets and stuff.

                    ELLIOT
              I love that.

                    MADDIE
What about that could you possibly love?

                    ELLIOT
Invading somebody's intimate space. Making it your own.

                    MADDIE
                    Creep.

                    ELLIOT
              I want to do it.

                    MADDIE
                  Have fun.

                    ELLIOT
For my birthday, that's what I want to do. You take me.

Elliot's getting excited. She turns, props herself up on her el-
        bow, her hand now on Maddie's face.

ELLIOT (CONT'D)

We go to some stranger's house, look through their shit, take some
stupid porcelain cat or something.

MADDIE

You're serious?

ELLIOT

As syphilis.

MADDIE

Which isn't that serious.

ELLIOT

The kind Al Capone died from.

MADDIE

(laughing) Horrible idea.

ELLIOT

You only turn thirty-one once.

MADDIE

You only turn every age once.

ELLIOT

Thank God.

MADDIE

What about probation?

ELLIOT

What about anything? Please, it will be fun. In and out. Can probably even sniff some panties or something.

Maddie laughs, turning to his right. He grabs a balled-up pair of
black panties. He sniffs them.

ELLIOT (CONT'D)

Pervert.

MADDIE

Did you even shower today?

ELLIOT

Fuck off.

Elliot reaches for her underwear, and Maddie turns, making himself into a cocoon as Elliot crawls on top of him trying to get back her panties. They laugh. Elliot eventually stops. She's draped over Maddie's turned body, her face next to his, but at a perpendicular angle.

> ELLIOT (CONT'D)
> Please.

> MADDIE
> You really want to do this?

> ELLIOT
> There's something beautiful about it.

> MADDIE
> Breaking and entering?

> ELLIOT
> (shaking her head)
> The loss of opportunities you didn't want in the first place.

INT. MADDIE'S CAR - NIGHT

Maddie drives down River Road. The Mississippi is on their right, a darkened snake at the bottom of crumbly sandstone bluffs. Million-dollar homes line their left side. Elliot takes a drink from a pint of gin, grimacing.

> ELLIOT
> No, too nice. They'll have security systems, not to mention wives making dinner.

> MADDIE
> Then where to?

> ELLIOT
> East side. Second and third shifters.

> MADDIE
> Criminal mastermind over there.

> ELLIOT
> You do remember I spent time in jail.

> MADDIE
> My little convict.

                    ELLIOT
                  Thug life.

                    MADDIE
                   (laughing)
            Please don't ever do that again.

        INT. MADDIE'S CAR - MOMENTS LATER

Maddie's creeping along a residential street. The houses are tiny
cubes, ramblers, most either gray or blue. There's an inch of
              freshly fallen snow.

                    ELLIOT
                     Here.

She points to a darkened house. It's nondescript in every aspect,
except for a concrete birdbath with what looks like a painted
              bowling ball in its bowl.

                    MADDIE
                     Yeah?

                    ELLIOT
                    Perfect.

Maddie parks his car and hits the lights. He reaches over and takes
two quick pulls from the gin. He sticks out his tongue, rubbing
it against his teeth as if trying to scrape the taste from its
surface. Maddie looks at Elliot. He's nervous but trying not to
          show it. She takes his face in her hands.

                 ELLIOT (CONT'D)
                   You Okay?

                    MADDIE
                   I'm okay.

                    ELLIOT
                  You love me?

                    MADDIE
                  I love you.

                    ELLIOT
Because I can have you drop me off at Chucky Cheese right now for my
stupid birthday party, and we can keep playing this sneak around—

Maddie opens his car door.
EXT. OUTSIDE OF BLUE-COLLAR HOME - CONTINUOUS

Maddie shuts his door, careful not to make much noise. Elliot gets
out. Maddie's looking around. Elliot starts toward the house.
Maddie follows.

At the front door, Elliot bends down, lifting a snow-covered welcome mat. There's no key. She looks up at Maddie. She's smiling.

Elliot walks to the side of the house. She runs her hand over the
top of a row of dilapidated shrubs. She stops at the birdbath. She
places her hand on the metallic orb, then rolls it to the side.

CLOSE UP of a house key resting underneath the bowling ball.

Elliot skips back over to the front door. She inserts the key,
then turns the handle.

ELLIOT
(whispering) Honey, I'm home.

INT. BLUE-COLLAR HOME - CONTINUOUS

The house is dark, but light enough to make out general shapes and
shades of color.

To the left, there's a tiny kitchen, just large enough to open the
refrigerator fully before hitting the opposite wall. A two-person
table partially blocks the entrance to the kitchen. To the right,
there's a love seat and a recliner, the recliner heavily worn on
the armrests.

CLOSE UP of an ashtray resting on the left arm of the recliner.
It's an upside-down sombrero with a cartoon mouse drunkenly sleeping in the center.

ELLIOT
That might be my keepsake.

Maddie hasn't moved an inch from the doorway. He nods.

ELLIOT (CONT'D)
Come on.

Elliot reaches out and takes Maddie's hand. She leads him down
a narrow hallway. There's nothing on the wall except a single

photograph, black and white, a stoic-looking woman's face shot in partial profile. Elliot runs her free hand over the picture.

INT. BLUE COLLAR BEDROOM - CONTINUOUS

The bedroom is sparse: a bed with no headboard, a TV resting on top of a three-drawer dresser, and a single nightstand made from a different type of wood. A quilt is folded nicely across the bottom third of the bed.

> MADDIE
> You think it's a couple?

Elliot doesn't respond. She bends down and checks under the bed.

> ELLIOT
> (speaking while still crouched)
> Two sets of slippers. One here, one on the other side.

Elliot gets on her stomach, reaching underneath the bed. She pulls out a shoebox. From her knees, she sets the box on the bed.

> ELLIOT (CONT'D)
> This is it.

> MADDIE
> Huh?

> ELLIOT
> Mementos. Keepsakes. Treasures.

Elliot opens the box. There aren't any pictures, just a small roll of twenties and a snub-nosed revolver. Elliot picks up the gun. She holds it with both hands, pointing it at Maddie.

> MADDIE
> Can you not point that thing at me.

> ELLIOT
> Told you I was all about thug life tonight.

> MADDIE
> Let's get that ashtray and bounce.

> ELLIOT
> Taking this.

Elliot stands, slipping the revolver into her waistband.

                    ELLIOT (CONT'D)
                    And this.

She puts the money in her pocket. She closes the box and slides it
              back underneath the bed.

                    MADDIE
         What are we going to do with a gun?

                    ELLIOT
Not about the gun. It's about taking something of importance. And
this guy keeps a pathetic stack of money and gun under his bed.
Practically screaming that this is his prized possession.

                    MADDIE
              It's a gun.

                    ELLIOT
Doing him a favor anyway. Can't tell me he isn't thinking about
putting it to his old lady's temple if she cooks him hamburger hot
              dish one more time.

Elliot walks to Maddie, putting her arms over his shoulder. She
              speaks into his mouth.

                    ELLIOT (CONT'D)
         I'm saving him from temptation.

              INT. MADDIE'S CAR - LATER

Elliot and Maddie are silent in his car, both lost in thought.
It's not hard to see them mulling over the question of what the
              hell they'd just done.

Elliot reaches out and takes Maddie's hand, motioning with her
head to a motel on their right. A neon sign advertises hourly
              rates.

                    ELLIOT
    Still have like forty minutes before birthday party hell.

                    CUT TO:
         INT. LAKE STREET INN - MOMENTS LATER

The CAMERA shows the inside of the room. It's passable, but dingy.
The white door is covered in black scuff marks.
The door opens, and Elliot walks backward while kissing Maddie.
They lay on the bed.

CUT TO:

INT. LAKE STREET INN - MOMENTS LATER

CLOSE UP of Elliot's face, her neck extended, Maddie's hands closing around it, squeezing, her facial expression ecstasy.

CUT TO:

INT. LAKE STREET INN - MOMENTS LATER

Maddie is lying on his back on the faded red comforter. He's naked.
Elliot rides him.

You can't hear her actual words, but you can read her lips.

ELLIOT (MOUTHED)
Tell me you love me.

ClOSE UP of Maddie's face.

MADDIE (MOUTHED)
I love you.

MEDIUM SHOT of Elliot. She's started riding Maddie again. There's
something completely unnerving about the look on her face.

ELLIOT (MOUTHED)
Fucking love you.

FADE TO BLACK.

INT. LAKE STREET INN - LATER

Maddie and Elliot are naked, sprawled out on the red comforter.
They're at odd angles, dead almost. The empty bottle of gin and
the revolver rest on the bedside table.

Elliot stirs, rolling over. She stretches. Then her eyes open
wide, panic on her face. She sits up.

ELLIOT
Fuck. Fuck. Fuck.

Maddie stirs awake.

Elliot bends over the bed, reaching for her purse.

ELLIOT (CONT'D)
My phone's dead. What time is it?

Maddie's still trying to come to his senses but gets his phone from
the pocket of his jeans.

MADDIE
Eleven-thirty.

ELLIOT
(screaming) Fuck!

Maddie lets his head hit the cheap headboard.

ELLIOT (CONT'D)
What are you doing? Let's go. We need to go.

MADDIE
It's too late.

ELLIOT
Too late for what? What are you talking about. Let's go. Now.

Elliot is frantic as she looks for her underwear. She finds them,
struggling to put them on while standing. The way she bends at the
waist to get her second leg in makes her stomach pouch out, her
stretchmarks spreading.

MADDIE
It's too late. Your party's over.

ELLIOT
Shut up and help me find my jeans.

Maddie climbs across the bed. He's still naked. At the edge of the
bed, he rights himself on his two knees.

MADDIE
Elliot.

Elliot ignores him, scouring the stained carpet for her jeans.
She's crying the tears of the panicked.

                    MADDIE (CONT'D)
                    Baby.

                    ELLIOT
                    Fuck.

Maddie grabs her wrist. She's still searching for her jeans, which
        hang off the far corner of the bed.

                    MADDIE
This is it. The moment you're always talking about. Right here,
                    right now.

                    ELLIOT
            No, this is...just help me —

Maddie pulls her close to him, still holding onto her wrists, which
            he pulls to his sides.

                    MADDIE
It might not be the best of circumstances, and like maybe we didn't
    plan it this way, but it's here, right here, right now.

                    ELLIOT
            (whiney) No, no, no.

                    MADDIE
                    Look at me.

Elliot looks at Maddie, but fleetingly, before giving the room
            another once-over for her jeans.

                    MADDIE (CONT'D)
                Baby, look at me.

CLOSE UP of Elliot looking at Maddie. Her face is blotchy with
sleep and alcohol and fear. With the CAMERA still on her face, we
                hear Maddie's words

                    MADDIE (CONT'D)
I love you. I love our daughter. We're a family. And we start
                    right now.

Elliot's crying, but the initial panic dissipates. Her face soft-
ens. There's a hint of a smile at the corner of her mouth.

INT. ROOM 113 - DAY

Maddie sits in the front of the class in one of three chairs turned
to face his peers. He's holding white pages. Two other peers sit
there with him.

MALE CLASSMATE
(reading)
Can you not point that fucking thing at me?

FEMALE CLASSMATE
(reading)
Told you I was all about thug life tonight.

MALE CLASSMATE
(reading)
Let's get that ashtray and bounce.

FEMALE CLASSMATE
(reading) Taking this.

MADDIE
(reading)
Elliot stands, slipping the revolver into her waistband.

Professor walks from the corner of the room, clapping.

PROFESSOR
Okay, I think that's a good stopping point. A round of applause
for Mr. Johnson and his readers.

The class gives a half-hearted round of applause. Professor turns
to the class.

PROFESSOR (CONT'D)
Comments? Questions? Concerns?

The class sits there looking somewhat bored. Finally, a chubby
blond sorority type raises her hand.

PROFESSOR (CONT'D)
Yes, Kate.

KATE
It's just, like, I don't get it. Like his motivation or whatever.
Why is he even doing all this stuff, you know?

Professor nods, giving a frowning shrug as if contemplating the
validity of Kate's comments.

PROFESSOR
Are you speaking about the breaking and entering, specifically?

KATE
(gaining a little confidence)
Yeah, that, but also like even loving her because it's so obvious
she doesn't love him. Plus, like, the daughter probably isn't even
his. It's just really unbelievable that he loves her in the first
place.

CLOSE UP of Maddie. He's staring down at his script, stoic, or
trying to be.

PROFESSOR
Yes, Joseph.

Joseph, a Midwestern type decorated as a hipster, leans forward
in his desk.

JOSEPH
It's as if the author is unsure if he's ripping off Alexander Payne
or Derek Cianfrance or...Tarantino.

PROFESSOR
(annoyed look on his face) How's that?

JOSEPH
The whole gun thing.

PROFESSOR
Like Chekov said, if a rifle is hanging on the wall in the first
chapter, it damn well better go off. And did we not see a gun in
the first scene?

Joseph wants to protest but doesn't.

PROFESSOR (CONT'D)
And are you not terrified to see the confluence of events that lead
up to that gun being fired?

Joseph concedes with a nod.

PROFESSOR (CONT'D)

And isn't that the point of any story, in any form? To unravel
the mystery of the protagonist's psyche at the precise moment he
snaps, after which nothing will ever be the same?

Professor gives Maddie a significant yet fleeting look.

EXT. COURTYARD - MOMENTS LATER

Elliot greets Maddie. She wraps her arm through his. She's upbeat,
happy if not manic.

ELLIOT

Did you crush?

MADDIE

Crushed.

ELLIOT

Because you're brilliant.

MADDIE

Something like that.

They walk amidst the hundreds of students. It's gray and overcast.

ELLIOT

(using a fake male voice) And, Elliot, how did your appointment go
with graduate admissions?

MADDIE

Sorry. How'd it go?

ELLIOT

(smiling)

Very well, thank you. They weren't sure how many credits would
transfer, but when I described my thesis work, plus my GRE scores,
they changed their tune right quick.

MADDIE

That's rad.

ELLIOT

Probably wouldn't be able to start until fall semester, but still.

INT. DORM COMPLEX - MOMENTS LATER

The building is Soviet-style concrete. Maddie and Elliot walk past students dressed in maroon and gold. They wait at an elevator.

ELLIOT
Also called about a sublet on Huron. Cheap as hell, like $400 a month, one bedroom, but the pictures were nice.

Maddie leans over and kisses Elliot.

The elevator chimes, then the smudged metallic door opens. Mrs. Johnson stands there dressed in a Columbia parka. She's about to step out, but stops, shrieks, her hand instantly going up to cover her mouth.

MADDIE
Mom? What...

MRS. JOHNSON
What are you...

Mrs. Johnson's stare darts between her son and Elliot and then she's crying and shaking her head and she storms past Maddie, jogging to the door.

Maddie exchanges a look with Elliot, then turns and runs after his mom.

EXT. OUTSIDE OF DORM COMPLEX - CONTINUOUS

Maddie jogs after his mother. He catches up to her without much trouble.

MADDIE
Mom.

Mrs. Johnson keeps running.

MADDIE (CONT'D)
Mom, would you please stop?

Mrs. Johnson stops, turning quickly, her face a mess of tears and emotion. Her mouth is open, but she can't find the words.

MADDIE (CONT'D)
It's not like that.

Beat.

MADDIE (CONT'D)
I love her. Okay. I love her.

MRS. JOHNSON
Don't.

MADDIE
She had my child.

Mrs. Johnson drops a plastic bag. Several items (Christmas Reese's Peanut Butter Cups, a Target gift card, a pair of Minnesota Vikings boxer shorts) fall out. We see Maddie realize this was a care package his mother was dropping off.

MADDIE (CONT'D)
Netta-Mae. Her daughter. Is mine.

Mrs. Johnson stares at her son.

MADDIE (CONT'D)
I love her.

Wet snow falls. Flakes stick for a second on Mrs. Johnson's face, but then melt.

MADDIE (CONT'D)
Say something.

Beat.

MADDIE (CONT'D)
Just say something. Yell. Scream. Hit me. Just say something.

Mrs. Johnson stares at her son. From her POV, we see Maddie, as if for the first time grown, a man, no longer hers.

MRS. JOHNSON
(her voice has an eerie distant quality)
You always wanted to be older.

MADDIE
Mom...

MRS. JOHNSON
And now you are.

                              MADDIE
          Can we please go somewhere and talk about this...

                            MRS. JOHNSON
              (shaking her head) I'm done, Madison.

                              MADDIE
                      What does that even —

                            MRS. JOHNSON
          With this. With trying to protect you. With paying your way. With
                              it all.

                              MADDIE
                  Mom, I love her, and I have —

                            MRS. JOHNSON
                              A child.
              Mrs. Johnson turns and walks away.

From Maddie's POV, we watch his mother walk away, then look down
at the white plastic gift bag from Target, its contents spilled
                          into the snow.

                        MONTAGE - VARIOUS
          (Radiohead's "Everything In Its Right Place" plays)

A) INT. MADDIE'S DORM ROOM - NIGHT - Maddie's shirtless, his back to
Elliot, also shirtless, who strokes his head with one hand, smokes
a joint with the other. She exhales over his shoulder, bringing
                    the joint to his mouth.

B) EXT. PARK BENCH - NIGHT - Maddie sits bundled up staring at the
Mississippi. The dim lights of St. Paul shimmer in the distance.

C) INT. DORM ROOM COMPLEX - DAY - Maddie walks in with Elliot.
He's stopped at the front desk by a campus security guard, who's
                  speaking, pointing at Elliot.

D) INT. LAKE STREET INN - NIGHT - The room looks lived in, clothes
all over, an empty pizza box by the door. Elliot sleeps. Switch to
Maddie's POV, and we see a discolored ceiling. There's the joint
              for a ceiling fan, but no actual fan.

E) INT. MADDIE's DORM ROOM - DAY - Maddie stuffs clothes into a
                          duffel bag.

MADDIE (V.O.)

Elliot told me that with age, comes the loss of options.

F) INT. ZUMIEZ - DAY - Maddie folds a stack of T-shirts. Right next to him, a teenage girl carelessly rifles through some jeans looking for her size.

G) INT. ICE PALACE - NIGHT - An OVERHEAD SHOT of Elliot and Maddie lying, smiling, staring up at the looming ice wall.

H) EXT. MRS. JOHNSON'S FRONT DOOR - DAY - Maddie's pleading with his mother, who stands there with both arms across her stomach. She turns and shuts the door behind her.

I) EXT. THE HOOD OF MADDIE'S CAR - NIGHT - Rachel stands in front of him. She drops her sweater, then her top. She turns and kicks off her pants and then walks into the pond.

J) INT. LAKE STREET INN - NIGHT - They sit in bed watching Charlie Brown's Christmas on TV. They aren't touching one another.

K) INT. MICKEY'S DINER - AFTERNOON - Maddie and Elliot sit at a dive. They're eating breakfast, even though the sun is setting. They're talking excitedly.

MADDIE (V.O.)

We lived in a crack motel for three weeks. We talked about getting loans. About finishing school. About becoming famous. We promised to better ourselves. To be responsible once financial aid rolled in.

(MORE)

MADDIE (V.O.) (CONT'D)

To find a nice place, somewhere with two rooms, one for Jacob, one for Netta-Mae, us the sacrificial parents coopting the common room with a mattress.

L) EXT. ICE PALACE - NIGHT - They're at the current year's version of the ice palace. They're walking down a different corridor, this one wider than the previous year. They hold hands. Dark purples from the floodlights flash against the wall.

MADDIE (V.O.)

And if we tried, I mean like really tried, we could convince ourselves that we were close to all those goals. That they were still obtainable. That we were even trying to reach them in the first place.

END MONTAGE

EXT. OUTSIDE OF SUBURBAN HOUSE - NIGHT

The house is big, a clone of those around it with its front-facing garage and steepled roof. Elliot's checking underneath the welcome mat, Maddie is looking for fake rocks.

MADDIE (V.O.)

And then we were out of money with ten days to go until my loans came through. We promised ourselves it'd be once, quick, an easy in and out, this time abandoning the pretense of doing anything other than robbery.

CLOSE UP of the front door. The door is divided into four panes of glass, each one five-by-eight.

MADDIE

And how do you propose we —

Elliot picks up a hand-sized rock from the landscaped area next to the door. She smashes it through the bottom right quadrant of the door. She reaches in, her coat covering her hand, and unlocks the latch.

She turns, smiling.

MADDIE (CONT'D)

That's great. Really doing the whole leave no trace thing well.

INT. SUBURBAN HOUSE - CONTINUOUS

Elliot and Maddie walk in. The house is nice, upper-middle class, mahogany furniture and oversized couches. They both stop in the foyer, their heads tilted. There's a faint beeping. They booth look around for a security system, but don't see anything.

MADDIE

Smoke alarm battery?

ELLIOT

Just hurry.

They jog up the carpeted stairs.

CAMERA ZOOMS to the wall on the opposite side of the stairs they're ascending. A white digital security system interface flashes red.

CLOSE UP of security system. It reads, "BREACH."

INT. SUBURBAN HOUSE MASTER BEDROOM - MOMENTS LATER

Elliot's at an ornate vanity, stuffing earrings and necklaces into her pocket.

A LONG SHOT shows Maddie in the bathroom rifling through prescription bottles.

ELLIOT
You good?

MADDIE
Our housewife suffers from boredom or anxiety. Every benzo known to man. And little Piper must have the world's worst case of ADD.

ELLIOT
Let's go.

Maddie comes into the bedroom. Elliot's uneasy but kisses him hard on the lips.

EXT. SUBURBAN HOUSE - MOMENTS LATER

Maddie and Elliot speed-walk toward his car. They hear sirens in the distance. They run to the car.

INT. MADDIE'S CAR - CONTINUOUS

They're both frantic, Maddie fumbling with his keys, Elliot hitting the dashboard.

ELLIOT
Go, go, go.

The engine sputters, turns, but doesn't catch.

EXT. SUBURBAN COMPLEX - CONTINUOUS
A patrol car turns the corner, lights and sirens on.

INT. MADDIE'S CAR - CONTINUOUS
The engine finally catches. Maddie hits the gas, then slows, realizing a car speeding away would look even worse.

CLOSE UP of rearview mirror. You can see flashing sirens in the distance. They're coming closer.

ELLIOT (O.S.)
I'm not going back.

Still in CLOSE UP. The patrol car stops in front of the house they
just robbed. The dark shapes of two policemen rush out of the car.
They become smaller and smaller as Maddie drives away.

INT. LAKE STREET INN - LATER

Elliot's sitting at the dingy card table. She appears shaken up,
vacant. Maddie's looking at the pills he stole. He takes two Xanax,
then one more.

MADDIE
So we're done.

Elliot doesn't respond.

CLOSE UP of her right hand. She's picking her thumb cuticle with
her index finger. There's a tiny bit of blood.

MADDIE (CONT'D)
Right?

ELLIOT
What are we doing?

MADDIE
Done. Fucking done. Never again, Okay? My financial aid is like a
week away, and then we're set. Put that behind us.

ELLIOT
Jacob started wetting the bed the first night I was in jail.

Maddie looks over at Elliot. She's staring at a stain on the wall.

MADDIE
Nobody's going to jail. It's over with. That shit was a wake-up
call, but we're okay, we're here, safe, like it's all good.

ELLIOT
The only way he wouldn't pee was to be curled next to Devon.

Maddie gets off the bed, walking over to Elliot. He kneels down,
taking her hands. He notices her bloody thumb.

                              MADDIE
                            Hey, hey.

        Elliot finally meets his gaze.

                          MADDIE (CONT'D)
                     You're fine. You're safe.

                              ELLIOT
                    What the fuck are we doing?

                              MADDIE
        We were stupid. Really stupid. But we're done with that.

                              ELLIOT
                         My milk is dry.

                              MADDIE
                           Come here.

        Maddie hugs Elliot, but she doesn't hug him back.

                          MADDIE (CONT'D)
        It's like we talked about, remember? Darkest before the dawn. Hard
        right now, but it's going to get better. We get Netta-Mae —

                              ELLIOT
                        He wets the bed.

                              MADDIE
                         And Jacob.

                              ELLIOT
        I'm a felon. What judge is going to give me custody?

                              MADDIE
        Hey, baby, you're freaking out. Totally understandable, because
        tonight was scary, but it's going to get better. We'll have a
            place, a nice place, two bedrooms, maybe three.

        Maddie's rubbing Elliot's hair. There's still a blank quality to
                           her gaze.

                          MADDIE (CONT'D)
                    And you'll be in grad school. And —

                    ELLIOT
          What the fuck is wrong with me?

                    MADDIE
And we'll get our daughter and your son, and it'll be better,
                 everything, perfect.

Maddie reaches into his pocket, pulling out the stolen bottle of
Xanax. He shakes two out. He places them in Elliot's hand. He
                    stands.

                  MADDIE (CONT'D)
            Let me get you some water.

Maddie walks over to the sink, fills a plastic cup with water. In
the reflection in the mirror, we see Elliot slip the pills into her
              pocket. Maddie walks back over.

                    ELLIOT
            Swallowed them already.

                    MADDIE
Good. We're all good. We just relax now. Like, watch some mindless
shit on TV and tomorrow everything's better. We'll be better. Put
                 this night behind us.

Elliot nods. Maddie helps her out of the chair. They walk over to
the bed. Maddie's tending to Elliot like she's an elderly sick
woman. He pulls the stained comforter around her chest. He turns
   on the TV. He strips. He hits the light and climbs into bed.

The light from the TV changes their faces from blue to yellow to
                     white.

                    ELLIOT
           You think I'm a good person?

                    MADDIE
              The fucking best.

                    ELLIOT
                 A good mom?

                    MADDIE
         Would've been lucky to have you.

                         ELLIOT
               Think they'll forgive me?

                         MADDIE
                The kids? Absolutely.

                         ELLIOT
                       And you?

                         MADDIE
                      Me what?

                         ELLIOT
                     Forgive me.

An OVERHEAD shot of the two of them on their pillows. Maddie turns.
               Elliot stares at the TV.

                         MADDIE
        Nothing you ever did to me needed forgiveness.

Elliot turns over, inching her back and butt into Maddie. He wraps
               his arm around her stomach.

                         ELLIOT
                  And you love me?

                         MADDIE
                      So much.

CLOSE UP of Elliot. Her eyes are open. The TV changes to red. She
                        blinks.

                    MADDIE (CONT'D)
         Nothing else matters besides you and our family.

              INT. LAKE STREET INN - MORNING

The CAMERA PANS from right to left around the motel room. Winter
sun shines through the dusty curtains. The room appears cleaner
than it did the night before, lacking clothes strewn around the
floor. The CAMERA makes its way to the bed, where Maddie is sprawled
                      out alone.

Maddie wakes. He struggles with the brightness of the sun, rubbing
his eyes, smacking his lips. He notices Elliot isn't next to him.

He makes a half-hearted attempt at raising his head and looking for her.

From Maddie's POV, the CAMERA pauses on the card table, minus her purse and coat. Then it pauses on the clear floor and its lack of her shoes.

Maddie bolts upright, stumbling around the corner to the empty bathroom. He's becoming frantic, his vision darting around the room. He rushes to the door and flings it open. There's an empty parking space next to his Civic where her truck had been.

Maddie's frantic, on the verge of tears, as he slams the door. It's here he notices the Bible propped open by the edge of the lamp.

He rushes over, seeing an inscribed note on the inside jacket.

CLOSE UP of handwritten note: I don't expect your forgiveness. She's not yours. I don't know what's wrong with me.

INT. LAKE STREET INN - NIGHT

Maddie sits shirtless at the card table. He's crushed the entire bottle of Ritalin. His nostrils are lined with yellow. He's leg won't stop bouncing.

He stands, walking over to the bathroom mirror. He holds a pock-etknife. His face is sunken, dead but twitchy. He holds the knife to his chest.

MADDIE (V.O.)
When I was eight years old, I cut my chest.

Looking into the mirror, Maddie presses the knife to his chest. A thin line of red sprouts up against his pale skin.

MADDIE (V.O.)
When my mom found out, she cried, screamed. Asked me why I'd hurt myself.

Maddie cuts another line in his chest.

MADDIE (V.O.)
I didn't really know but said the first thing that came to mind: I don't like it when you're unhappy.

CUT TO:

INT. LAKE STREET INN - MOMENTS LATER

Maddie leans over the card table, snorting the last of the Ritalin. He grabs his keys off the table, then the revolver, stuffing it into the back of his jeans.

INT. MADDIE'S CAR - MOMENTS LATER

Maddie drives, spun, his jaw quivering. Each passing car casts a yellow LENS FLARE. The Velvet Underground's "Oh! Sweet Nothing" plays at a low volume from the stereo.

                    MADDIE (V.O.)
My mom sent me to a psychologist. The only thing I really remember is playing this game where you rolled plastic pigs and gained points depending upon how they landed.

Maddie drives by Roseville Mall. The lights from the parking lot are almost blinding.

                    MADDIE (V.O.)
That and something about it not being my job to make my mom happy. That sometimes your family felt bad.
                       (MORE)

                 MADDIE (V.O.) (CONT'D)
That I needed to distance myself from these feelings, learn that I was okay even if those around me weren't.

EXT. ROSEVILLE APARTMENT COMPLEX - MOMENTS LATER

Maddie pulls into the parking lot of Devon and Elliot's apartment. He parks. He hits the lights.

                    MADDIE (V.O.)
The psychologist told me that the only thing I could control were my actions.

Maddie gets out of the car. He's holding a crowbar. He walks through the snow to the third set of windows on the left.

                    MADDIE (V.O.)
She told me about making decisions that were best for me. How this was a sense of empowerment that no amount of people-pleasing or self-harm could come close to achieving. She told me once I realized this, and acted upon this realization, I'd start to feel

happiness outside of the love from the women around me.

Maddie struggles with prying the crowbar inside of the window. He eventually jimmies it open a few inches, enough to reach his arm through, which he does, knocking out the screen.

INT. THE SVENDSON-HESTER APARTMENT - CONTINUOUS

Maddie climbs through the window. His jacket rides up, exposing the butt of the revolver. He's high, both scared and scary. He walks past the sofa, where Devon sleeps with a fleece blanket, to the back of the apartment. He puts his ear to a closed door, then turns the knob.

INT. NETTA-MAE'S NURSERY - CONTINUOUS

The nursery is spotless. There's a white matching crib and changing table, a white rug, a rocker with a matching side table. An electronic night light projects cartoon animals around the wall in a clockwise motion.

MEDIUM SHOT of Maddie walking over to the crib. He's staring down at his daughter. He's crying but smiling.

From over his shoulder, a shape steps into the doorway.

> DEVON
> What the fuck?

Maddie spins around. Devon doesn't hesitate, charging Maddie. Devon barrels into Maddie, who goes flying, smacking his mouth against the post of the crib.

> ELLIOT (O.S.)
> I've called the cops!

Maddie's on his back, his mouth bloodied. Netta-Mae starts screaming. The CAMERA is at GROUND LEVEL, and Devon's descending on Maddie, at which point Maddie grabs the crowbar and swings, striking Devon square across the face. He slumps over.

Maddie rights himself, picks up a screaming Netta-Mae, and pauses, seeing the ugly pink monster he'd purchased her. He grabs it and rushes from the room.

EXT. THE SVENDSON-HESTER APARTMENT - CONTINUOUS

Maddie pauses, looking at the closed door to the master bedroom and the exit. He rushes to the exit.

INT. MADDIE'S CAR - MOMENTS LATER

Maddie's driving with one hand, trying to console a crying Netta-Mae with the other. She lays in his lap. Blood drips down Maddie's mouth. He's rocking her, trying to get her to calm down.

CLOSE UP of Maddie's phone. Elliot's calling. He rolls the window down and throws it out of the window.

FADE TO BLACK.

EXT. COMO LAKE - LATER

The lake is a frozen sheet of white. The sky is so close to waking up. The playground is deserted, as is the path around the lake. Snow blows. Maddie's Civic pulls into the empty parking lot.

INT. MADDIE'S CAR - CONTINUOUS

Maddie parks. He's crying, but Netta-Mae isn't. She's close to being asleep. Warm air blows across her few fine hairs. She stares up at Maddie, who's stroking her face.

MADDIE (V.O.)
Maybe it's not beginnings we search for. Maybe it's alternate endings. Maybe that's what you're really thinking about when everything gets completely fucked up, and options are down to one.

Maddie's holding Netta-Mae. He's making cooing sounds. He stares out at the frozen lake, the sky gray as the sun is about to rise.

MADDIE (V.O.)
And you're imagining how it could've been. You're thinking about having met the love of your life six months later. You're thinking about never agreeing to get your girlfriend a sandwich.
You're thinking about never breaking into a house. You're thinking about divorce, finality, happily ever after, you and your family together amassing the luxuries and resentments of the middle class.

EXT. COMO LAKE - CONTINUOUS

Elliot's truck comes speeding into the parking lot. Devon's driving, Elliot riding shotgun.

272

INT. MADDIE'S CAR - CONTINUOUS

Maddie positions Netta-Mae just-so on the driver's seat. He reaches into his waistband and takes out the revolver.

                    MADDIE (V.O.)
        You're thinking about the happiest moments of your life...

                    JUMP CUT TO:
                INT. ICE PALACE - NIGHT

OVERHEAD shot of Maddie and Elliot starring up at the multicolored wall of ice.

                    JUMP CUT TO:
                INT. THE CABOOZE - NIGHT

The CAMERA spins circles around the slow dancing Elliot and Maddie.

                    JUMP CUT TO:
        EXT. COMO PARK - LIFE GAURD TOWER - DUSK

Maddie holds Netta-Mae in his lap. His lips rest on her soft hair. Elliot leans her head on his shoulder. They stare out at the lake and the setting sun.

                    JUMP CUT TO:
            EXT. COMO LAKE - CONTINUOUS

Maddie steps out of his Civic. He places his parka over Netta-Mae, then turns. Elliot and Devon are standing twenty feet away. They freeze when they see his gun.

                    MADDIE (V.O.)
But you're not thinking about those moments as beginnings. You're thinking about them as endings. The exact moments you wish could be encapsulated in time. The shit you could die to, happy or at least close, content maybe.

                    ELLIOT
            Maddie, what the fuck?

                    MADDIE
            Get on your knees.

ELLIOT
(pleading)
Maddie, you don't have to do this.

Maddie waves the revolver in a downward motion. The calm tranquil-
ity he'd been exhibiting a moment before is gone, now replaced with
panic, hurt, tears.

Devon and Elliot kneel.

DEVON
Just don't hurt our daughter.

Maddie laughs, rubs the back of his hand across his bloodied mouth.
Netta-Mae cries from the car. Sirens can be heard in the distance.

ELLIOT
Please.

MADDIE
Is she?

ELLIOT
Please don't do this.

MADDIE
(screaming)
Is she my fucking daughter?

Elliot's crying. She has her hands pressed to her chest and then
her head starts shaking no.

CLOSE UP of Maddie's face. He closes his eyes to the point of
ruptured blood vessels.

LONG SHOT of a cavalcade of police cruisers speeding toward the
lake.

CLOSE UP of Maddie's face. His eyes burst open violently, and he
screams an animalistic scream of the caged and dying.

MEDIUM SHOT of Maddie raising the gun. It shakes. He's crying. He
pulls the hammer back.

MADDIE (V.O.)
Elliot told me getting older was nothing but the loss of options.
She said that was the tragedy of age.

                        Beat.

                    MADDIE (V.O.)
                 I didn't believe her.

The deafening sirens abruptly cut out to complete silence. The
CAMERA jumps between CLOSE UPs of Devon and Elliot and Netta-Mae.

Maddie raises the revolver, screaming, and fires three shots into
                        the air.

                    FADE TO BLACK.

        EXT. COMO PARK - LIFE GAURD TOWER - DUSK

Maddie, Elliot, and Netta-Mae sit there as a family, in love,
still, content. Cold air blows across their faces. The final seconds of The Velvet Underground's "Oh! Sweet Nothing" play.

                    MADDIE (V.O.)
        I didn't believe her because I was still a kid.

                    ROLL CREDITS END

Right-sized; Anonymous
(Jacob Svendson-Hester's Common Application essays)
Jacob Svendson-Hester
339 Western Ave,
St. Paul, MN 55105

Office of Admissions and Financial Aid
Harvard University
86 Brattle Street
Cambridge, MA 02138

Common Application Essay Question Number 1: Some students have a background or story that is so central to their identity that they believe their application would be incomplete without it. If this sounds like you, then please share your story.

My name is one that causes people to pause, to scrunch their faces, to squint as they try to place its familiarity in the vast reserves of pointless information inside of their minds. Most of the time, this facial distortion of memory recall is a short process, followed by a shrug, an air of indifference, a my bad, thought I recognized your name.

My "story," on the other hand, is a different matter. People know that. You know that. You know me as the hapless little bystander of an illicit love affair between a woman and a high school boy, as made famous by the movie STATUTORY. You know me from three to four years old. You know me as a symbol of parental negligence, a victim, a forgotten layer of gravitas.

It's a strange sensation, being trapped in the communal consciousness as a four-year-old. Although I am in no way comparing myself to a child star, I imagine the lasting effects may be similar. Adoration and support and unnecessary attention from everyone, from the person bagging your groceries to your second grade teacher, it does something to a boy, something—and excuse my clichéd metaphor here—resembling the flipping of one's worldview lens, so that instead of one's vision being corrected to a singular point, his outward vision blurs, becomes nothing but smudges of confusing movement, all the while affording others a more crystalline look at him. Eventually, when age catches up with people's millisecond-long attention spans for sensationalized stories, the lens rights itself. The child star sees the world for what it actually is for the first time in a decade. It is with this correction of the perversion that a realization of one's cultural importance is either accepted or rejected (obviously, most highly covered stories are of a child star's rejection of said realization, and his subsequent spiral into self-destruction). It is this moment that you, the consumer of STATUTORY and *We, Adults,* don't know about me.

This essay question is obviously about identity. I would surmise that most of the responses are about the reluctant accepting of ethnicity, sexuality, and religion. If I was a minority or confused sexually or believed in God, I'd probably have written the same thing. But my epiphany, however fleeting, was basically the opposite of anything I'd highlight to set me apart from ninety-five percent of your applicants. It was about assimilation into white suburbia. It was about becoming a face among many. It was about introducing myself as Jake, which I hate, both the phonetic sound of it and what it implies about men with that name. It was about becoming invisible, which, in a strange way, was fully realized, or at least I acknowledged in my freshman year of high school.

I was at a new school, this one private, my father teaching at the neighboring girl's campus. We went around the room and introduced ourselves, giving one interesting thing we did over the summer and our favorite book. I was nervous to the point of dry heaves. I imagined my new peers staring at me, instantly placing my name, my picture eleven years in the past, my mother and father. There was Tim who loved Harry Potter and then there was Peter who went to soccer camp in Virginia and then it was my turn and I told myself to stay calm, to breathe, to be normal.

"I'm Jake. I worked at CVS this summer. It was horrible and fun all at once. My favorite book is *Catcher in the Rye.*"

A few people mumbled a hello. Nobody cared what I'd said. Nobody even looked at me. This silence and lack of recognition, still to this day, was one of the happiest moments of my life.

Which brings me back to identity: I am the Caucasian kid dressed in nondescript jeans and T-shirts, receiving a 4.0 at the twenty-ninth ranked prep school in the country; the kid who doesn't watch movies because "based on a true story" is a lie that no person in America questions; the peer who never sleeps over at people's houses because my friendships are only lunch-period deep, part of the anonymous tapestry of school sporting event fans, assembly cheers, and hallway jostling.

So that's my story. The real one. The one that happened from five years old onward. I became something other than a symbol of my mother's poor choices. I became a person. An individual. Right sized. Anonymous. And unlike the actor who played my life, whom, I believe at this time is in a rehabilitation center for opiate abuse, I gladly accepted the reversal of my metaphorical lens. I have done nothing worthy of attention or praise or pity. But I have done everything in my power to place myself in the advantageous position to be accepted by Harvard, to be sitting in class with the best young minds in the world, to receive the education that will allow me to go forward and introduce myself as Jacob Svendson-Hester, causing people to pause, scrunch their faces, this time smiling, recognizing my name as somebody worthy of esteem, this time earned.

Jacob Svendson-Hester
339 Western Ave,
St. Paul, MN 55105

Office of Undergraduate Admissions
Stanford University
Montag Hall
355 Galvez Street
Stanford, CA 94305

Common Application Essay Question Number 2: Describe a place or environment where you are perfectly content. What do you do or experience there, and why is it meaningful to you?

I live in a fly-over state. It's miserably cold in the winter and hot and humid in the summer. It's a five-hour drive from Canada. We're a homogenized bunch of Norwegians, happy to accept our replicas of urban shopping in malls with skylights and fake cobblestone. This is St. Paul, Minnesota. This is a place where the tradition of a winter carnival excites the million-plus people scattered like buckshot around our decaying downtown. This is a city that's more like a town, a place with its prized structure being constructed in ice every year, only to melt by the baseball season opener.

As a child, our holiday excitement wasn't so much about the bounty of goods that Santa was sure to bring, but about our trip to the ice palace. The palace was different every year, sometimes with spires, sometimes with different levels, one year with a three-story ice slide wrapped around the back entrance, but the one thing you could count on, especially as a child, was the sheer enormity of it. It seemed miles long, football fields high, the cavernous rooms inside endless. The fact that it was sculpted from ice only added to its enchantment and mysticism. Everything was cold to the touch. Everything had a fluid quality—the technicolored spotlights, the ornately carved statues, the soft drips in warmer corners—as if the whole thing was submerged in water, floating, ready to return to its natural state.

My mother took my younger sister and me every year. We'd run around, roasted nuts spilling from paper cones, screaming, amazed at our echoing voices fading but never completely disappearing. Eventually, after thorough exploration, we'd find a quiet nook of the ice palace.

We'd lie down on the cold floor. We'd stare up at the overarching wall. We'd frighten ourselves with the thought of it crashing down upon us. But then we'd just lie there. My sister and I never knew how long we were supposed to be still for, but we'd be good, understanding, on some level, that this was a moment of meditation for our mother. She'd hold us close. She'd tell us she loved us. She'd kiss our foreheads. We'd feel safe.

I've always believed that a place, regardless of its inherent qualities, exists primarily in relation to the person experiencing that particular place. Or rather, the significance of any given place is contingent upon one's interaction within the setting, what he was experiencing during the time of exploration, what the place symbolized/dredged up within himself rather than the place itself (Ex: The Grand Canyon is unquestionably stunning, but when recalling the Grand Canyon, a person thinks about whom he saw it with, what events were going on in his life, ascribing personal significance rather than the significance of the place itself). Within this framework, the meaning of any given place can radically change depending upon the construct the person comes to the place armed with. And much like the entire aura of the ice palace, this relationship is fluid, as I discovered at eleven years old when I stayed up late one night to watch STATUTORY, the film about my parents' life, which until then, I knew nothing about.

One of the central images of the film was the ice palace. It was routinely circled back to, emphasized as a point of purity, of love, of beginnings. An actress who looked vaguely similar to my mother laid on her back, staring up at the purple-and-orange-lit ice walls. She said, "I don't you, either." She looked happy. She probably felt safe.

Suddenly, the ice palace's meaning completely shifted. It no longer was a place of maternal refuge, but something dirty, a secret aired to the world, an admission of regret and longing on my mother's part. After the movie came out, the three of us, as a group, never stepped foot in the ice palace again.

But I did. I was sixteen, my younger sister twelve. I'd recently started driving, and volunteered to take Netta-Mae shopping for Christmas presents for our parents. We went to the mall, picked out a sweater for my father, a set of orange mixing bowls for my mother. Then I took her to the ice palace. She'd seen the movie as well, and although she was still young, still unable to fully grasp the place's significance in our mother's life, and in turn, her own, she intuited enough to start crying. I held her hand. We walked to a forgotten corner. We lay on our backs. We stared at the wall and its lights. We did as we'd done as children; we did as our mother had done in the film. We didn't talk. We didn't say we loved one another. But maybe she felt it, my love for her, because she put her head on my shoulder. I didn't feel safe, but I wanted to.

Jacob Svendson-Hester
339 Western Ave,
St. Paul, MN 55105

Office of Undergraduate Admissions
Yale University
P.O. Box 208234
New Haven, CT 06520

Common Application Essay Question Number 3: Discuss an accomplishment or event, formal or informal, that marked your transition from childhood to adulthood within your culture, community, or family.

We live in a vast nation, one pocked with every sort of topography, home to both Arctic and equator, one that begs to be explored, conquered; a nation streamlined for efficiency by an unimaginatively drawn interstate system. So like every other young man on the verge of adulthood (i.e. brushing up on the age when it's legal to die for oil wars), some part of me itched for the "rite of passage" voyage of a road trip. Truckers and cornfields and Nebraska, pitching tents and seedy motels and illicit drugs done with no abandon. Or so I told my parents. A trip from Minnesota to California and back, ten days total. I told them I needed to exercise some freedom. To feel alive. They conferred and then agreed.

The reality was I had no such desire for a road trip, or rather, the extracurricular activities that the term "road trip" conjures. Nothing could've interested me less. My sole objective was to drive to Hollywood and meet Madison Johnson, writer and director du jour, multi-million-aire, gossip-magazine-cover regular, and ask him one question.

The drive to California was long and tedious. I don't smoke and I don't do drugs, so the flats of our nation's breadbasket were a particularly harsh rung of Dante's hell. My parents insisted upon me staying at decent hotels, nothing worse than a Holiday Inn Express, so that's what I did. Twice, I ate at a connected Applebee's. I usually fell asleep by nine o'clock.

Three days later, I arrived in Los Angeles. The city was what I expected—cars on top of cars, sprawl, palm trees, fat tourists and beautiful gas station attendants. I'd done my research (looked online) and knew where Madison Johnson lived. I drove up hills and switchbacks until I arrived at his address. His house wasn't as big as I'd imagined, nor was it white with glass walls. It was an ugly blob of stucco, two stories tall, a Tuscan rip-off with a well-manicured lawn.

Of course I was nervous, but I told myself my mission was simple, concise, probably no more than a thirty second Q&A, and then I was free to go home. I got out of the car. I rang the doorbell. I adjusted myself. I waited. Nothing. I rang again. I wiped the palms of my hands against my jeans. Nothing.

I went back to my car and opened the windows and sat there. I half expected some security guard to come kick me out, but after a half-hour, when that didn't happen, I relaxed, until I realized Madison Johnson could easily not be in California, but maybe on vacation or shooting his horrible sounding new action-thriller in South America. I turned on my car and let the AC lull me to sleep, which in fact happened, me not waking up until the sun had set and somebody was knocking against the window of my car.

Madison Johnson was both more and less beautiful in person than he appeared in the tabloids. His features were all overly sculpted, a perfection of geometrical proportions, his mouth the clear focal point. But his eyes, even in the half-dark of his driveway, were somewhat dull or maybe diluted, little stretches of wrinkles exploding in every direction around their sockets.

"Excuse me, man, what are you…you can't be here."

I climbed out of my car. This evidently made Madison Johnson a little nervous, as he took several steps backward and reached into his pocket, retrieving his phone.

"Private property, man, gonna have to ask you to bounce."

I looked at him. I imagined myself as Elliot, the female lead in Madison Johnson's first hit film, STATUTORY, as my mother. I imagined seeing him twelve years before working at Roseville Mall, him younger, more energetic, more charismatic. I imagined myself as having run home to Minnesota with a child in tow, a marriage shattered by a husband's infidelity. I imagined thinking here was an alternate ending, a happy ending, his perfect teeth and oversized Adam's apple the only evidence I needed.

"All right, man, calling the cops and stepping inside."

"My name's Jacob Svendson-Hester."

Madison Johnson's whole demeanor changed, or rather, it went through a clear and distinct metamorphosis, each stage apparent (shocked, confused, quizzical, pitying). He rubbed his mouth with his hand not holding the phone. "Jesus Christ, man. Wow. It's been…do your parents know you're out here?"

I nodded.

"You want to come in or something?"

I shook my head. It was here when Madison Johnson's demeanor changed once more, this time becoming rigid, frightened, obviously running through the scenario of me having adjusted poorly, pinning my angst on his involvement in my life, a gun about to raise from my side.

"I have one question," I said.

Madison Johnson nodded, still unsure how to take me.

"Did my mother plan on taking me as well?"

Madison Johnson furrowed his brow as if he wasn't following, then nodded, smiled his famous smile. "Back then?"

I nodded.

"That was the plan the entire time. Both you and your sister."

"It wasn't just Netta?"

"No, man, both of you. Start a—"

"Family."

"Yeah," Madison Johnson said.

I nodded and turned around. Madison Johnson was saying things about coming inside and grabbing something to eat, about maybe calling my mom just so she knew I was okay, but I didn't respond. I got in my car. I turned it on. The headlights lit him up. He looked small and alone standing in front of his ugly stucco house. I imagined myself as my mother driving away from a motel, back to her children and unfaithful husband, back to her family.

I'd originally believed that the real point to any road trip was to trick oneself into the notion of achieving freedom through exploration. But this is a falsity. The interstates are thruways from one area of commerce to another. Every city, every town, every exit with a gas station, is planned, is produced, is exactly the same as the hundreds of other thousands dotting our country. So freedom, as sought through the car, has to be more of a result of distance between those people we know than the places we are actually exploring. It is through this distance from the people in our lives that we are afforded the smallest glimpse of retrospection, as if our homes become a form of our pasts, and distance becomes a measurement of time. Our journeys become an exercise in nostalgia. Each mile marker is a memory. The sunrise in Nevada becomes our mother running around the house in her underwear, screaming about a snake, you and your sister laughing hysterically at your gag placed in the cupboard. The salt flats of Utah become a winter's night when your mother knocks on your door, a cup of Russian Tea (Tang and cinnamon) in hand. The white wooden crosses staked alongside never-ending stretches of Nebraskan highway become bed-time stories—just one more, okay, honey, one more—the ends of your mother's hair silky between your fingers.

As your home approaches, as the distance shortens, you're brought closer to the present. A sense of immediacy constricts your chests. You're left searching for the ease of your past. And it is here—contrary to what I originally believed—where the mythical freedom of the road trip rite of passage lays: you either keep driving or return home. You ei-ther accept the fleeting epiphanies you've been searching for as enough to tide you over, or you reject your present, your family. Madison John-son told me my mother had planned on returning for me. Part of me believed him. I exited 94, turning through the sleepy streets of St. Paul, knowing somehow I was changed, had found an answer to a question I wasn't even posing correctly, my realization all but disappearing as the combination of distance and retrospect became zero, my car idling in the driveway, my mom opening the door, the lights illuminating her slender frame, her smiling, relieved that I'd returned back to her.

Jacob Svendson-Hester
339 Western Ave,
St. Paul, MN 55105

Office of Undergraduate Admissions
Dartmouth College
6016 McNutt Hall
Hanover, NH 03755

Common Application Essay Question Number 4: Recount an incident or time when you experienced failure. How did it affect you, and what lessons did you learn?

At fourteen years old, I was denied emancipation from my parents. I sat in a small Ramsey County courthouse, really nothing more than a rectangular room with a table, no wooden throne housing a stoic judge. My parents sat in a neighboring room, this one even smaller. I was asked questions about sexual, physical, and verbal abuse. I answered no to each one. Then I was asked about my level of care, if I felt my base needs were met. Yes. I was asked about my parents' level of interest in my life: did they attend my sporting events (I don't play sports); did they help me with my schoolwork (if I ever needed their help, I'm sure they would); do your parents ever express their love for you (yes, all the time).

It was here the judge—a large man, African American, handsome with a large swath of pink gums that showed every time he spoke— asked, what exactly, was my reasoning for seeking emancipation.

I'd typed a response. It was two pages long, a self-pitying tale about growing up in the shadow of my mother's scandalized affair. The typed response discussed postpartum depression's lasting effects on a woman, citing a Swedish study from the early part of 2015, which demonstrated those who'd suffered one or more times with severe postpartum, were three hundred times more likely to experience future, non-pregnancy related swings of emotional attachment and detachment. The written statement also spoke to infidelity, how a child learns from his parents, how my parents each had indiscretions, my father's evidently a lifelong vice. My statement concluded with a self-righteous paragraph about seeking individuality, how it was ingrained in us as Americans, cherished, prized above all else, us humans molded individually in the image of God. It talked about how I needed this independence. To, for once, become my own person. To be something other than a boy fossilized at four-years-old, always a victim, always a character to be pitied.

Sitting in the courtroom, which wasn't really a courtroom, my hands sweaty on the printed sheets of paper, I cleared my throat. I was about to start reading when I set the paper down. I thought about the questions the judge had asked. Have either of your parents ever sexually abused you? Are you ever forced to go to sleep without having eaten dinner? Do they express their love toward you? I realized these were the children in need of emancipation. These were the unfortunate ones forced to grow up at fourteen, to become adults in the eyes of the law, to sign leases on apartments, to be allowed to gain driver's licenses in order to get between school and work. I, on the other hand, was impatient. Entitled. Selfish in my need to claim to the world that I was not my parents' mistakes. All these realizations hit me at once, and I felt juvenile, immature, and strangely, never more in need of my mother and father.

I apologized to the judge. I made something up about having been angry with them and sought out emancipation as a form of punishment. The judge sighed. He lectured me on wasting his time, the state's time, and more importantly, devastating my parents who were doing their best to raise a loved boy.

My parents drove me home. We didn't talk. I sat in the backseat, both of them in the front. At one point, I watched my father reach out and clasp my mother's hand. Something about this gesture—probably the infrequency of physical contact between them—struck me as heartbreaking. I wanted them to start yelling. I wanted them to threaten me. I wanted to be grounded, loss of computer privileges for a month, a year, until I left for college, which, while we're on the subject, they'd say, you are now going to have to pay for by yourself.

But they didn't.

Instead, my father parked in front of Snuffy's. It was a '50s style malt shop, lots of pink and turquoise, the air heavy with grease. We filed out of the car. We sat in a booth. The Beach Boys played. I wasn't hungry and said so. My mother ordered a chocolate malt, split three ways. I kept waiting for the yelling or the shaking of heads or admissions of hurt feelings. "Barbara Ann" came on the jukebox. Our malts arrived. My mother's portion was the only one with a cherry, which she picked up and dropped in my plastic cup.

And here—as I've been instructed by my college advisors—is where

I explicitly spell out what this experience of failure taught me: parents are parents. They're people, broken in all the ways the world breaks them, scared, terrified, desperately going through life with the façade of not drowning in loneliness. They are us in twenty-five years. They are doing the best they possibly can, even if that best falls short of what we think we deserve. It can always be worse; they can always be worse. And sometimes, just sometimes, when we fail to achieve what we think is best for us, we're afforded the briefest moments of selflessness as our egos reel inward in self-defense, and we're given the gift of empathy. We can see these towering figures of our lives without the capitalized pronouns of Father and Mother, and just as people, as ourselves. And in these times, a simple statement—I've always loved these malts—says everything we can't begin to express about forgiveness and gratitude.

ACKNOWLEDGEMENTS

I want to thank Jaynie Royal, Pam Van Dyk, and all the other rockstars at Regal House Publishing for believing in this strange mutant of a novel. I am so grateful for your faith, guidance, and patience along the way.

I would also like to thank my agent, Jim McCarthy. Your help fleshing out the characters and shaping this novel were everything.

I can't forget to thank Rob Lane, the first reader for everything I write. While it's embarrassing sending my unedited work to you, your help trimming my typos and malaprops down to one-per-page is invaluable.

I would also like to thank everyone I've worked with at various retail jobs over the past twenty years. This novel was born from those experiences. Sure, the pay is shit and the customers are horrible, but the comradery of working any service industry job is to die for. Jokes, bullshitting, commiserating, feeling a misguided sense of pride when sales are good even though it makes no difference to your paycheck, all of it made those years not only bareable, but fun. Thank you.

Lastly, I'd like to thank my family. My parents have always encouraged me, even when I was writing angsty, emo poems in elementrary school. My brother told me my first stab at a novel when I was eighteen (an artful epic about the son of a donkey show performer) wasn't half bad. My three children are the joy of my silly little life. Plus, they know Daddy is a hell of a lot more pleasant to be around if they allow him to write in the morning, and thusly afford me that time. And my wife, whom this novel is dedicated to. You've been my ride-or-die since I was nineteen. You are a beautiful person, inside and out. You have supported my passions and writing every step of the way, somehow knowing when I need to be told to quit feeling sorry for myself and when I need a gentle smile-frown of empathy. You are my best friend. I love you.

Oh, and I need to thank The Velvet Underground, because according to Spotify, I listened to "Oh! Sweet Nothin'" 1,332 times over the eighteen months it took to write this novel.